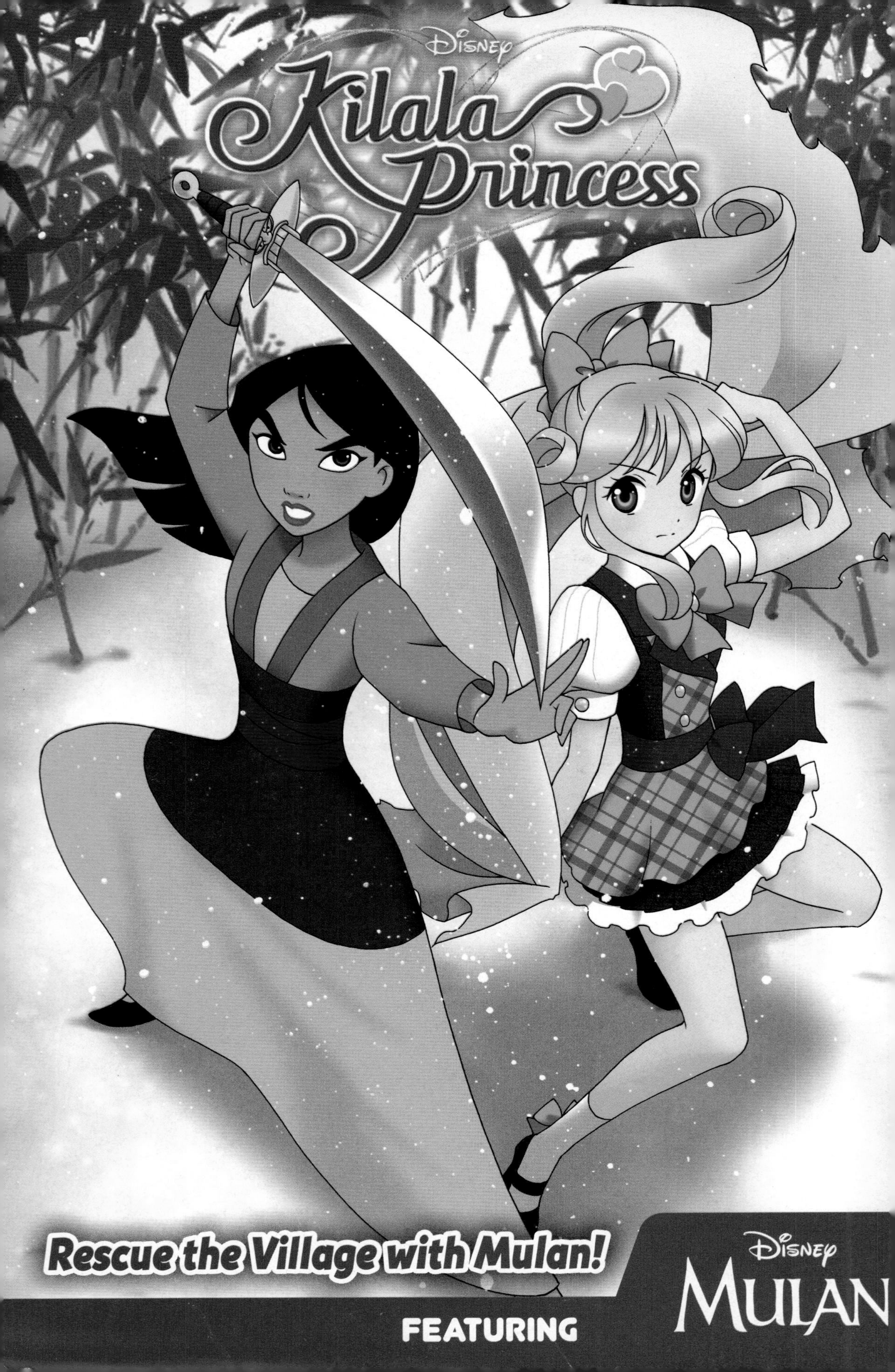
Disney
Kilala Princess
Rescue the Village with Mulan!
FEATURING
Disney
MULAN

Disney

Kilala Princess

Rescue the Village with Mulan!

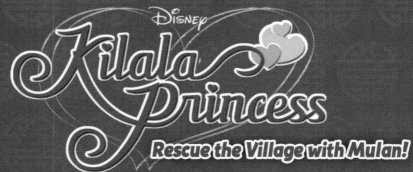

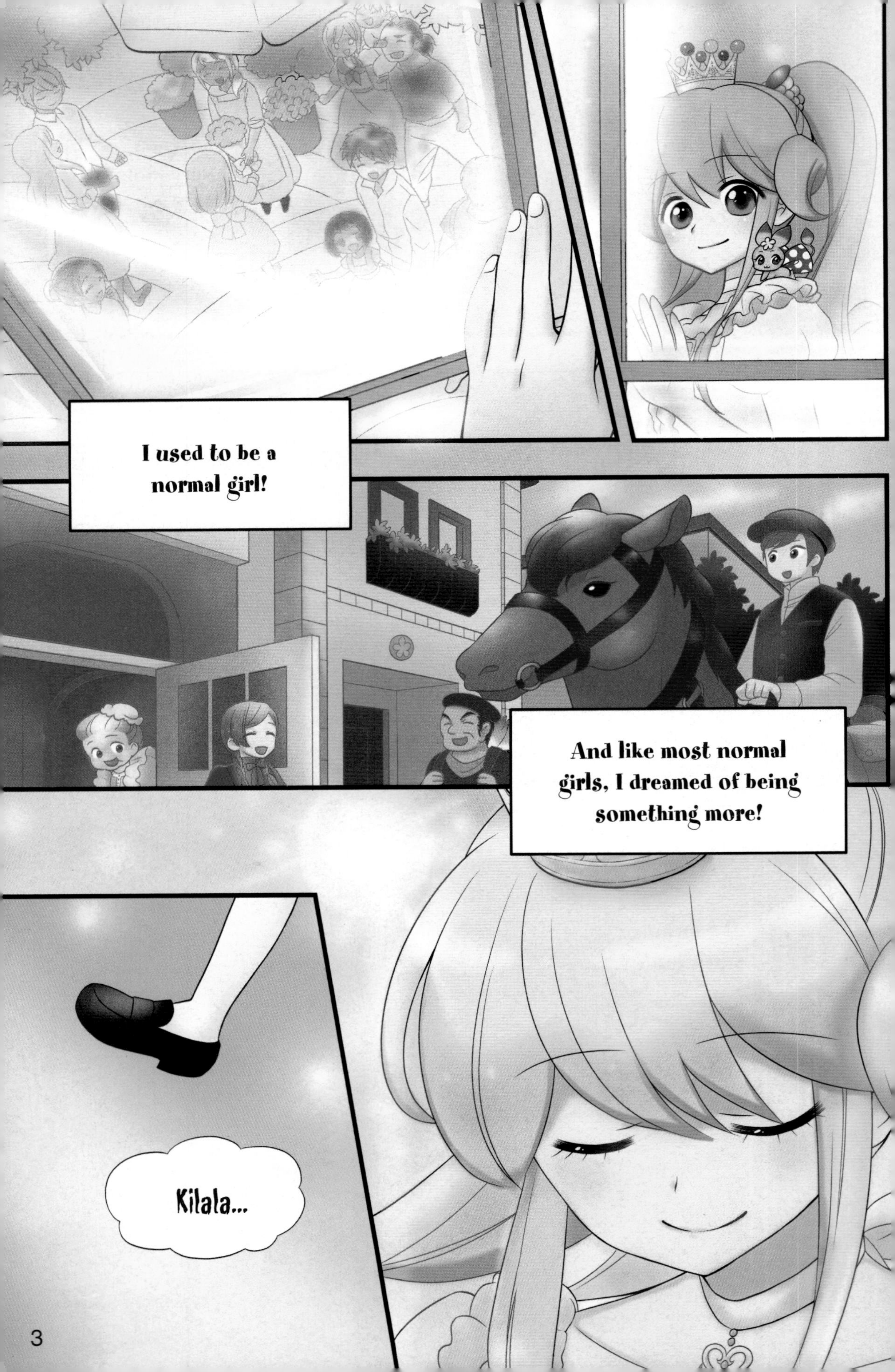
I used to be a normal girl!
And like most normal girls, I dreamed of being something more!
Kilala...

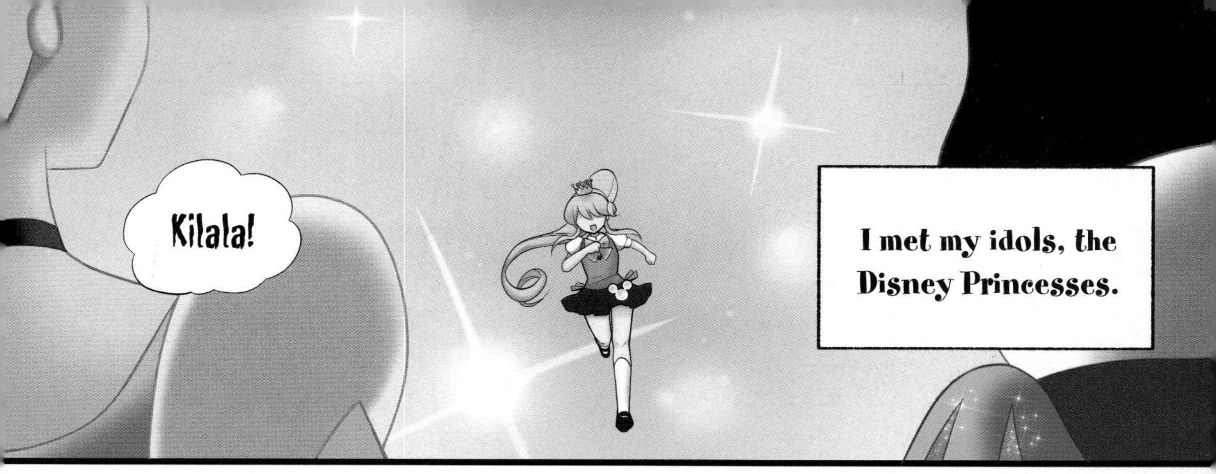
Kilala!
I met my idols, the Disney Princesses.

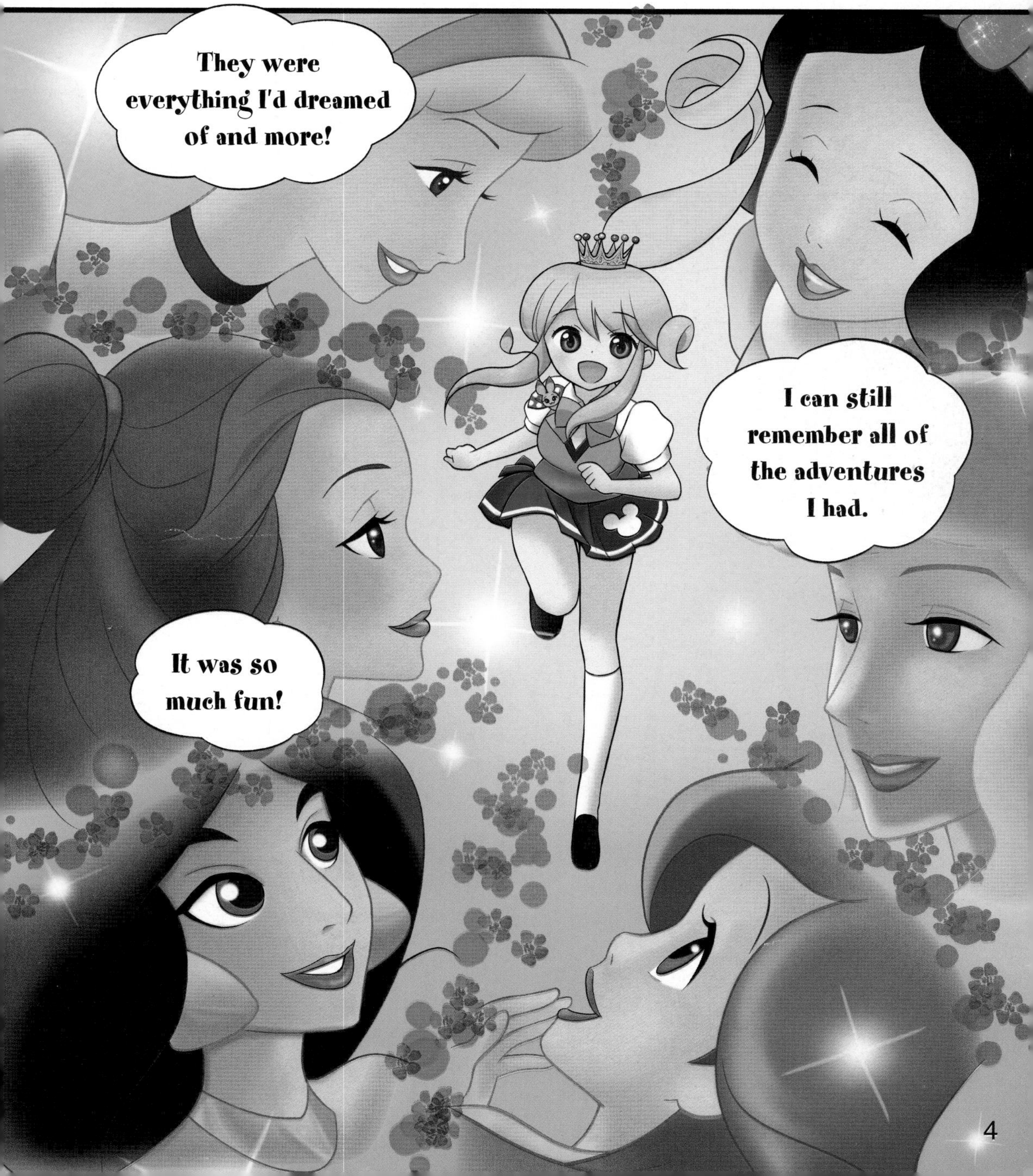
They were everything I'd dreamed of and more!
I can still remember all of the adventures I had.
It was so much fun!

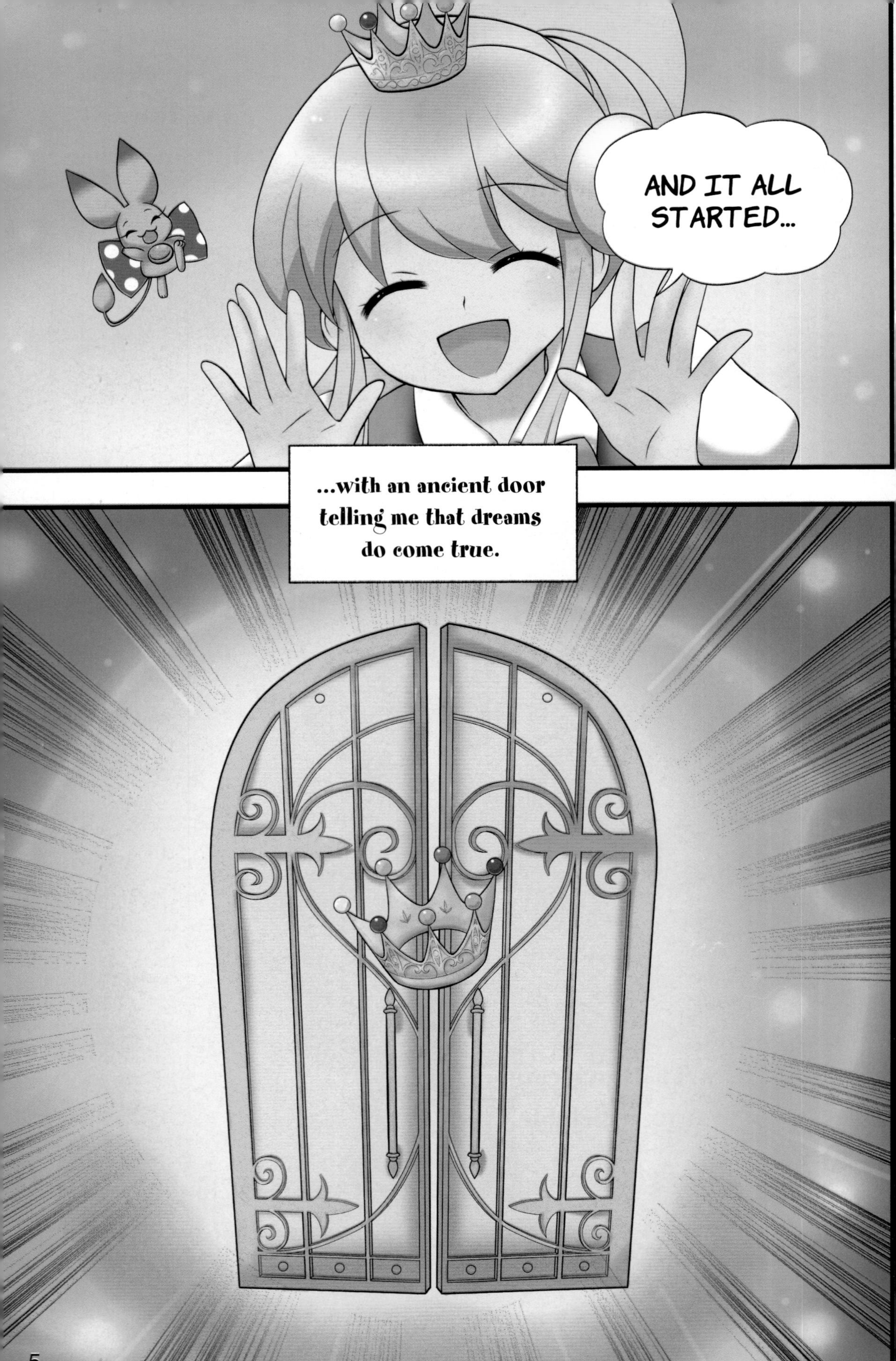
AND IT ALL STARTED...
...with an ancient door telling me that dreams do come true.

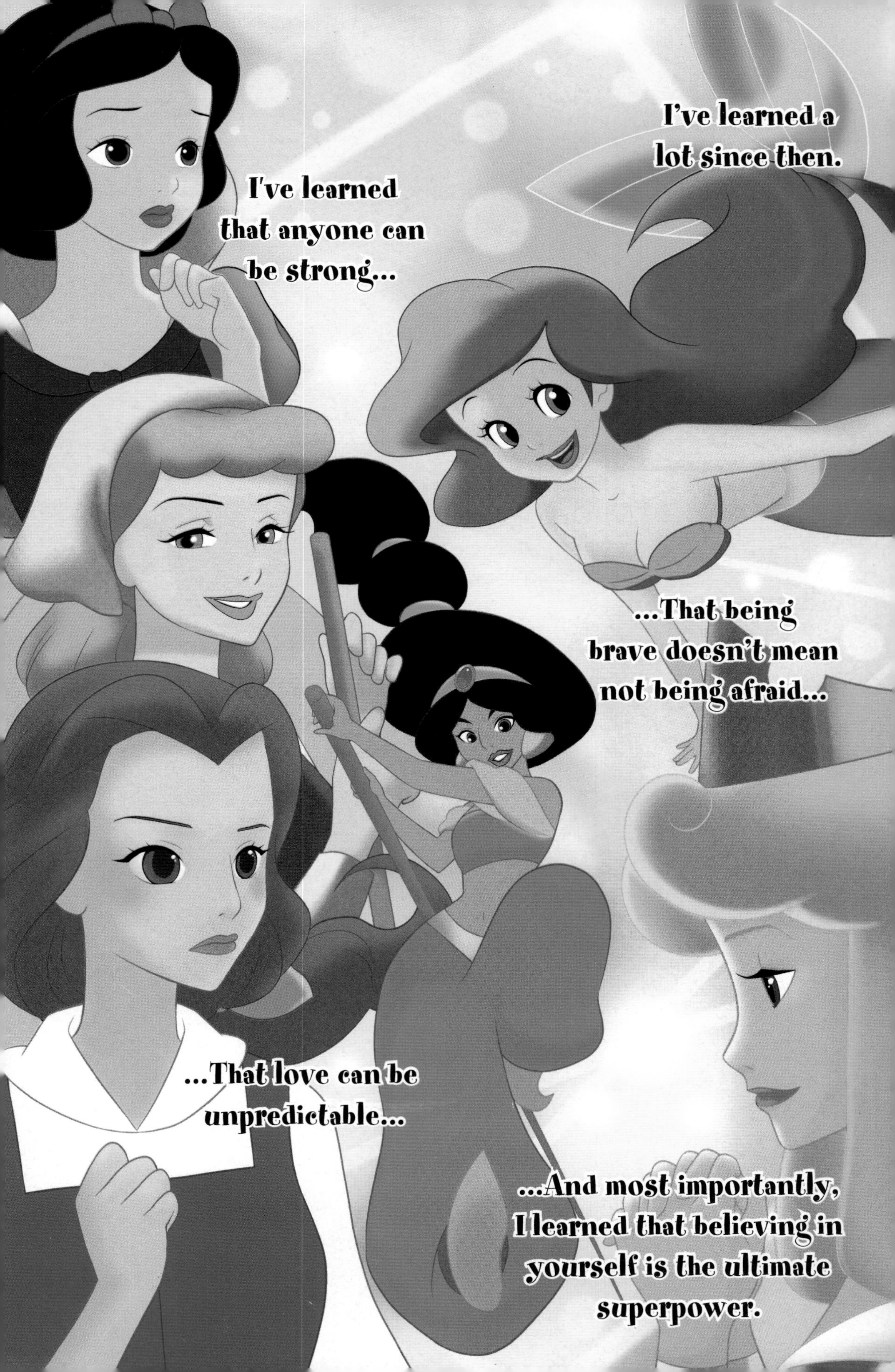
I've learned a lot since then.
I've learned that anyone can be strong...
...That being brave doesn't mean not being afraid...
...That love can be unpredictable...
...And most importantly, I learned that believing in yourself is the ultimate superpower.

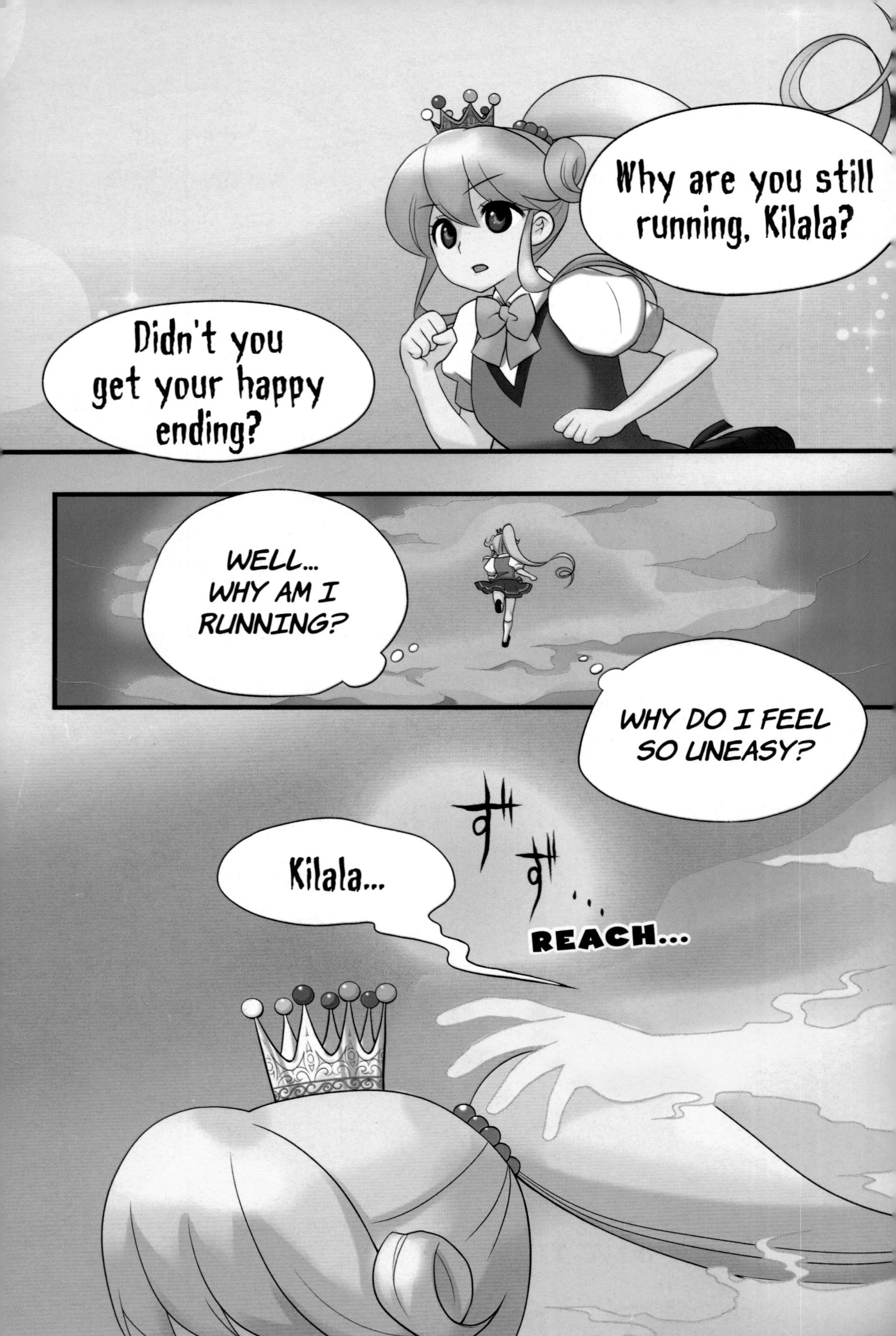
Why are you still running, Kilala?
Didn't you get your happy ending?
WELL... WHY AM I RUNNING?
WHY DO I FEEL SO UNEASY?
Kilala...
ず ず...
REACH...

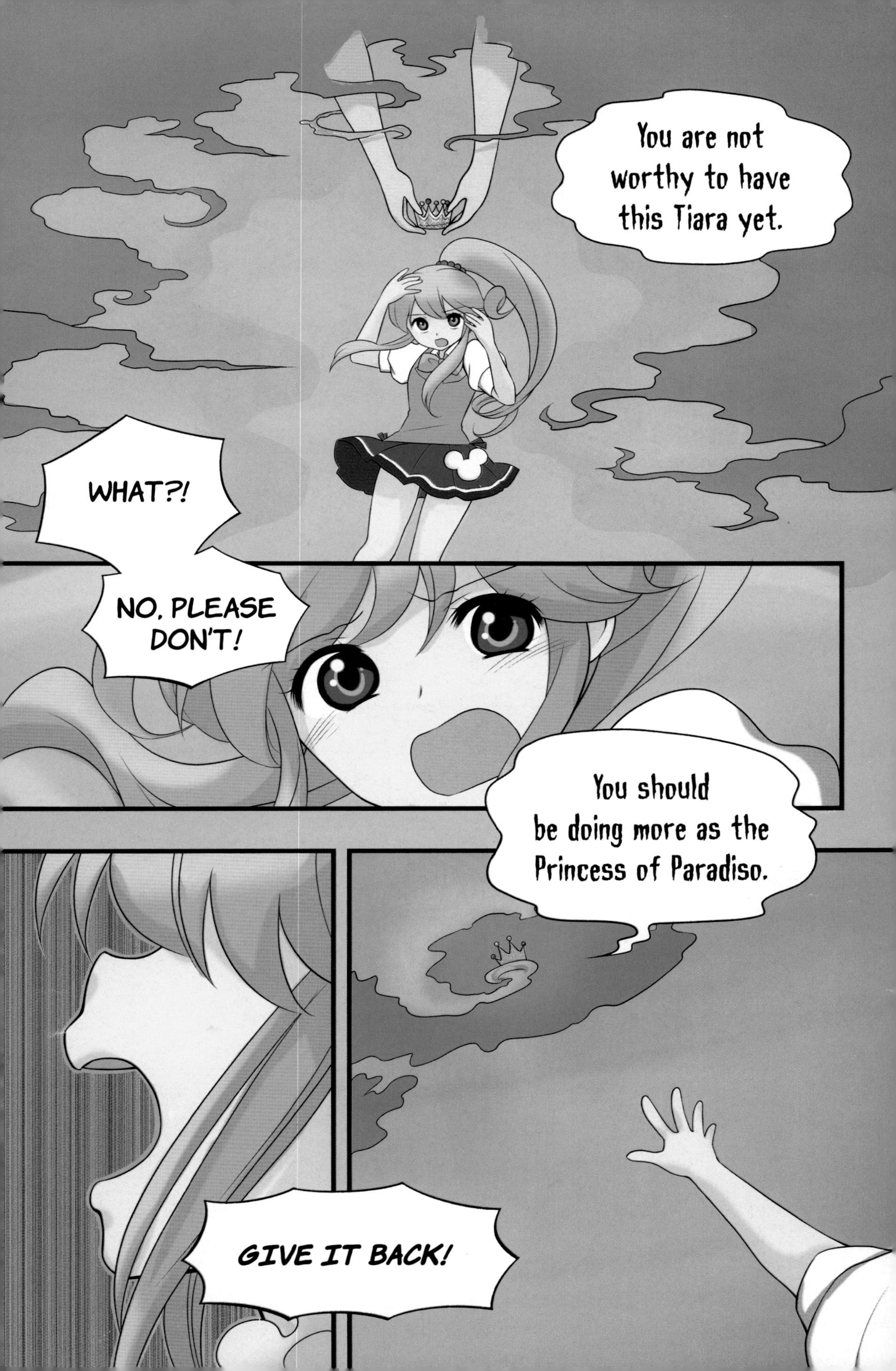
You are not worthy to have this Tiara yet.
WHAT?!
NO, PLEASE DON'T!
You should be doing more as the Princess of Paradiso.
GIVE IT BACK!

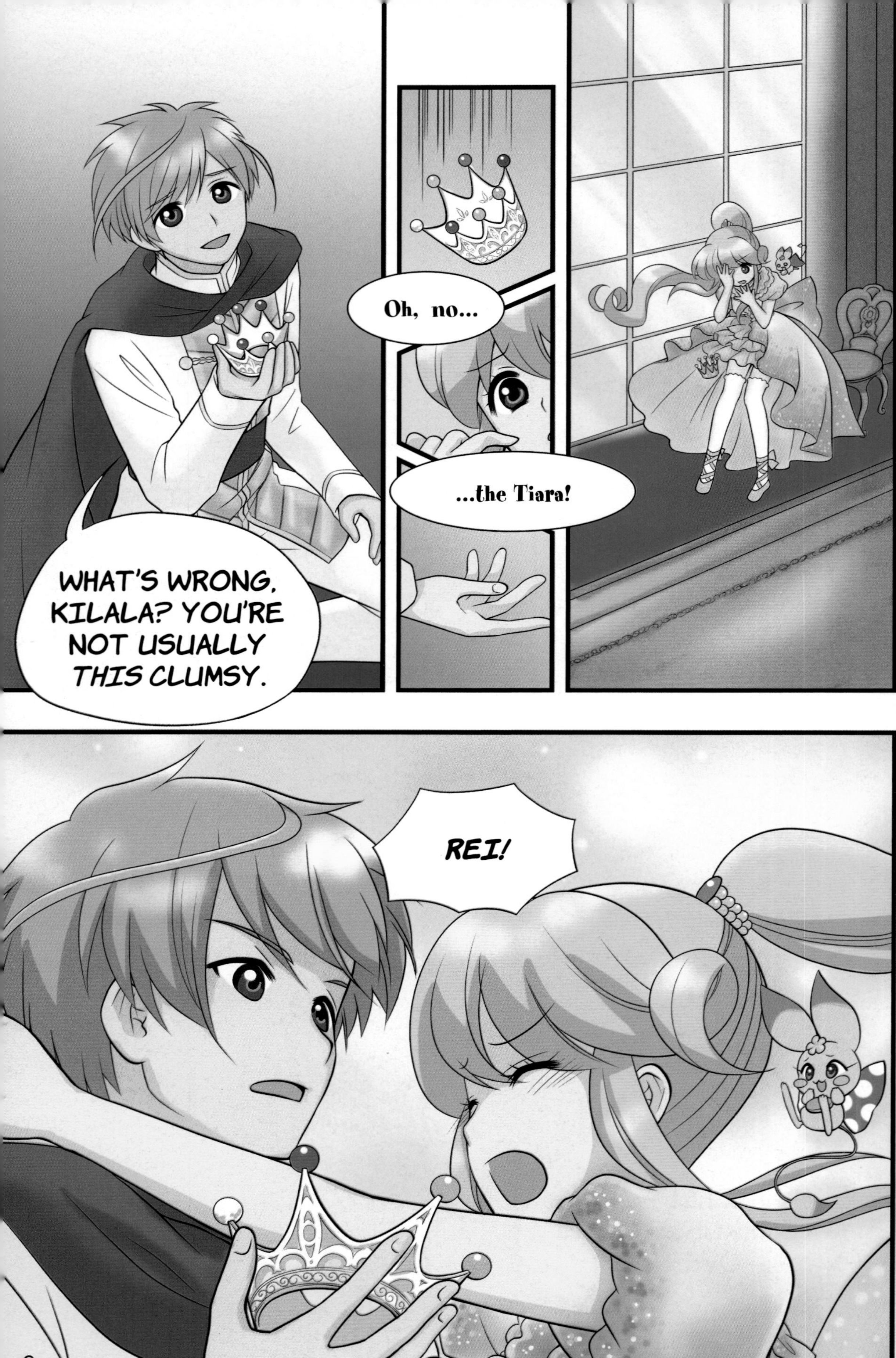
WHAT'S WRONG, KILALA? YOU'RE NOT USUALLY THIS CLUMSY.
Oh, no...
...the Tiara!
REI!

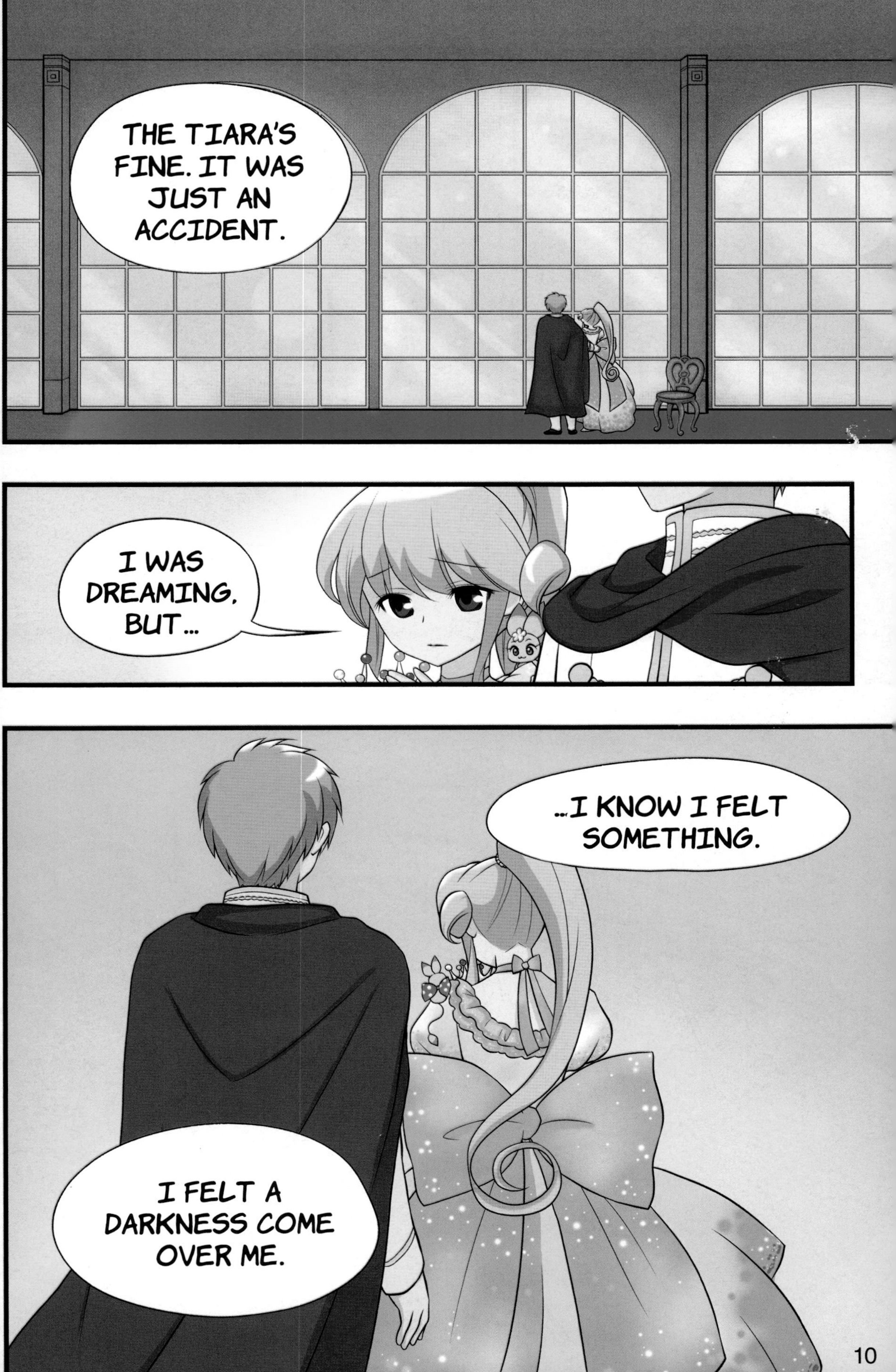
THE TIARA'S FINE. IT WAS JUST AN ACCIDENT.
I WAS DREAMING, BUT...
...I KNOW I FELT SOMETHING.
I FELT A DARKNESS COME OVER ME.

I WAS SO AFRAID I WASN'T WORTHY...

...BUT THE TIARA CHOSE ME. IT COULDN'T HAVE BEEN WRONG... COULD IT?

LOOK AT THIS, REI!

THERE ARE MORE JEWEL SETTINGS!

REI, I WAS RIGHT!

RIGHT ABOUT WHAT?

SOMETHING'S HAPPENING.

SOMEONE NEEDS OUR HELP! EVEN IF IT'S OUTSIDE THE GATES, IT MIGHT AFFECT PARADISO!

WELL, THEN...
LET'S HELP THEM
TOGETHER.

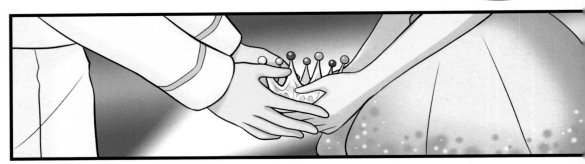

13

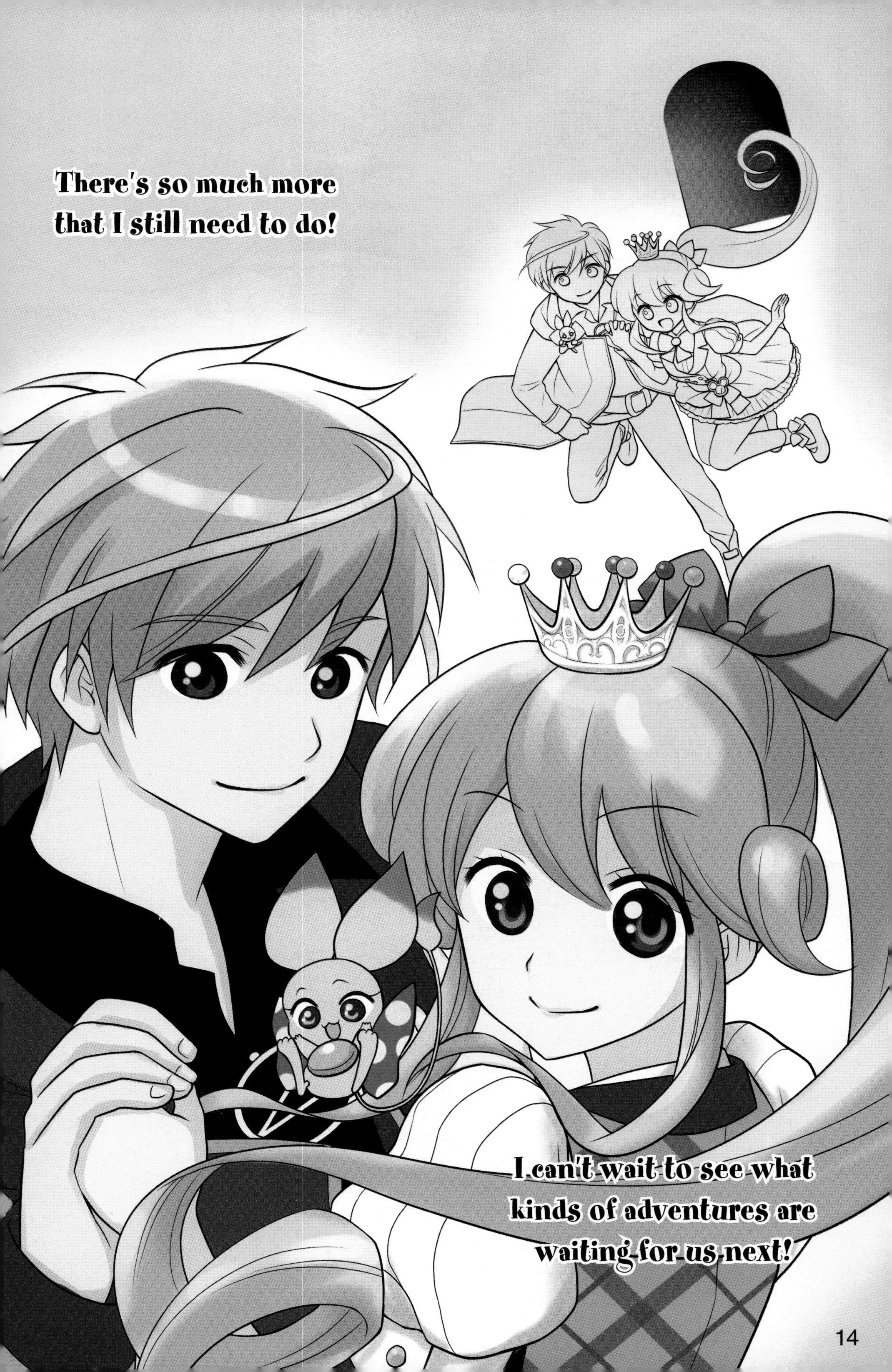
There's so much more that I still need to do!
I can't wait to see what kinds of adventures are waiting for us next!

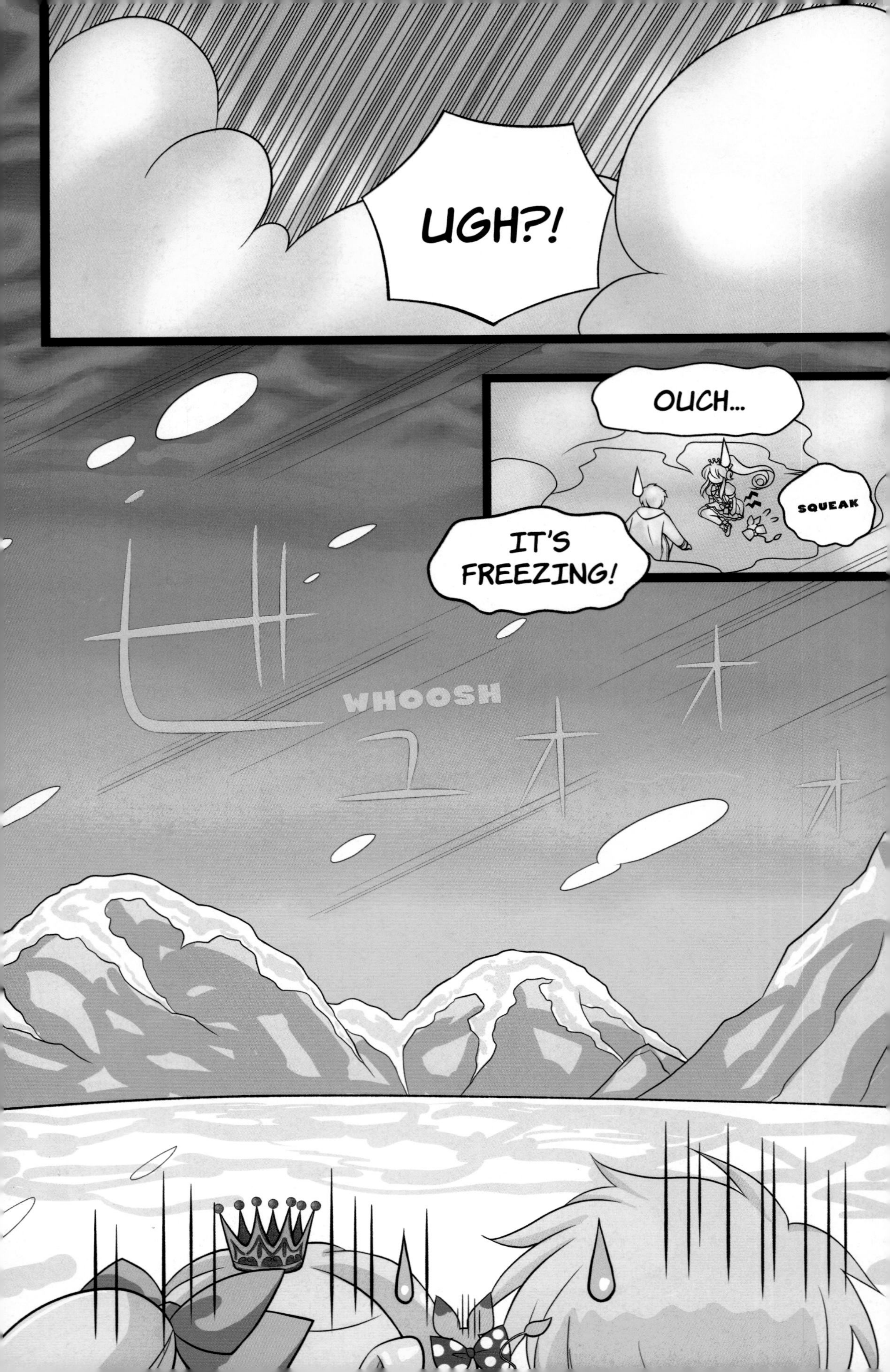
UGH?!
OUCH...
SQUEAK
IT'S FREEZING!
ヒュオオオ
WHOOSH

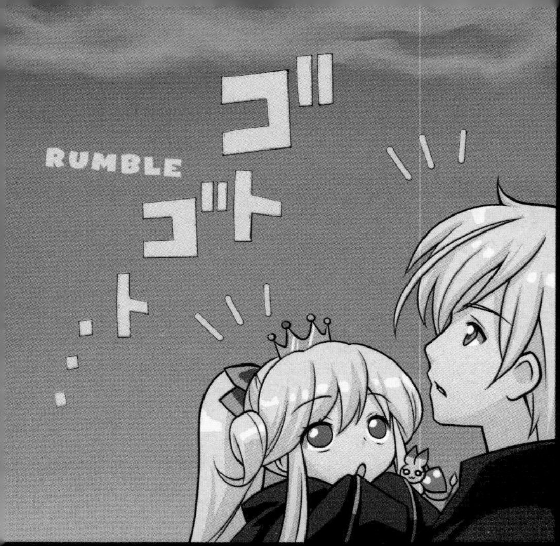
RUMBLE
ゴゴゴ
ト ト

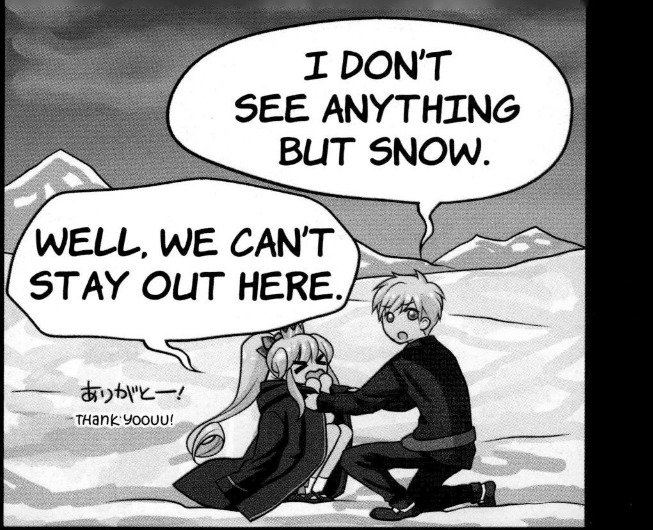
I DON'T SEE ANYTHING BUT SNOW.
WELL, WE CAN'T STAY OUT HERE.
ありがとー!
THANK YOOUU!

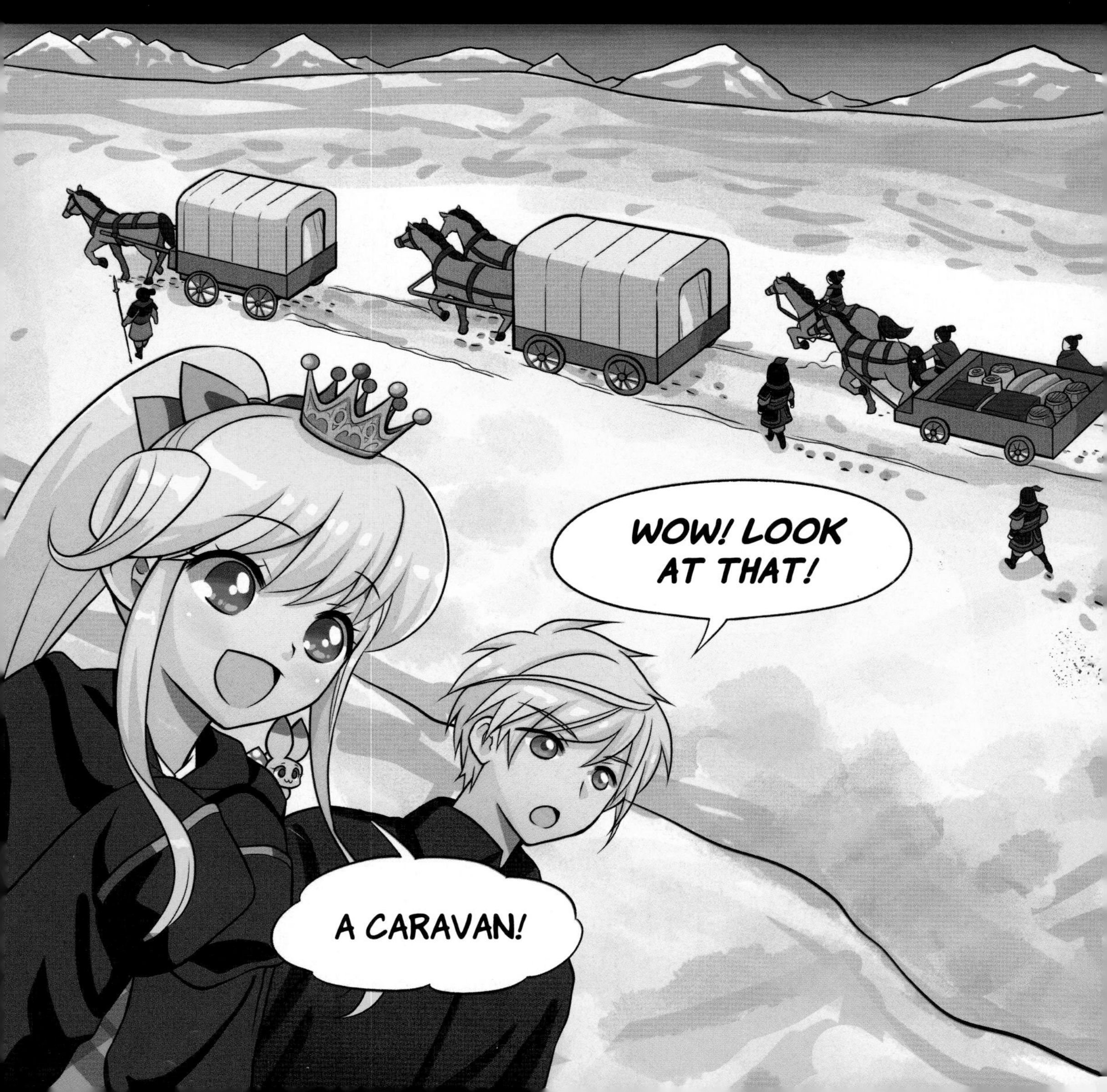
WOW! LOOK AT THAT!
A CARAVAN!

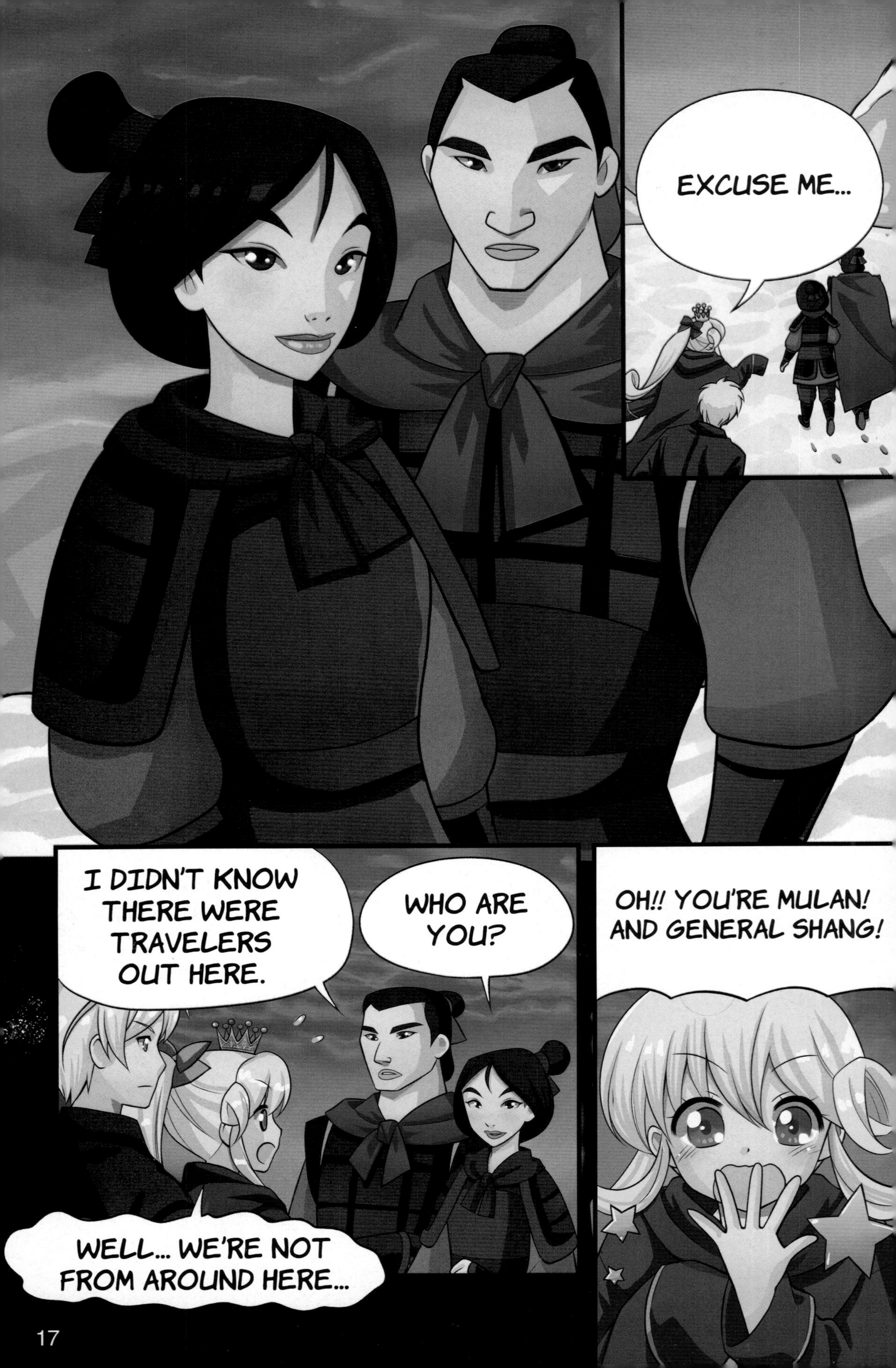
EXCUSE ME...
I DIDN'T KNOW THERE WERE TRAVELERS OUT HERE.
WHO ARE YOU?
WELL... WE'RE NOT FROM AROUND HERE...
OH!! YOU'RE MULAN! AND GENERAL SHANG!

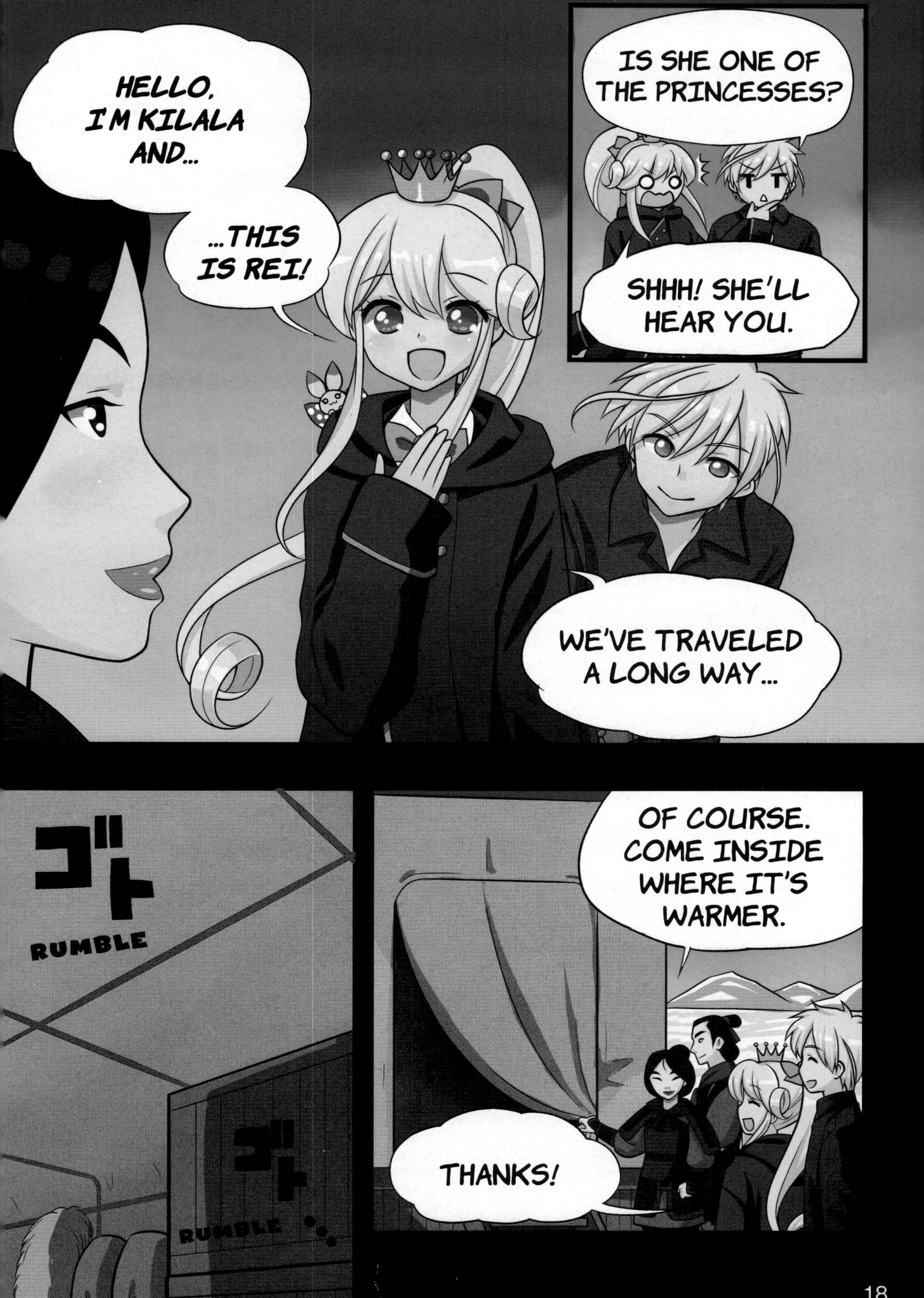
HELLO, I'M KILALA AND...
...THIS IS REI!
IS SHE ONE OF THE PRINCESSES?
SHHH! SHE'LL HEAR YOU.
WE'VE TRAVELED A LONG WAY...
ゴト
RUMBLE
ゴト
RUMBLE
OF COURSE. COME INSIDE WHERE IT'S WARMER.
THANKS!

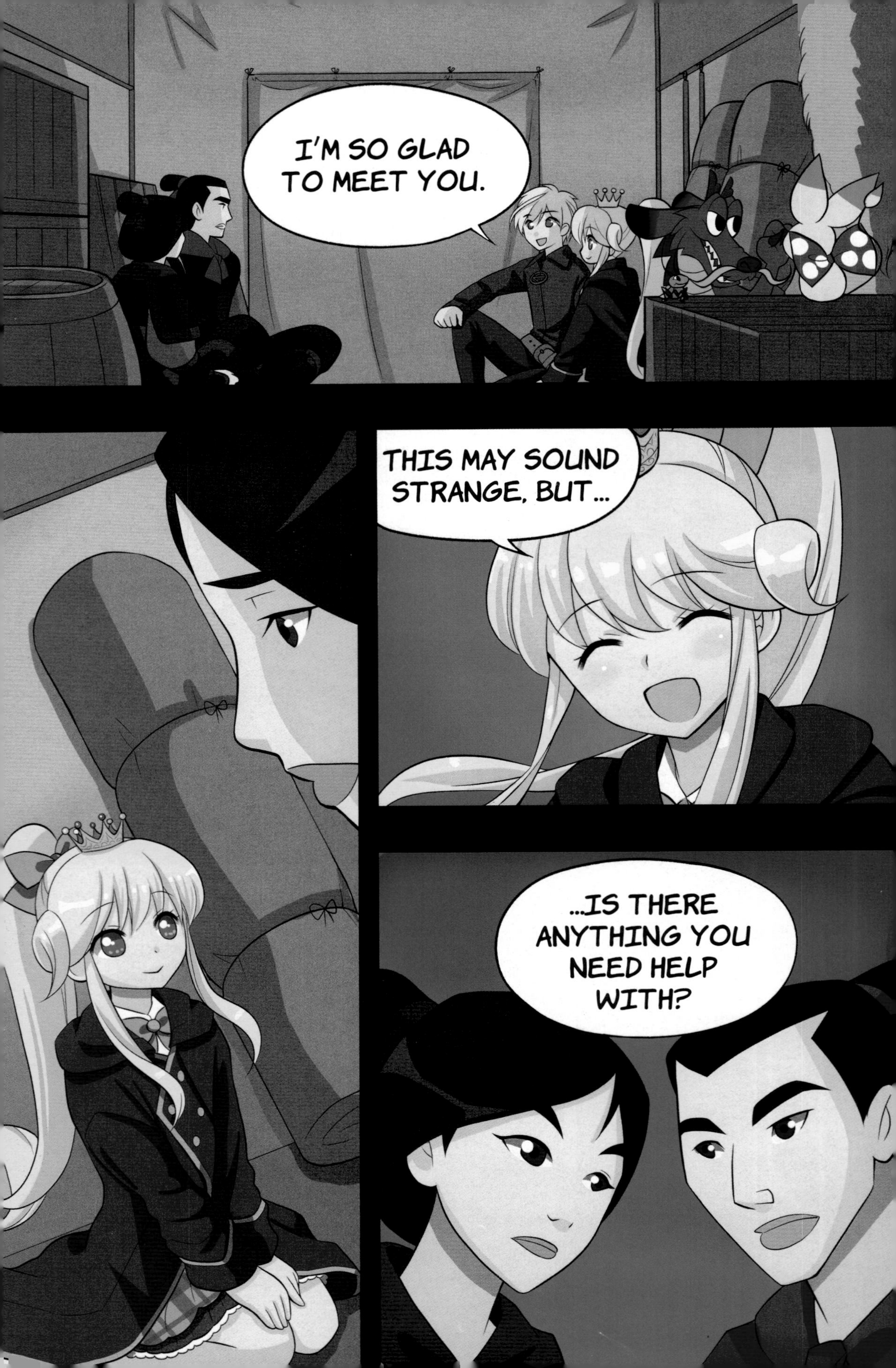
I'M SO GLAD TO MEET YOU.
THIS MAY SOUND STRANGE, BUT...
...IS THERE ANYTHING YOU NEED HELP WITH?

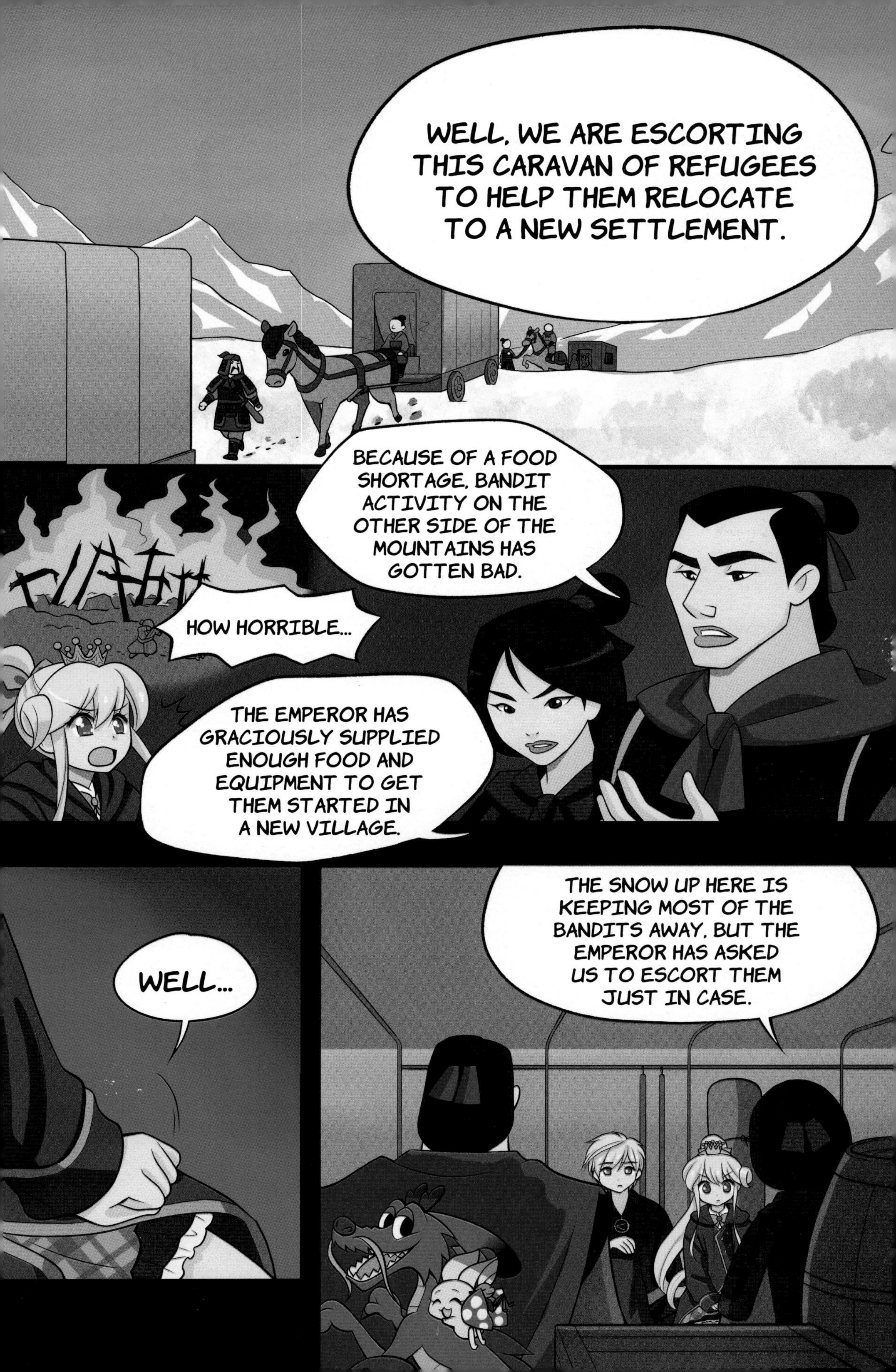

WELL, WE ARE ESCORTING THIS CARAVAN OF REFUGEES TO HELP THEM RELOCATE TO A NEW SETTLEMENT.
BECAUSE OF A FOOD SHORTAGE, BANDIT ACTIVITY ON THE OTHER SIDE OF THE MOUNTAINS HAS GOTTEN BAD.
HOW HORRIBLE...
THE EMPEROR HAS GRACIOUSLY SUPPLIED ENOUGH FOOD AND EQUIPMENT TO GET THEM STARTED IN A NEW VILLAGE.
WELL...
THE SNOW UP HERE IS KEEPING MOST OF THE BANDITS AWAY, BUT THE EMPEROR HAS ASKED US TO ESCORT THEM JUST IN CASE.

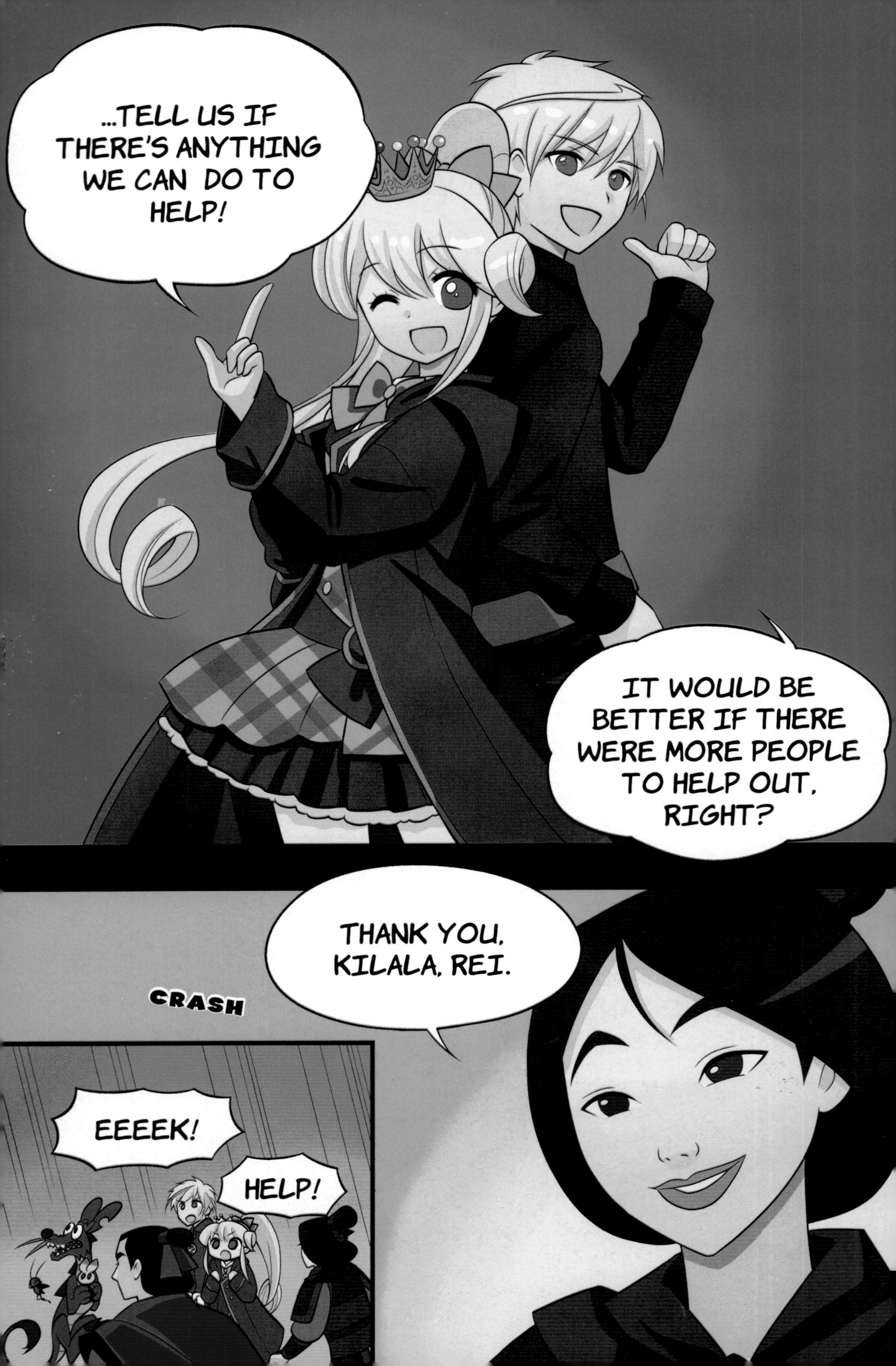
...TELL US IF THERE'S ANYTHING WE CAN DO TO HELP!
IT WOULD BE BETTER IF THERE WERE MORE PEOPLE TO HELP OUT, RIGHT?
CRASH
EEEEK!
HELP!
THANK YOU, KILALA, REI.

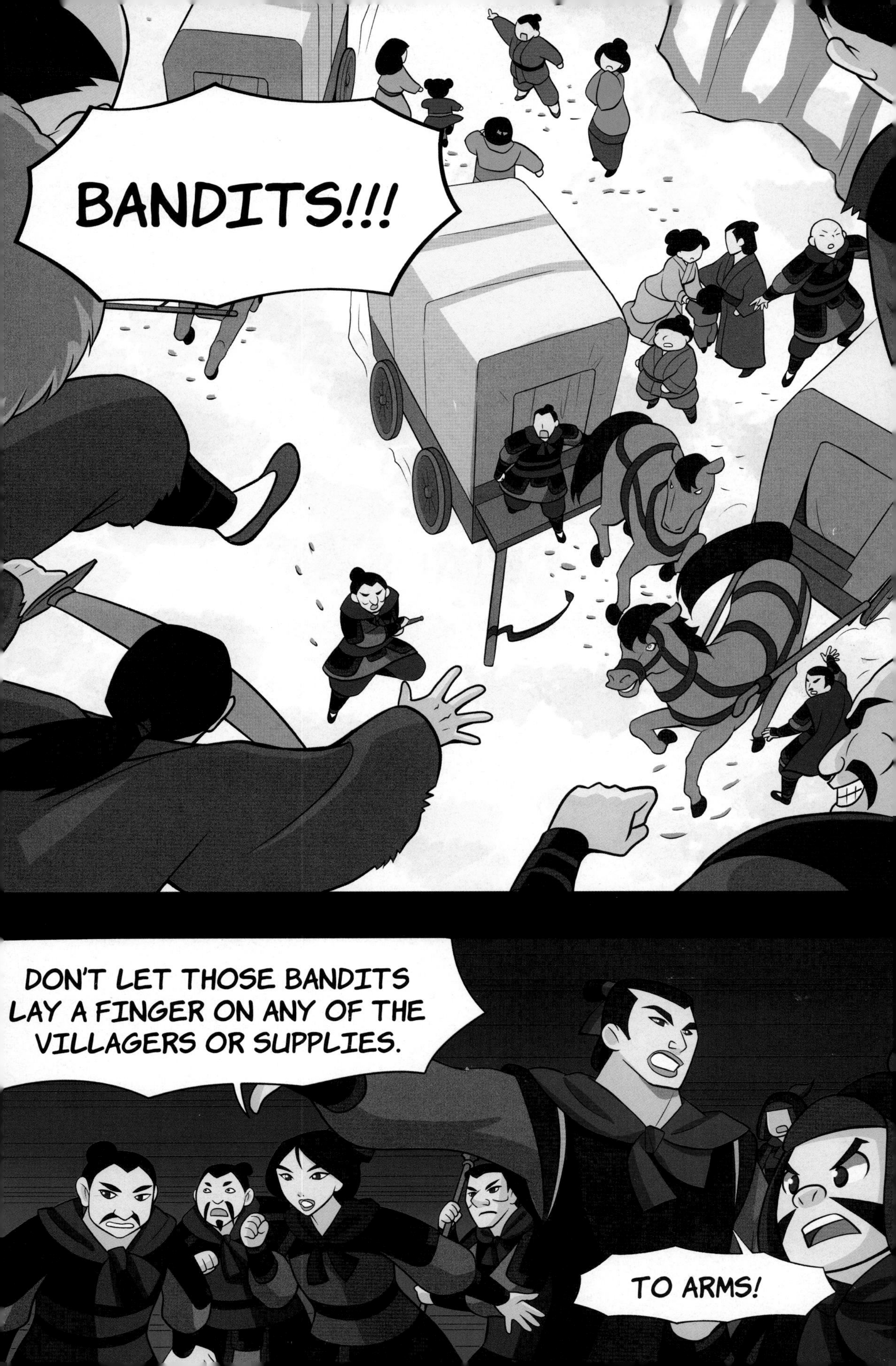
BANDITS!!!
DON'T LET THOSE BANDITS LAY A FINGER ON ANY OF THE VILLAGERS OR SUPPLIES.
TO ARMS!

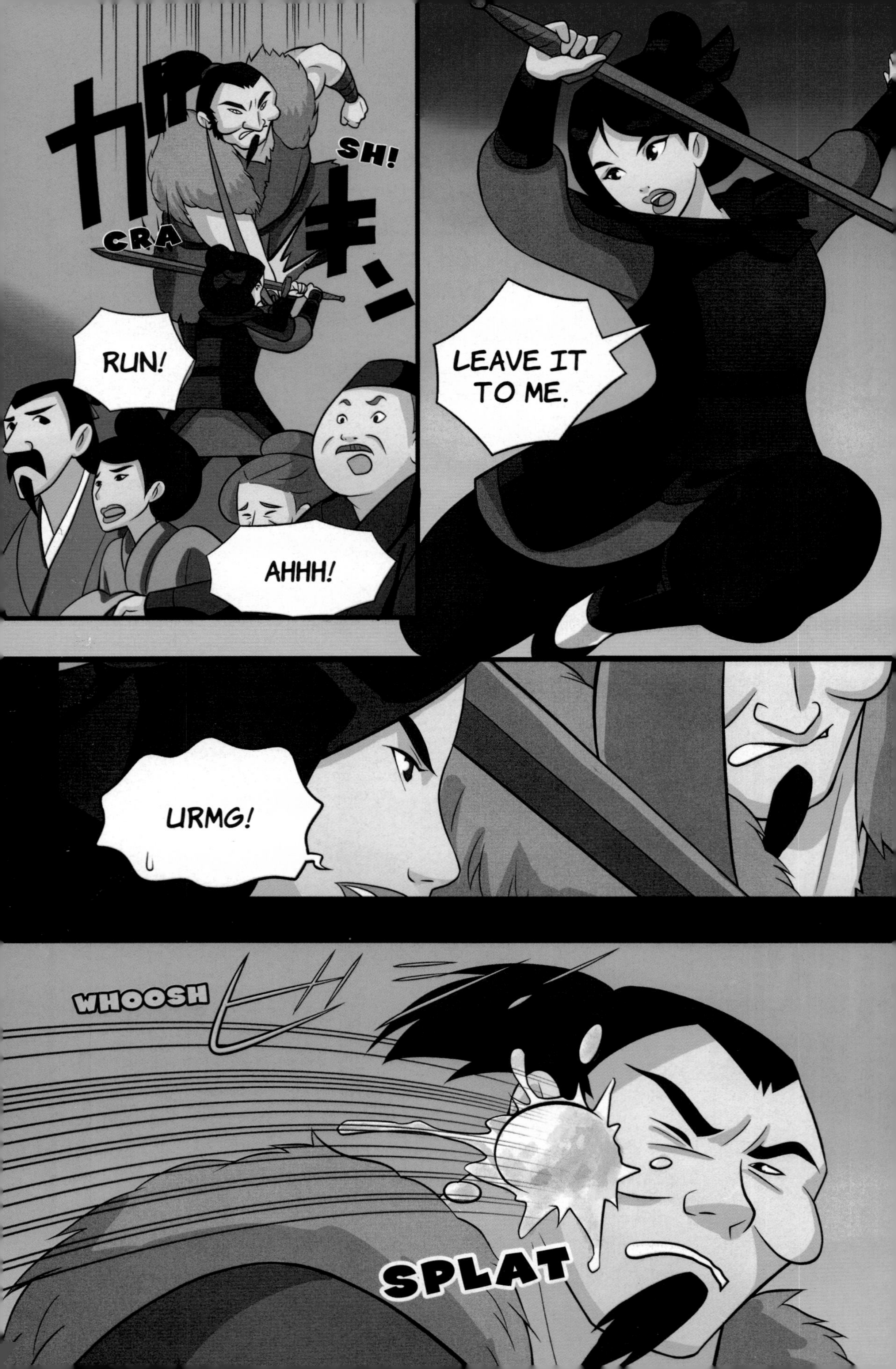
カキーン
CRA
SH!
RUN!
AHHH!
LEAVE IT TO ME.
URMG!
WHOOSH
SPLAT

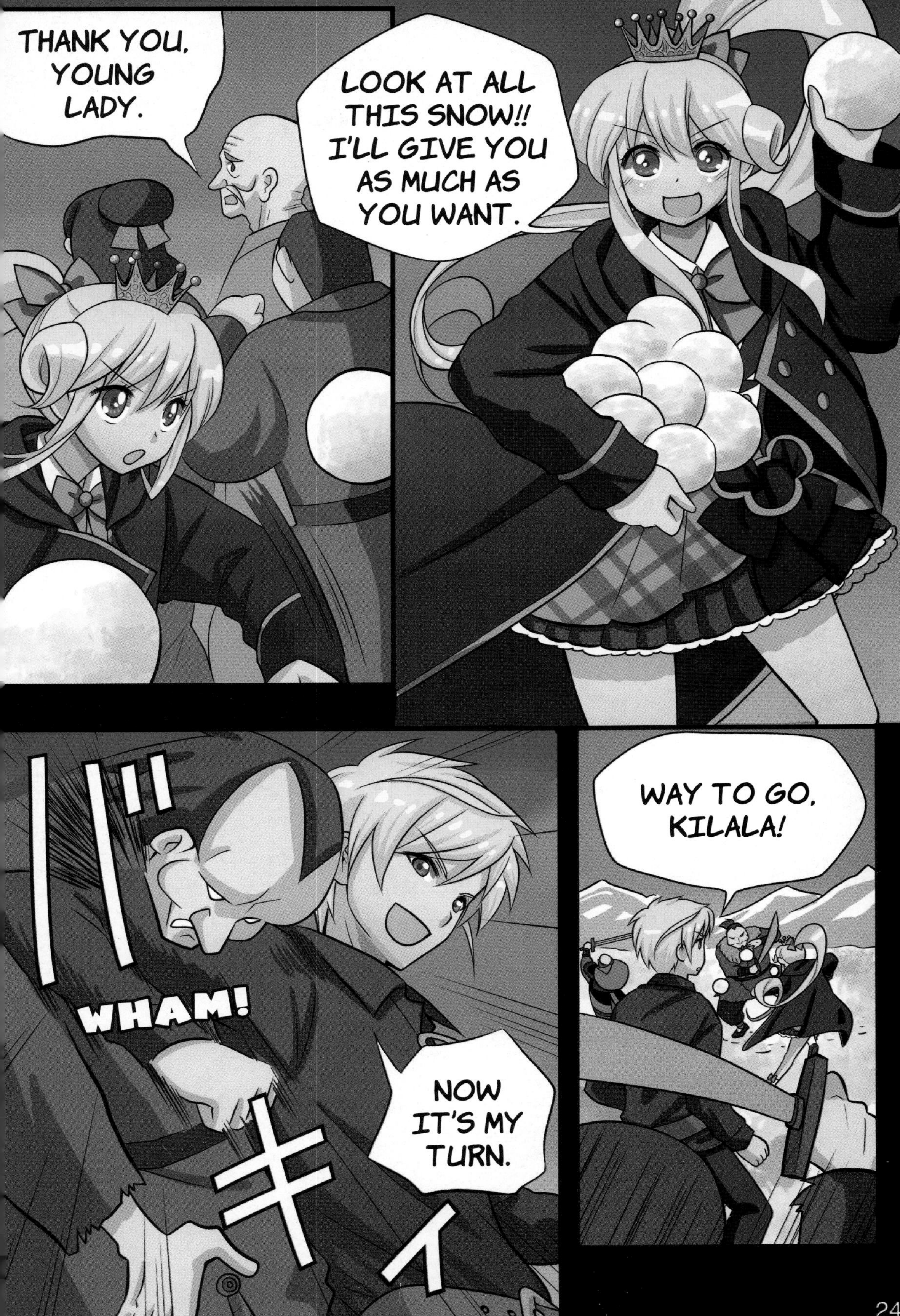
THANK YOU, YOUNG LADY.
LOOK AT ALL THIS SNOW!! I'LL GIVE YOU AS MUCH AS YOU WANT.
バ
WHAM!
キイ
NOW IT'S MY TURN.
WAY TO GO, KILALA!

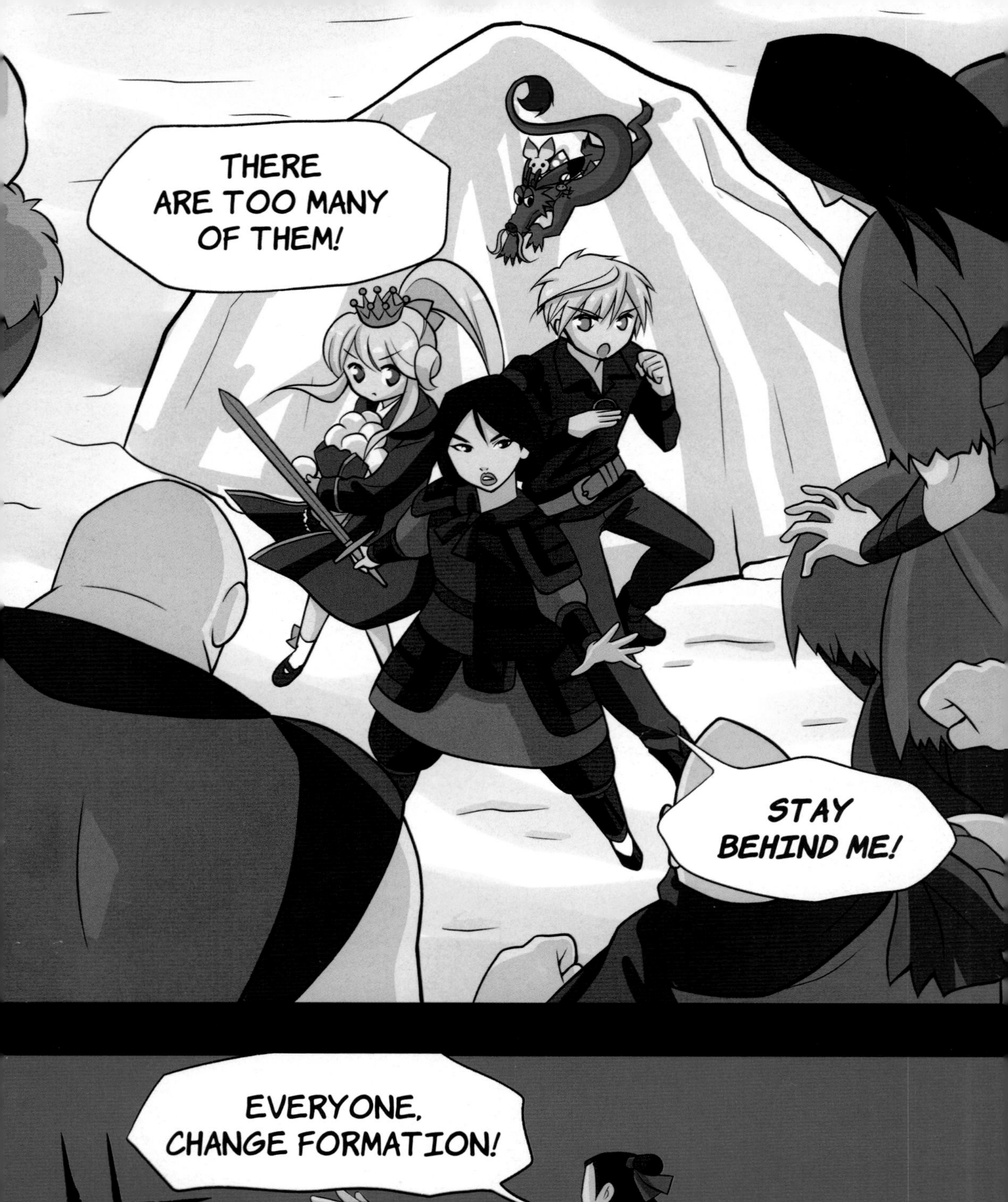
THERE ARE TOO MANY OF THEM!
STAY BEHIND ME!

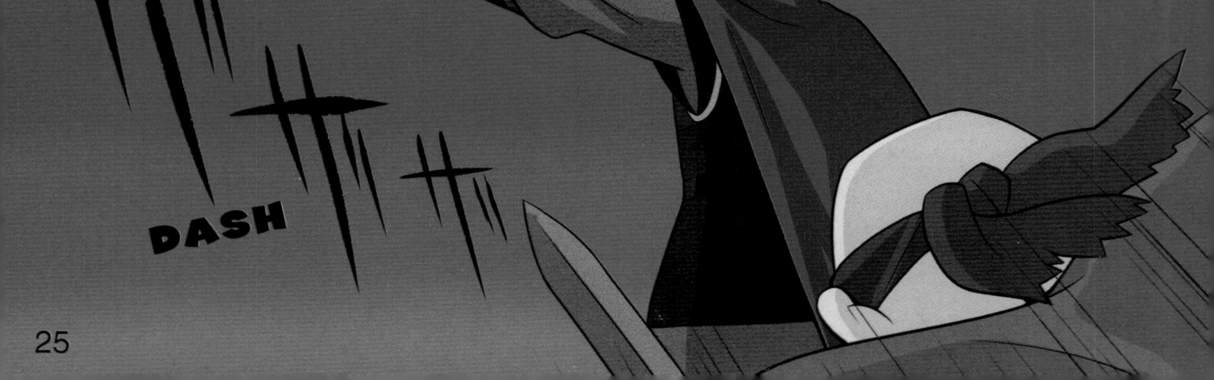
EVERYONE, CHANGE FORMATION!
DASH

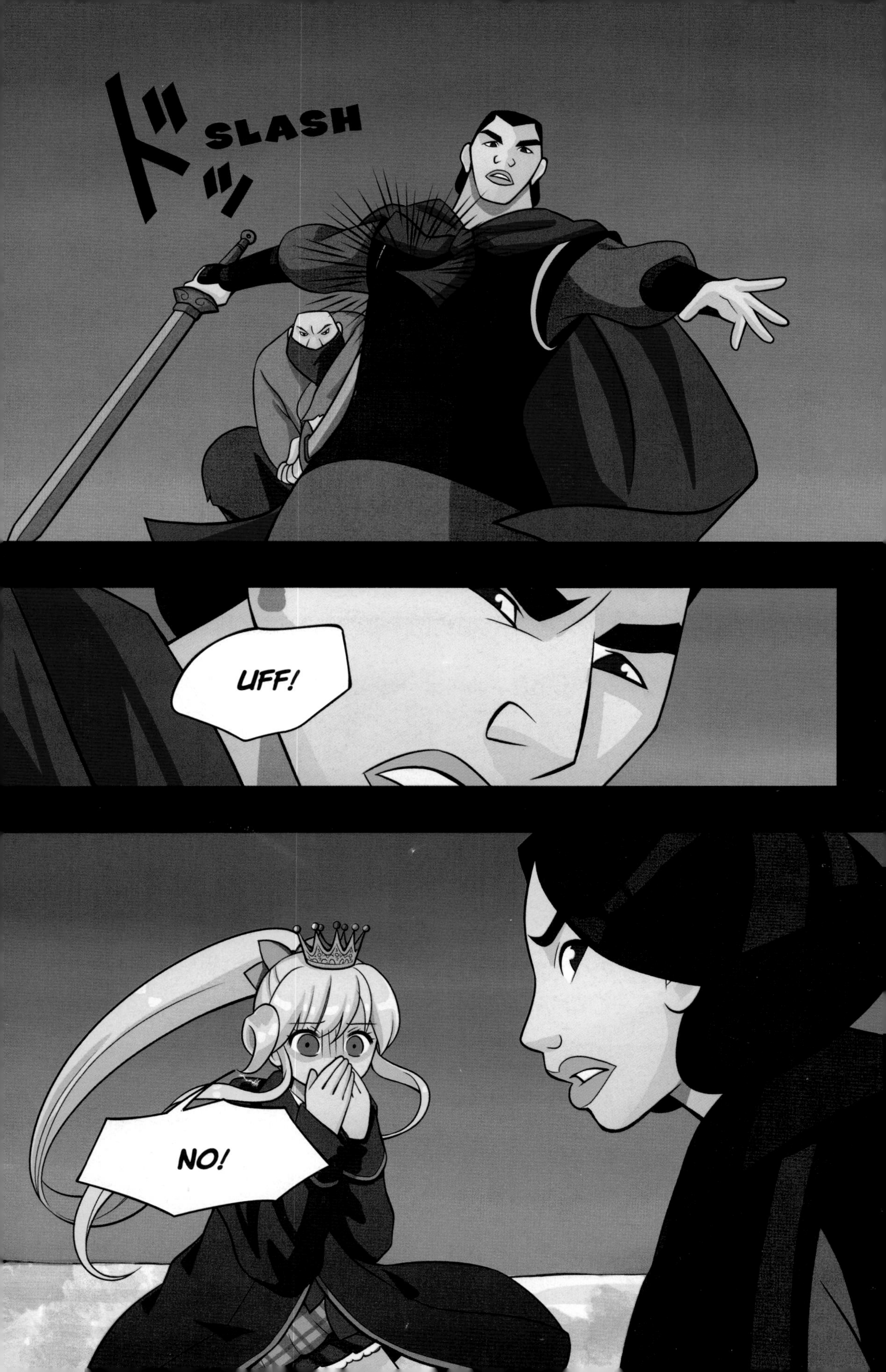
ドッ
SLASH
UFF!
NO!

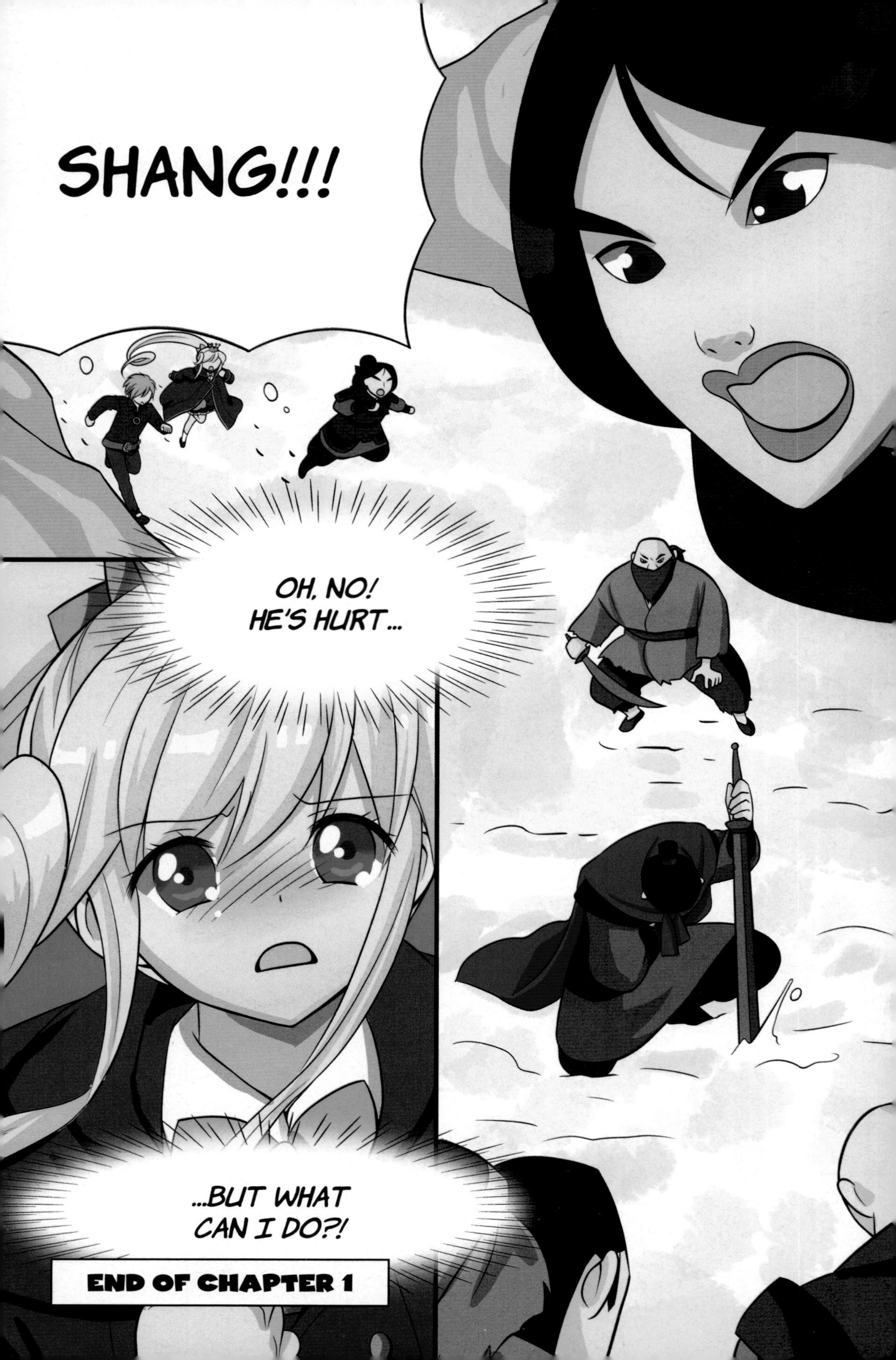
SHANG!!!
OH, NO! HE'S HURT...
...BUT WHAT CAN I DO?!
END OF CHAPTER 1

Disney

Kilala Princess

Rescue the Village with Mulan!

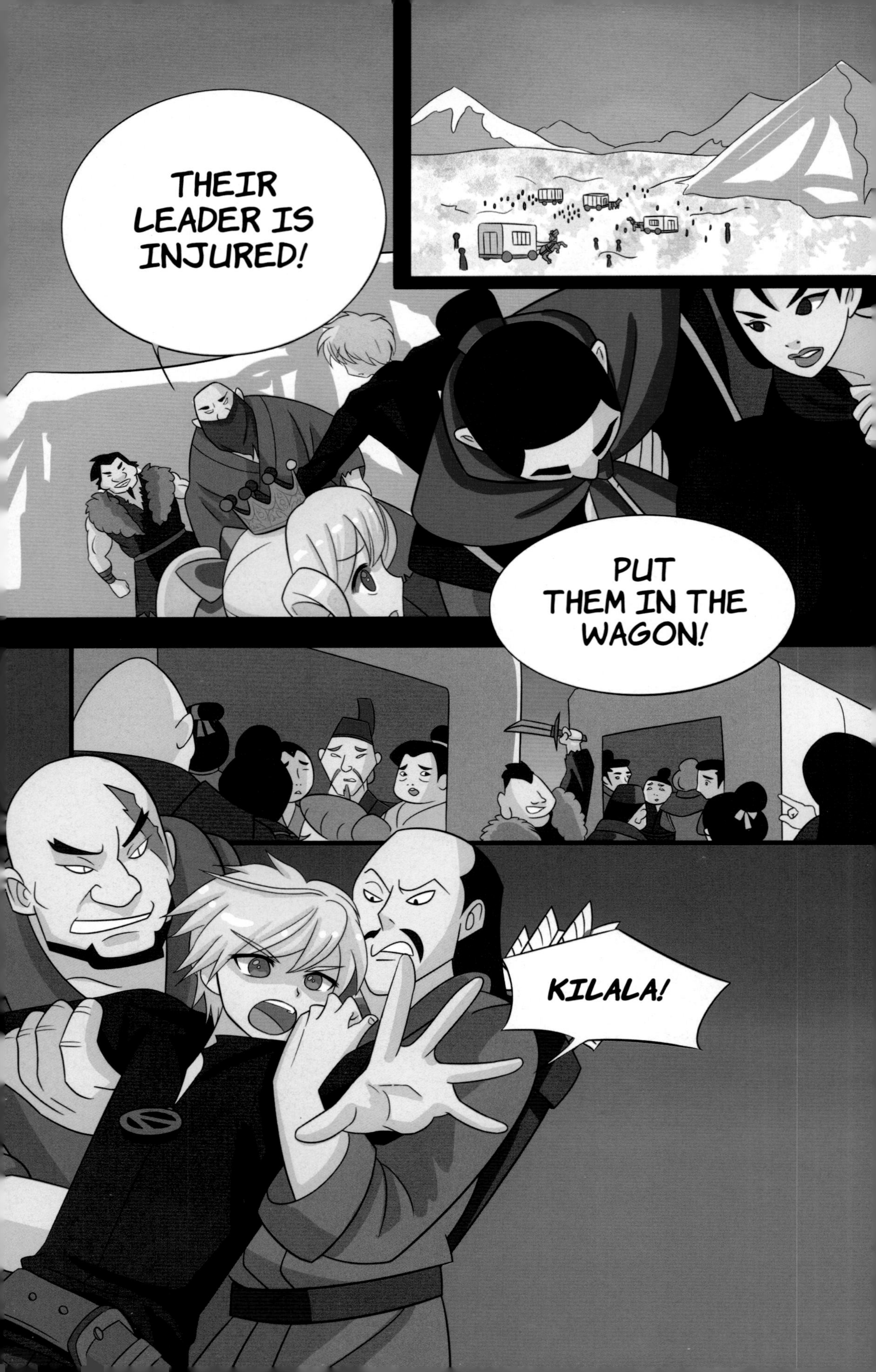
THEIR LEADER IS INJURED!
PUT THEM IN THE WAGON!
KILALA!

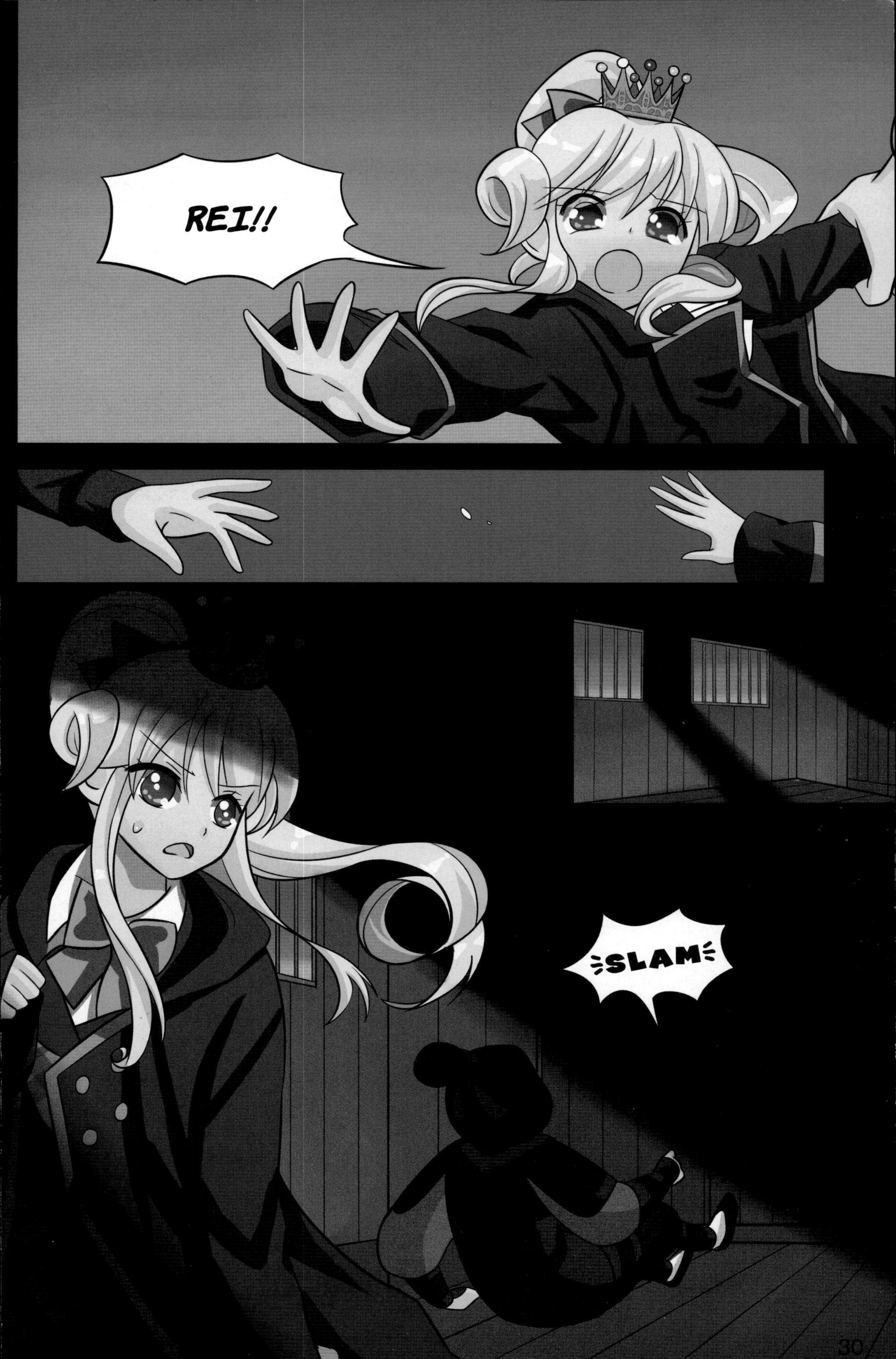
REI!!
SLAM

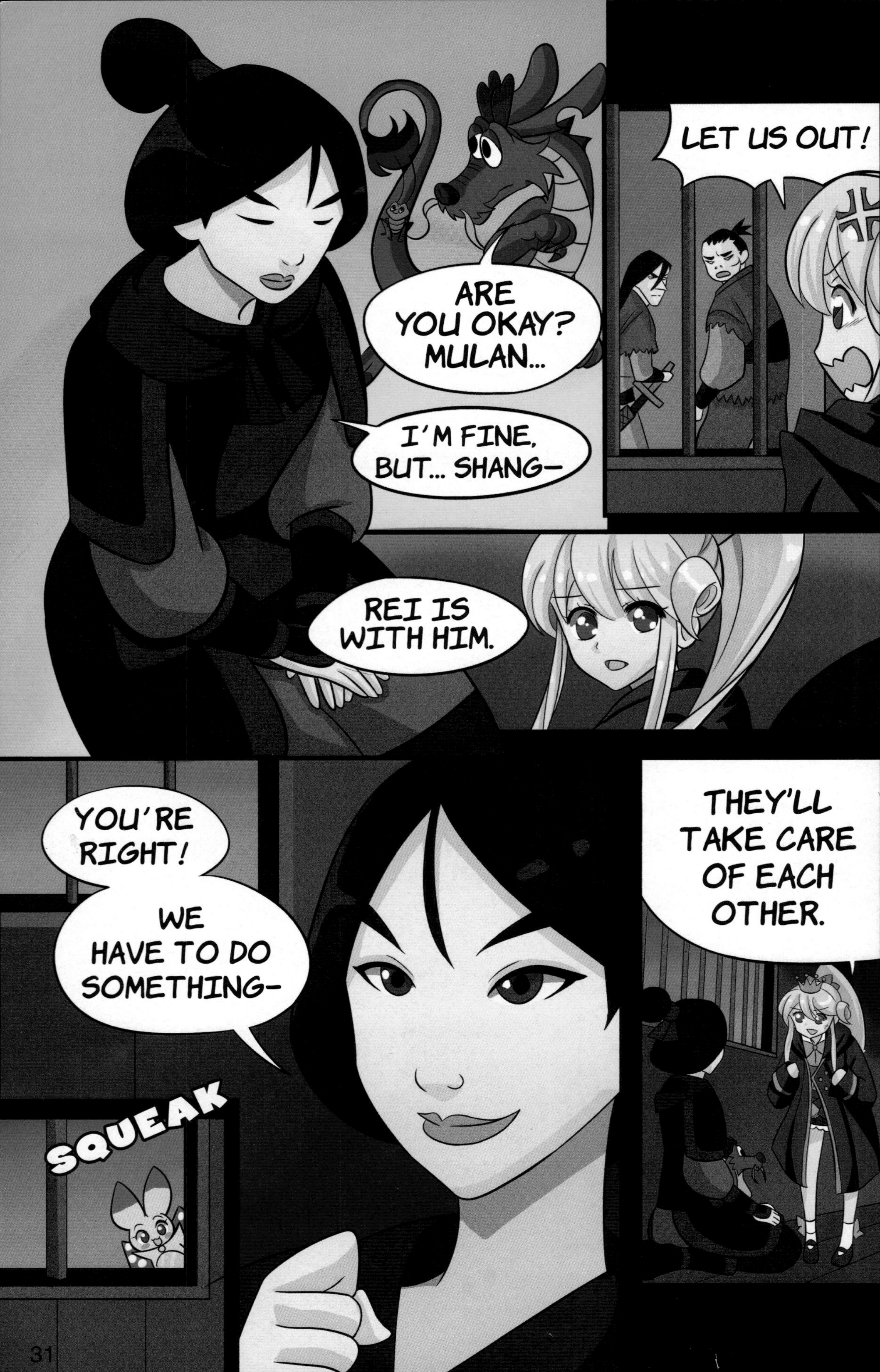
ARE YOU OKAY? MULAN...
I'M FINE, BUT... SHANG—
LET US OUT!
REI IS WITH HIM.
YOU'RE RIGHT!
WE HAVE TO DO SOMETHING—
SQUEAK
THEY'LL TAKE CARE OF EACH OTHER.

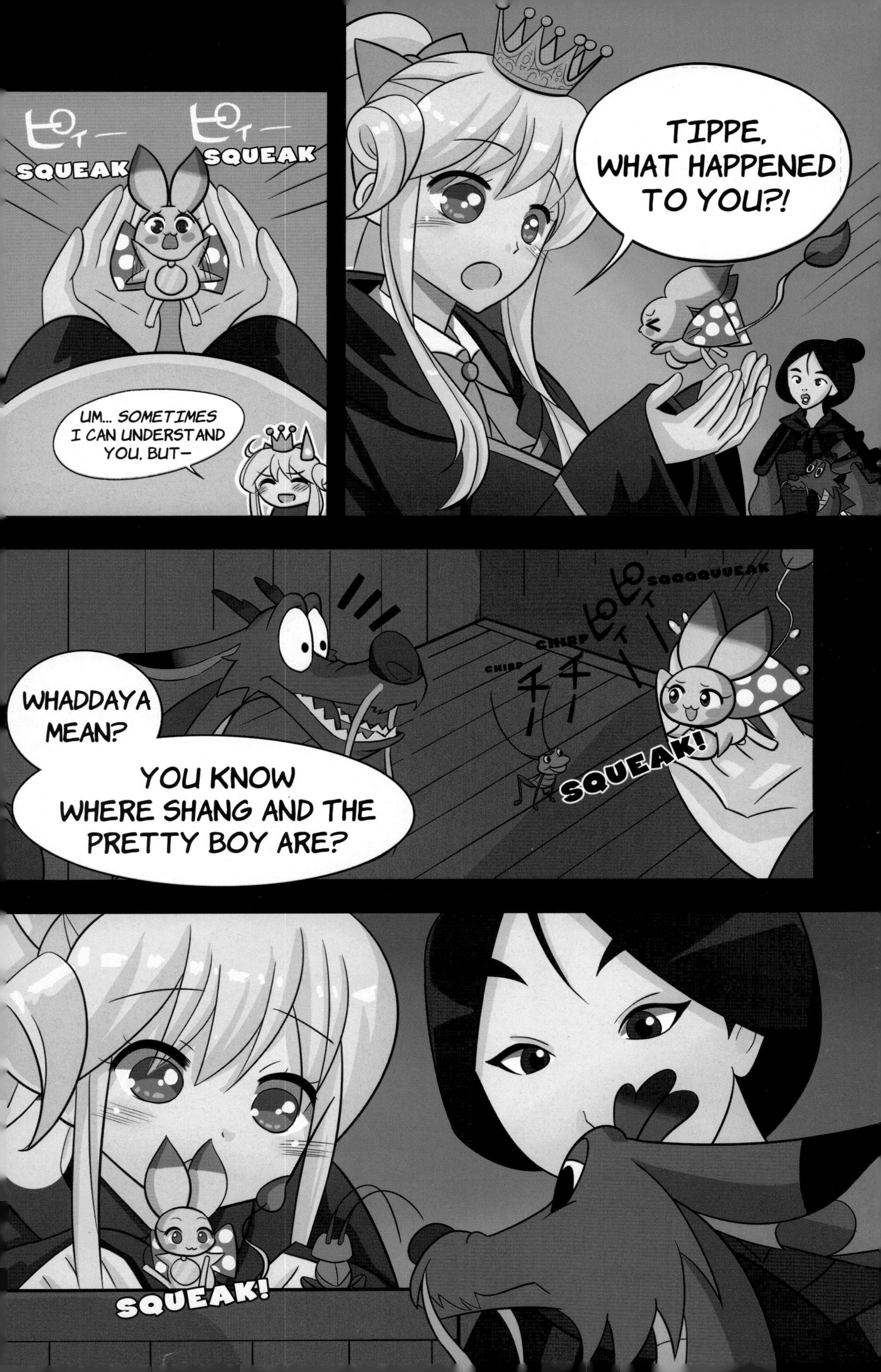

ピィー
SQUEAK
ピィー
SQUEAK
UM... SOMETIMES I CAN UNDERSTAND YOU, BUT–
TIPPE, WHAT HAPPENED TO YOU?!
WHADDAYA MEAN?
YOU KNOW WHERE SHANG AND THE PRETTY BOY ARE?
CHIRP
チー
CHIRP
チー
ピィピィー
SQQQQUUEAK
SQUEAK!
SQUEAK!

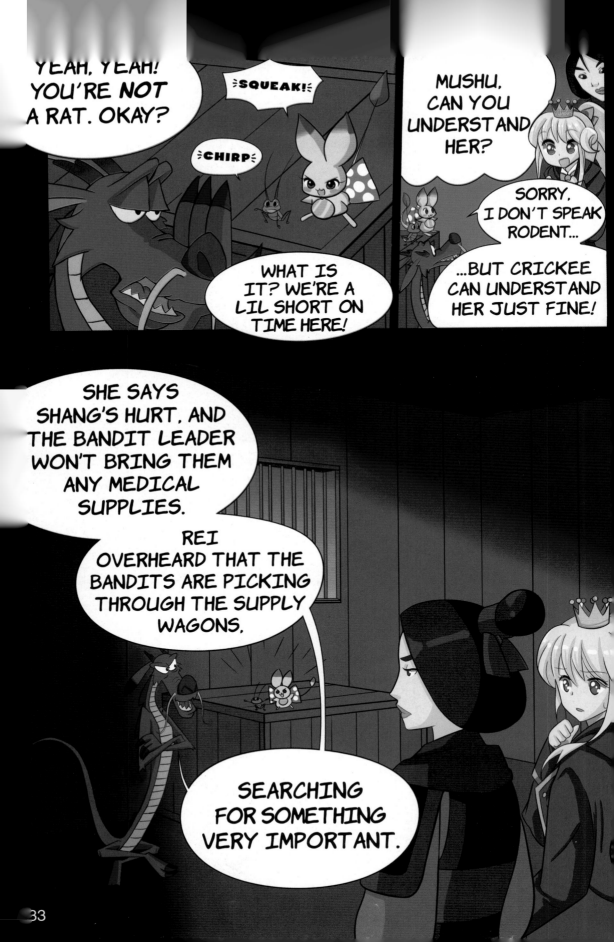

YEAH, YEAH! YOU'RE **NOT** A RAT. OKAY?

≷SQUEAK!≶

≷CHIRP≶

WHAT IS IT? WE'RE A LIL SHORT ON TIME HERE!

MUSHU, CAN YOU UNDERSTAND HER?

SORRY, I DON'T SPEAK RODENT...

...BUT CRICKEE CAN UNDERSTAND HER JUST FINE!

SHE SAYS SHANG'S HURT, AND THE BANDIT LEADER WON'T BRING THEM ANY MEDICAL SUPPLIES.

REI OVERHEARD THAT THE BANDITS ARE PICKING THROUGH THE SUPPLY WAGONS,

SEARCHING FOR SOMETHING VERY IMPORTANT.

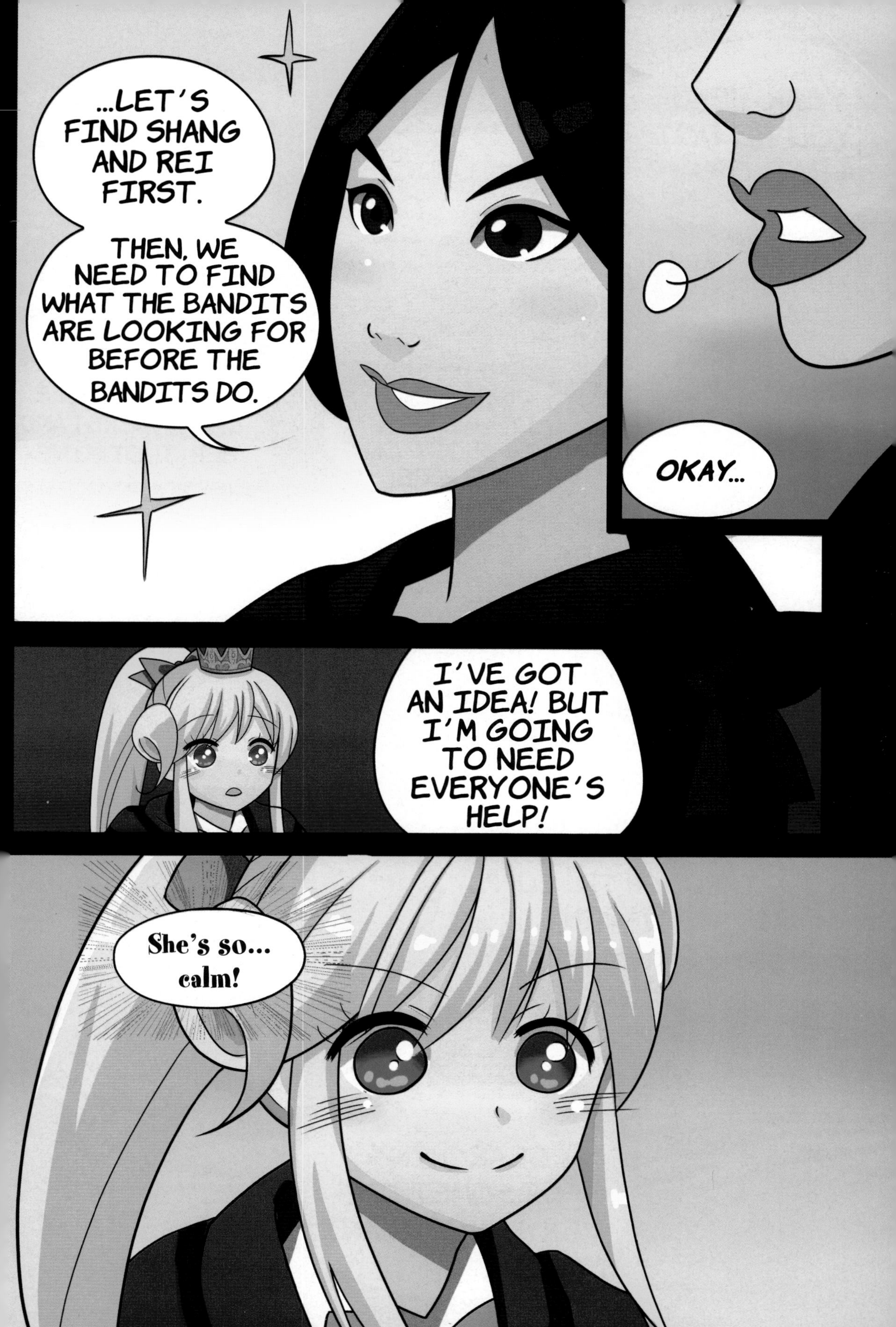
...LET'S FIND SHANG AND REI FIRST.
THEN, WE NEED TO FIND WHAT THE BANDITS ARE LOOKING FOR BEFORE THE BANDITS DO.
OKAY...
I'VE GOT AN IDEA! BUT I'M GOING TO NEED EVERYONE'S HELP!
She's so... calm!

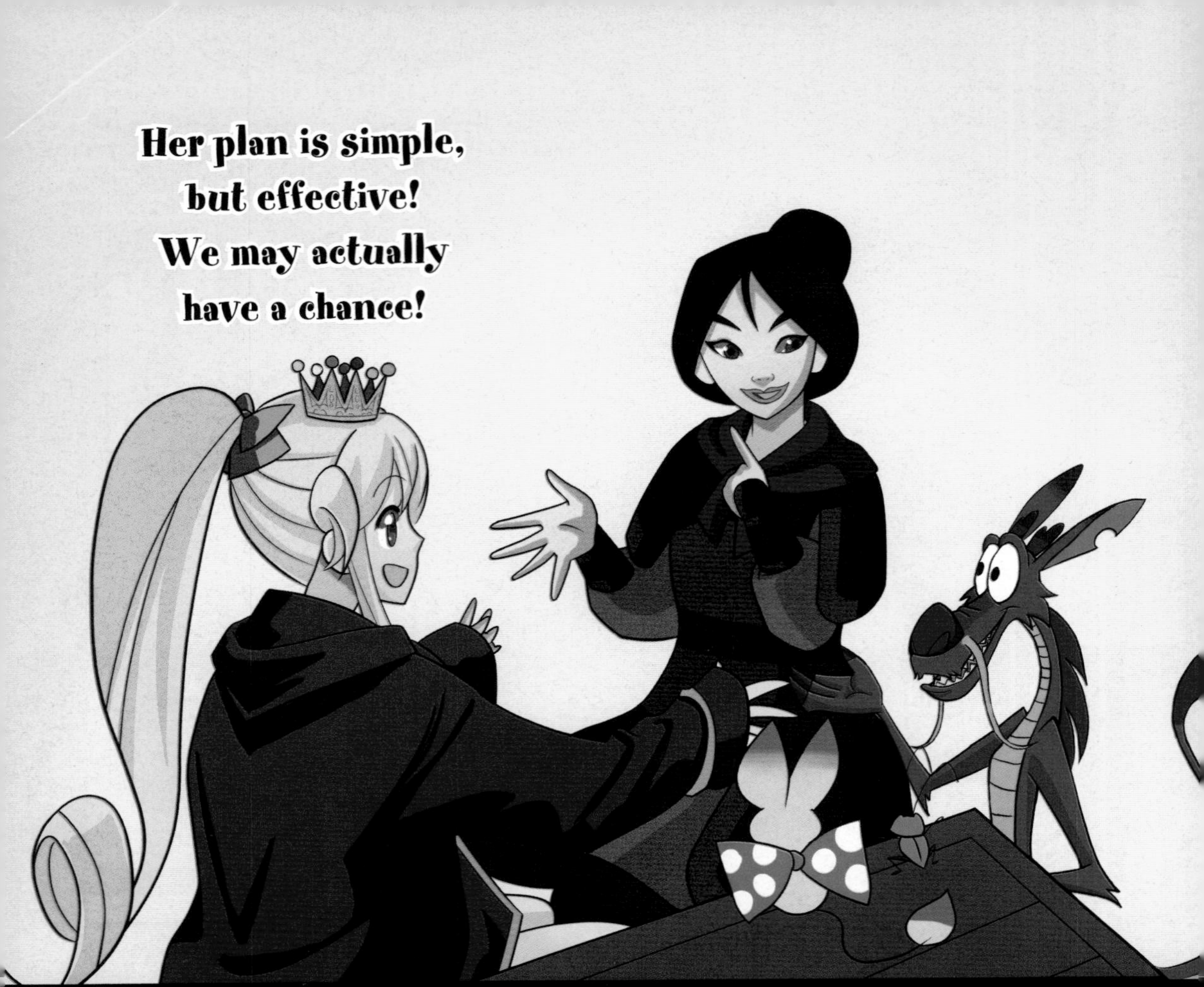
Her plan is simple, but effective! We may actually have a chance!

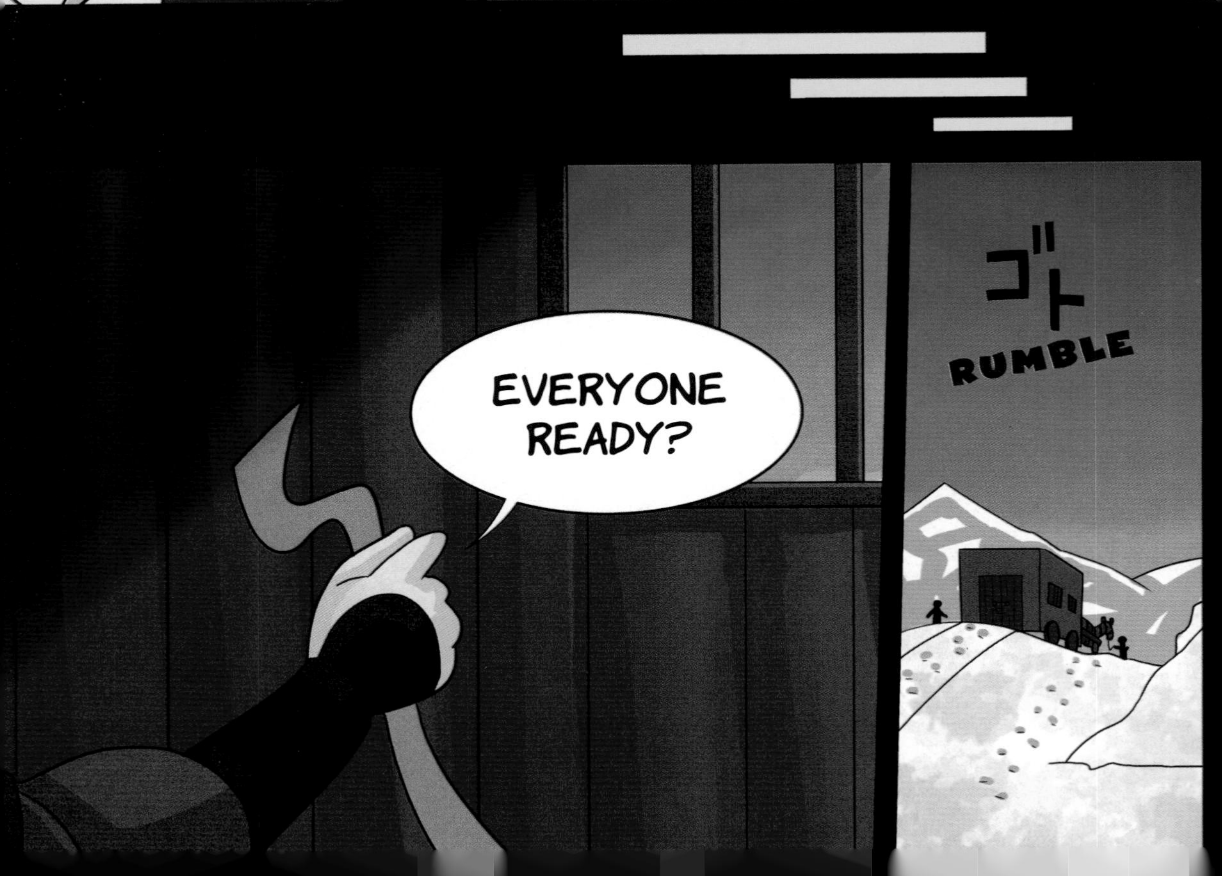
ゴト
RUMBLE
EVERYONE READY?

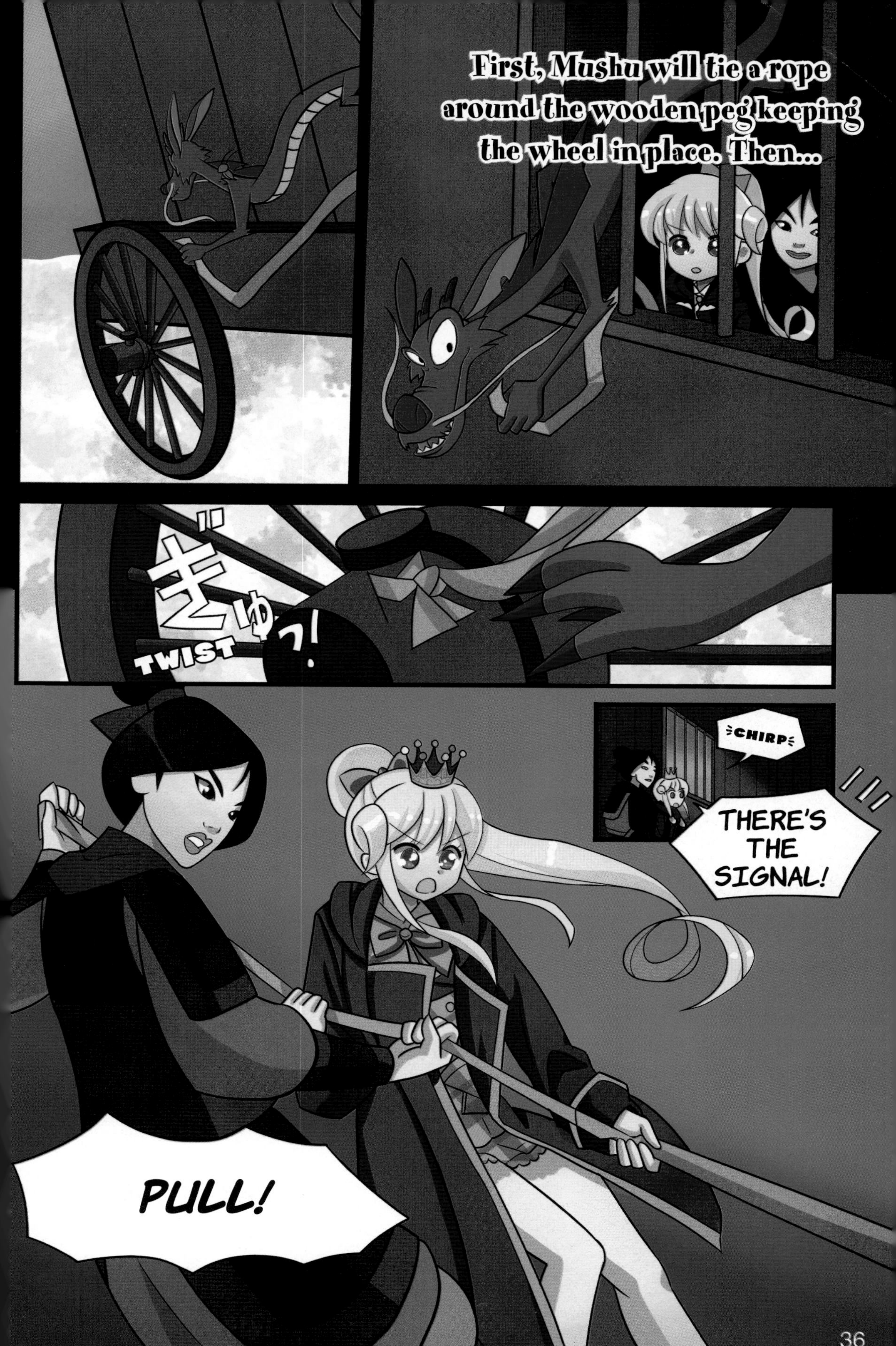

First, Mushu will tie a rope around the wooden peg keeping the wheel in place. Then...
ぎゅっ!
TWIST
CHIRP
THERE'S THE SIGNAL!
PULL!

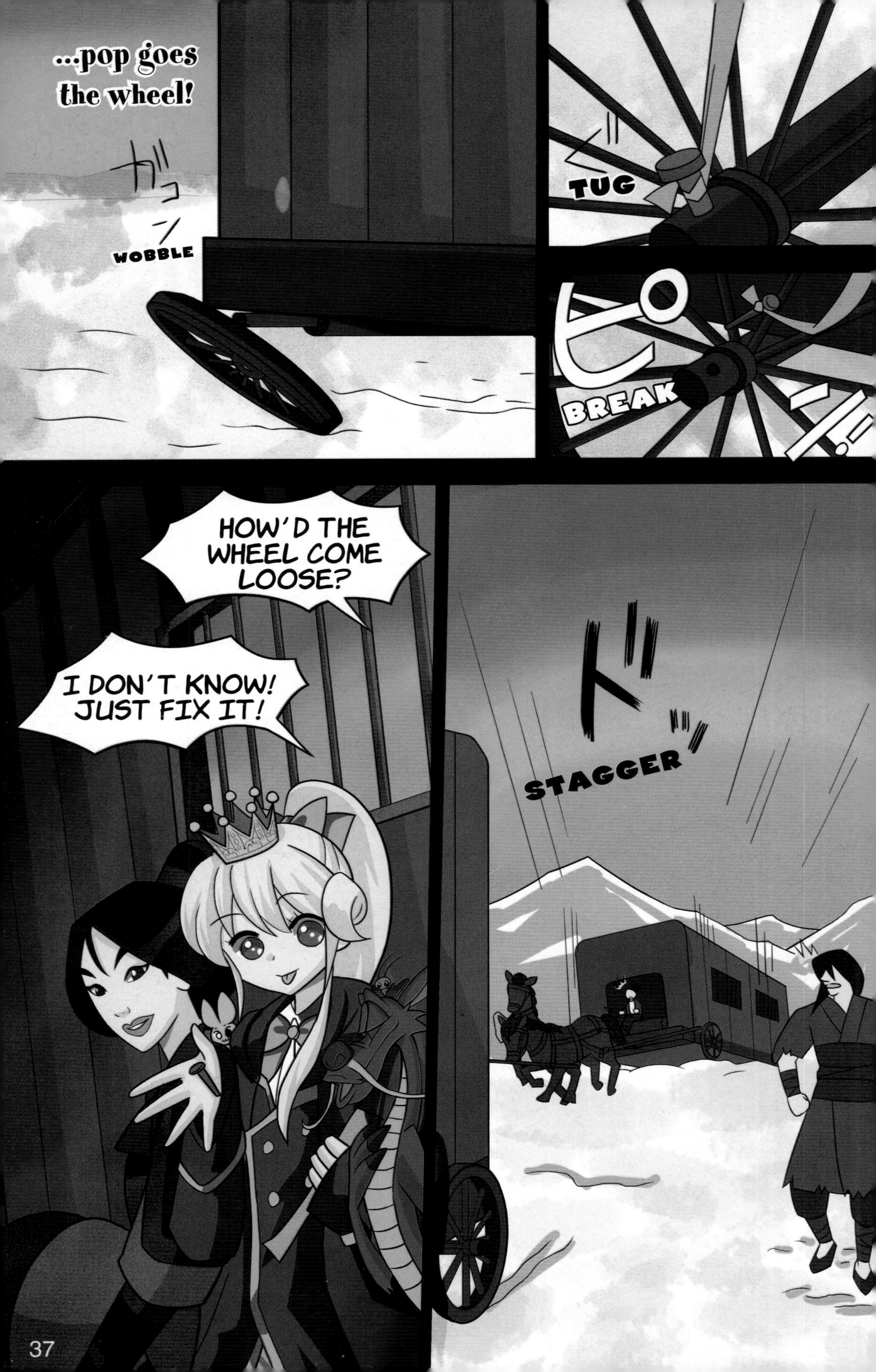
...pop goes the wheel!
ガコン
WOBBLE
TUG
BREAK
HOW'D THE WHEEL COME LOOSE?
I DON'T KNOW! JUST FIX IT!
STAGGER

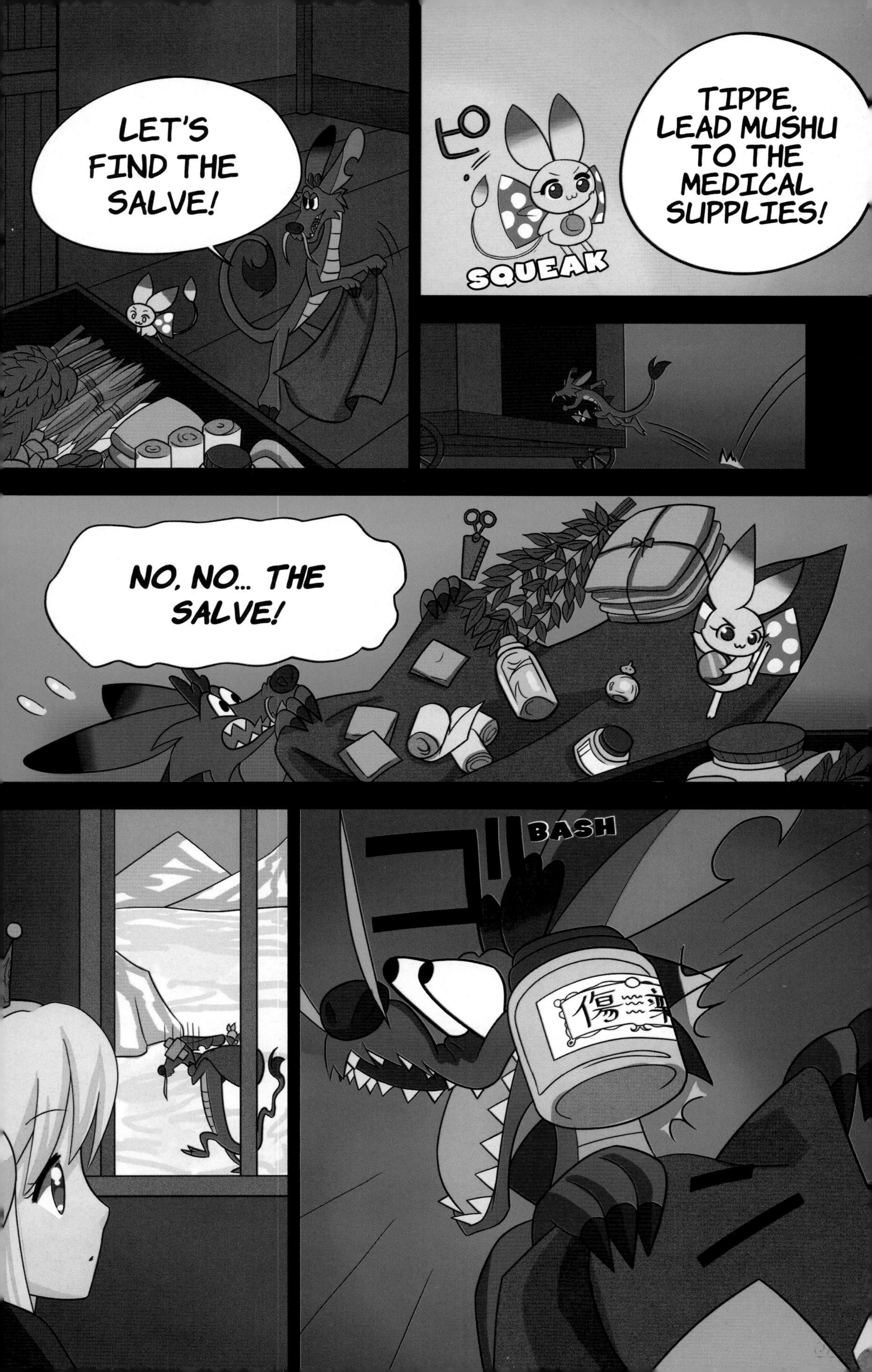
LET'S FIND THE SALVE!
TIPPE, LEAD MUSHU TO THE MEDICAL SUPPLIES!
SQUEAK
NO, NO... THE SALVE!
BASH

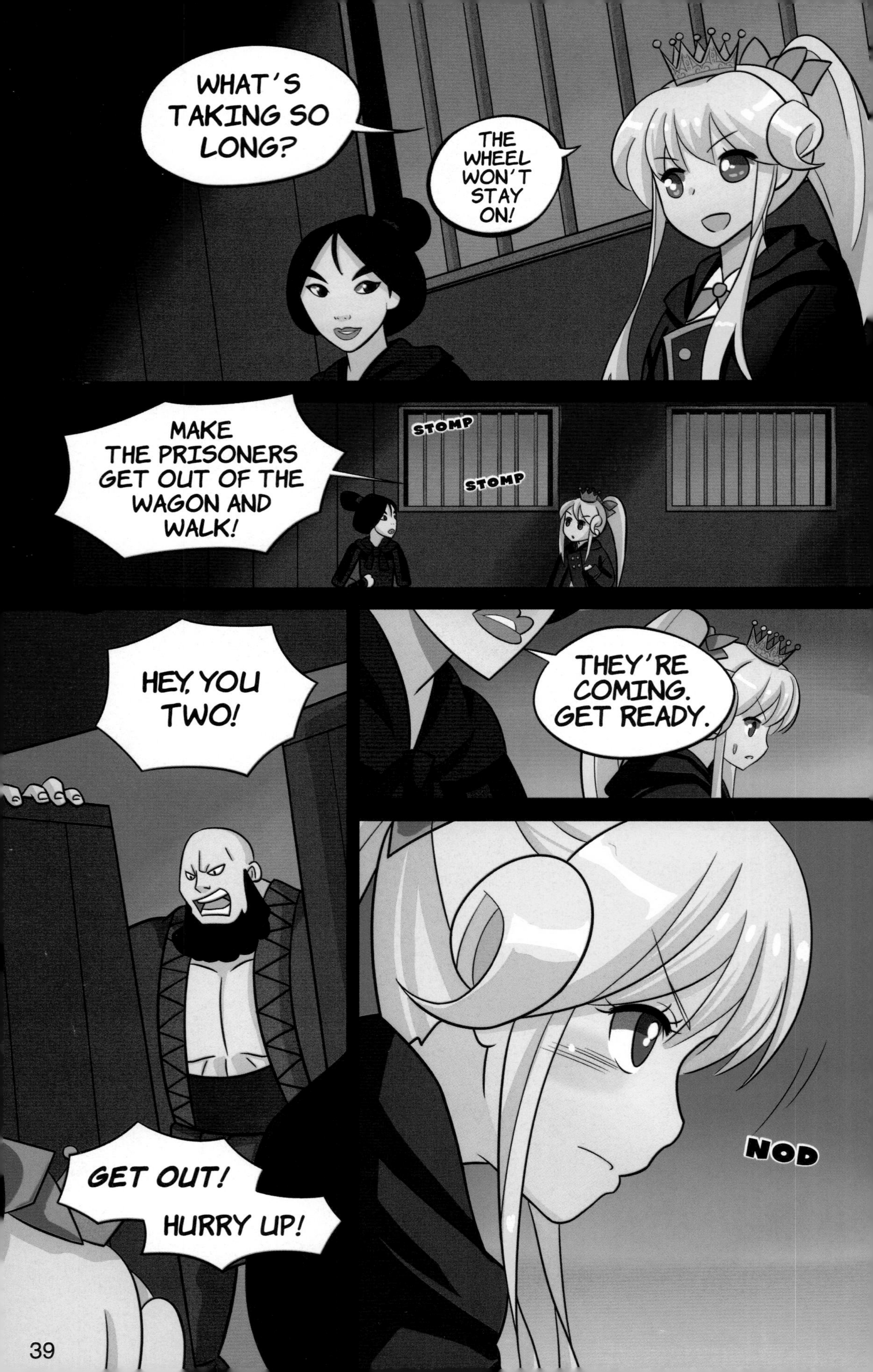
WHAT'S TAKING SO LONG?
THE WHEEL WON'T STAY ON!
MAKE THE PRISONERS GET OUT OF THE WAGON AND WALK!
STOMP
STOMP
HEY, YOU TWO!
GET OUT!
HURRY UP!
THEY'RE COMING. GET READY.
NOD

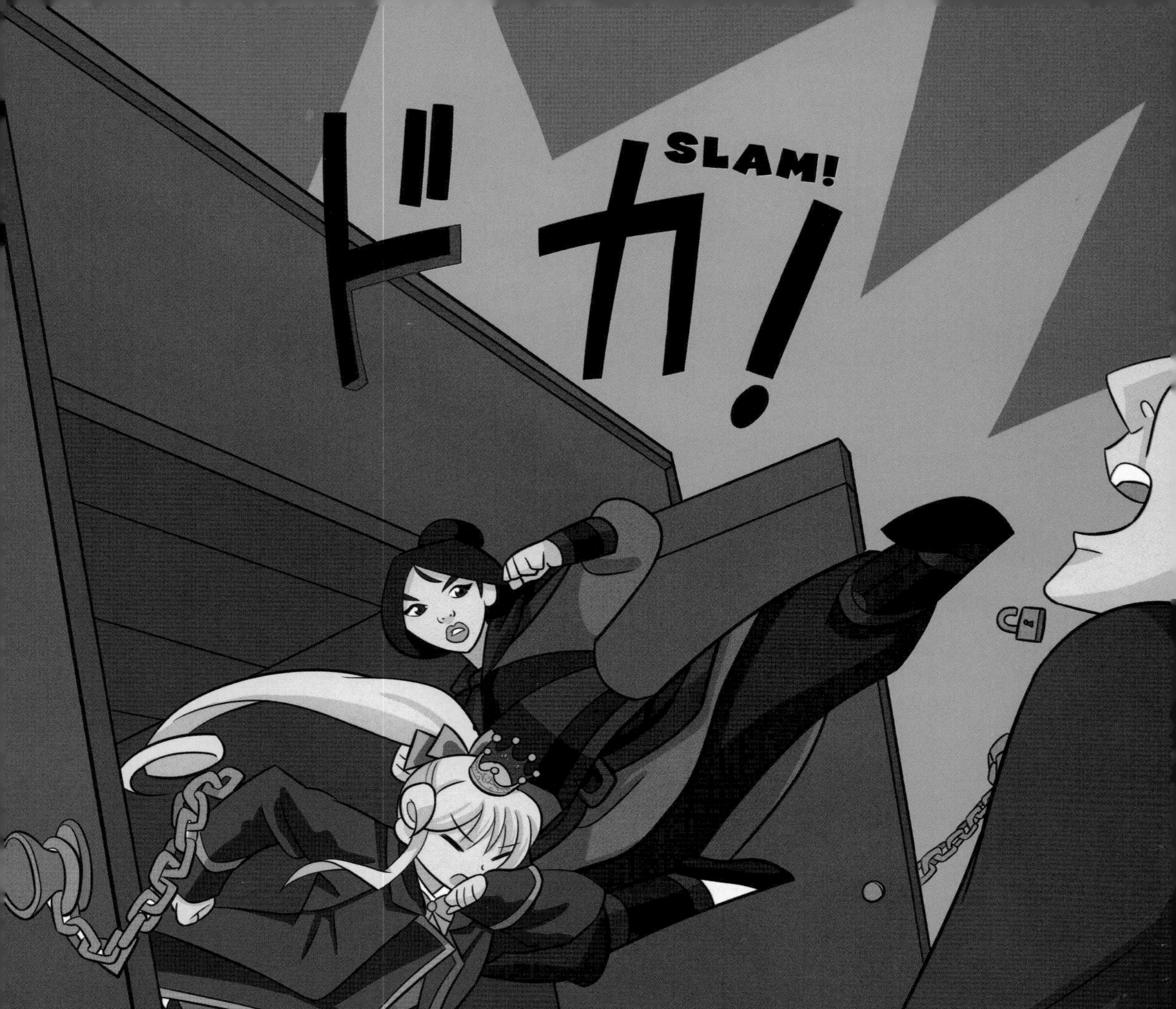
ドカ!
SLAM!
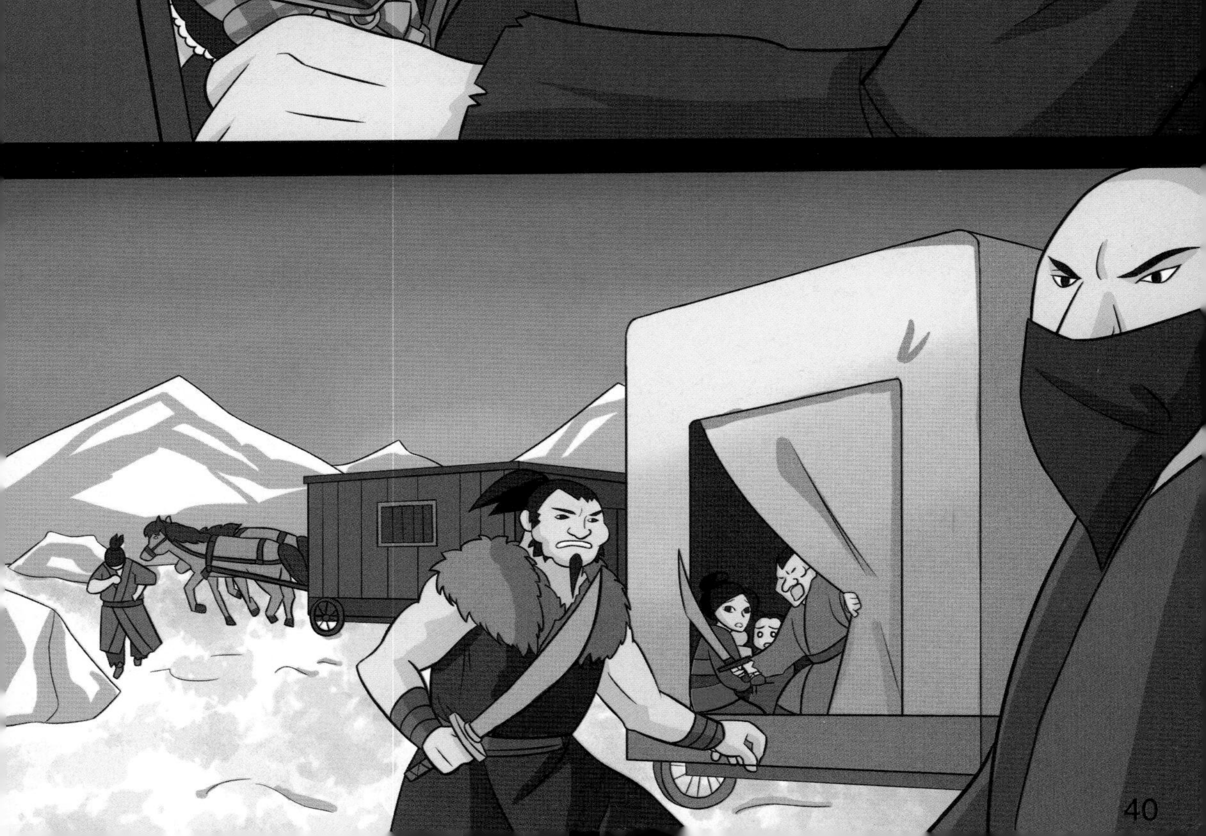

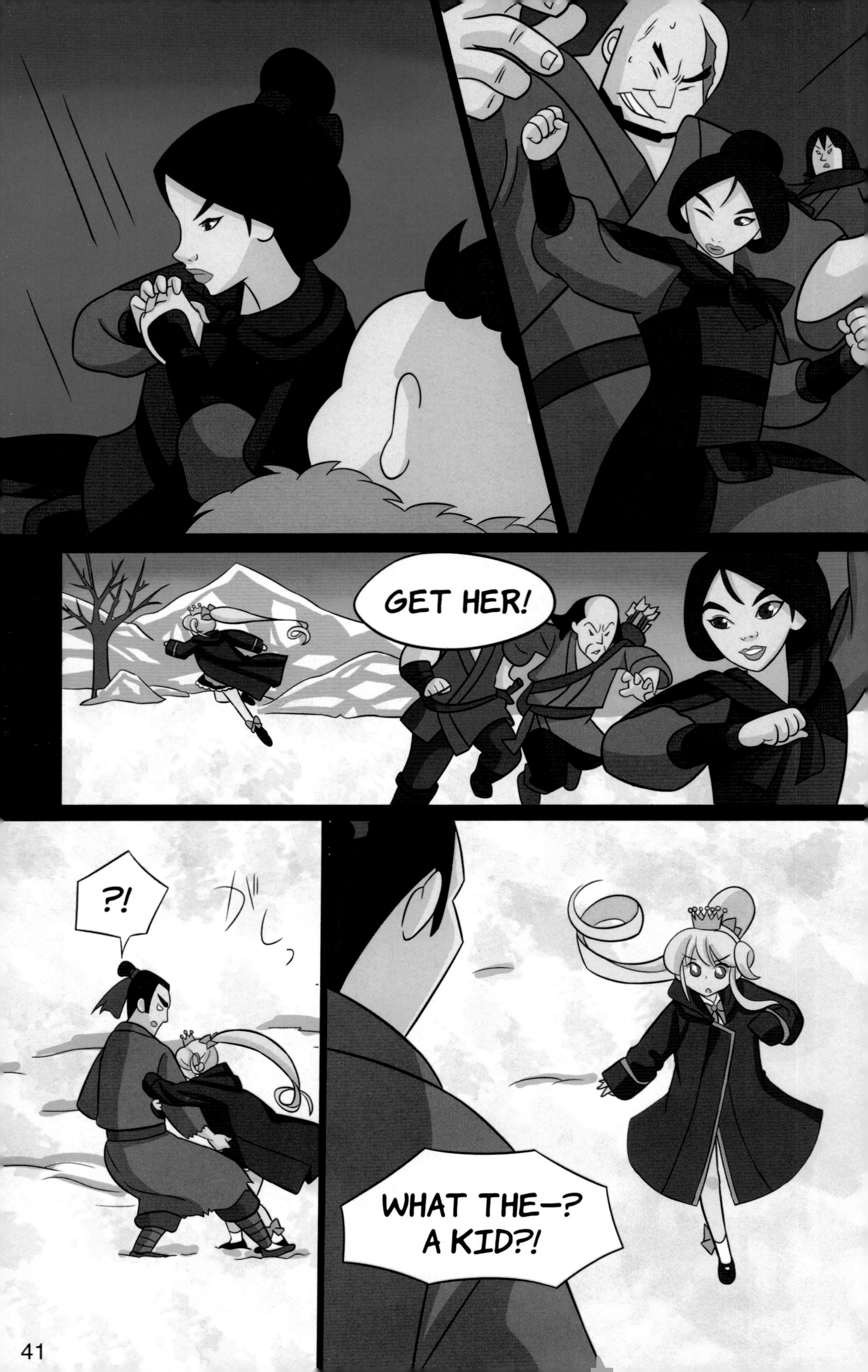
GET HER!
?!
がしっ
WHAT THE—? A KID?!

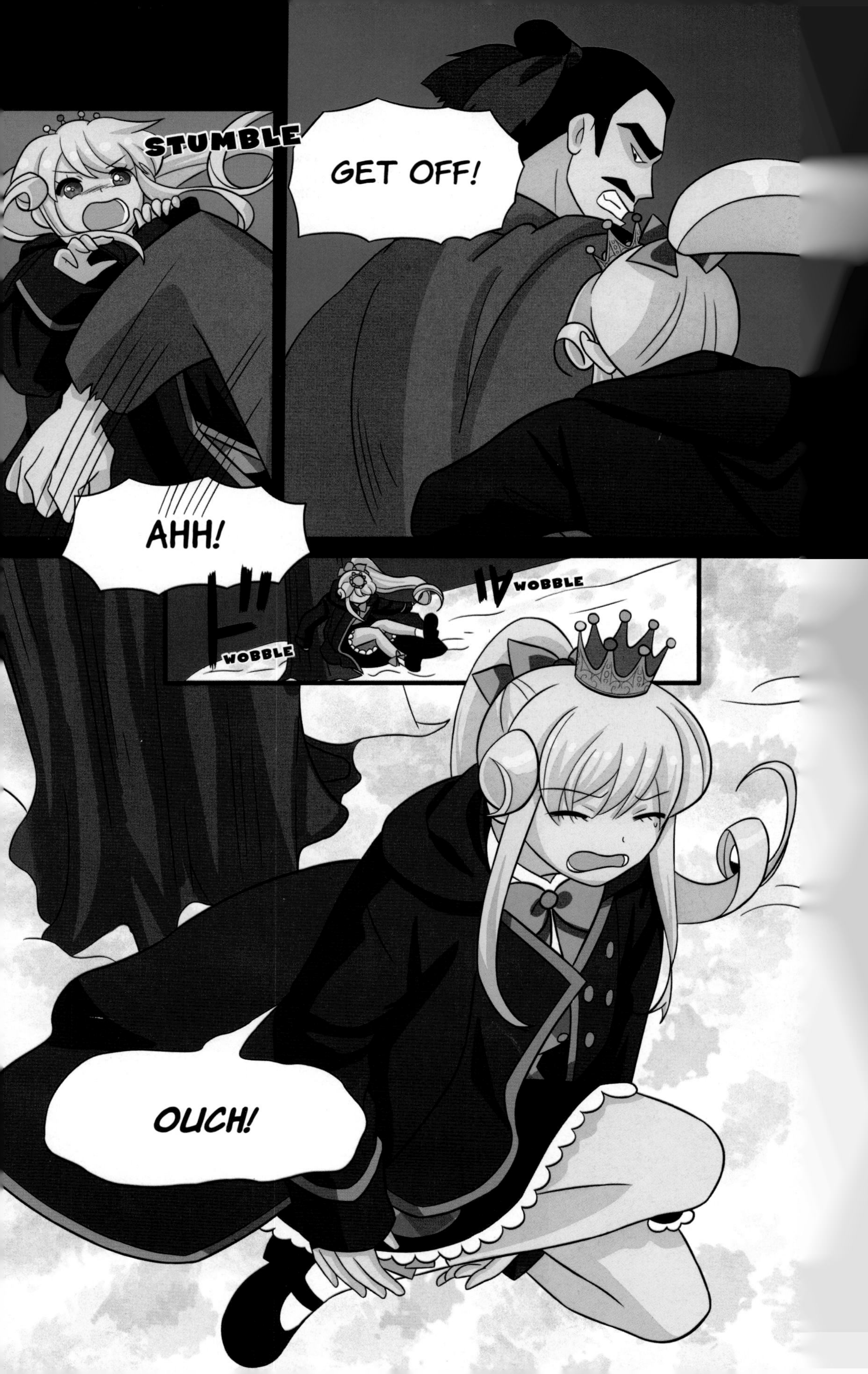
STUMBLE
AHH!
GET OFF!
WOBBLE
WOBBLE
OUCH!

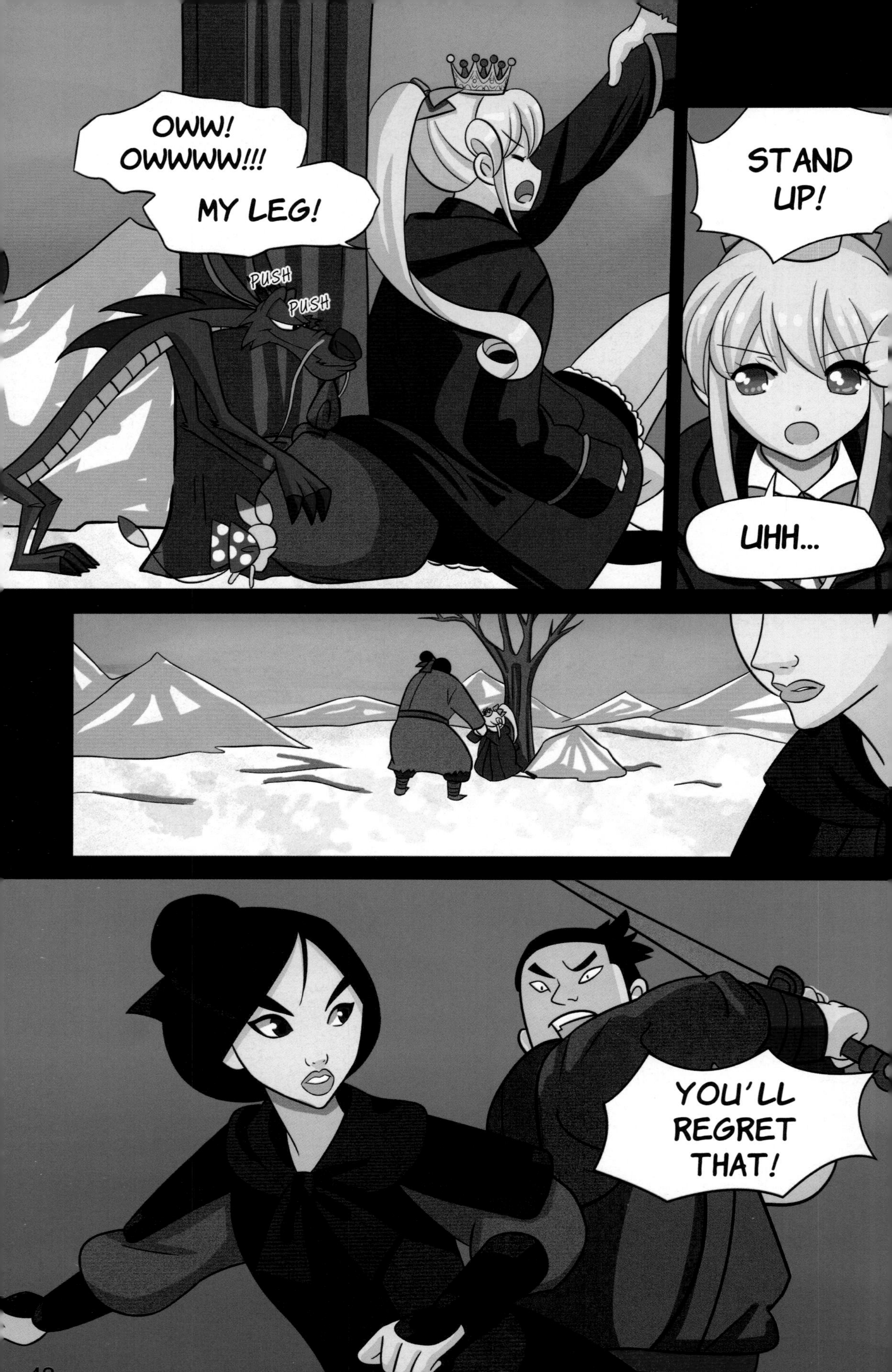
OWW! OWWWW!!!
MY LEG!
PUSH
PUSH
STAND UP!
UHH...
YOU'LL REGRET THAT!

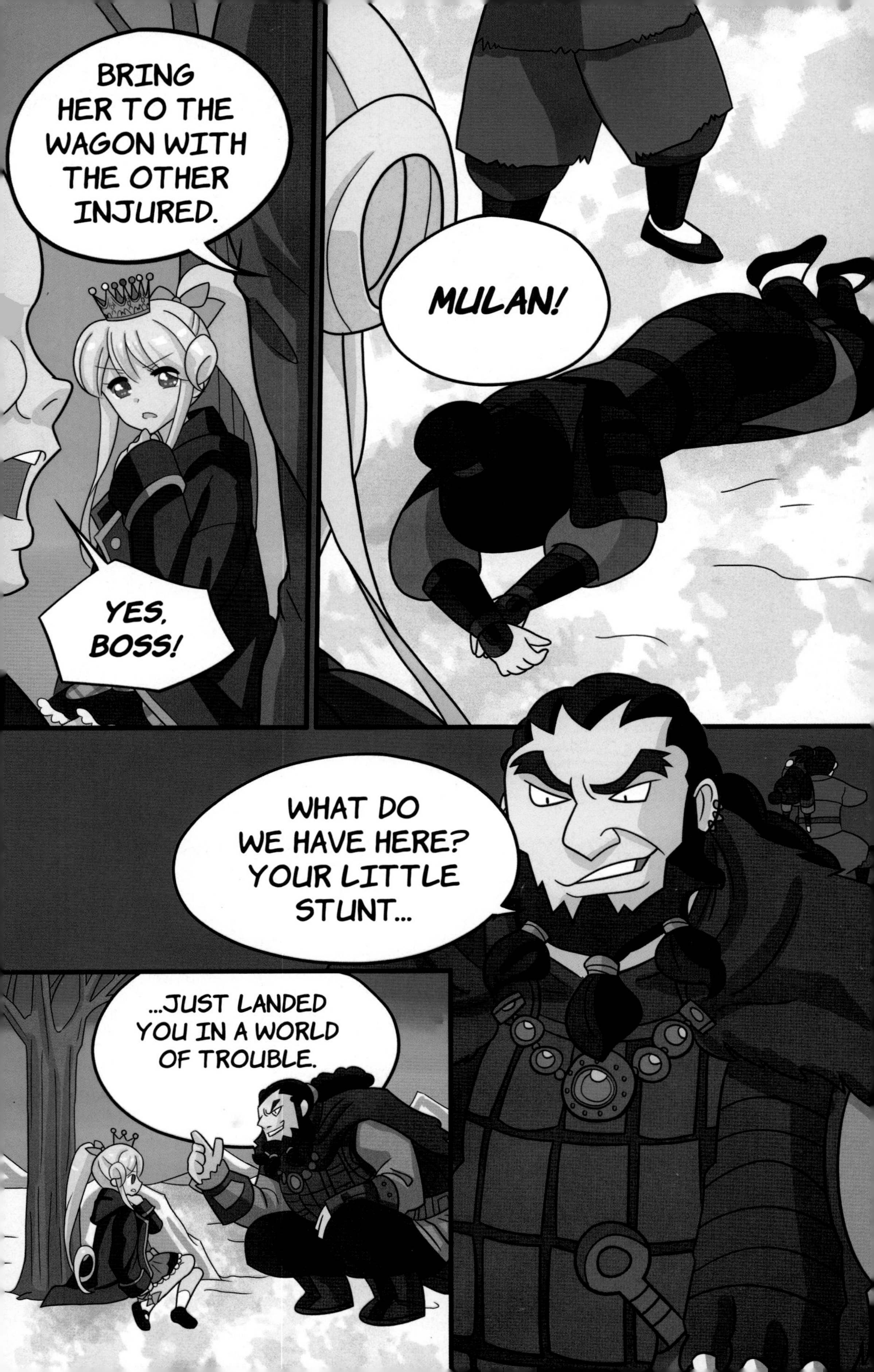
BRING HER TO THE WAGON WITH THE OTHER INJURED.
YES, BOSS!
MULAN!
WHAT DO WE HAVE HERE? YOUR LITTLE STUNT...
...JUST LANDED YOU IN A WORLD OF TROUBLE.

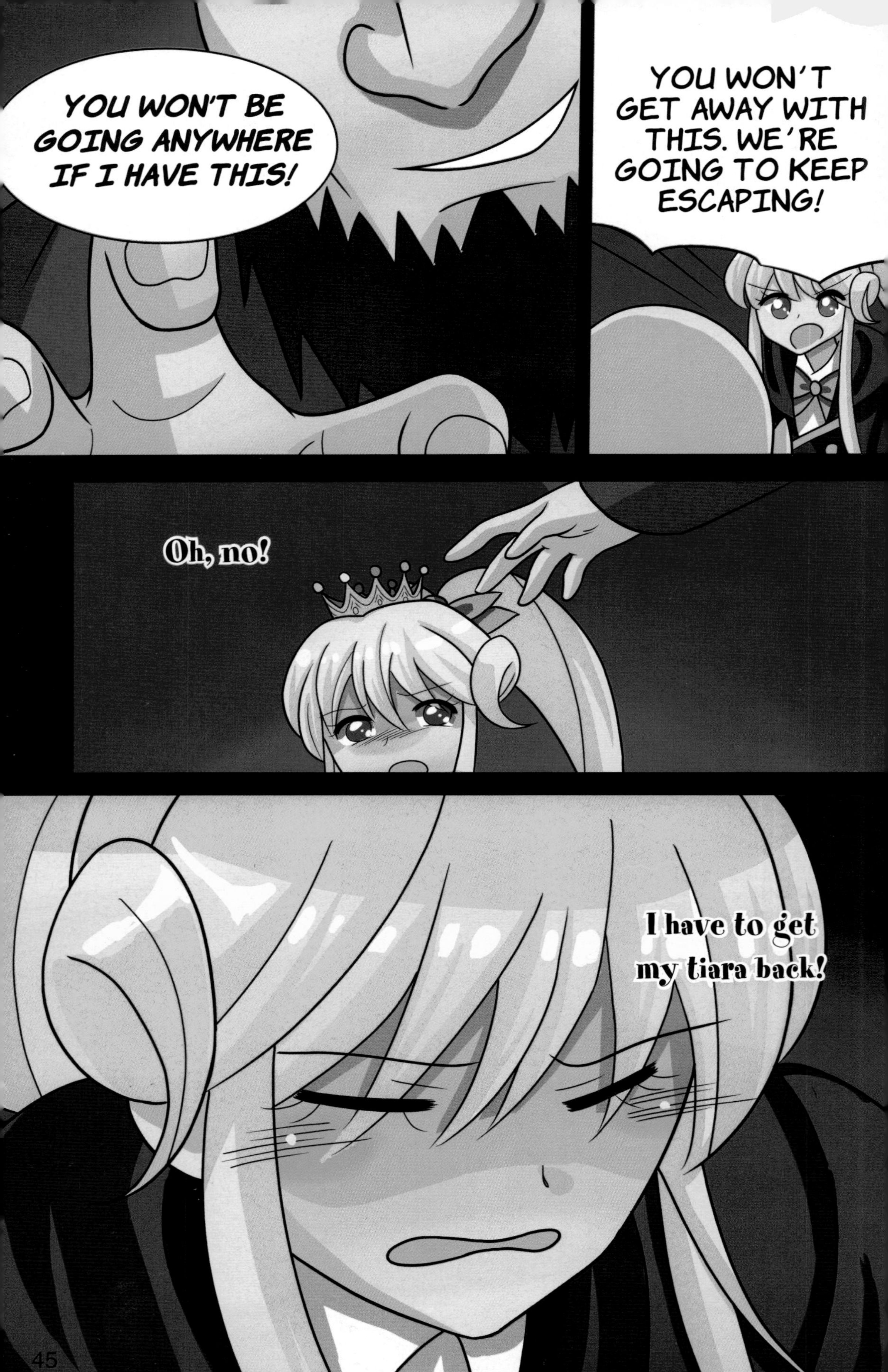
YOU WON'T BE GOING ANYWHERE IF I HAVE THIS!
YOU WON'T GET AWAY WITH THIS. WE'RE GOING TO KEEP ESCAPING!
Oh, no!
I have to get my tiara back!

...I'll get the tiara back somehow!

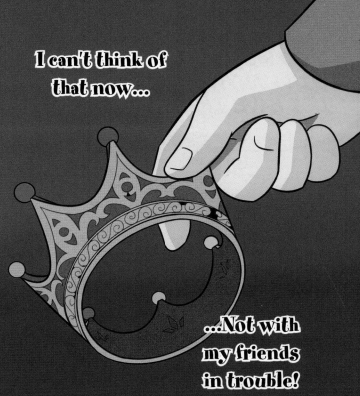

I can't think of that now...

...Not with my friends in trouble!

SLAM

GET INSIDE! STAY PUT!

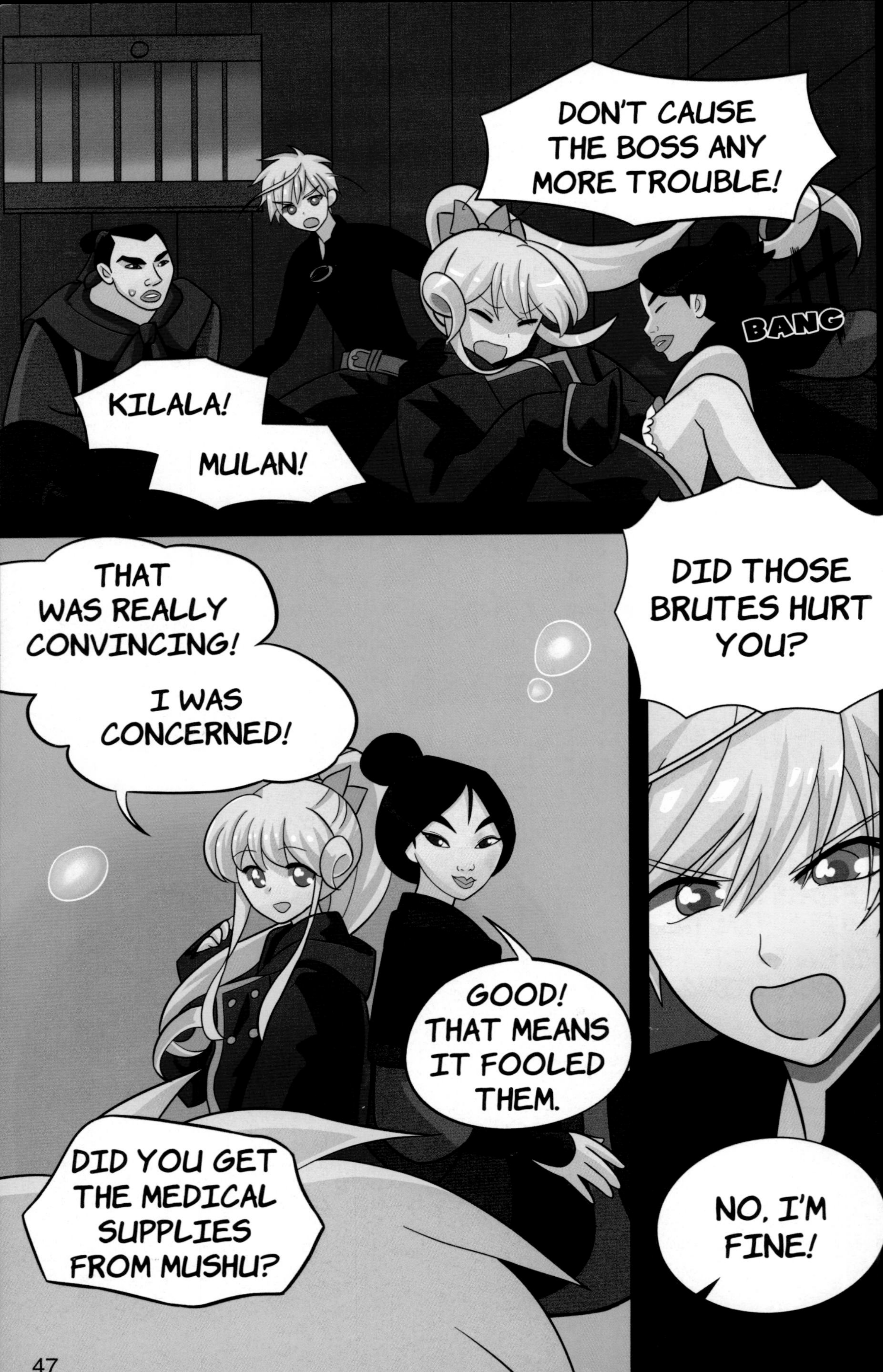

DON'T CAUSE THE BOSS ANY MORE TROUBLE!
BANG
KILALA!
MULAN!
THAT WAS REALLY CONVINCING!
I WAS CONCERNED!
GOOD! THAT MEANS IT FOOLED THEM.
DID YOU GET THE MEDICAL SUPPLIES FROM MUSHU?
DID THOSE BRUTES HURT YOU?
NO, I'M FINE!

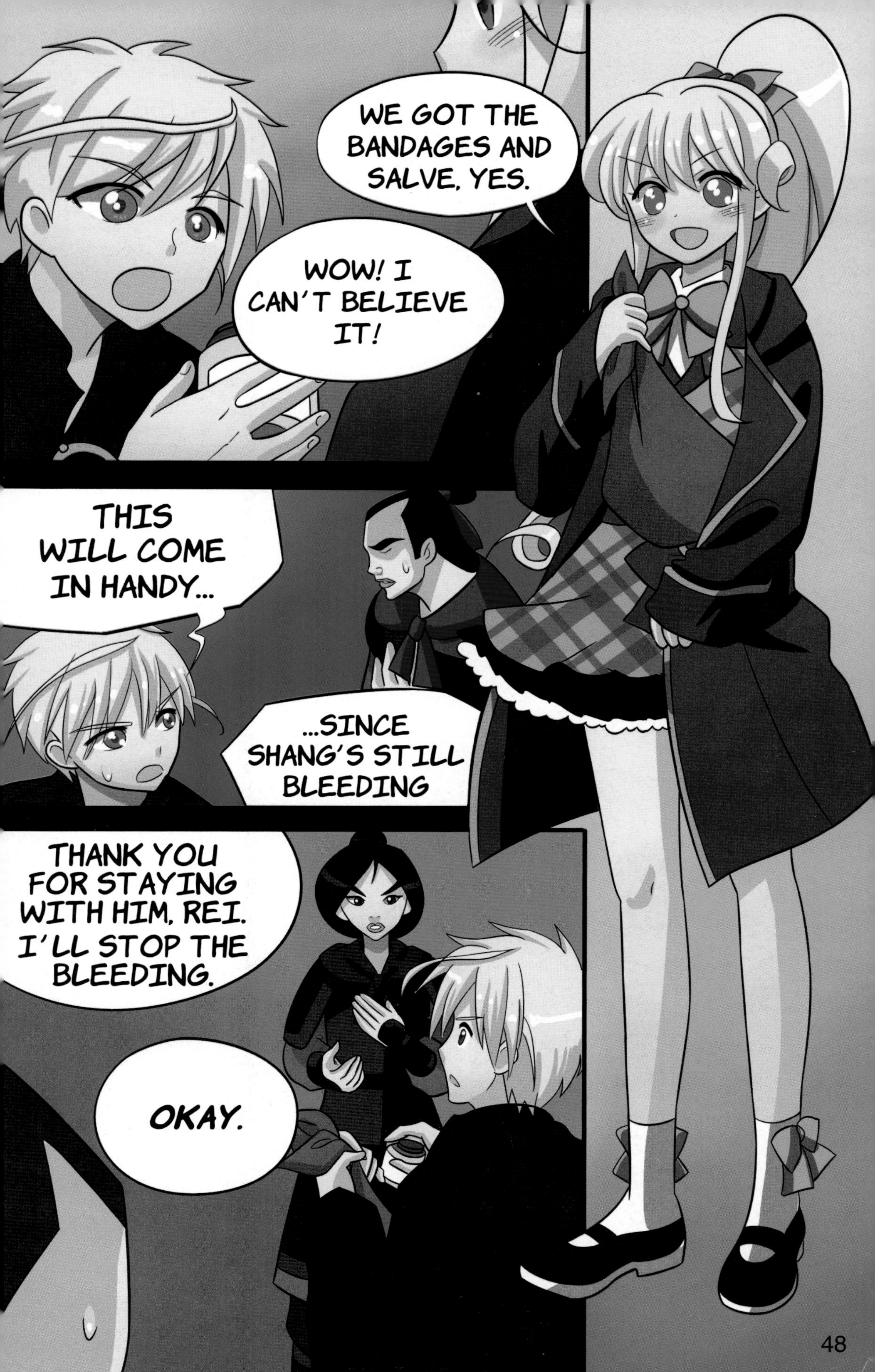
WE GOT THE BANDAGES AND SALVE, YES.
WOW! I CAN'T BELIEVE IT!
THIS WILL COME IN HANDY...
...SINCE SHANG'S STILL BLEEDING
THANK YOU FOR STAYING WITH HIM, REI. I'LL STOP THE BLEEDING.
OKAY.

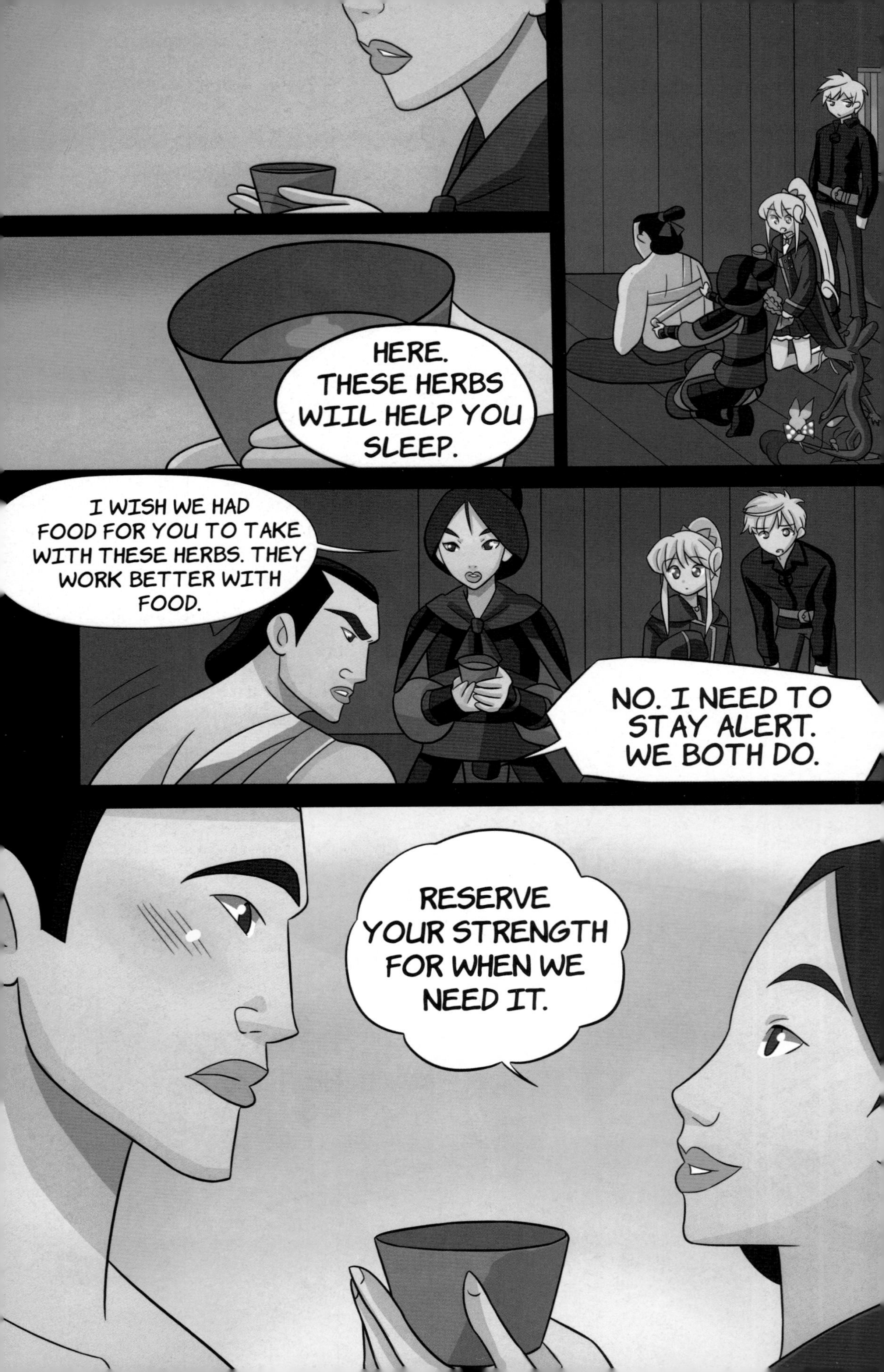
HERE. THESE HERBS WIIL HELP YOU SLEEP.
I WISH WE HAD FOOD FOR YOU TO TAKE WITH THESE HERBS. THEY WORK BETTER WITH FOOD.
NO. I NEED TO STAY ALERT. WE BOTH DO.
RESERVE YOUR STRENGTH FOR WHEN WE NEED IT.

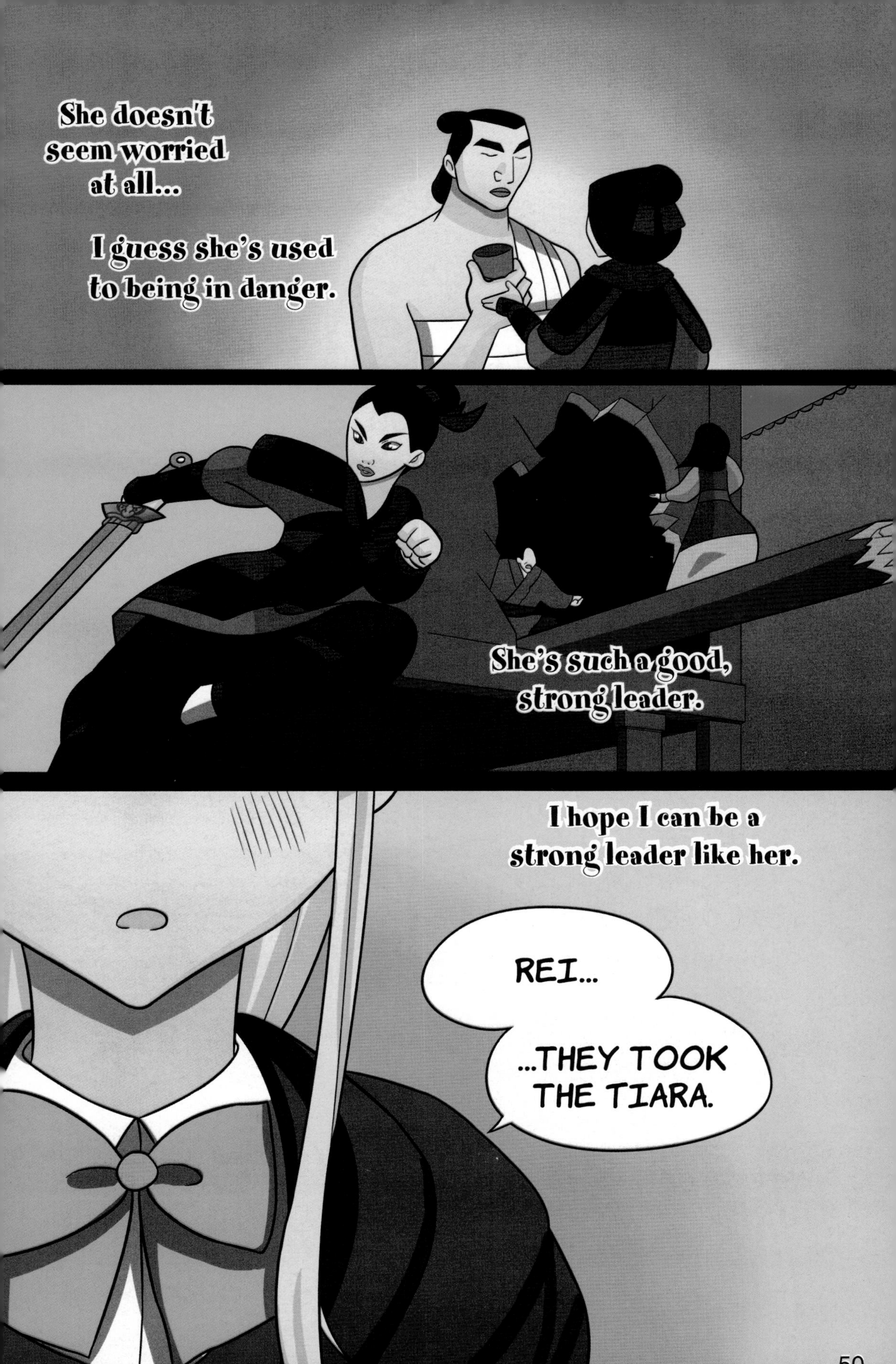
She doesn't seem worried at all...
I guess she's used to being in danger.
She's such a good, strong leader.
I hope I can be a strong leader like her.
REI...
...THEY TOOK THE TIARA.

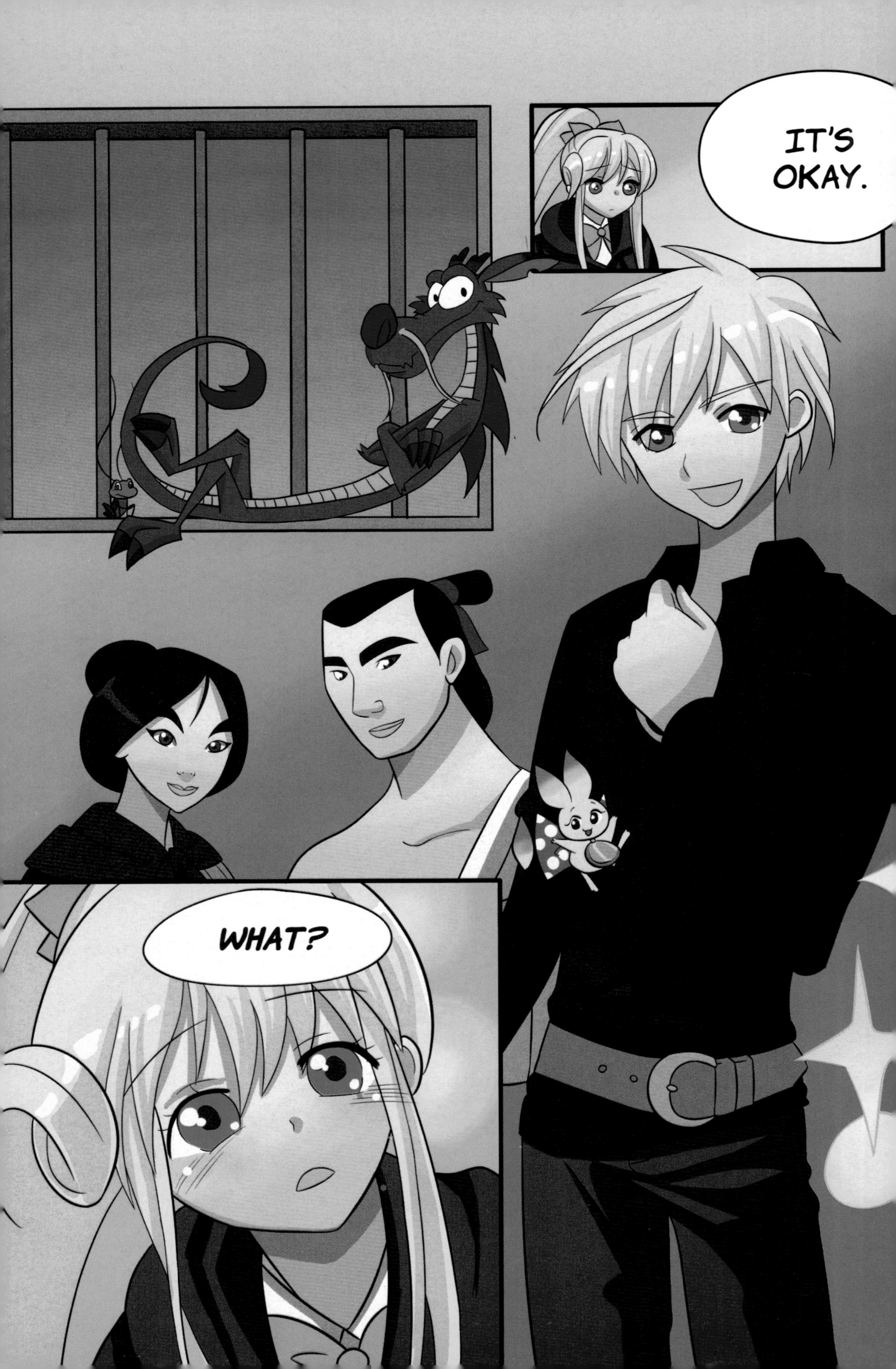
IT'S OKAY.
WHAT?

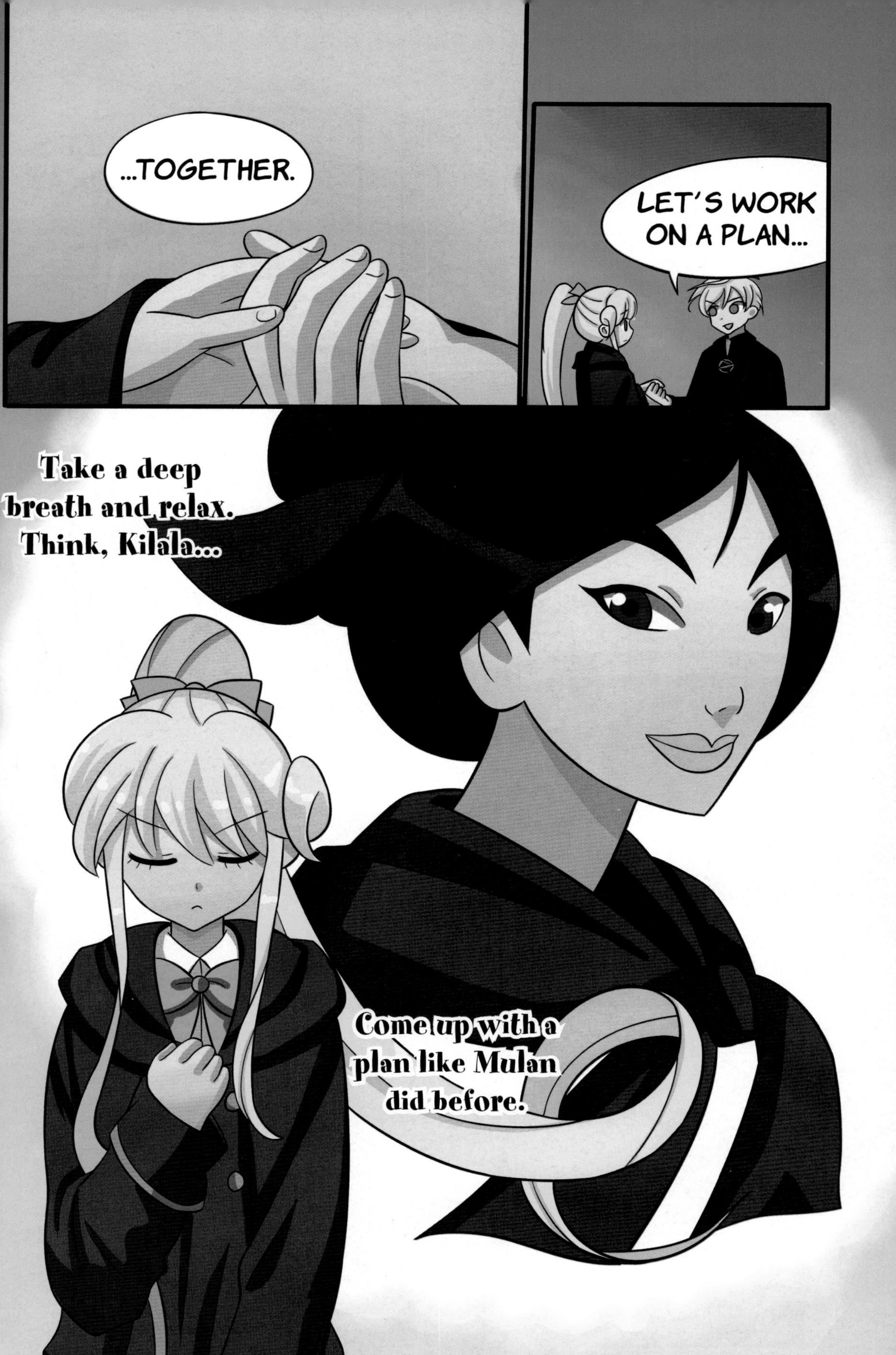
...TOGETHER.
LET'S WORK ON A PLAN...
Take a deep breath and relax. Think, Kilala...
Come up with a plan like Mulan did before.

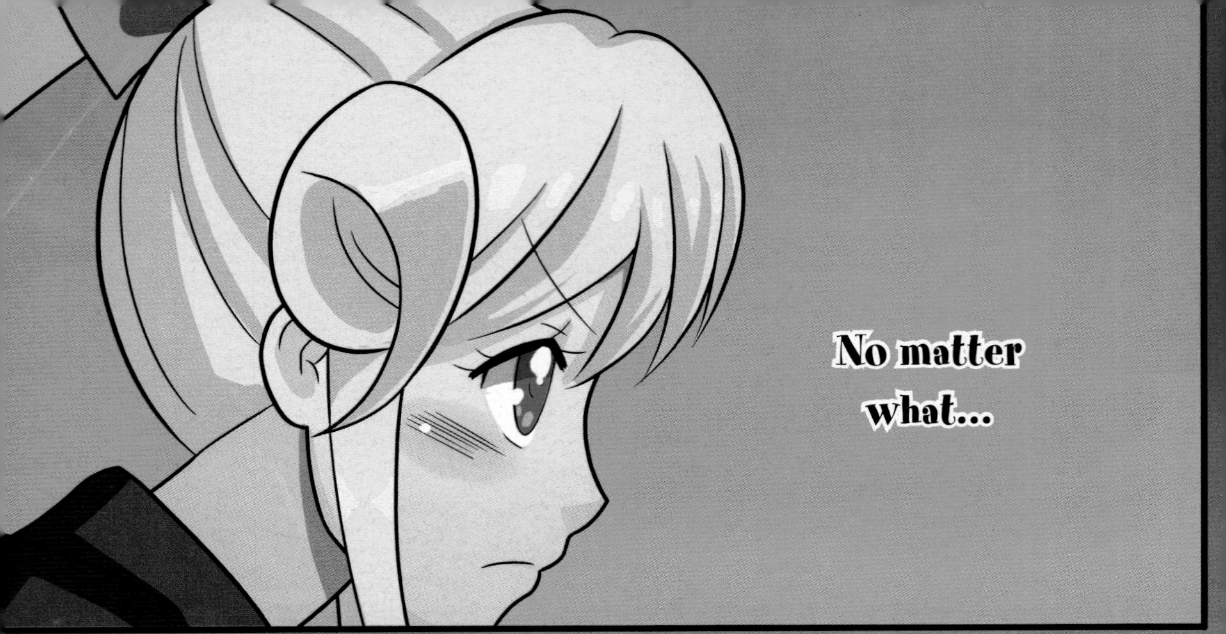
No matter what...

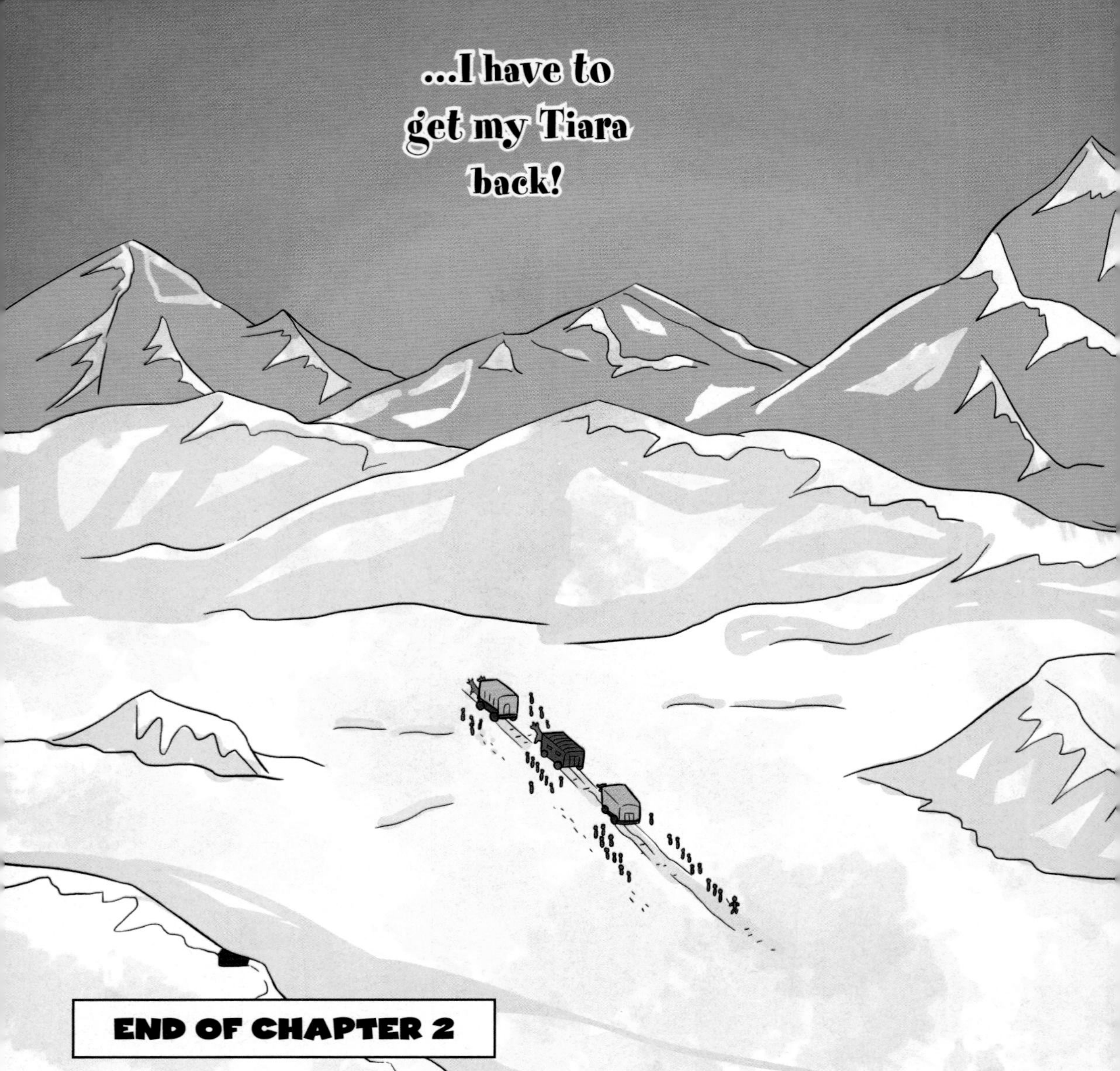
...I have to get my Tiara back!
END OF CHAPTER 2

Disney

Kilala Princess

Rescue the Village with Mulan!

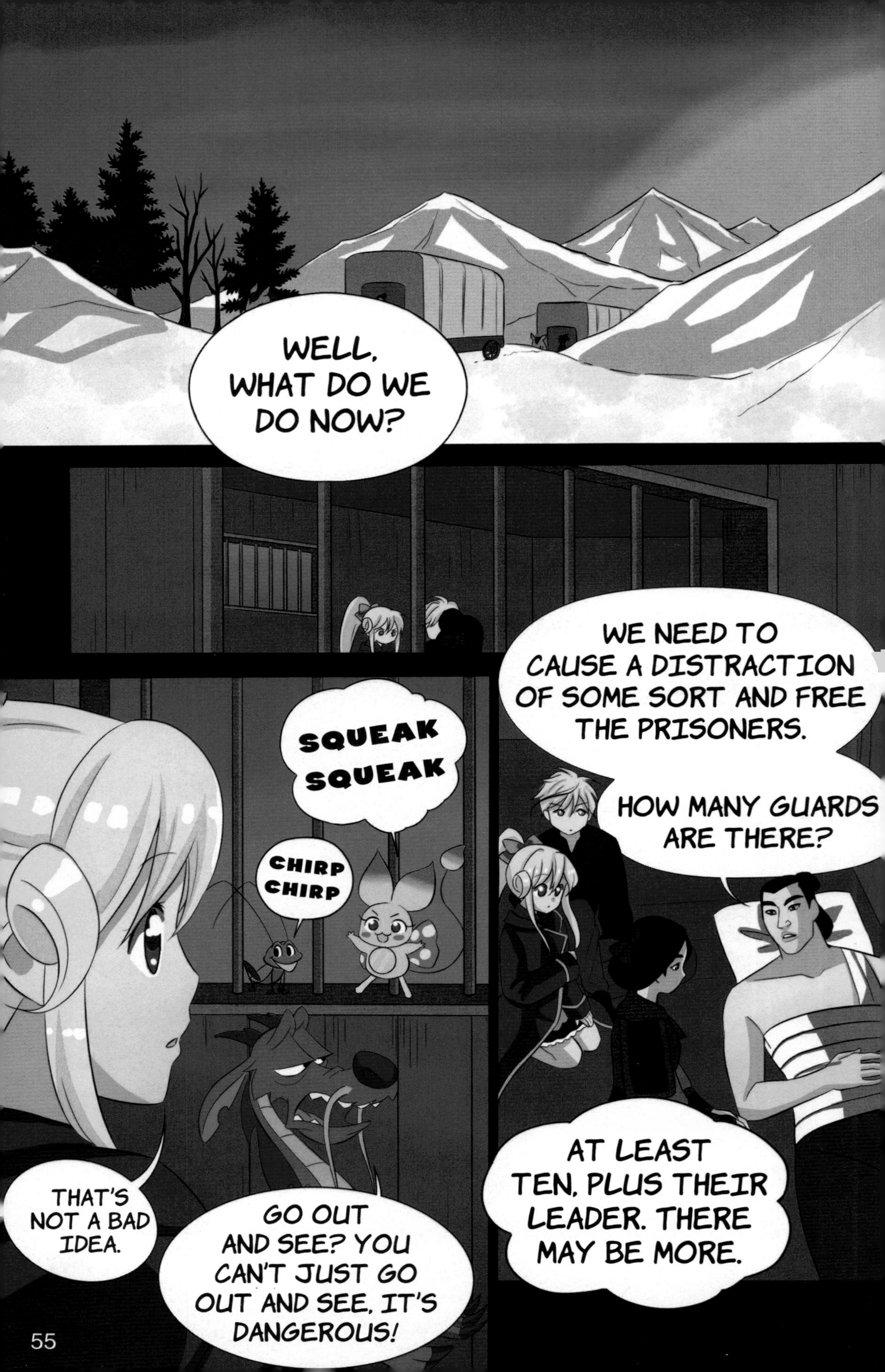
WELL, WHAT DO WE DO NOW?
SQUEAK SQUEAK
CHIRP CHIRP
THAT'S NOT A BAD IDEA.
GO OUT AND SEE? YOU CAN'T JUST GO OUT AND SEE. IT'S DANGEROUS!
WE NEED TO CAUSE A DISTRACTION OF SOME SORT AND FREE THE PRISONERS.
HOW MANY GUARDS ARE THERE?
AT LEAST TEN, PLUS THEIR LEADER. THERE MAY BE MORE.

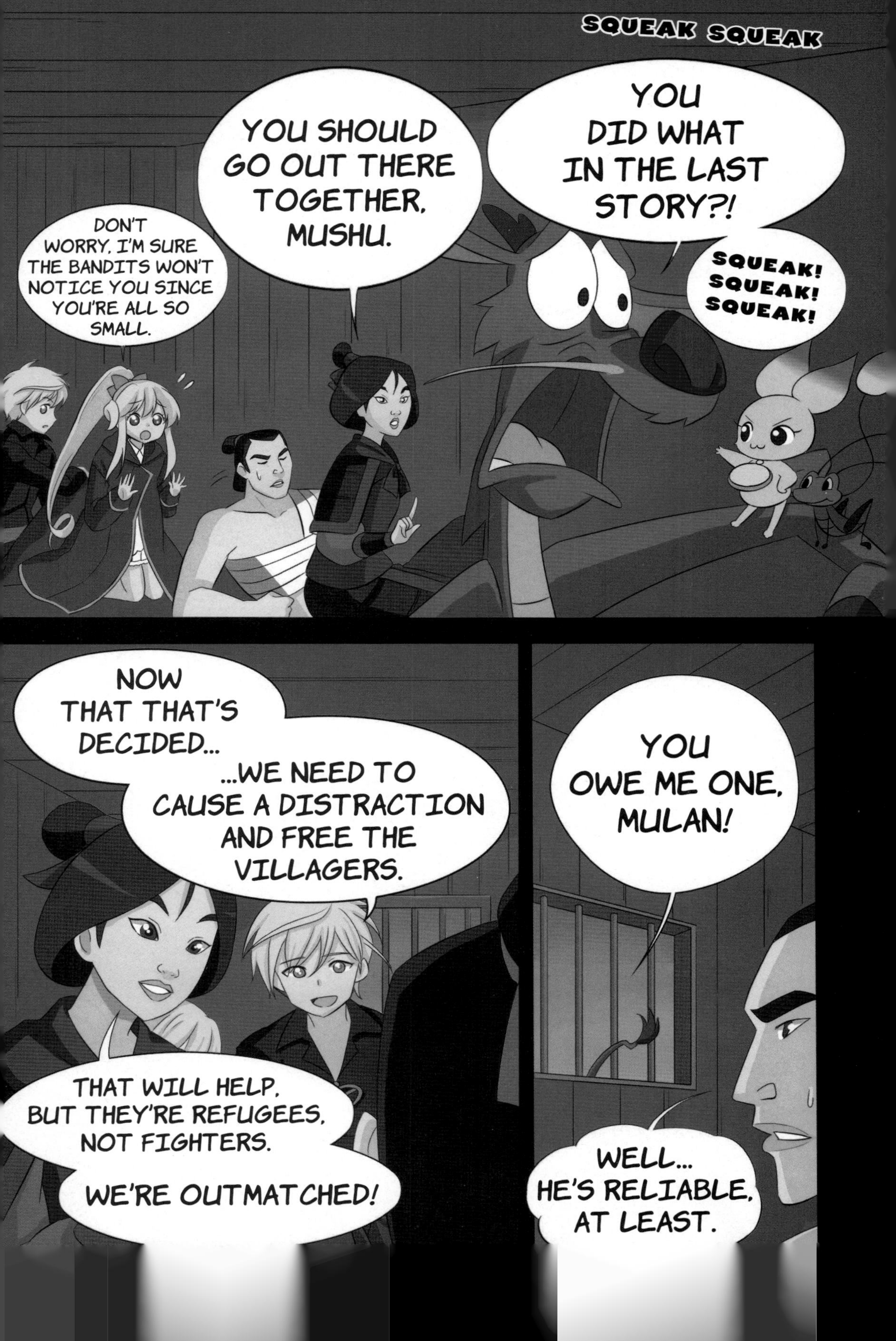
SQUEAK SQUEAK
DON'T WORRY, I'M SURE THE BANDITS WON'T NOTICE YOU SINCE YOU'RE ALL SO SMALL.
YOU SHOULD GO OUT THERE TOGETHER, MUSHU.
YOU DID WHAT IN THE LAST STORY?!
SQUEAK! SQUEAK! SQUEAK!
NOW THAT THAT'S DECIDED...
...WE NEED TO CAUSE A DISTRACTION AND FREE THE VILLAGERS.
THAT WILL HELP, BUT THEY'RE REFUGEES, NOT FIGHTERS.
WE'RE OUTMATCHED!
YOU OWE ME ONE, MULAN!
WELL... HE'S RELIABLE, AT LEAST.

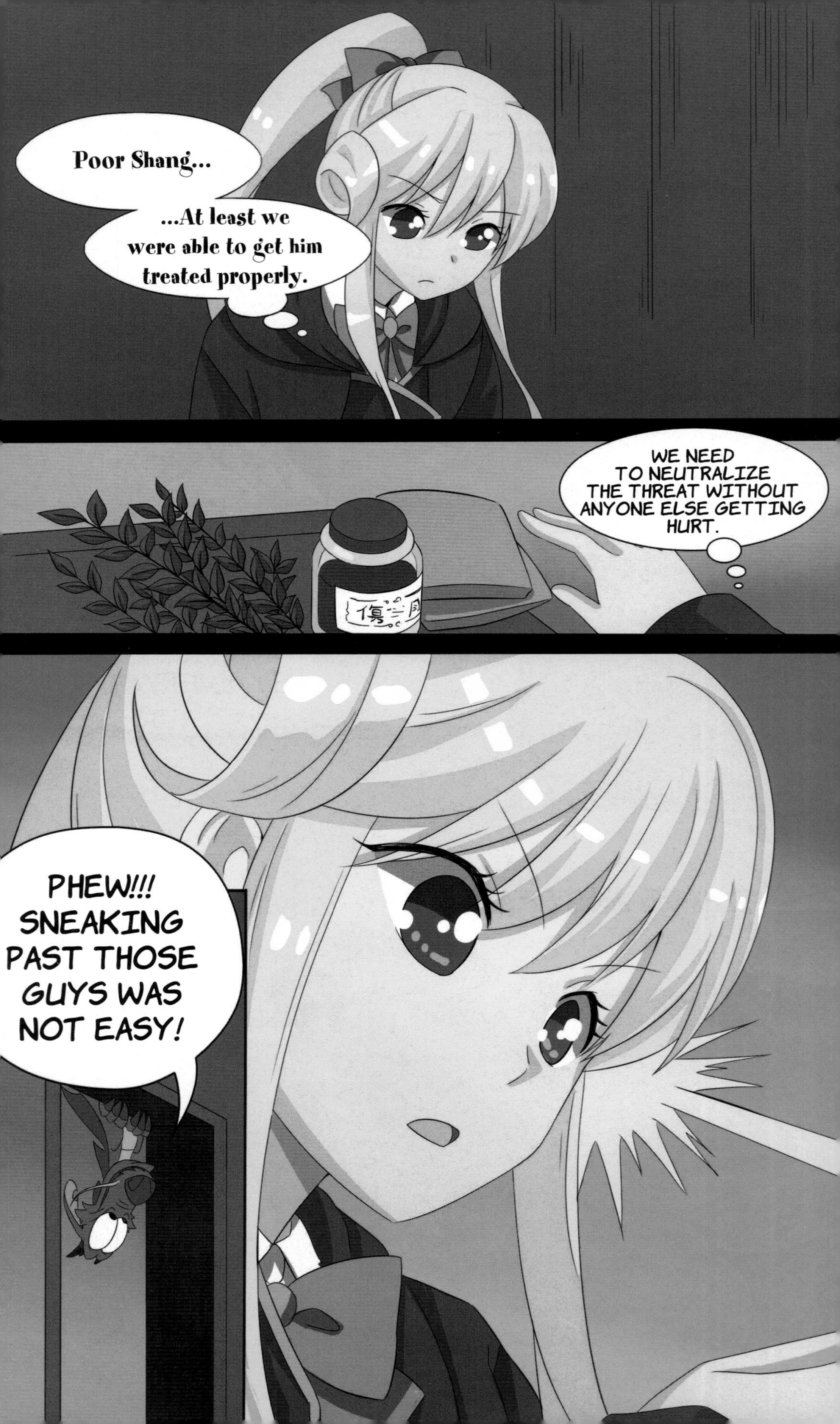
Poor Shang...
...At least we were able to get him treated properly.
WE NEED TO NEUTRALIZE THE THREAT WITHOUT ANYONE ELSE GETTING HURT.
PHEW!!! SNEAKING PAST THOSE GUYS WAS NOT EASY!

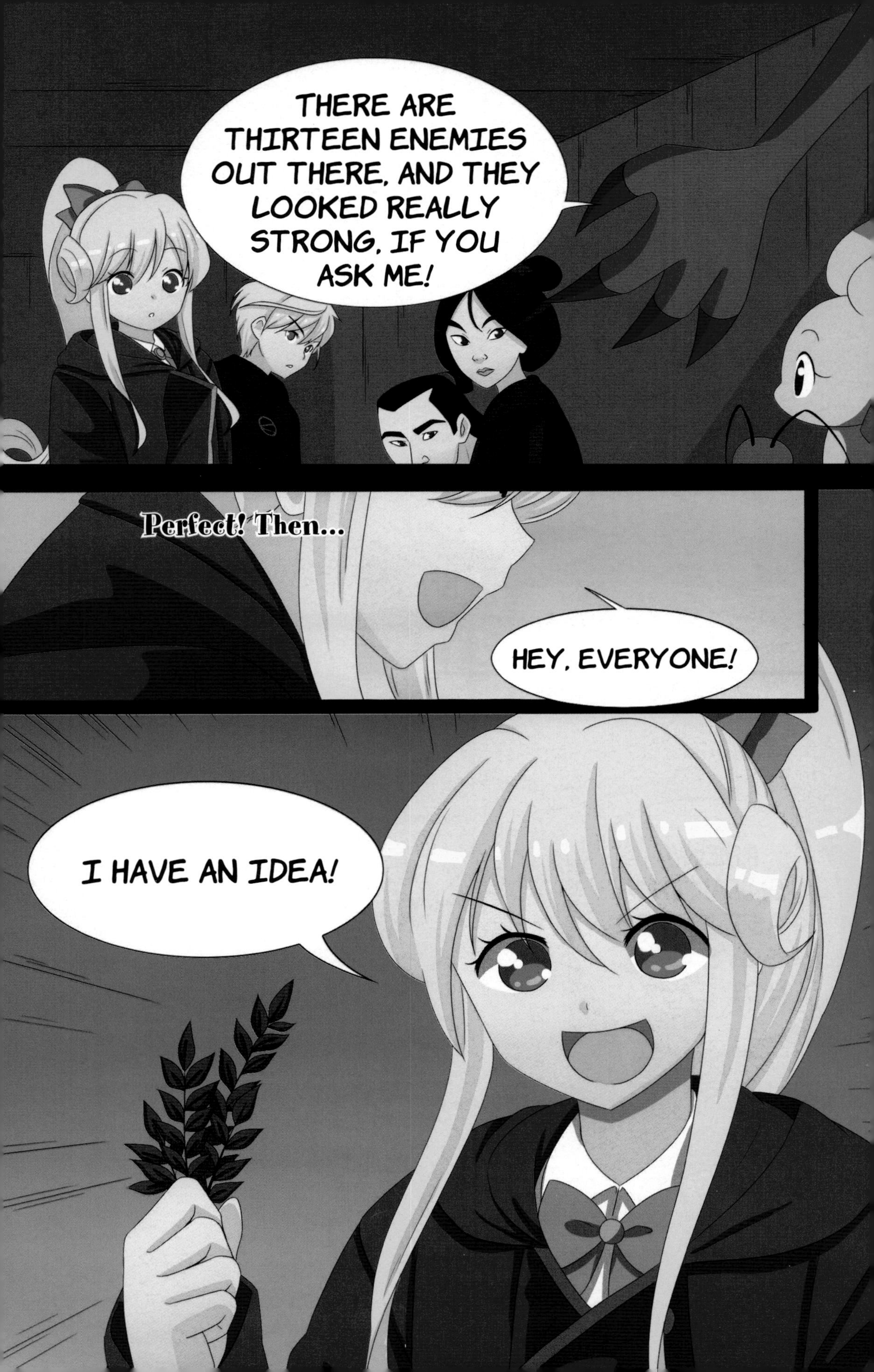
THERE ARE THIRTEEN ENEMIES OUT THERE, AND THEY LOOKED REALLY STRONG, IF YOU ASK ME!
Perfect! Then...
HEY, EVERYONE!
I HAVE AN IDEA!

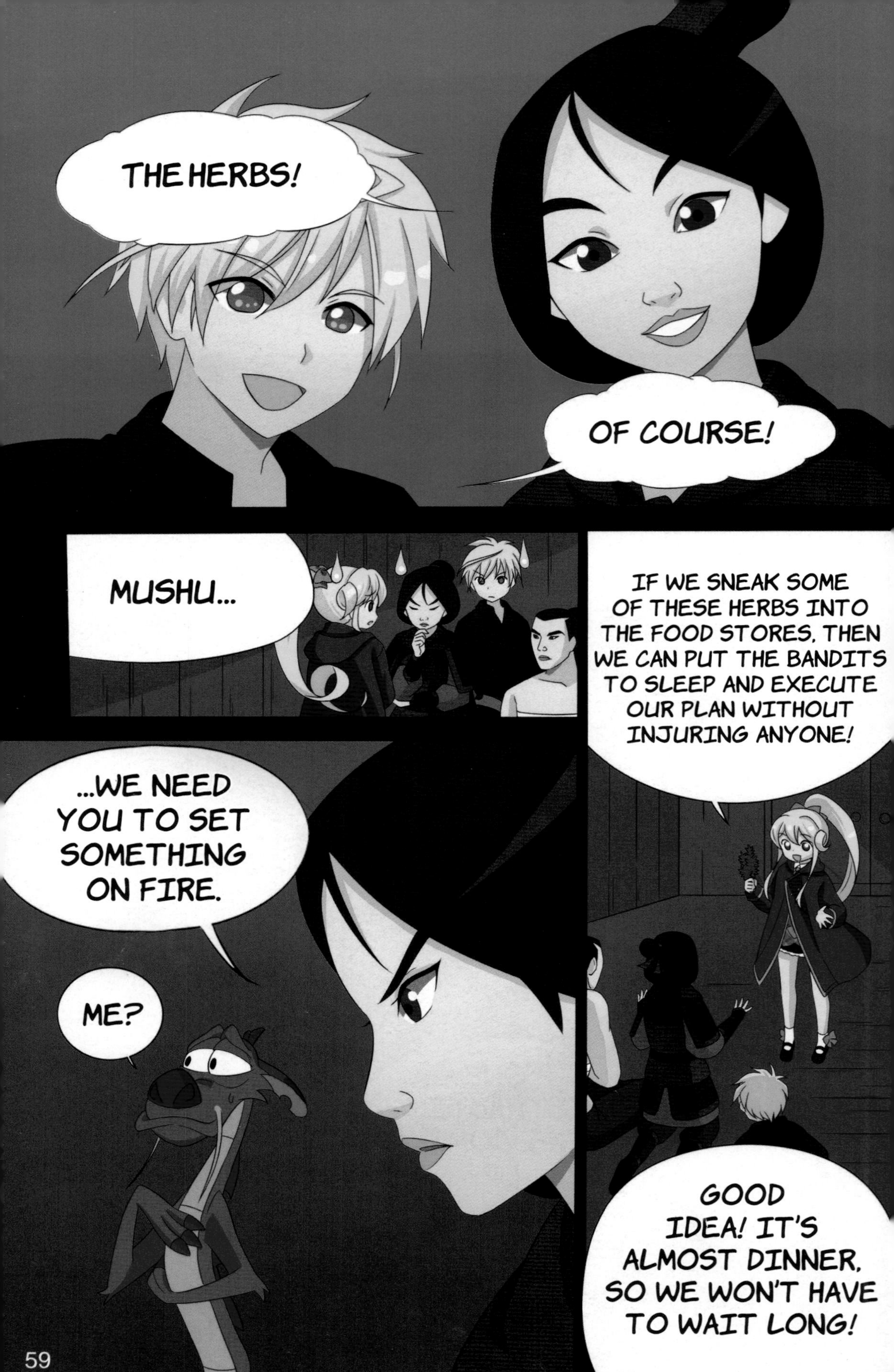

THE HERBS!
OF COURSE!
MUSHU...
IF WE SNEAK SOME OF THESE HERBS INTO THE FOOD STORES, THEN WE CAN PUT THE BANDITS TO SLEEP AND EXECUTE OUR PLAN WITHOUT INJURING ANYONE!
...WE NEED YOU TO SET SOMETHING ON FIRE.
ME?
GOOD IDEA! IT'S ALMOST DINNER, SO WE WON'T HAVE TO WAIT LONG!

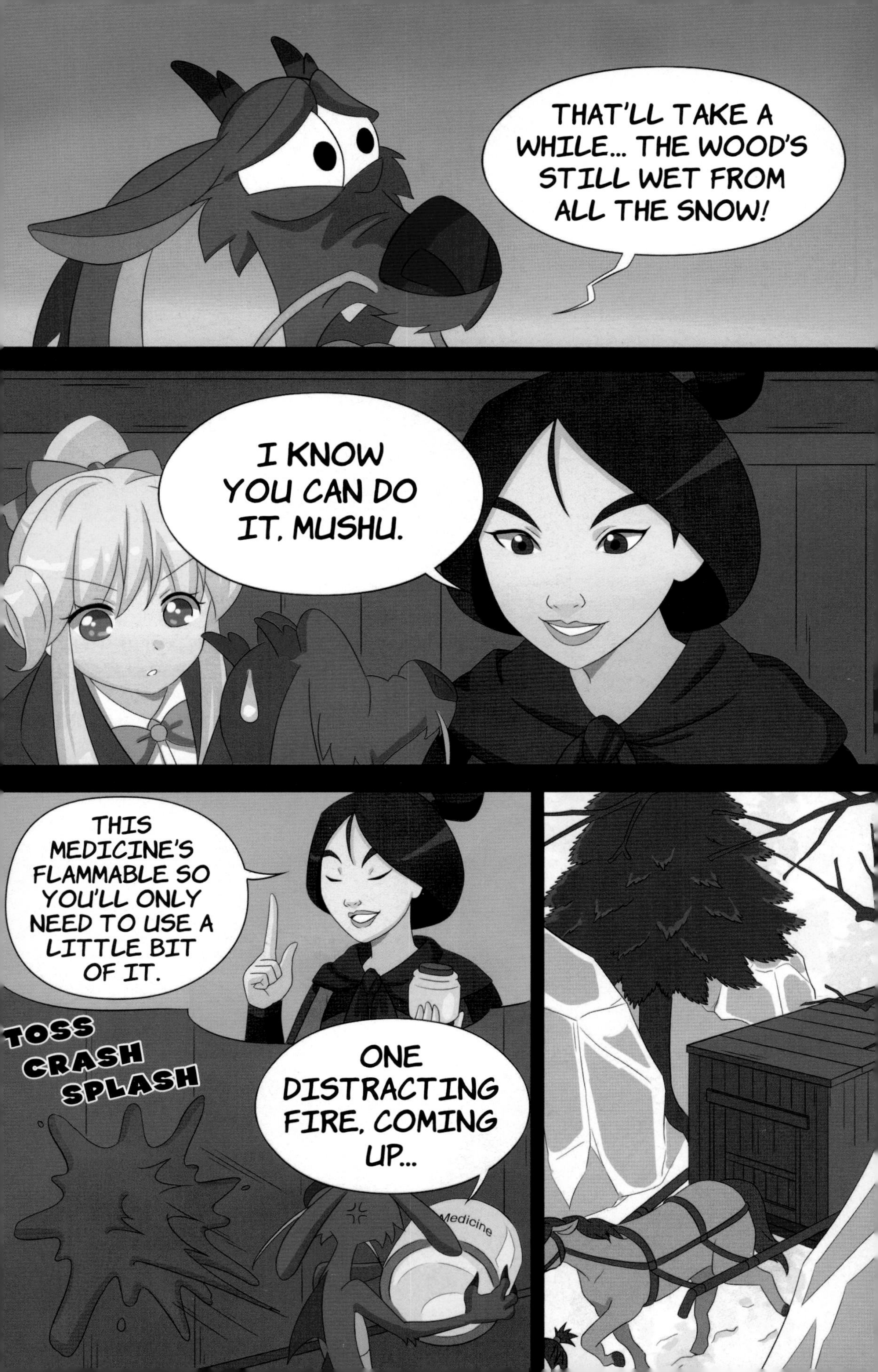
THAT'LL TAKE A WHILE... THE WOOD'S STILL WET FROM ALL THE SNOW!
I KNOW YOU CAN DO IT, MUSHU.
THIS MEDICINE'S FLAMMABLE SO YOU'LL ONLY NEED TO USE A LITTLE BIT OF IT.
TOSS
CRASH
SPLASH
ONE DISTRACTING FIRE, COMING UP...
Medicine

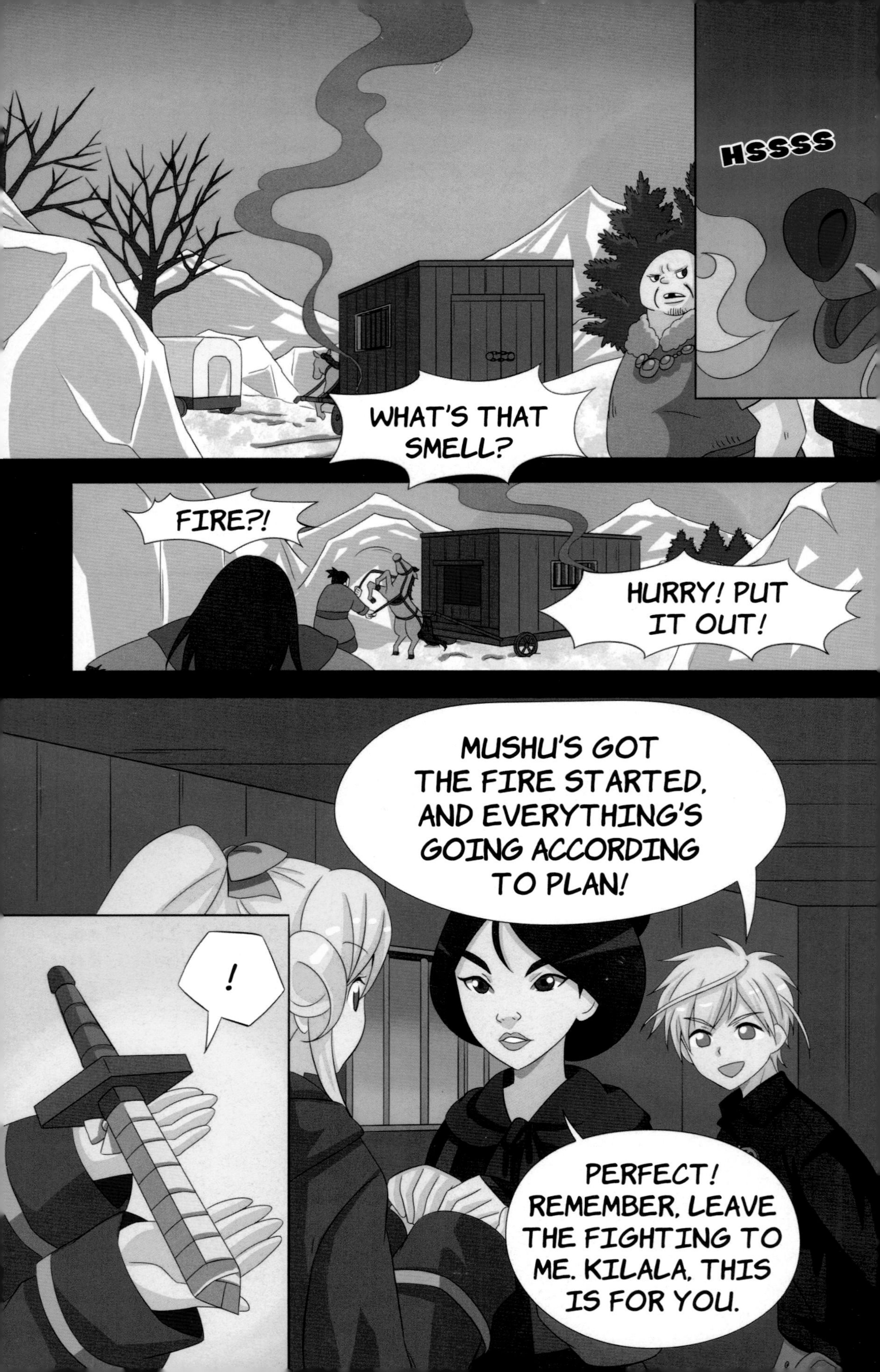

WHAT'S THAT SMELL?
HSSSS
FIRE?!
HURRY! PUT IT OUT!
MUSHU'S GOT THE FIRE STARTED, AND EVERYTHING'S GOING ACCORDING TO PLAN!
!
PERFECT! REMEMBER, LEAVE THE FIGHTING TO ME. KILALA, THIS IS FOR YOU.

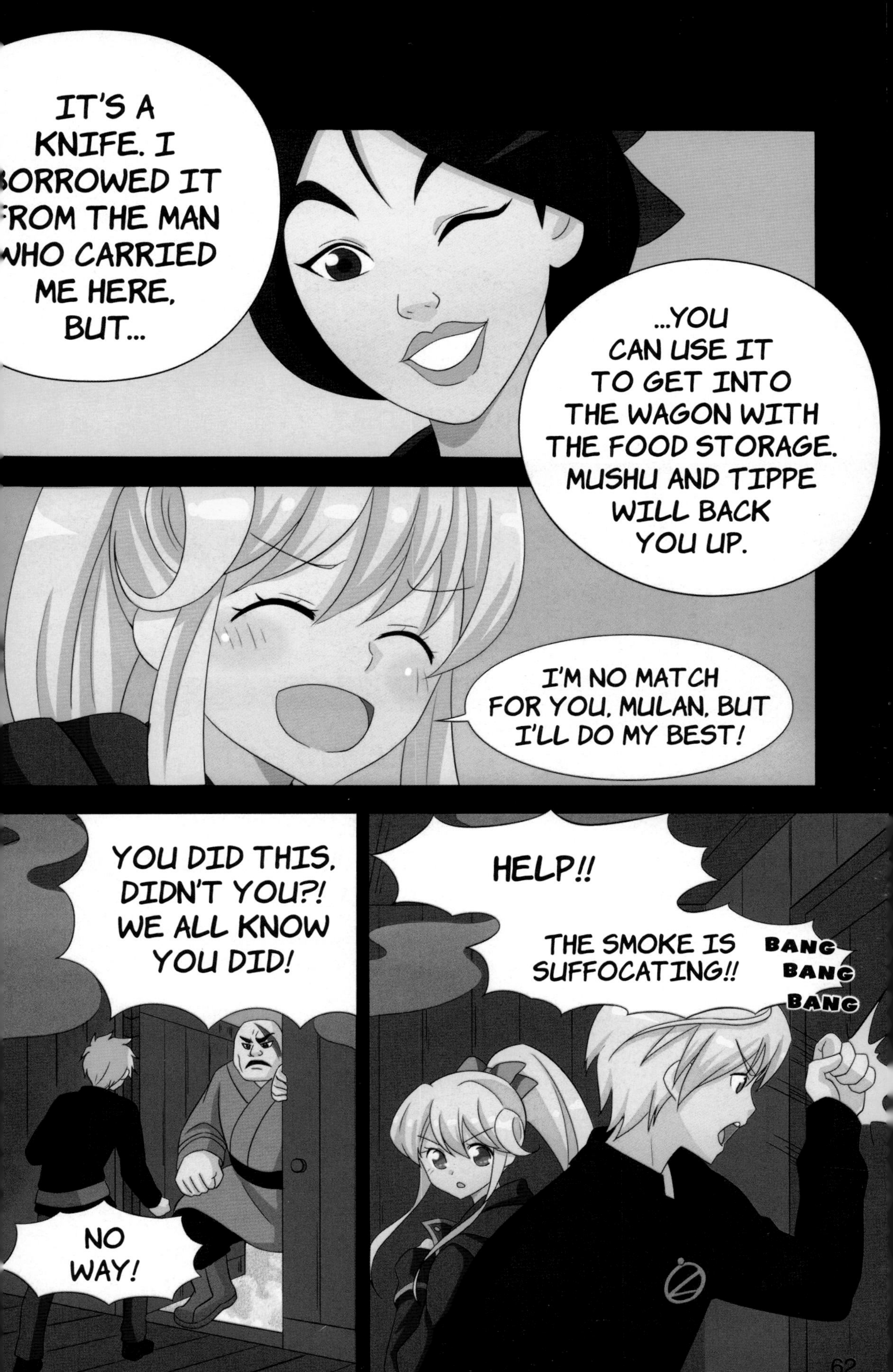
IT'S A KNIFE. I BORROWED IT FROM THE MAN WHO CARRIED ME HERE, BUT...
...YOU CAN USE IT TO GET INTO THE WAGON WITH THE FOOD STORAGE. MUSHU AND TIPPE WILL BACK YOU UP.
I'M NO MATCH FOR YOU, MULAN, BUT I'LL DO MY BEST!
YOU DID THIS, DIDN'T YOU?! WE ALL KNOW YOU DID!
NO WAY!
HELP!!
THE SMOKE IS SUFFOCATING!!
BANG
BANG
BANG

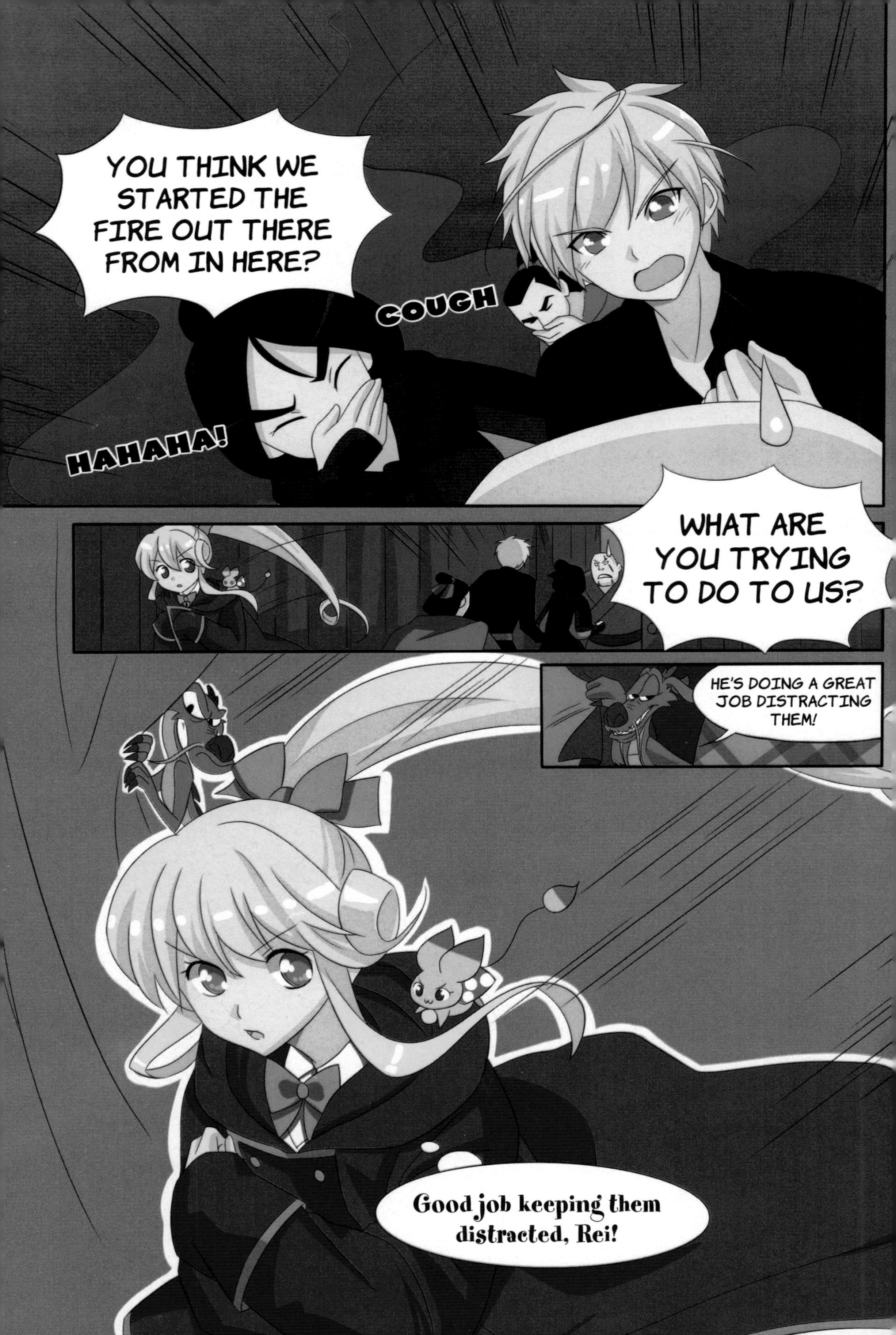
YOU THINK WE STARTED THE FIRE OUT THERE FROM IN HERE?
COUGH
HAHAHA!
WHAT ARE YOU TRYING TO DO TO US?
HE'S DOING A GREAT JOB DISTRACTING THEM!
Good job keeping them distracted, Rei!

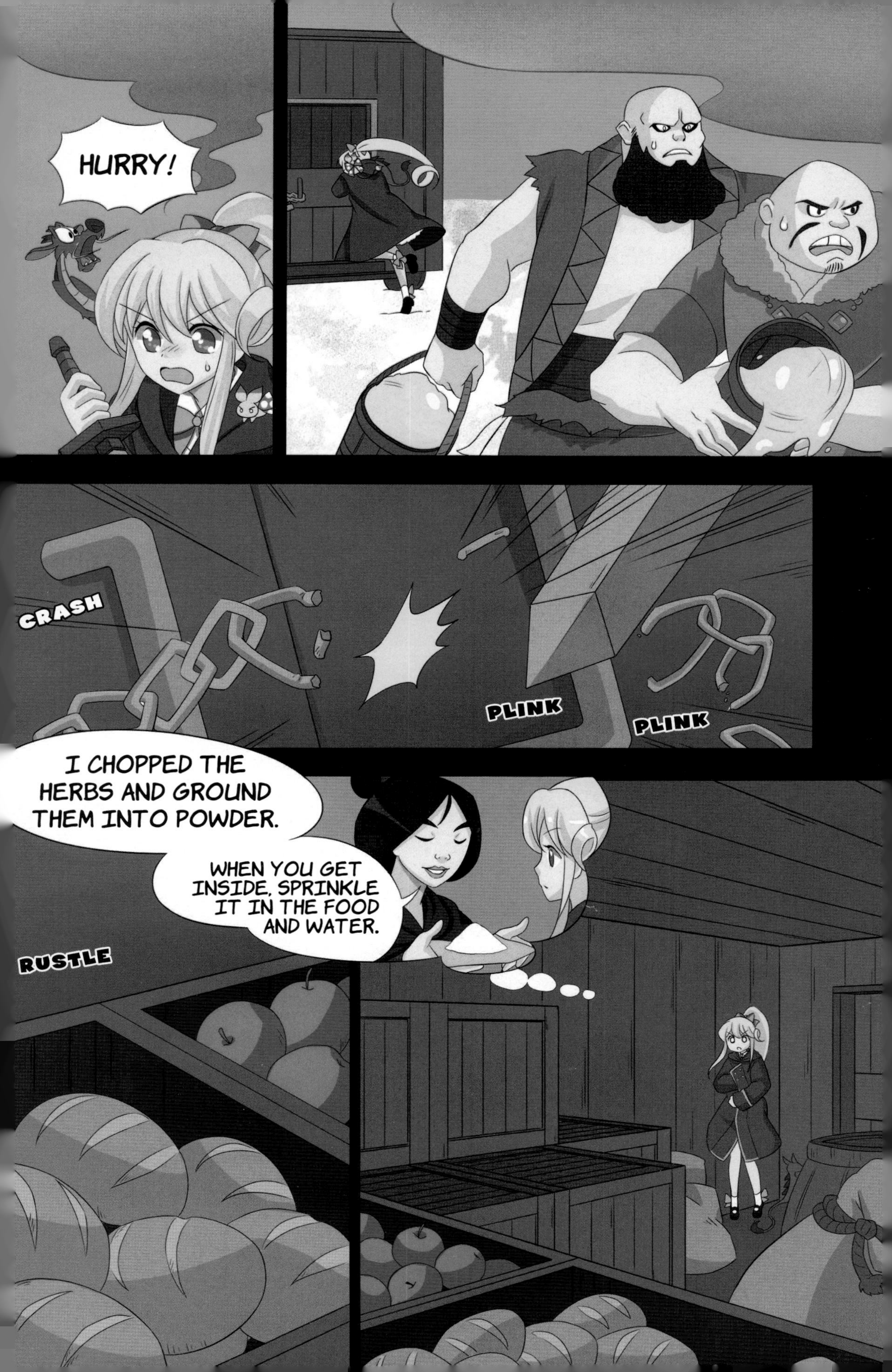
HURRY!
CRASH
PLINK
PLINK
I CHOPPED THE HERBS AND GROUND THEM INTO POWDER.
WHEN YOU GET INSIDE, SPRINKLE IT IN THE FOOD AND WATER.
RUSTLE

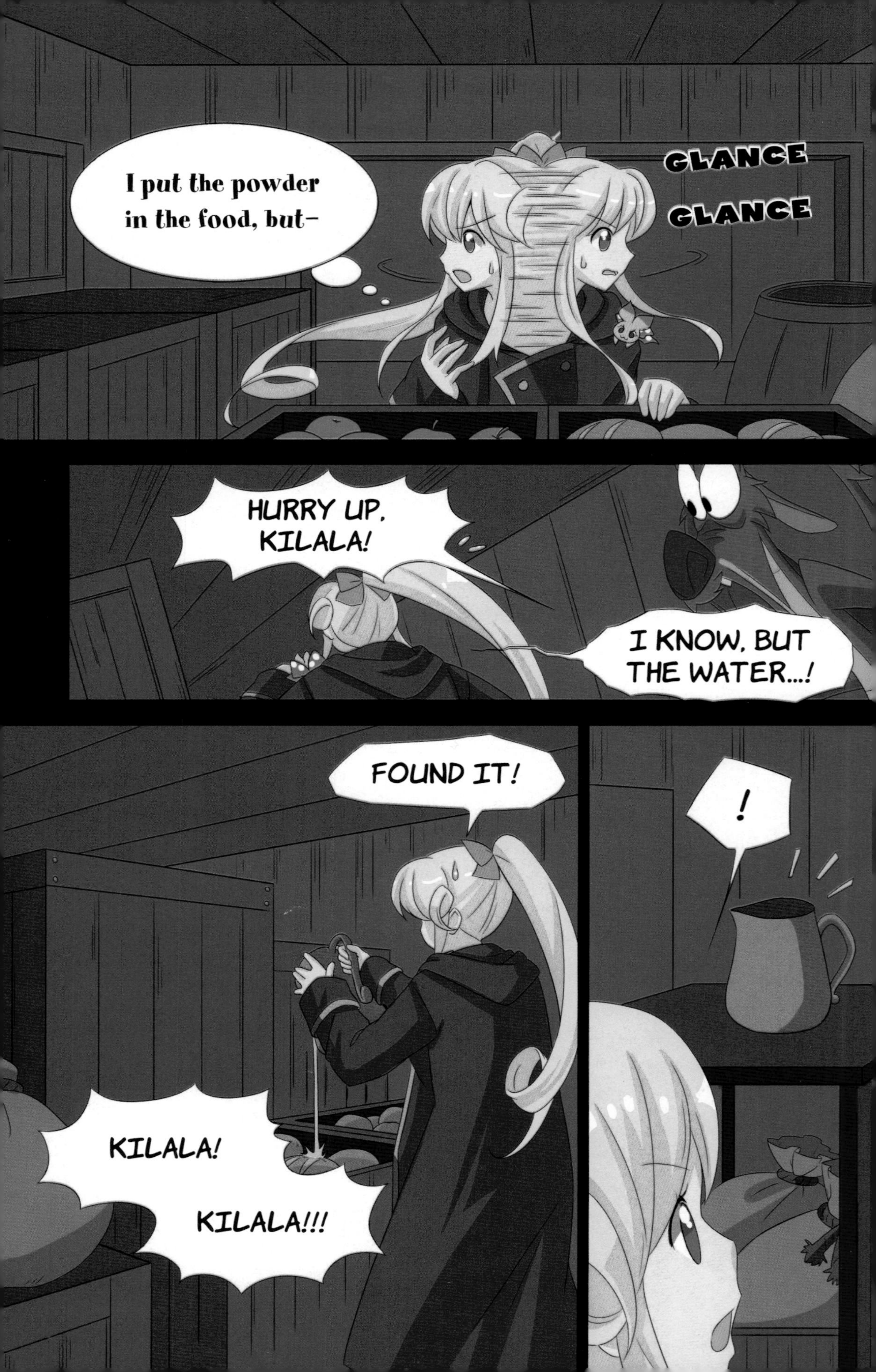
I put the powder in the food, but–
GLANCE
GLANCE
HURRY UP, KILALA!
I KNOW, BUT THE WATER...!
FOUND IT!
KILALA!
KILALA!!!
!

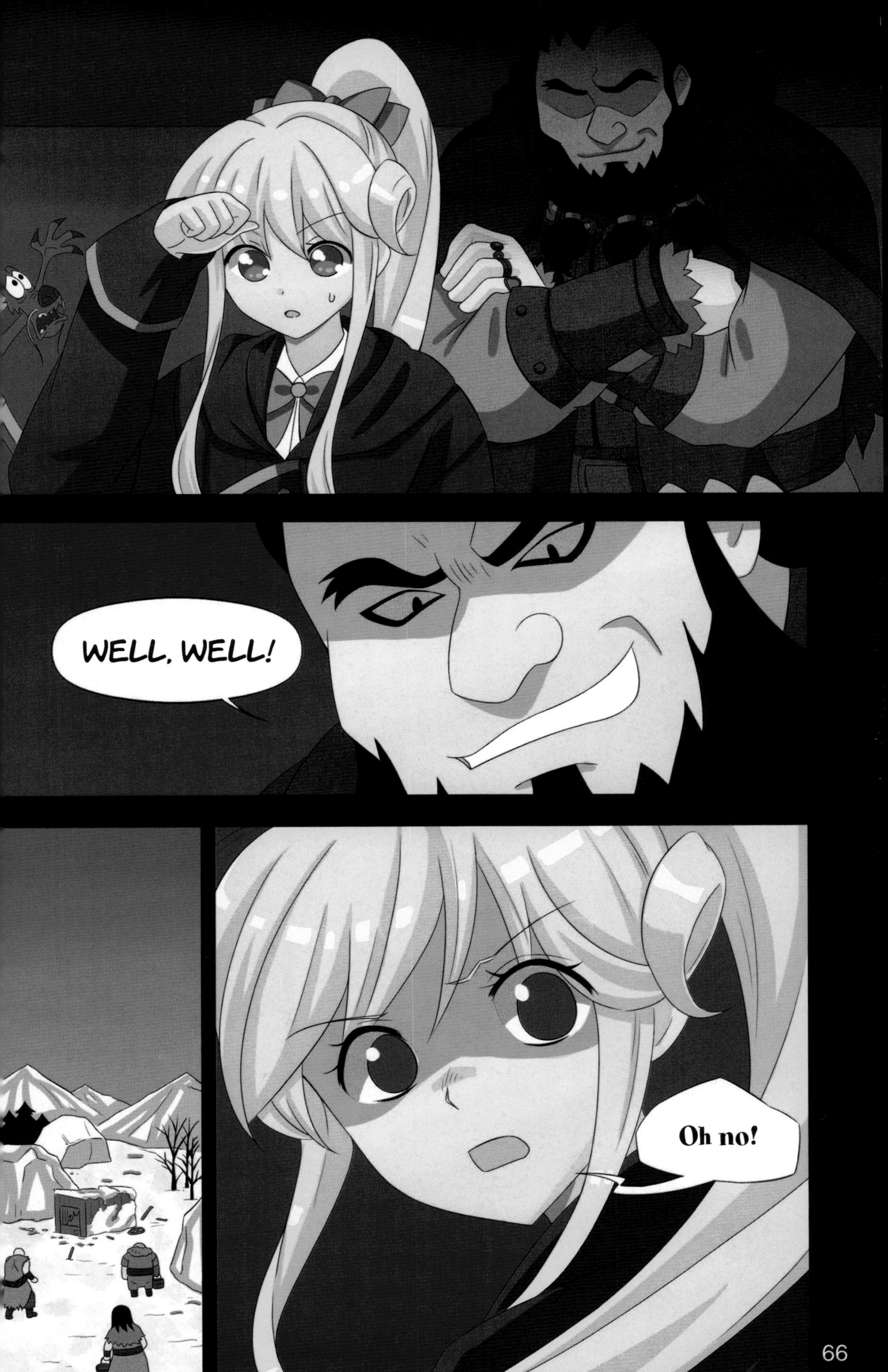
WELL, WELL!
Oh no!

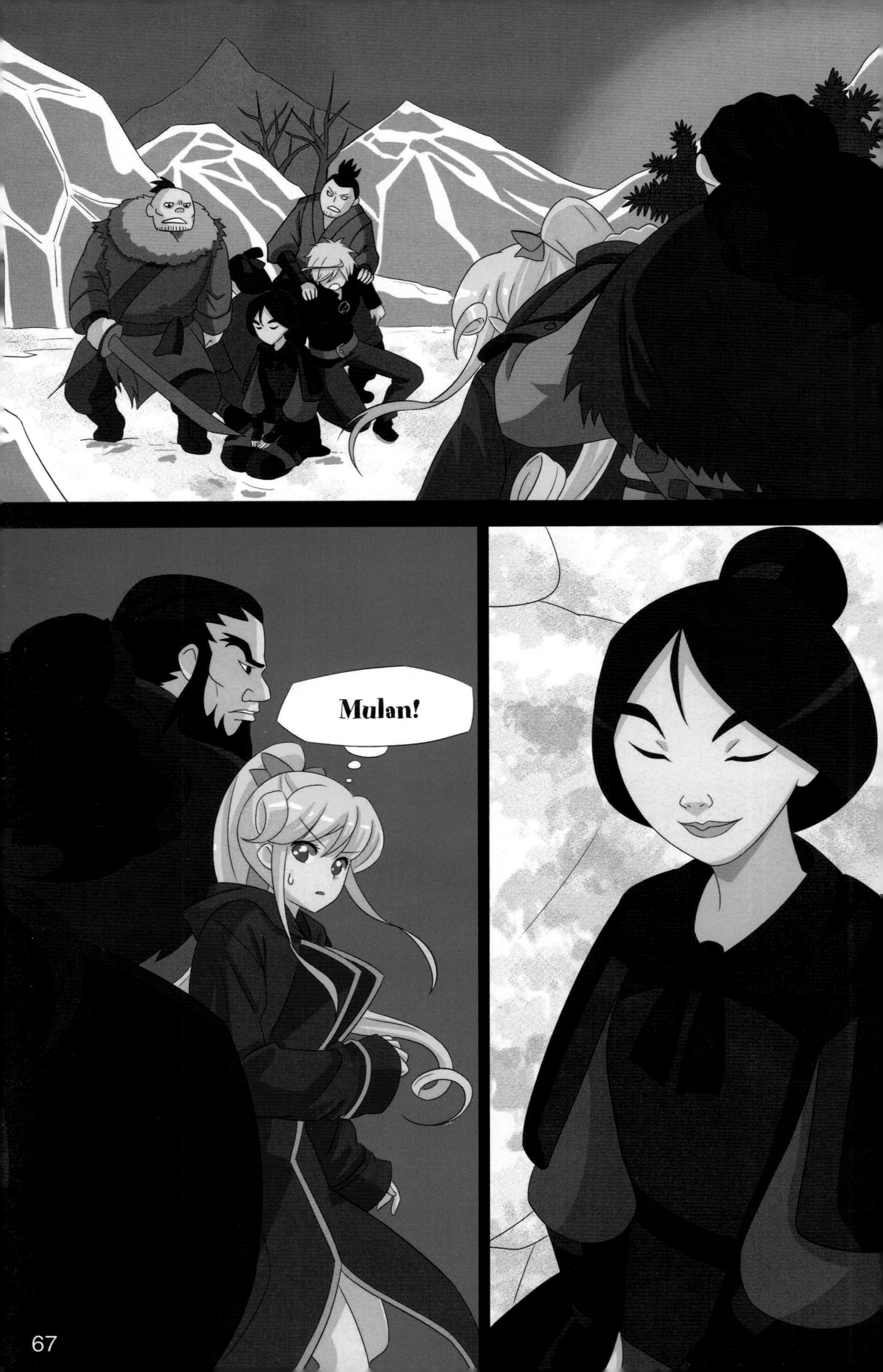
Mulan!

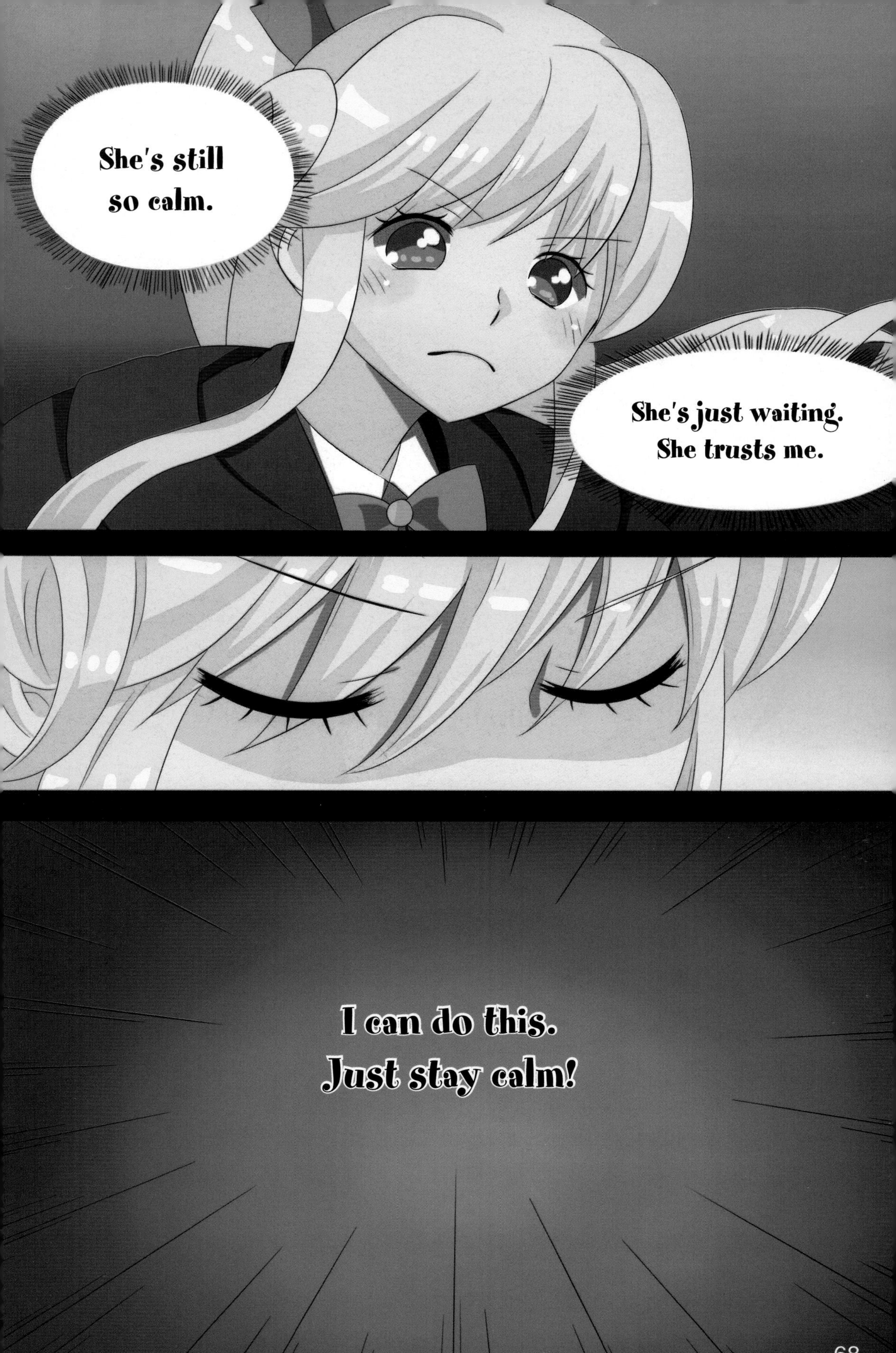
She's still so calm.
She's just waiting. She trusts me.
I can do this. Just stay calm!

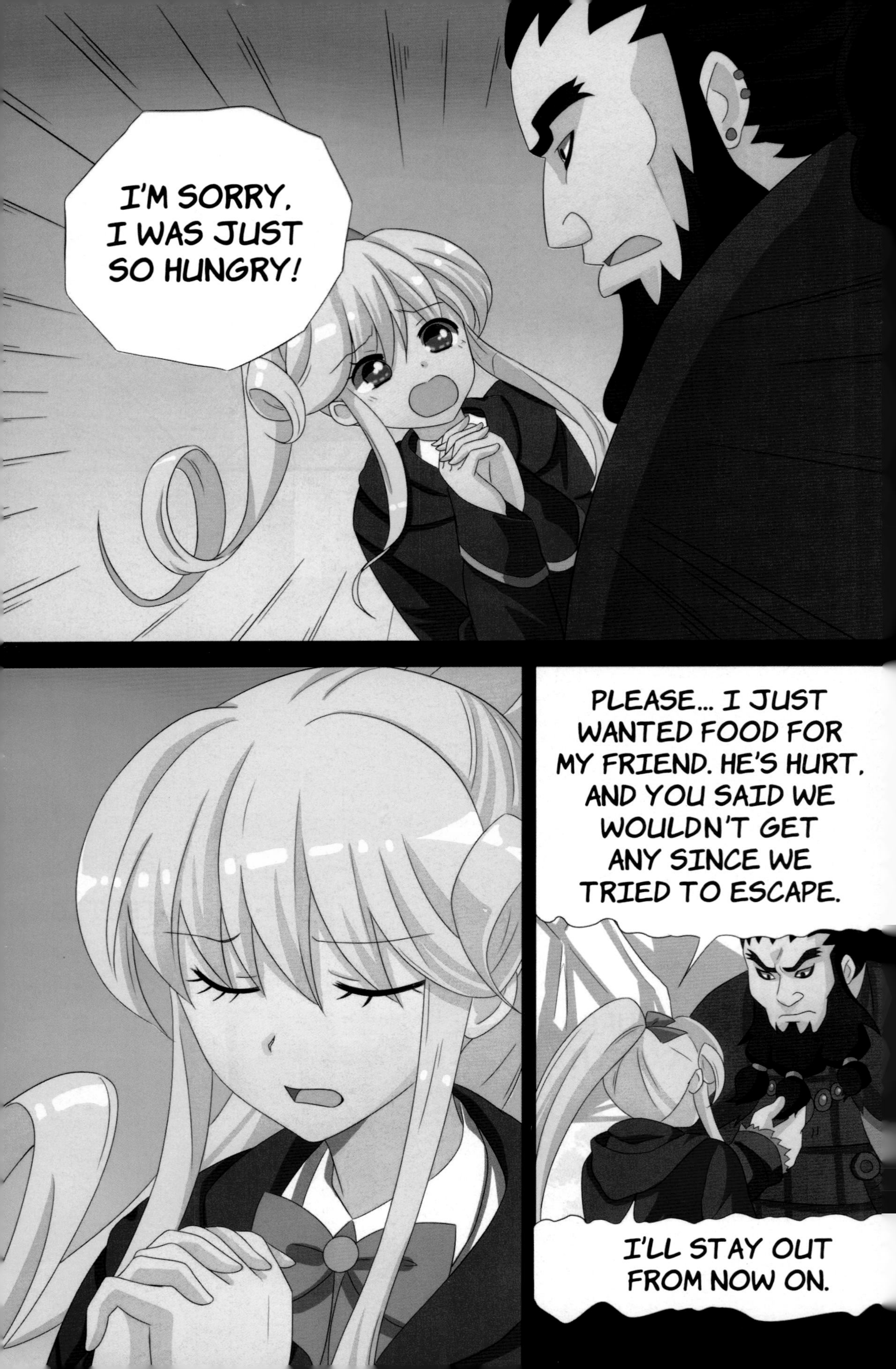
I'M SORRY, I WAS JUST SO HUNGRY!
PLEASE... I JUST WANTED FOOD FOR MY FRIEND. HE'S HURT, AND YOU SAID WE WOULDN'T GET ANY SINCE WE TRIED TO ESCAPE.
I'LL STAY OUT FROM NOW ON.

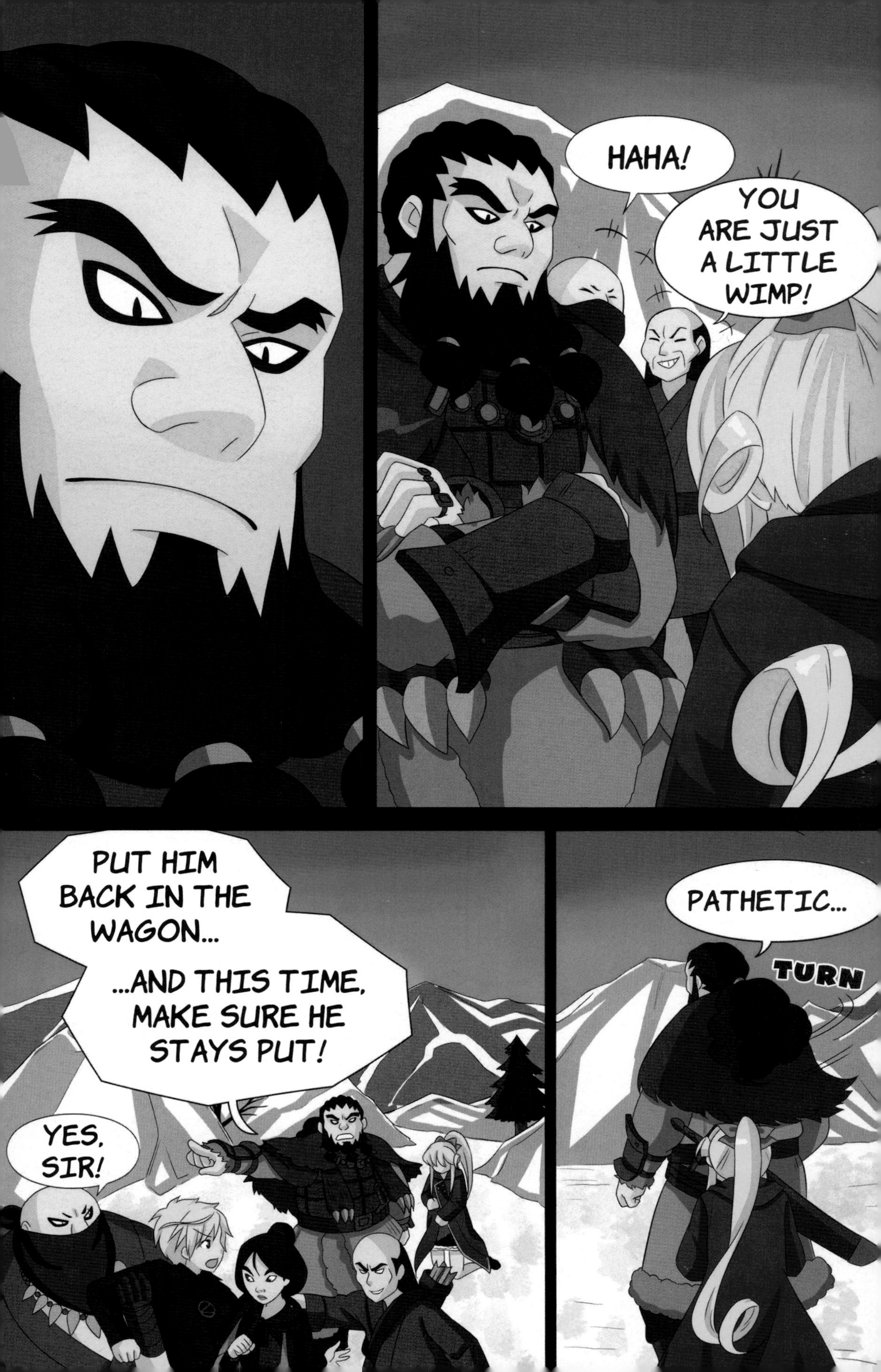
HAHA!
YOU ARE JUST A LITTLE WIMP!
PUT HIM BACK IN THE WAGON...
...AND THIS TIME, MAKE SURE HE STAYS PUT!
YES, SIR!
PATHETIC...
TURN

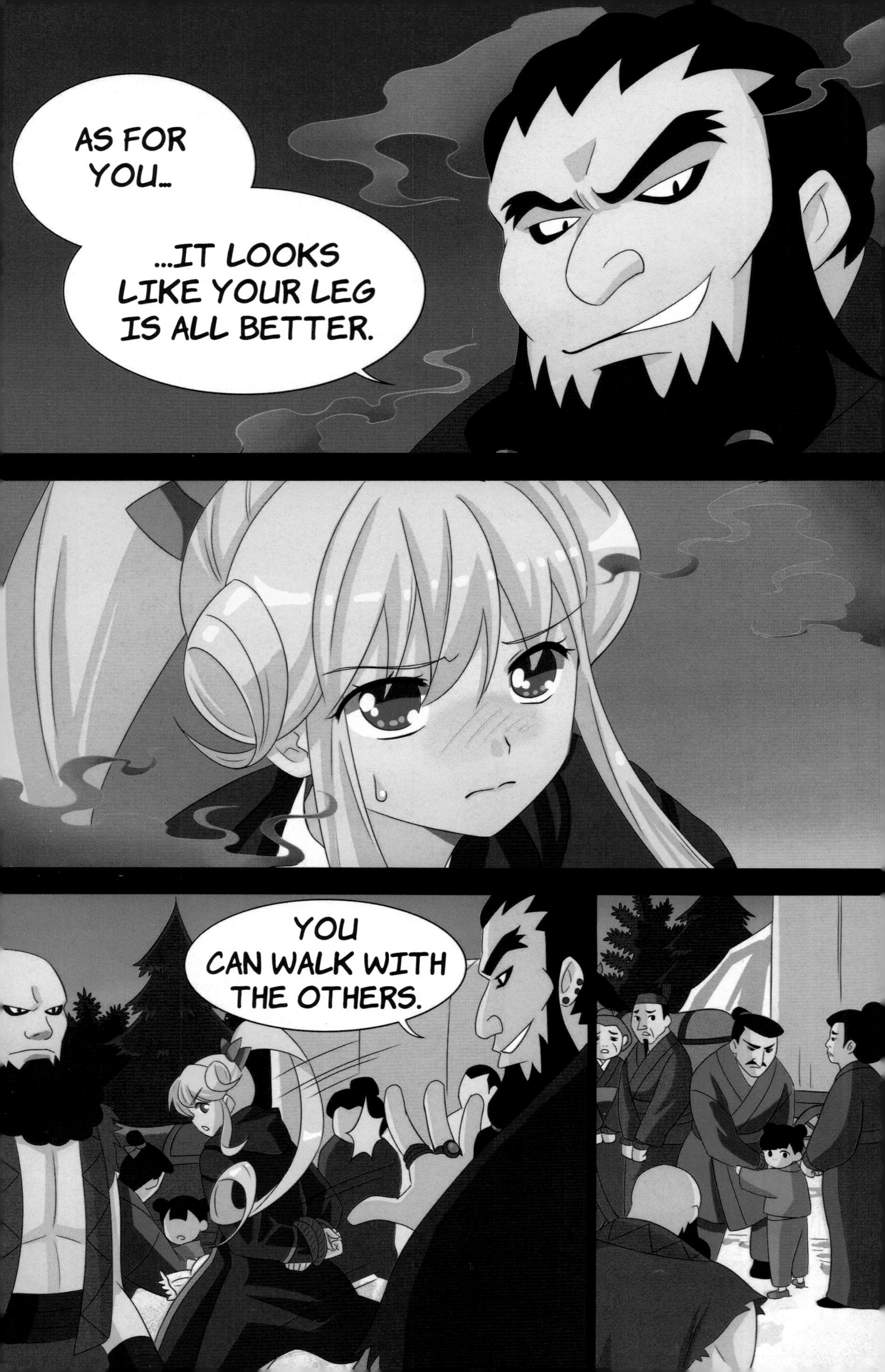
AS FOR YOU...
...IT LOOKS LIKE YOUR LEG IS ALL BETTER.
YOU CAN WALK WITH THE OTHERS.

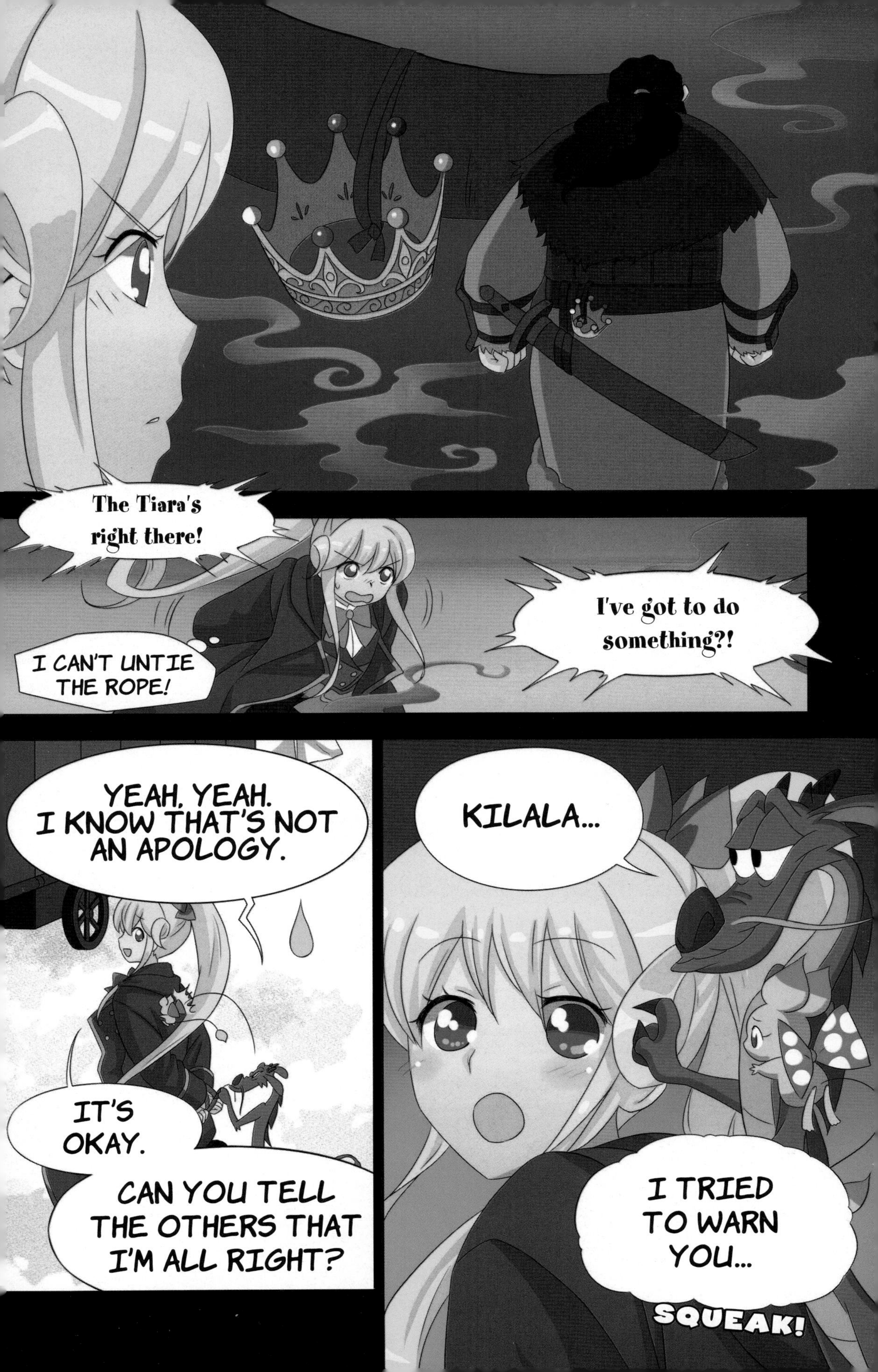
The Tiara's right there!
I CAN'T UNTIE THE ROPE!
I've got to do something?!
YEAH, YEAH. I KNOW THAT'S NOT AN APOLOGY.
IT'S OKAY.
CAN YOU TELL THE OTHERS THAT I'M ALL RIGHT?
KILALA...
I TRIED TO WARN YOU...
SQUEAK!

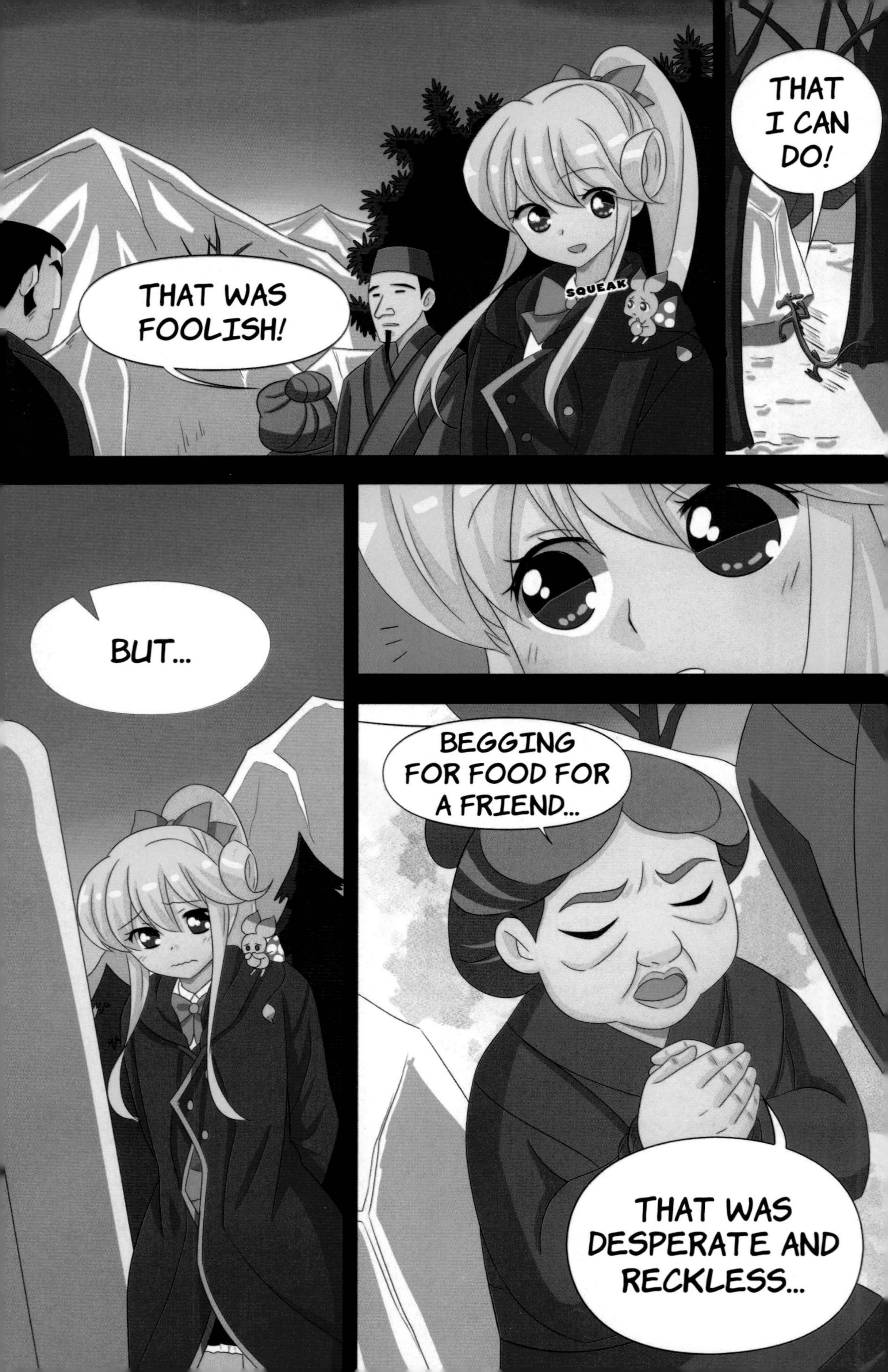
THAT WAS FOOLISH!
SQUEAK
THAT I CAN DO!
BUT...
BEGGING FOR FOOD FOR A FRIEND...
THAT WAS DESPERATE AND RECKLESS...

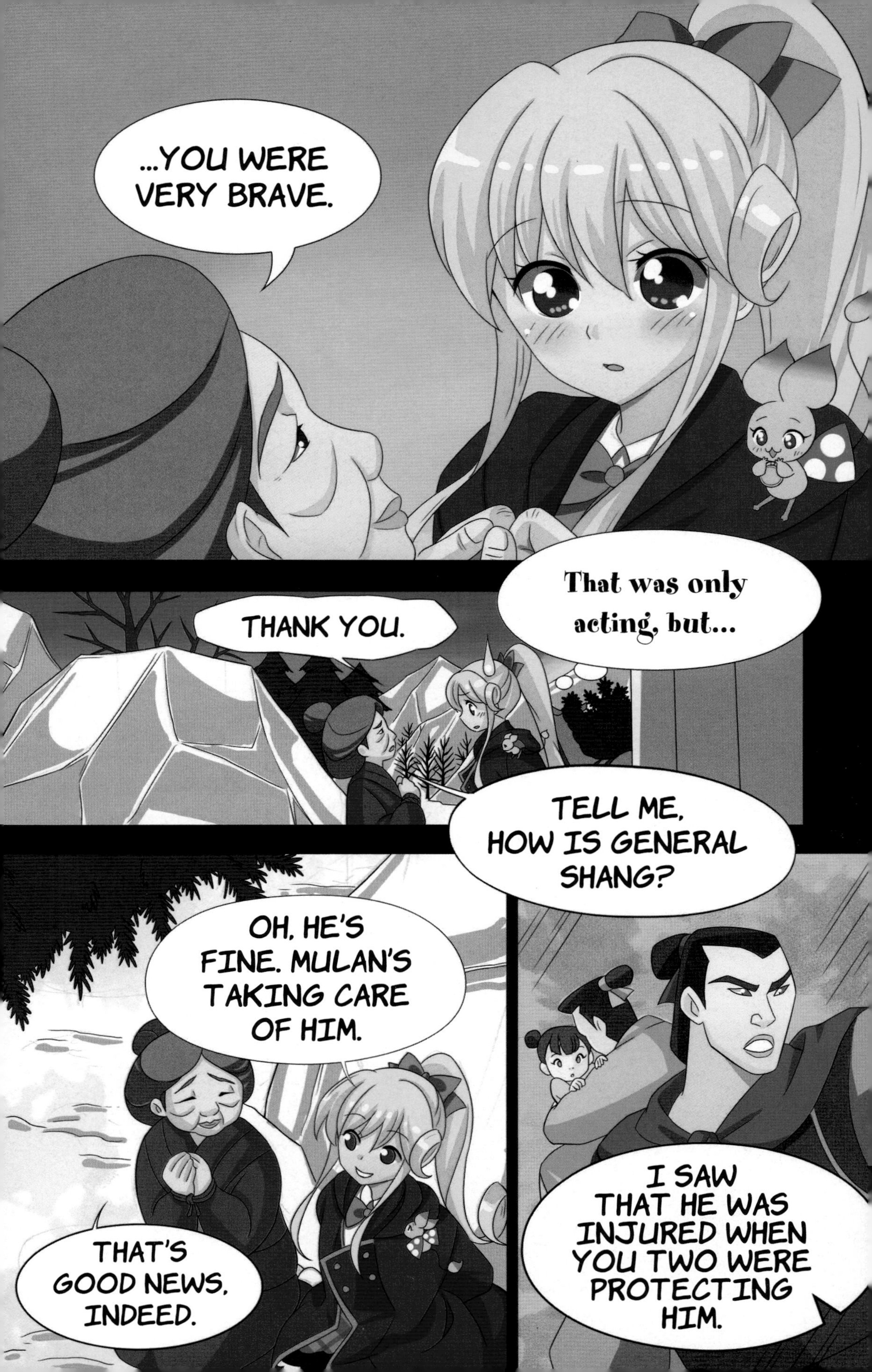
...YOU WERE VERY BRAVE.
THANK YOU.
That was only acting, but...
TELL ME, HOW IS GENERAL SHANG?
OH, HE'S FINE. MULAN'S TAKING CARE OF HIM.
THAT'S GOOD NEWS, INDEED.
I SAW THAT HE WAS INJURED WHEN YOU TWO WERE PROTECTING HIM.

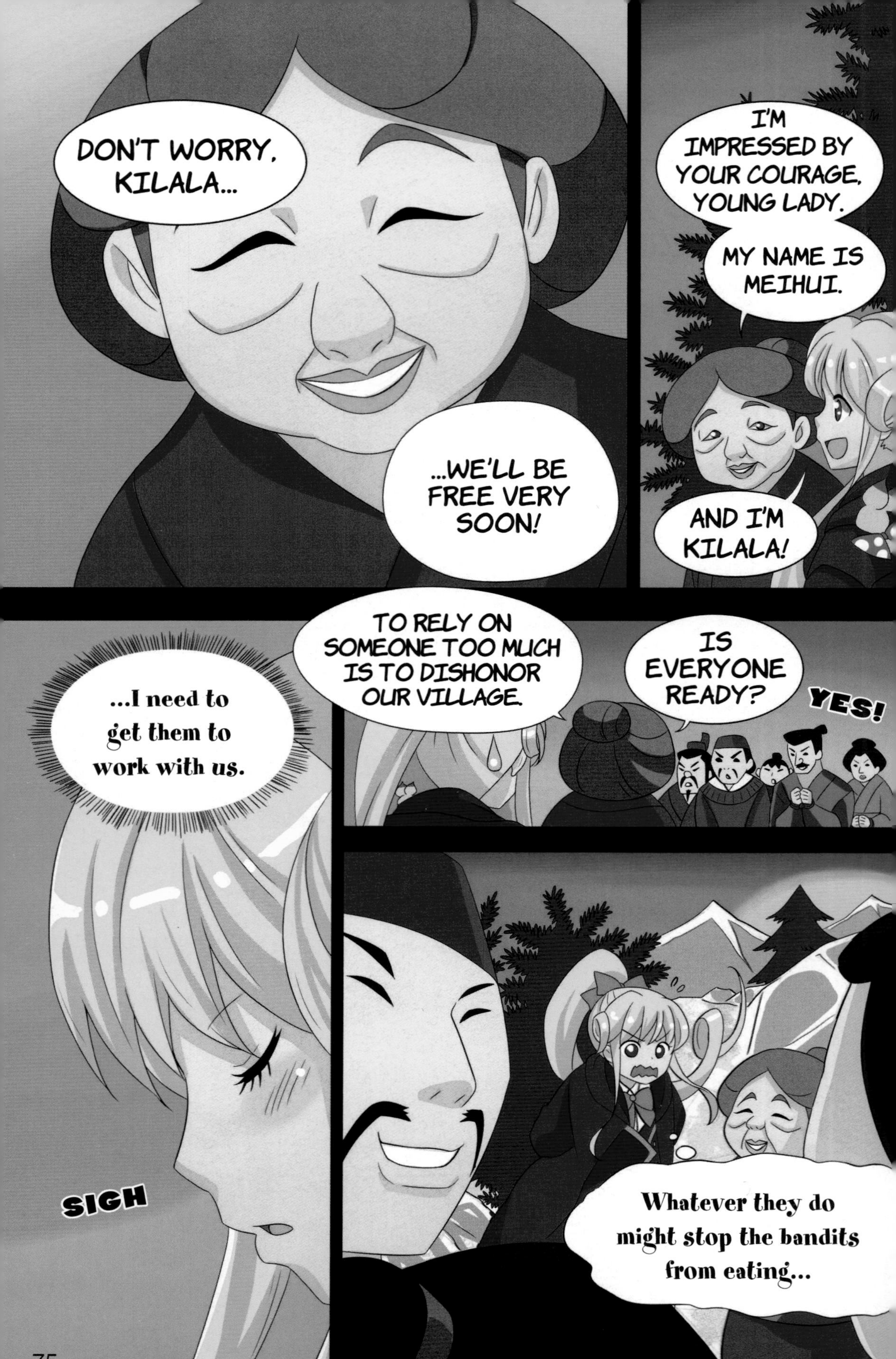
DON'T WORRY, KILALA...
...WE'LL BE FREE VERY SOON!
I'M IMPRESSED BY YOUR COURAGE, YOUNG LADY.
MY NAME IS MEIHUI.
AND I'M KILALA!
...I need to get them to work with us.
SIGH
TO RELY ON SOMEONE TOO MUCH IS TO DISHONOR OUR VILLAGE.
IS EVERYONE READY?
YES!
Whatever they do might stop the bandits from eating...

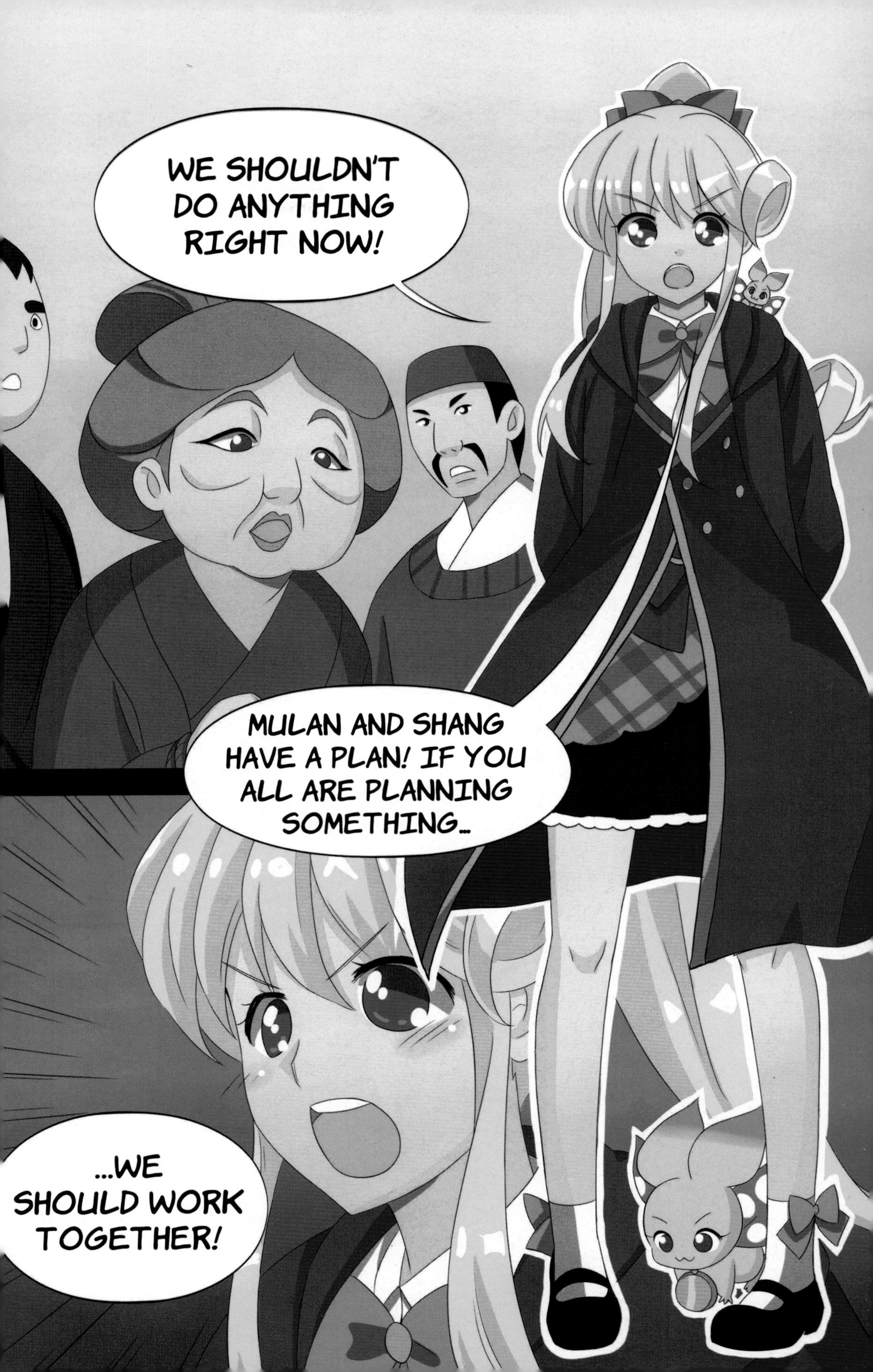
WE SHOULDN'T DO ANYTHING RIGHT NOW!
MULAN AND SHANG HAVE A PLAN! IF YOU ALL ARE PLANNING SOMETHING...
...WE SHOULD WORK TOGETHER!

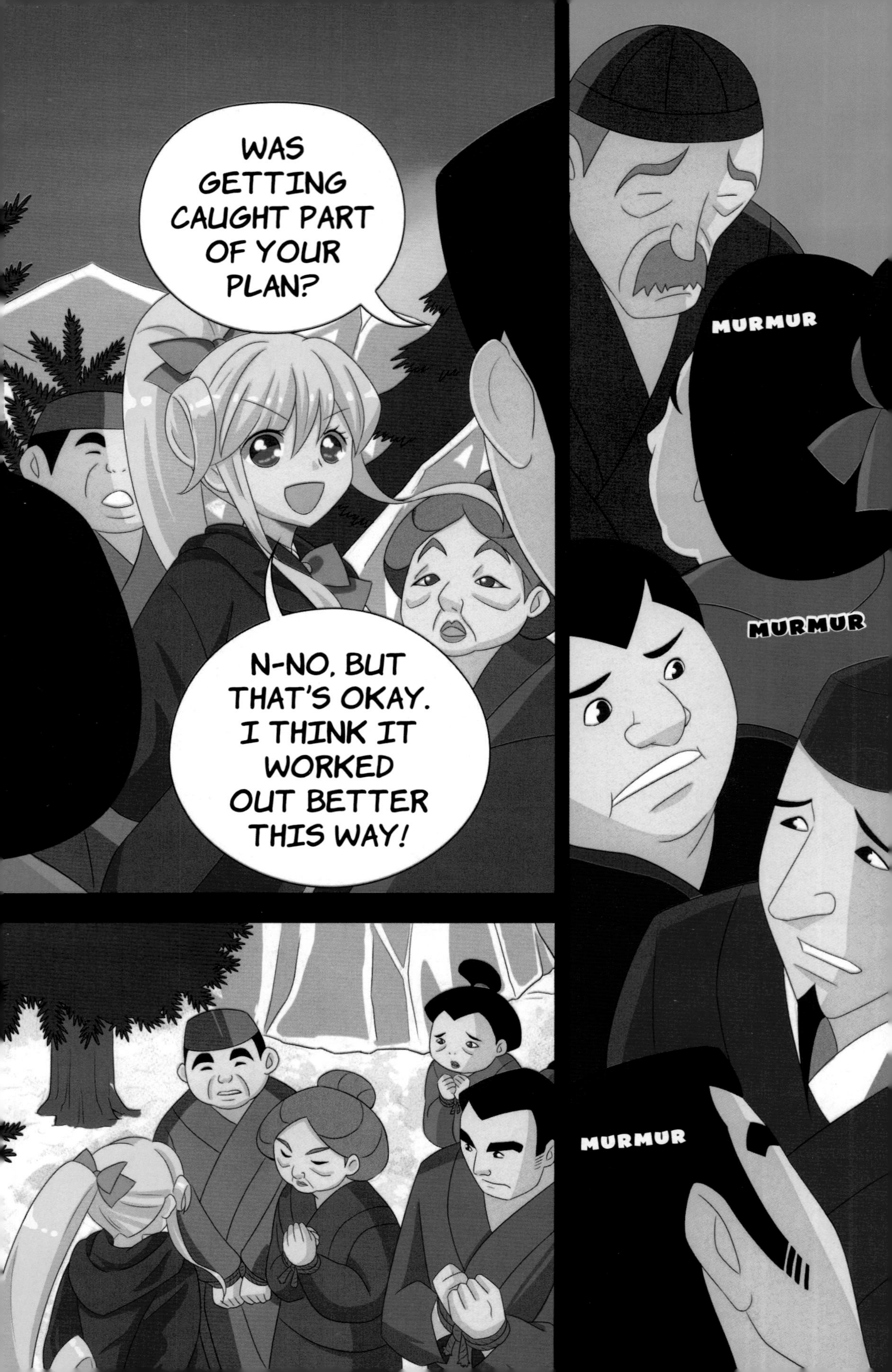
WAS GETTING CAUGHT PART OF YOUR PLAN?
N-NO, BUT THAT'S OKAY. I THINK IT WORKED OUT BETTER THIS WAY!
MURMUR
MURMUR
MURMUR

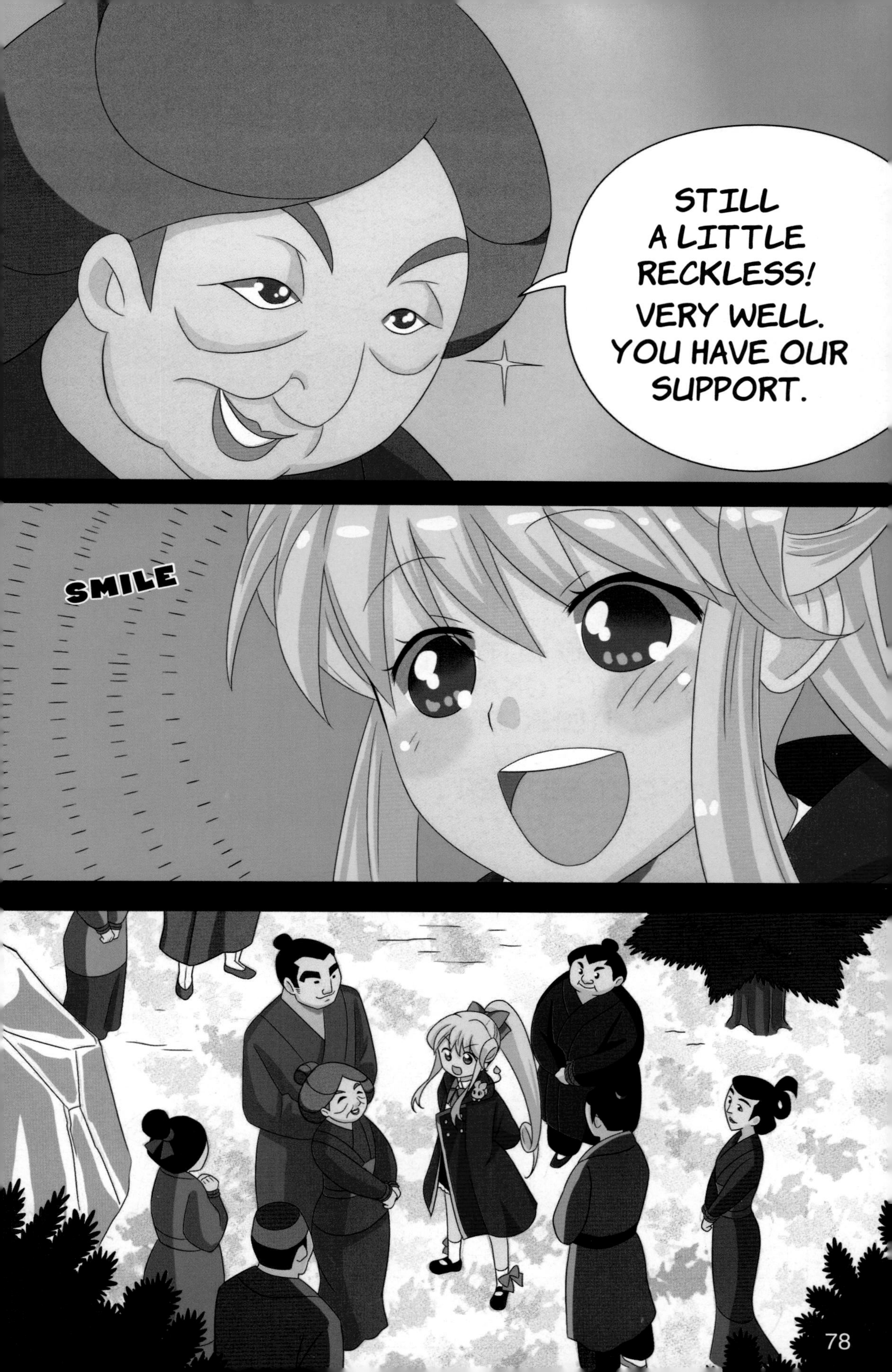
STILL A LITTLE RECKLESS! VERY WELL. YOU HAVE OUR SUPPORT.
SMILE

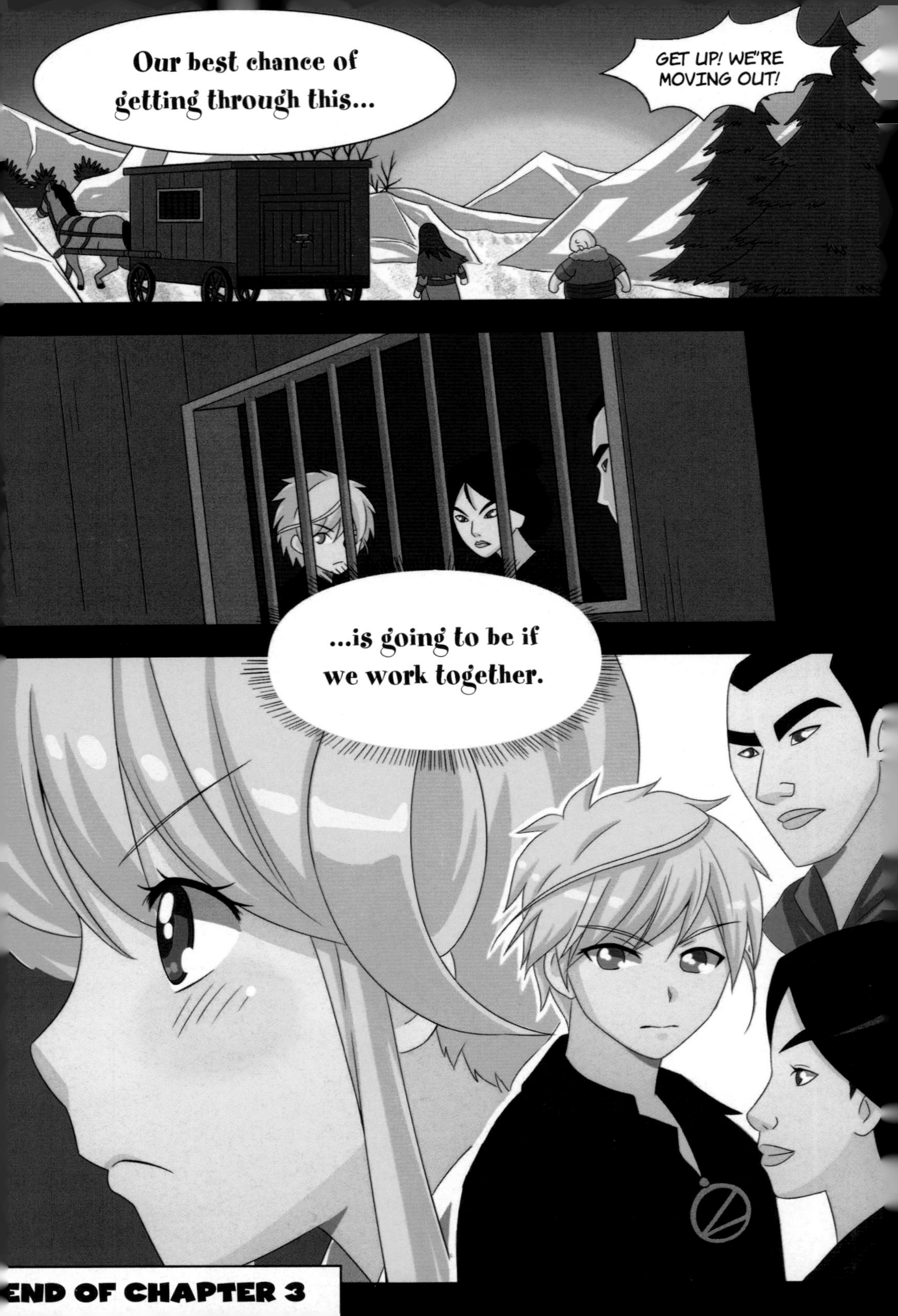
Our best chance of getting through this...
GET UP! WE'RE MOVING OUT!
...is going to be if we work together.
END OF CHAPTER 3

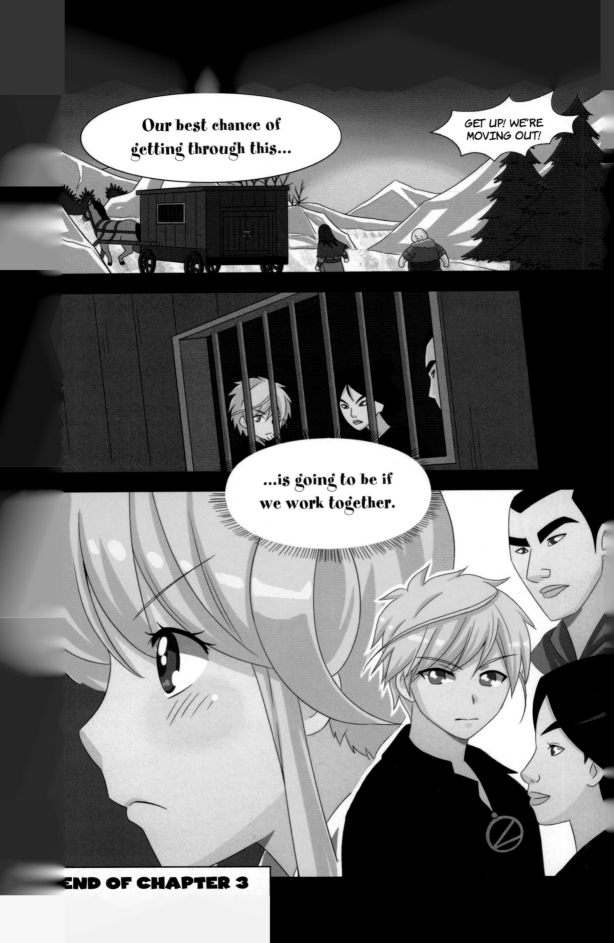

Disney

Kilala Princess

Rescue the Village with Mulan!

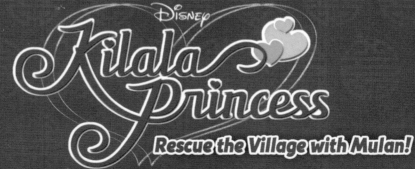

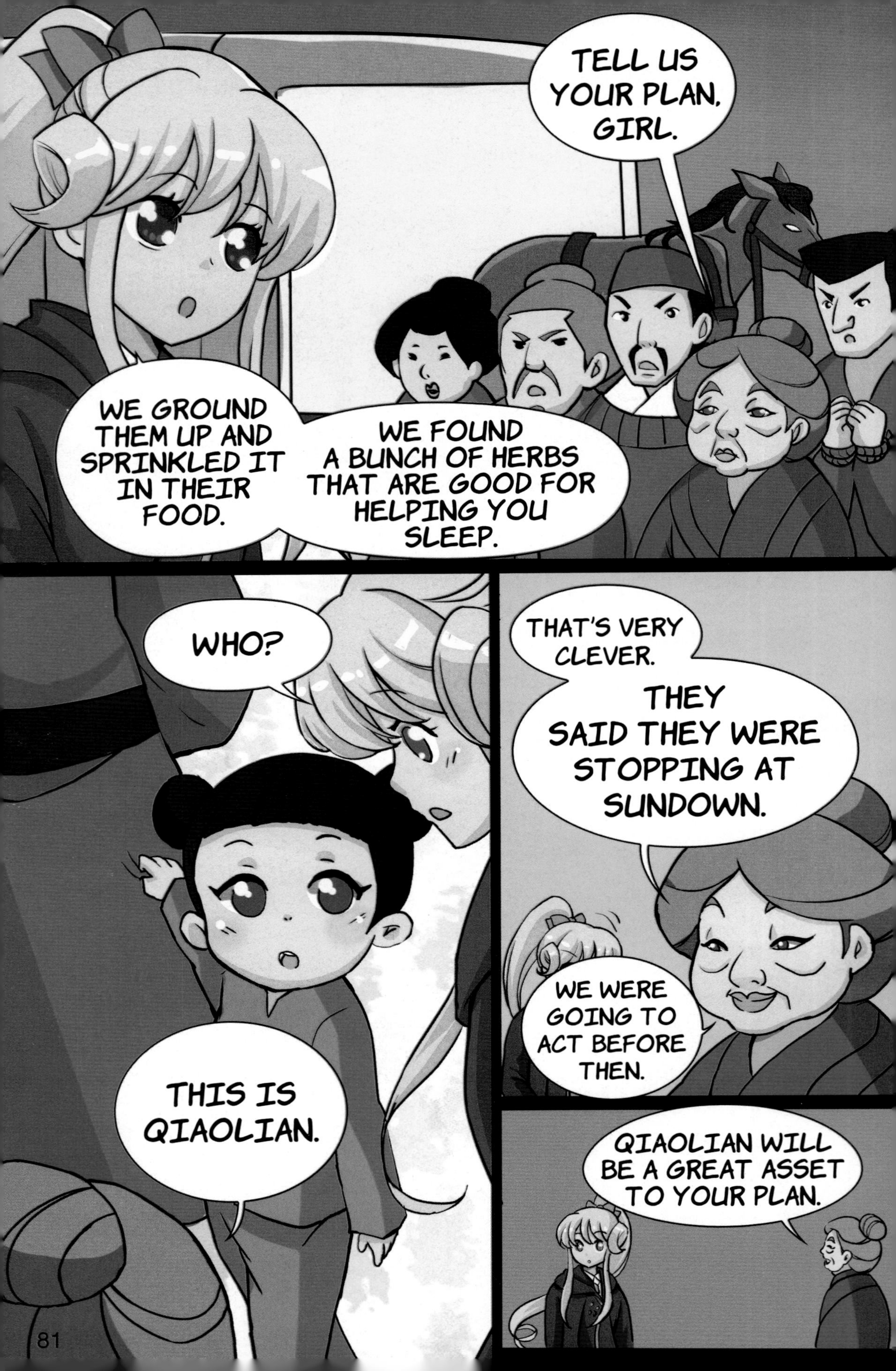
TELL US YOUR PLAN, GIRL.
WE FOUND A BUNCH OF HERBS THAT ARE GOOD FOR HELPING YOU SLEEP.
WE GROUND THEM UP AND SPRINKLED IT IN THEIR FOOD.
WHO?
THIS IS QIAOLIAN.
THAT'S VERY CLEVER.
THEY SAID THEY WERE STOPPING AT SUNDOWN.
WE WERE GOING TO ACT BEFORE THEN.
QIAOLIAN WILL BE A GREAT ASSET TO YOUR PLAN.

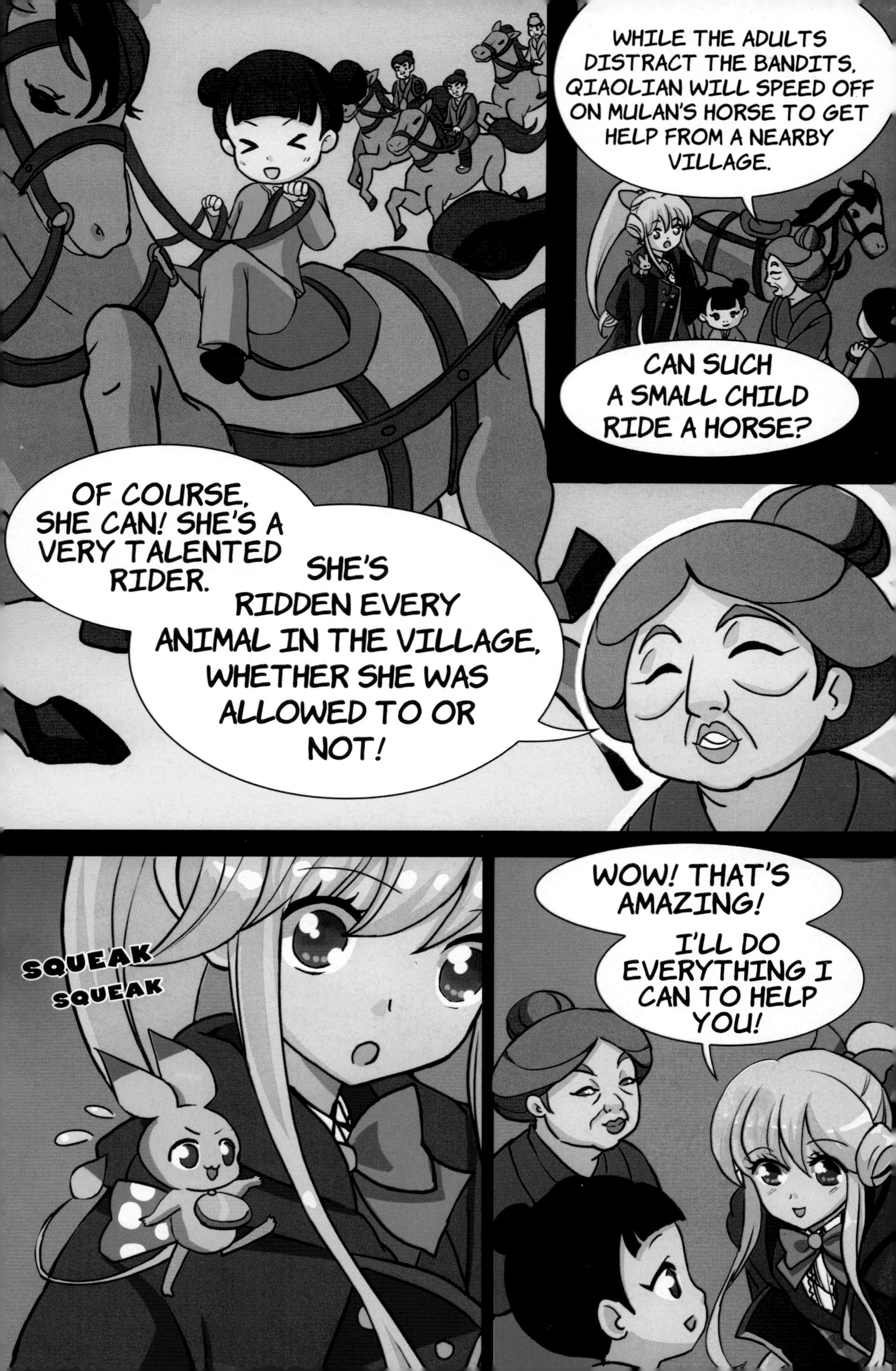
WHILE THE ADULTS DISTRACT THE BANDITS, QIAOLIAN WILL SPEED OFF ON MULAN'S HORSE TO GET HELP FROM A NEARBY VILLAGE.
CAN SUCH A SMALL CHILD RIDE A HORSE?
OF COURSE, SHE CAN! SHE'S A VERY TALENTED RIDER.
SHE'S RIDDEN EVERY ANIMAL IN THE VILLAGE, WHETHER SHE WAS ALLOWED TO OR NOT!
SQUEAK
SQUEAK
WOW! THAT'S AMAZING!
I'LL DO EVERYTHING I CAN TO HELP YOU!

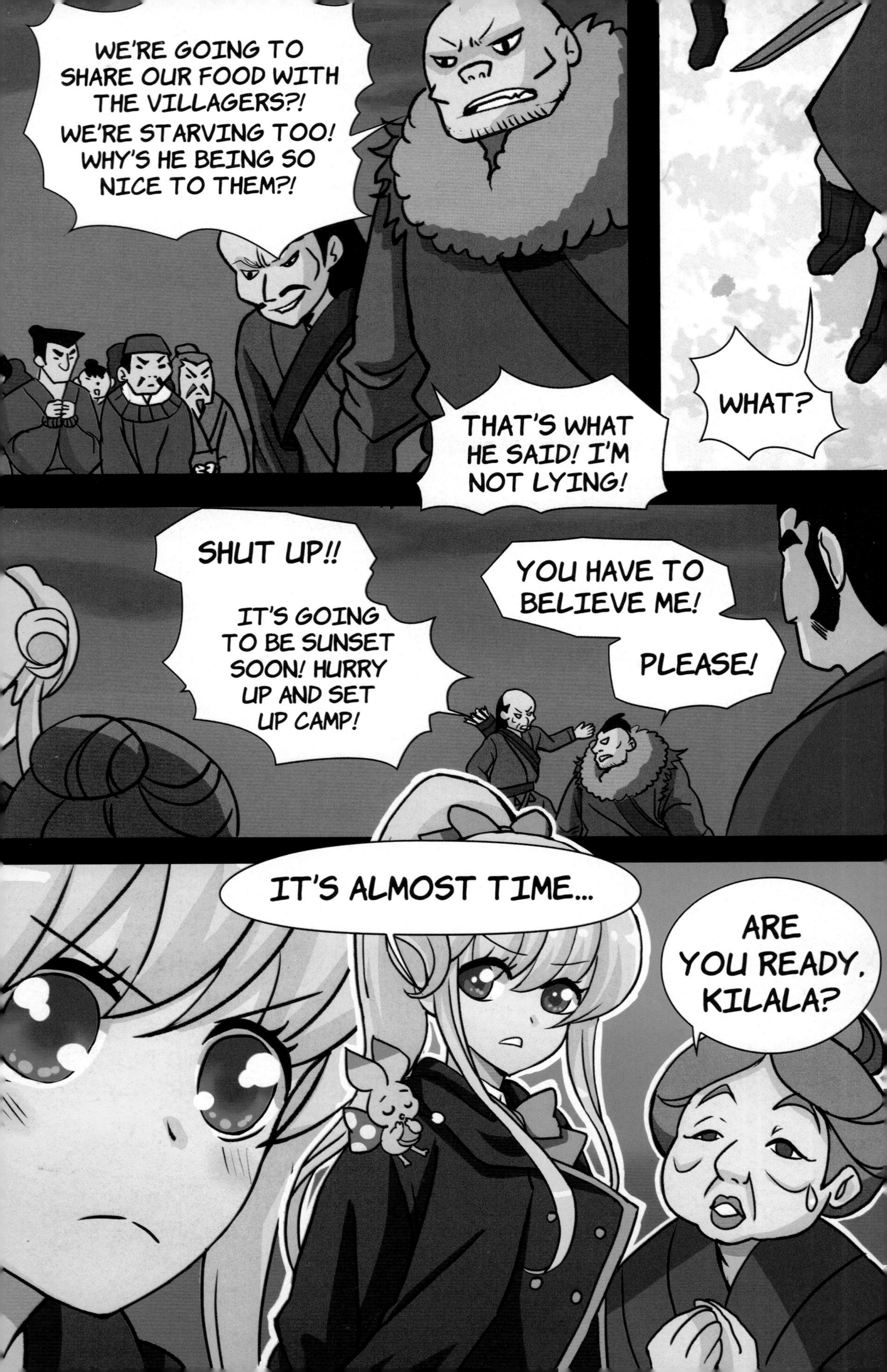
WE'RE GOING TO SHARE OUR FOOD WITH THE VILLAGERS?! WE'RE STARVING TOO! WHY'S HE BEING SO NICE TO THEM?!
THAT'S WHAT HE SAID! I'M NOT LYING!
WHAT?
SHUT UP!!
IT'S GOING TO BE SUNSET SOON! HURRY UP AND SET UP CAMP!
YOU HAVE TO BELIEVE ME!
PLEASE!
IT'S ALMOST TIME...
ARE YOU READY, KILALA?

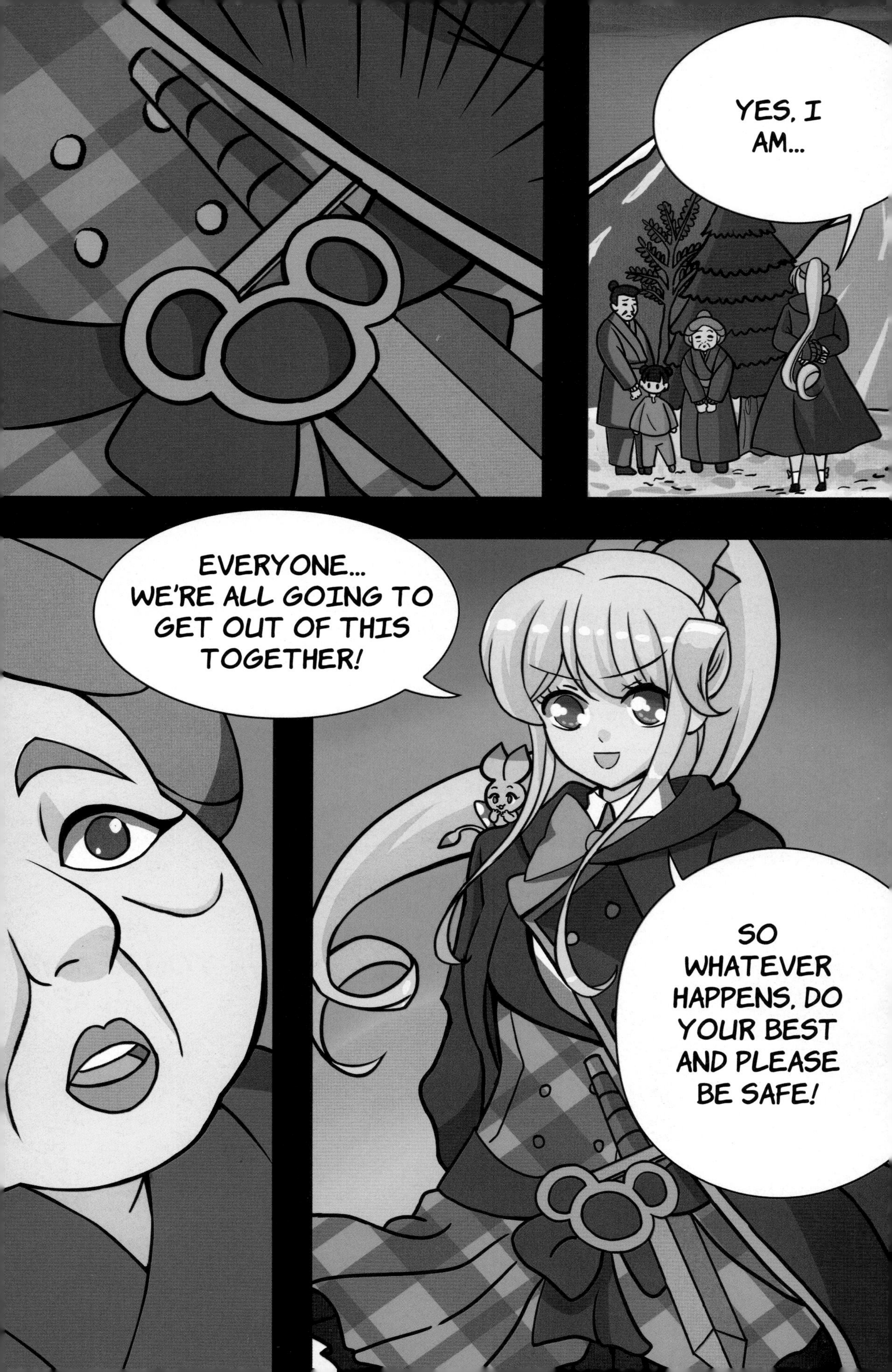
YES, I AM...
EVERYONE... WE'RE ALL GOING TO GET OUT OF THIS TOGETHER!
SO WHATEVER HAPPENS, DO YOUR BEST AND PLEASE BE SAFE!

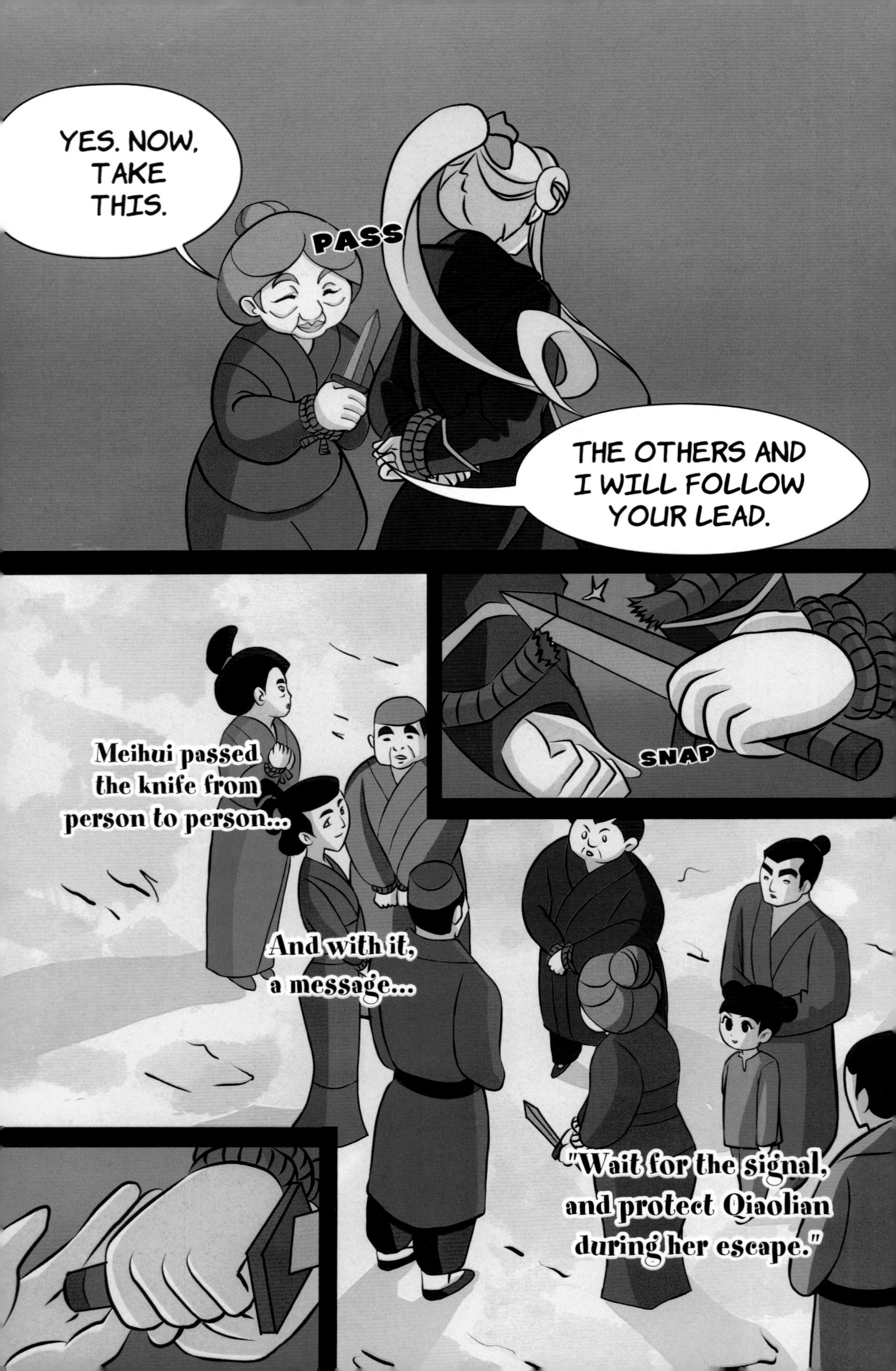
YES. NOW, TAKE THIS.
PASS
THE OTHERS AND I WILL FOLLOW YOUR LEAD.
Meihui passed the knife from person to person...
SNAP
And with it, a message...
"Wait for the signal, and protect Qiaolian during her escape."

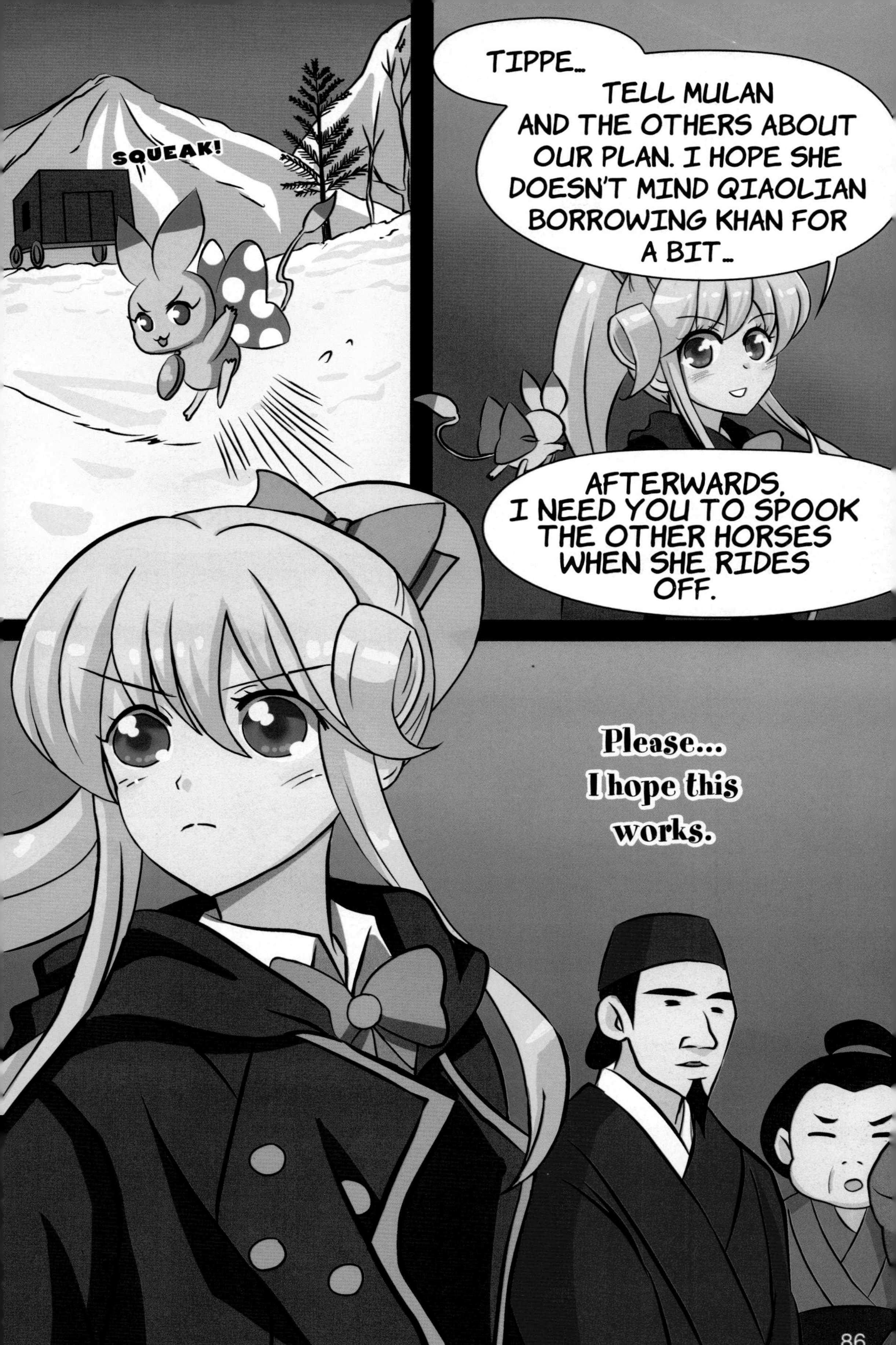
SQUEAK!
TIPPE... TELL MULAN AND THE OTHERS ABOUT OUR PLAN. I HOPE SHE DOESN'T MIND QIAOLIAN BORROWING KHAN FOR A BIT...
AFTERWARDS, I NEED YOU TO SPOOK THE OTHER HORSES WHEN SHE RIDES OFF.
Please... I hope this works.

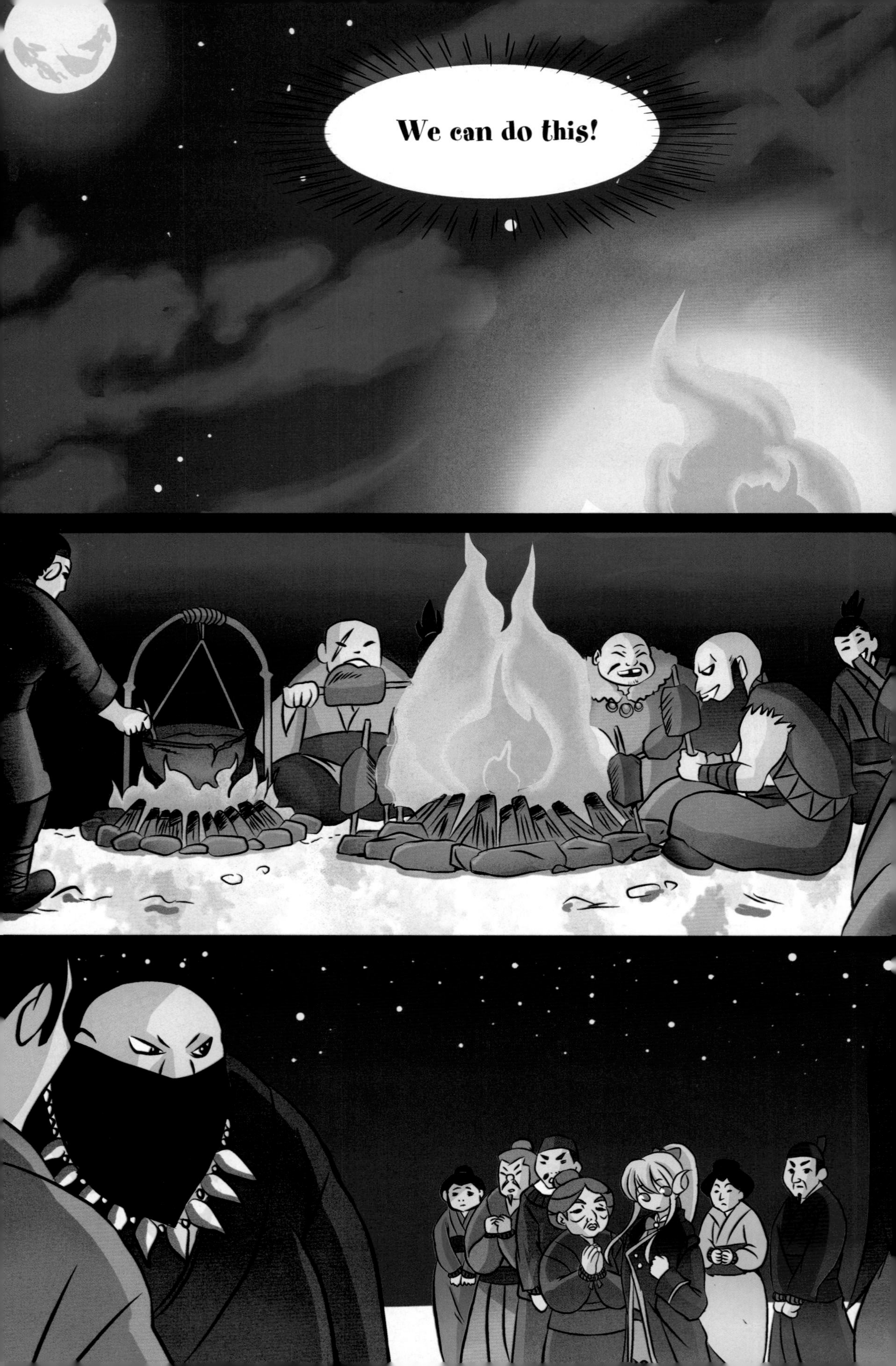
We can do this!

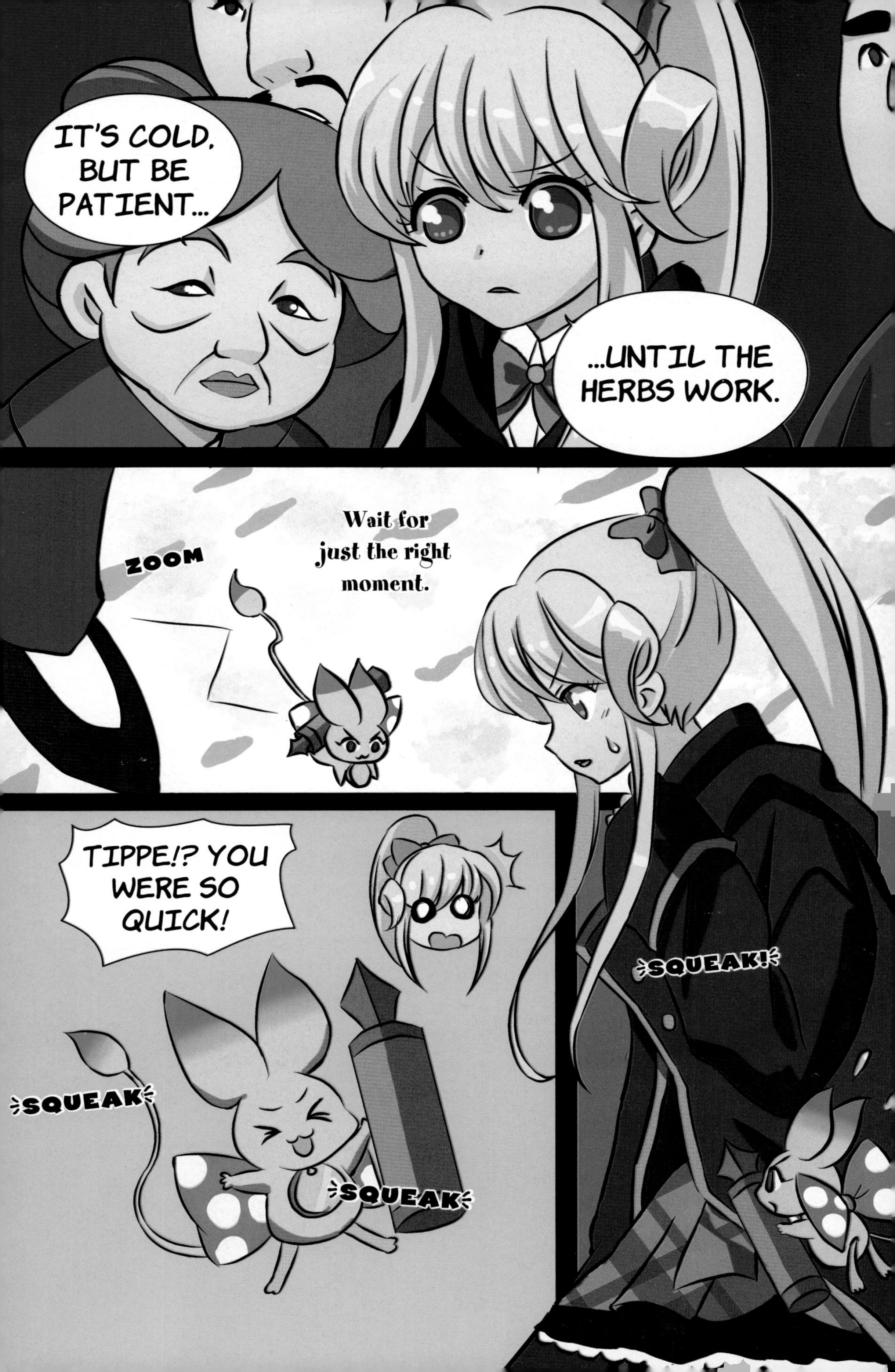

IT'S COLD, BUT BE PATIENT...
...UNTIL THE HERBS WORK.
ZOOM
Wait for just the right moment.
TIPPE!? YOU WERE SO QUICK!
SQUEAK
SQUEAK
SQUEAK!

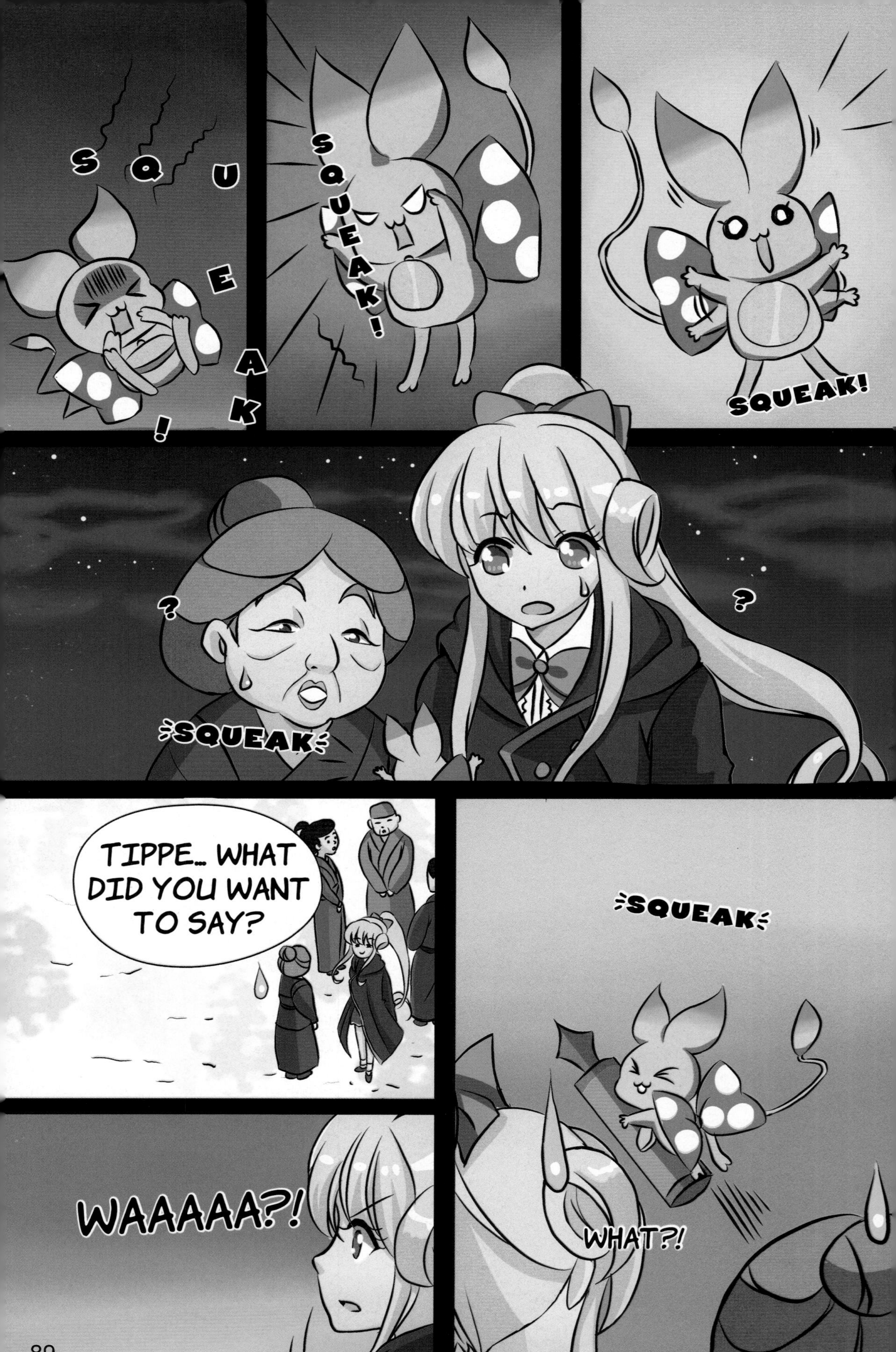
SQUEAK!
SQUEAK!
SQUEAK!
?
?
SQUEAK
TIPPE... WHAT DID YOU WANT TO SAY?
SQUEAK
WAAAAA?!
WHAT?!

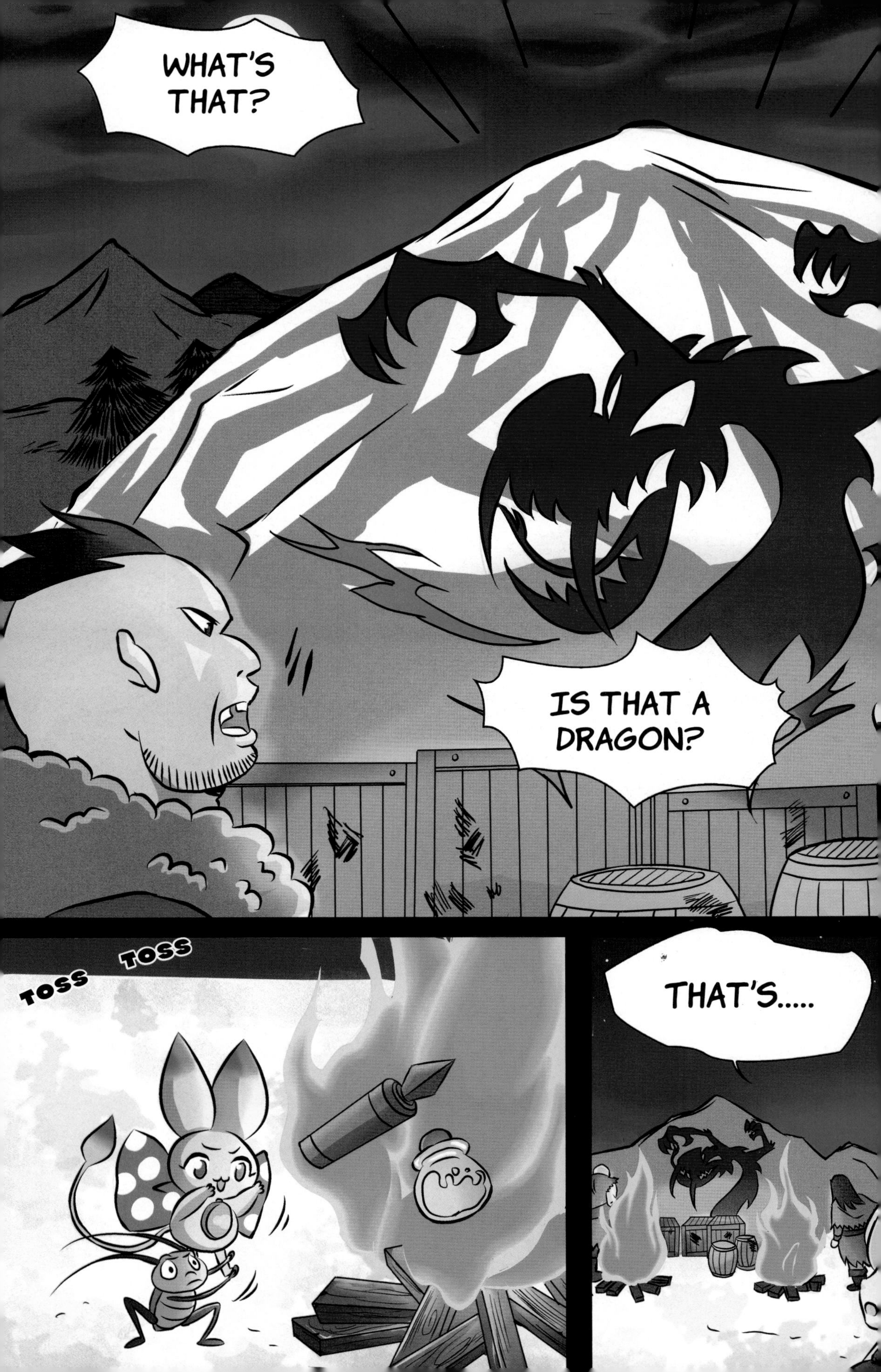
WHAT'S THAT?
IS THAT A DRAGON?
TOSS
TOSS
THAT'S.....

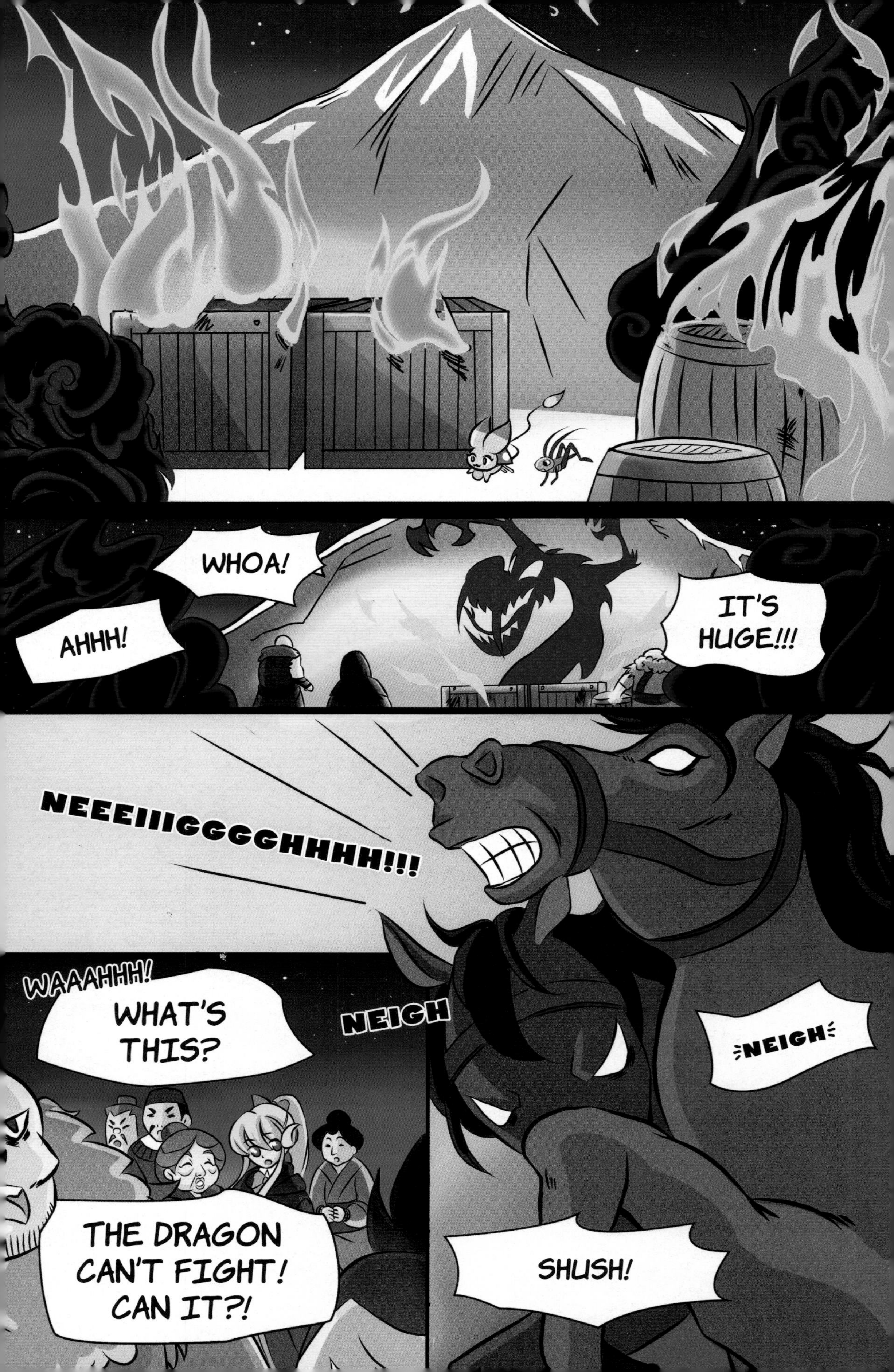
WHOA!
AHHH!
IT'S HUGE!!!
NEEEIIIGGGGHHHHH!!!
WAAAHHH!
WHAT'S THIS?
NEIGH
THE DRAGON CAN'T FIGHT! CAN IT?!
NEIGH
SHUSH!

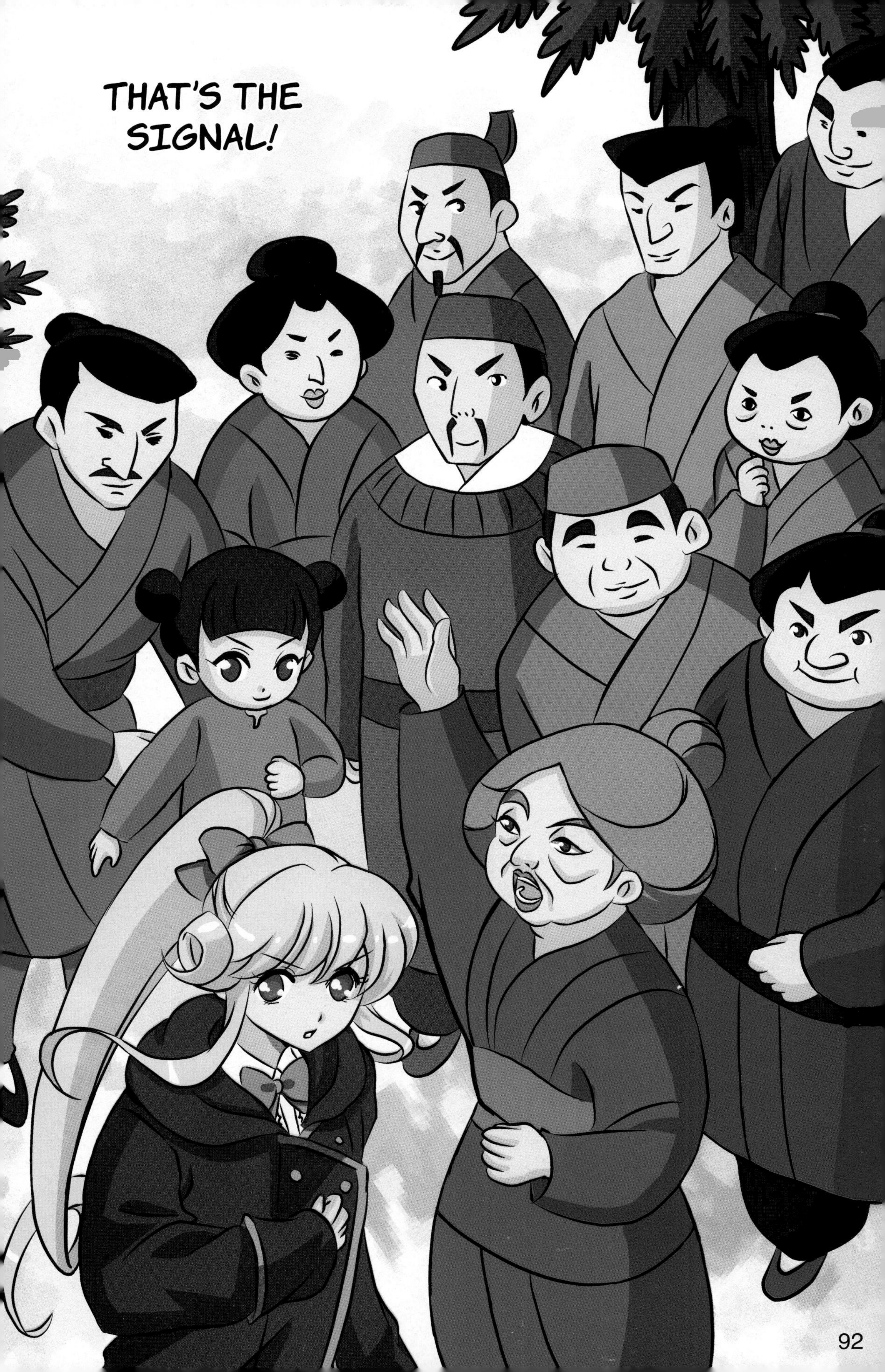
THAT'S THE SIGNAL!

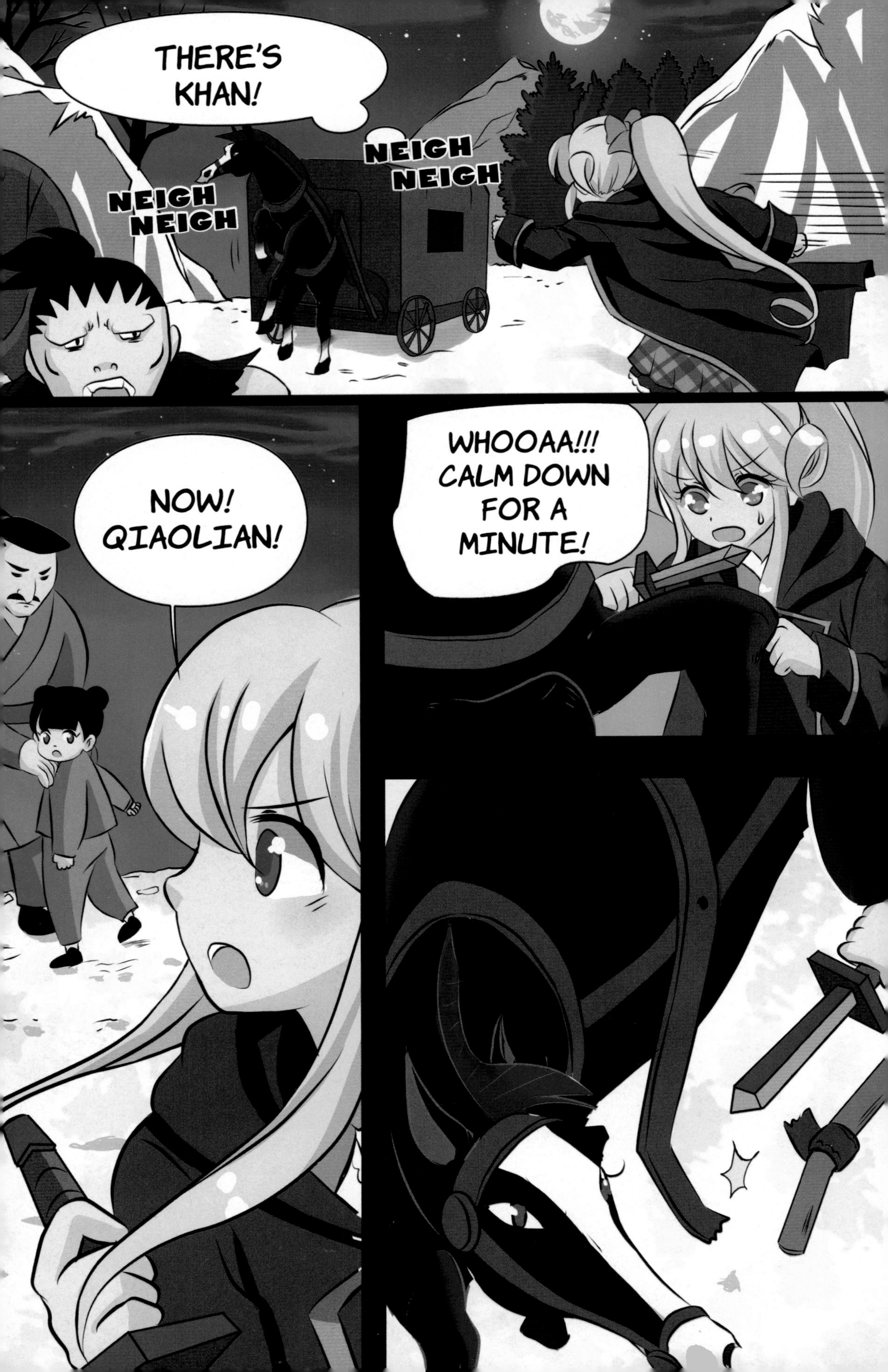
THERE'S KHAN!
NEIGH NEIGH
NEIGH NEIGH
NOW! QIAOLIAN!
WHOOAA!!! CALM DOWN FOR A MINUTE!

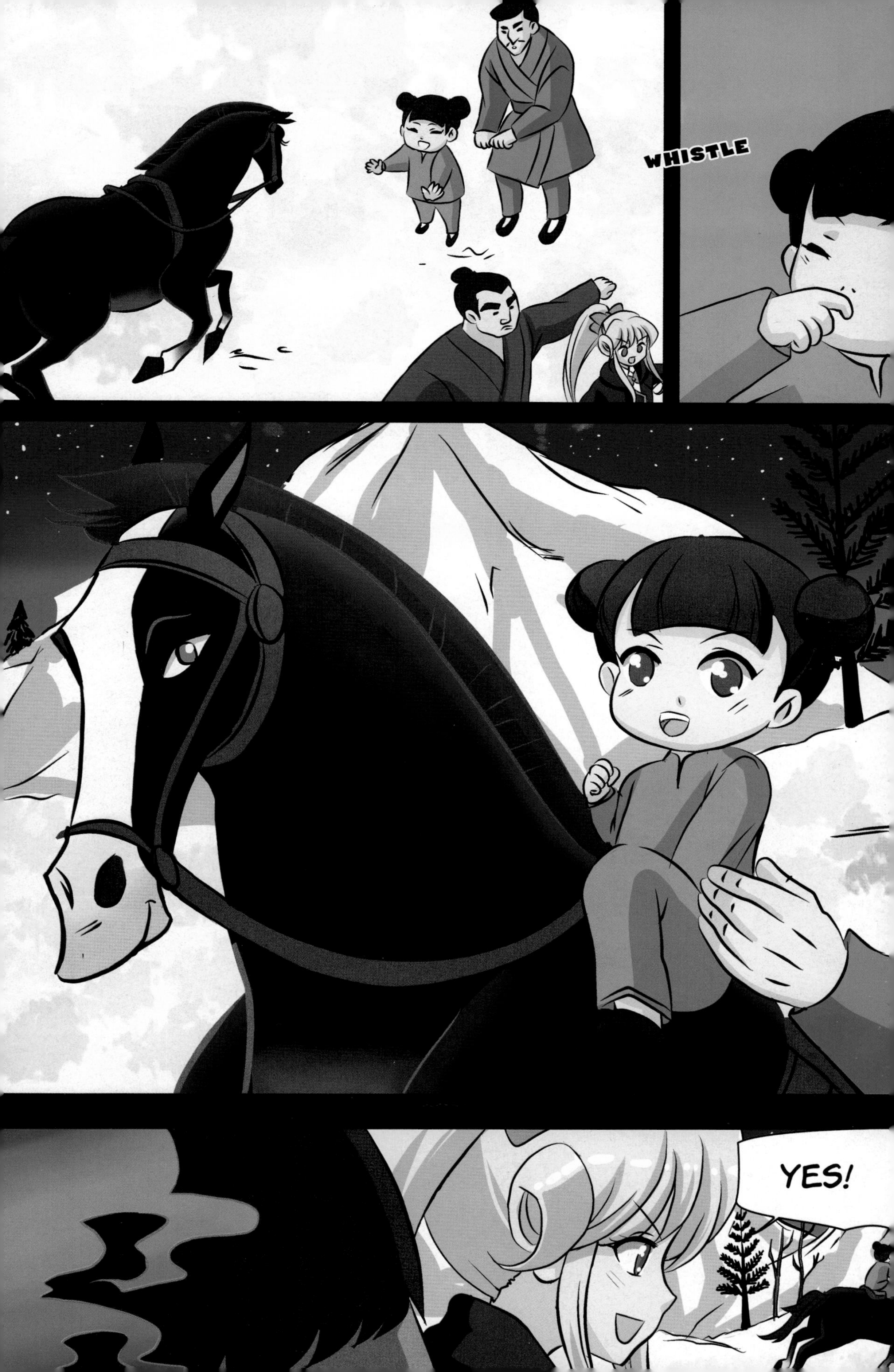
WHISTLE
YES!

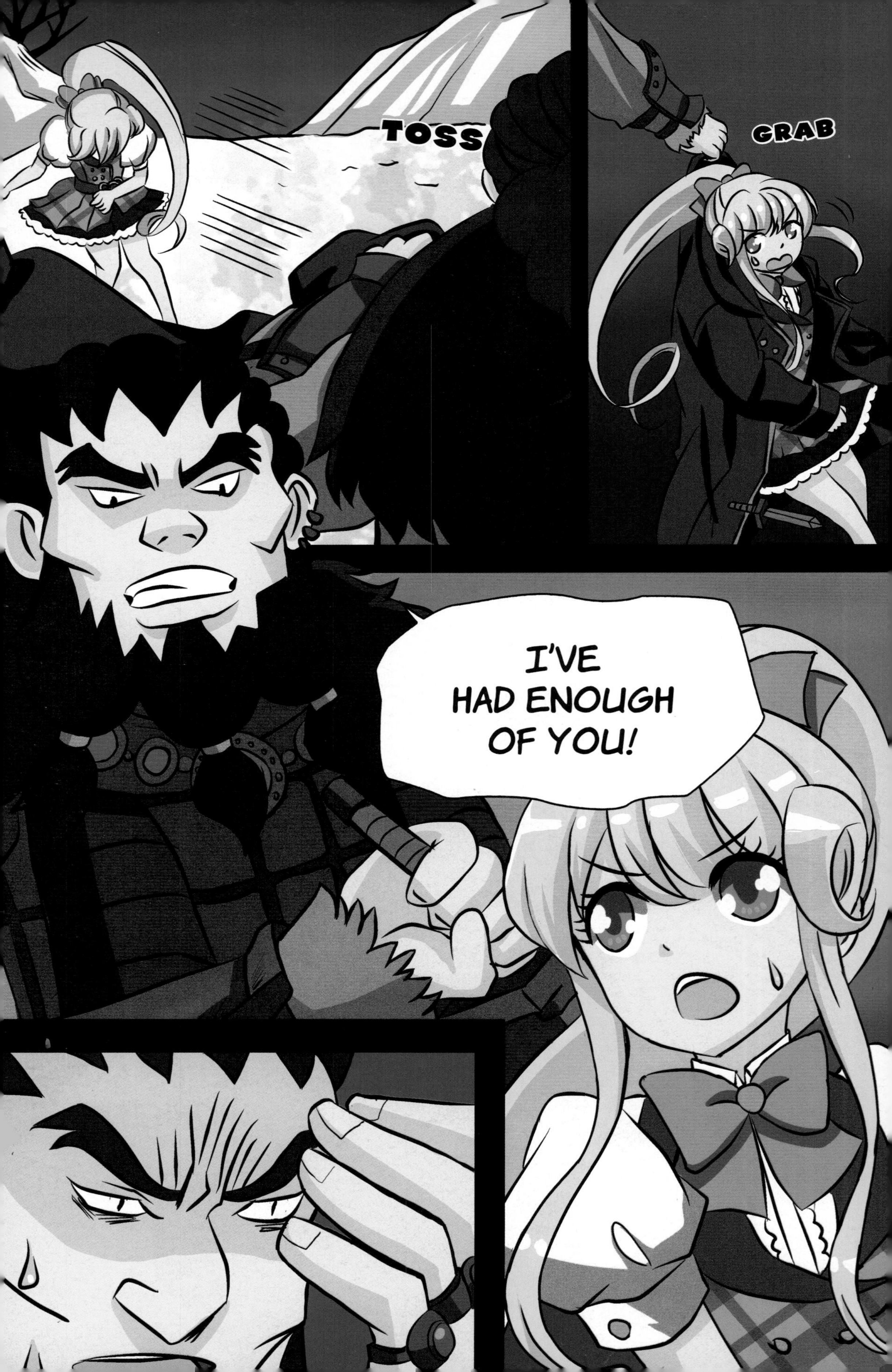
TOSS
GRAB
I'VE HAD ENOUGH OF YOU!

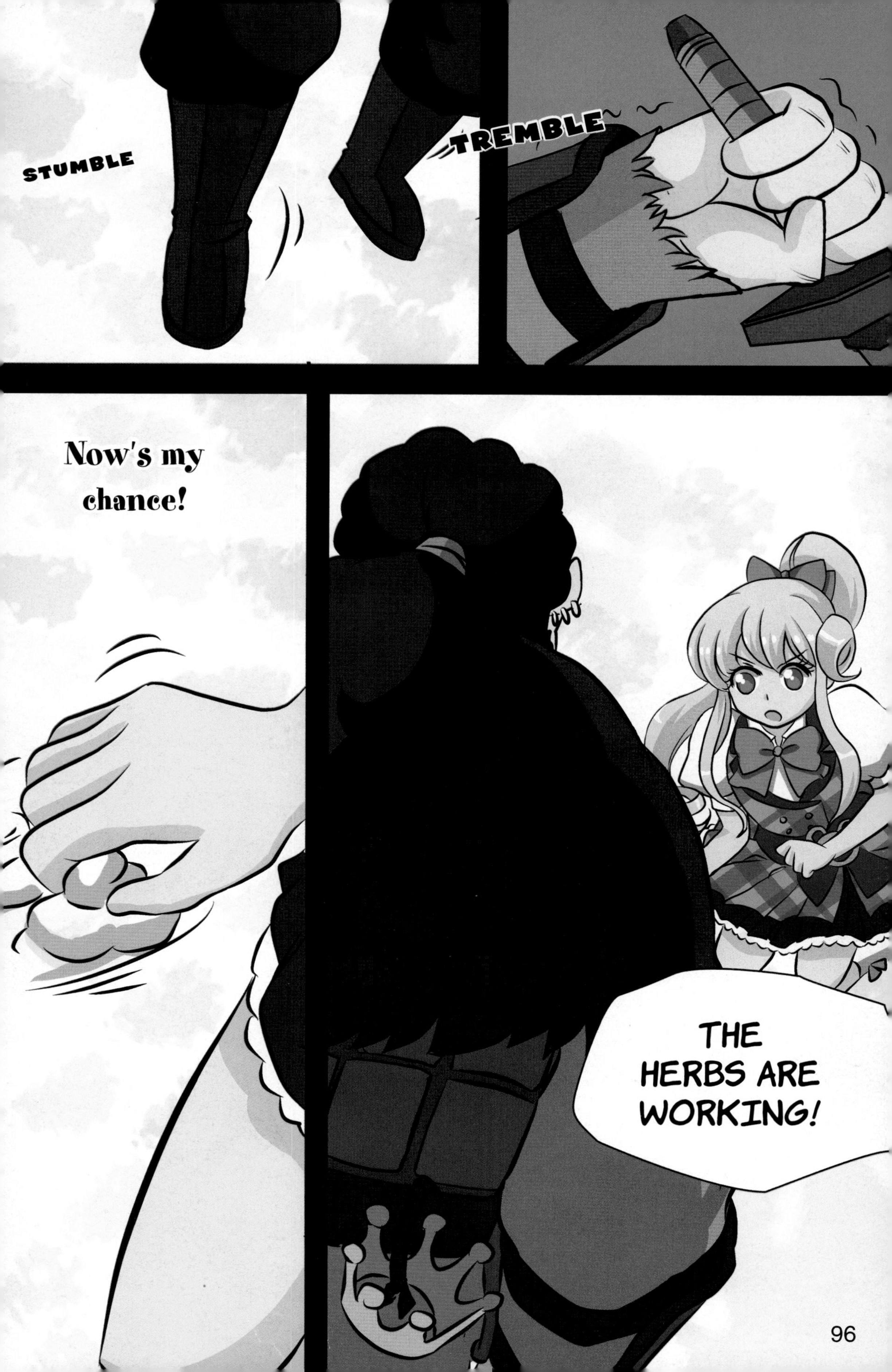
STUMBLE
TREMBLE
Now's my chance!
THE HERBS ARE WORKING!

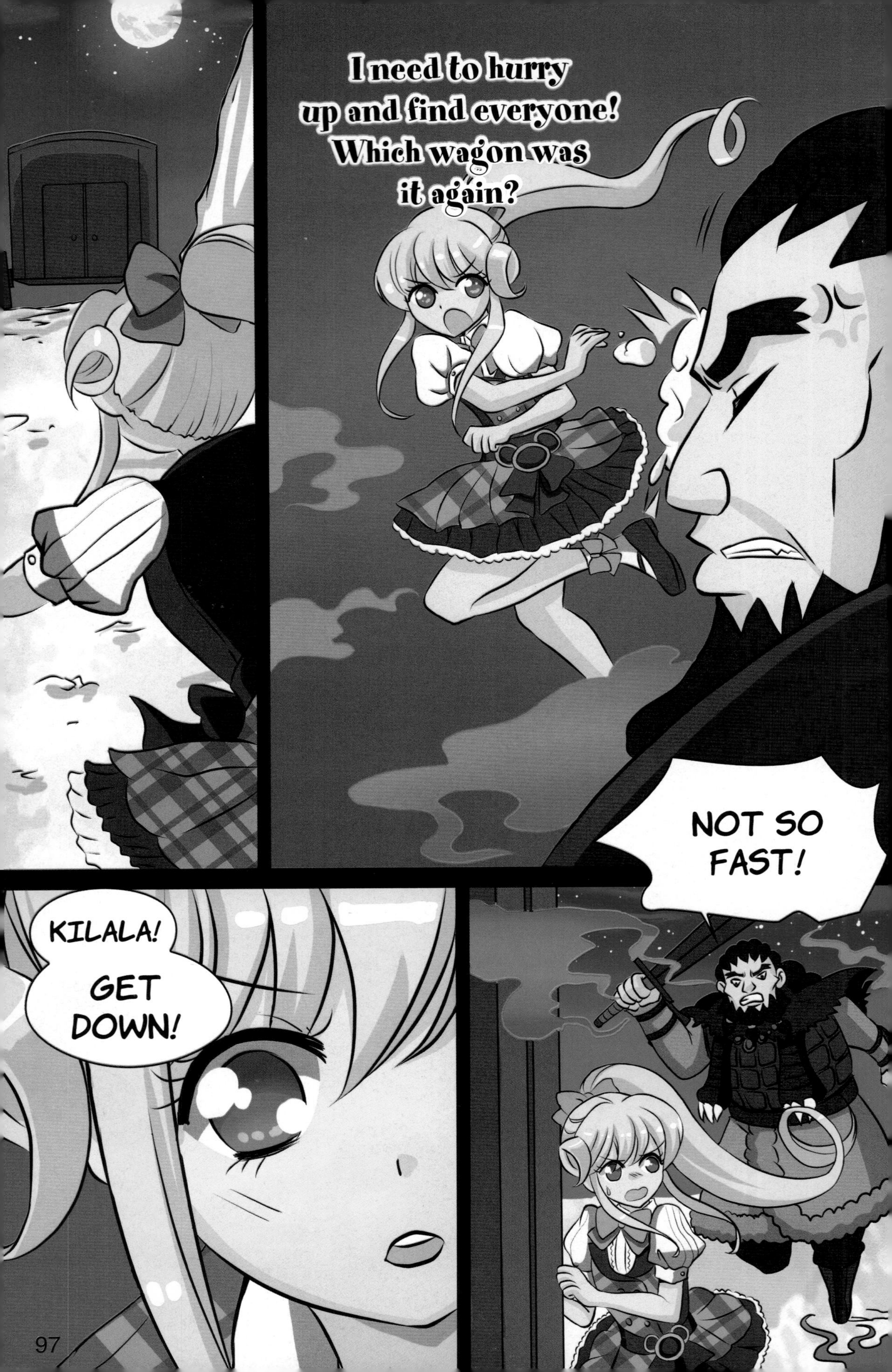
I need to hurry up and find everyone! Which wagon was it again?
NOT SO FAST!
KILALA!
GET DOWN!

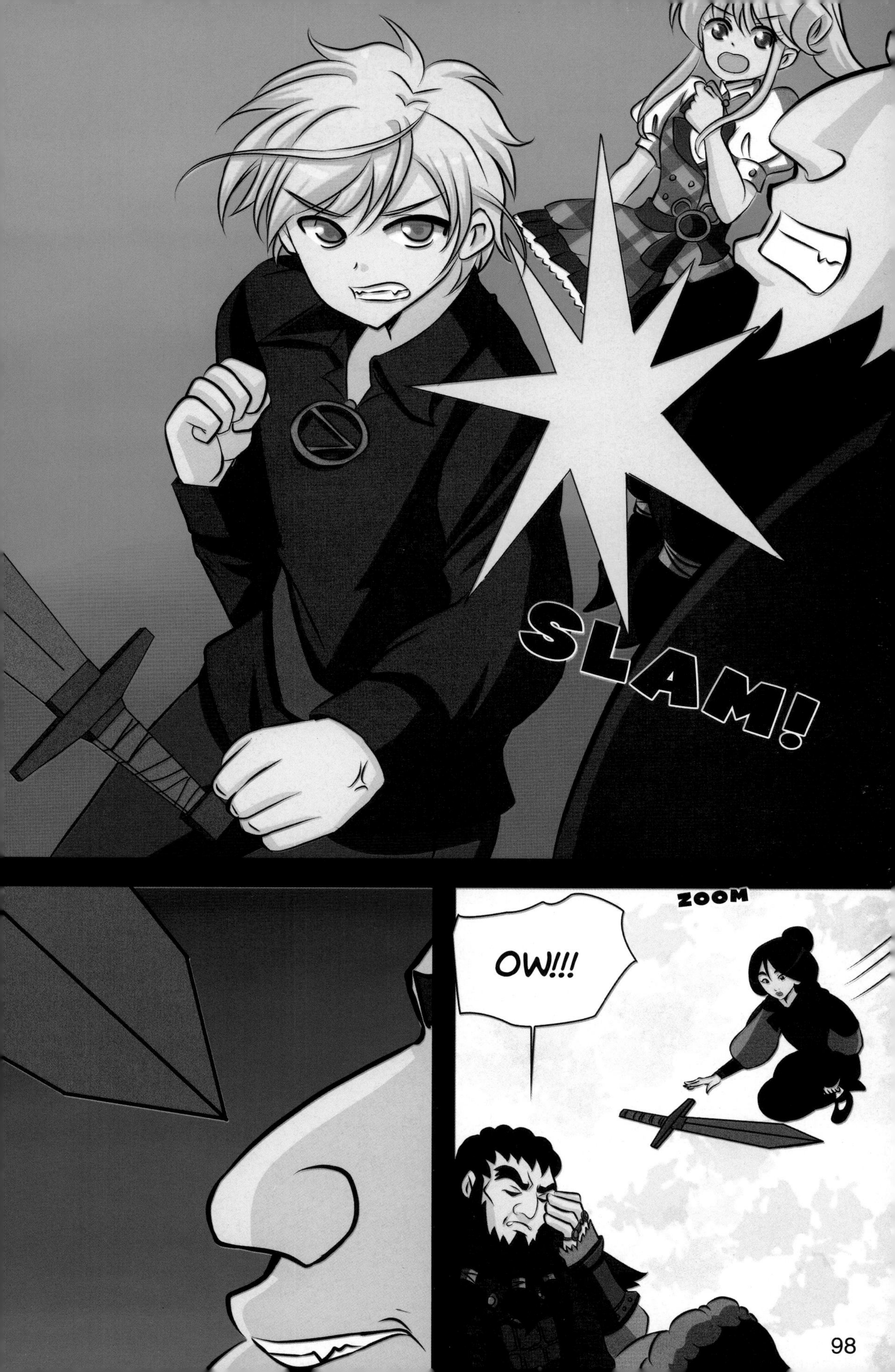
SLAM!
ZOOM
OW!!!

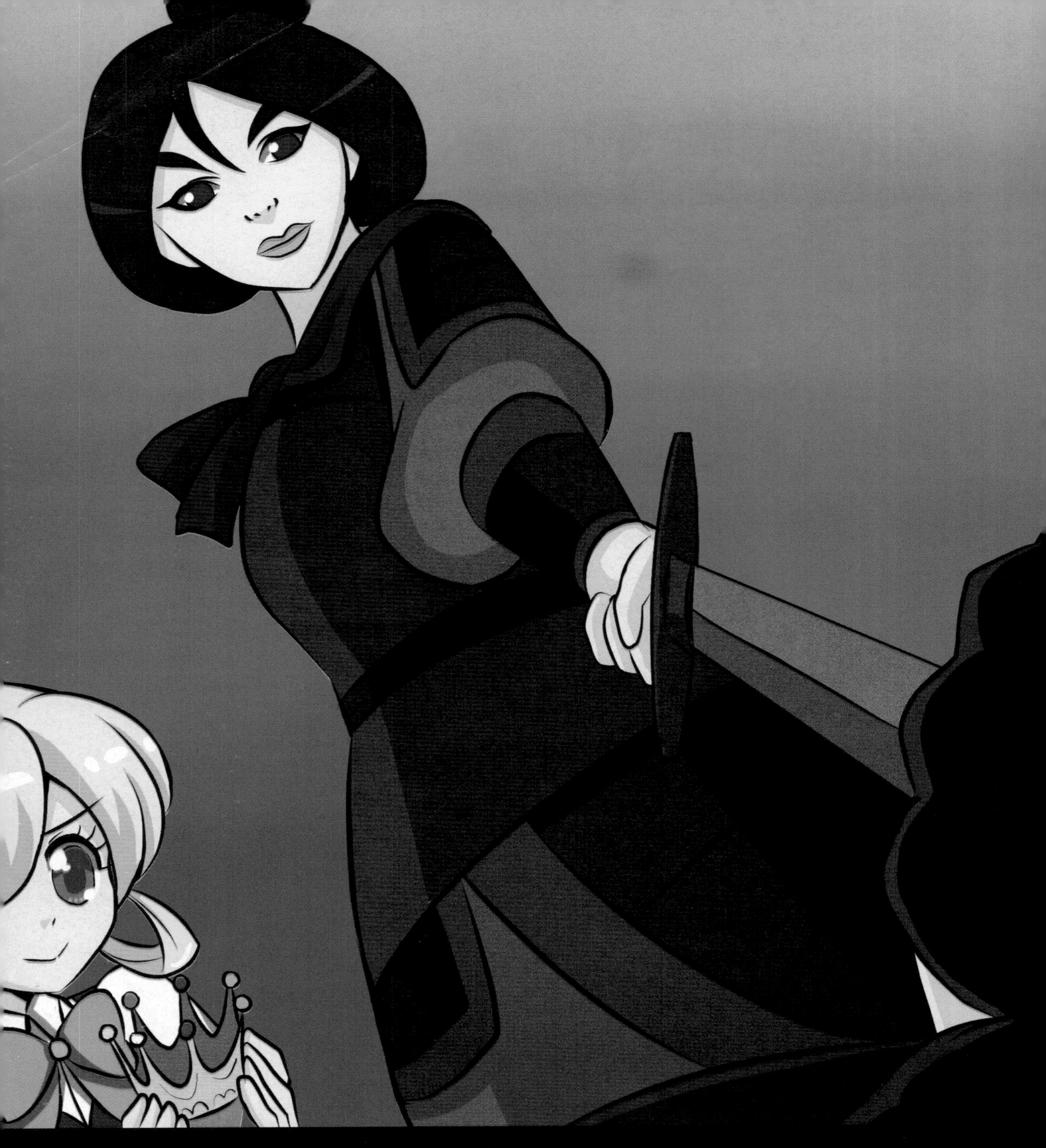
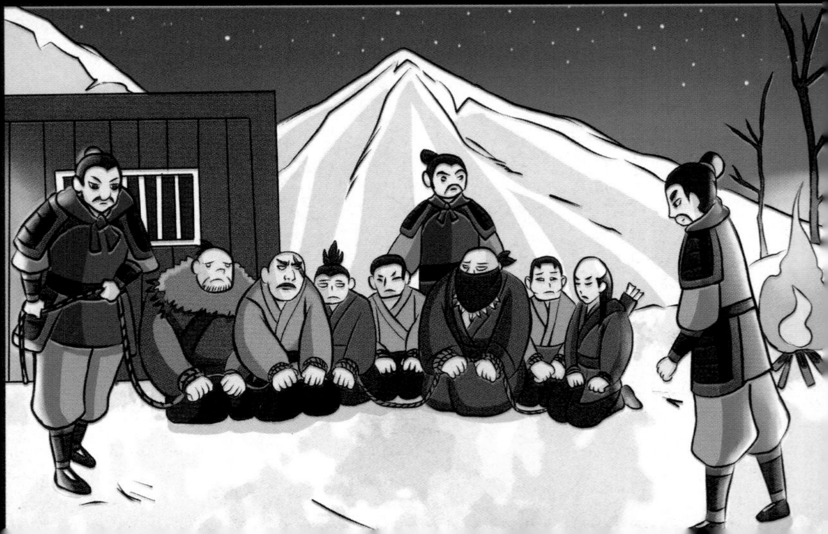
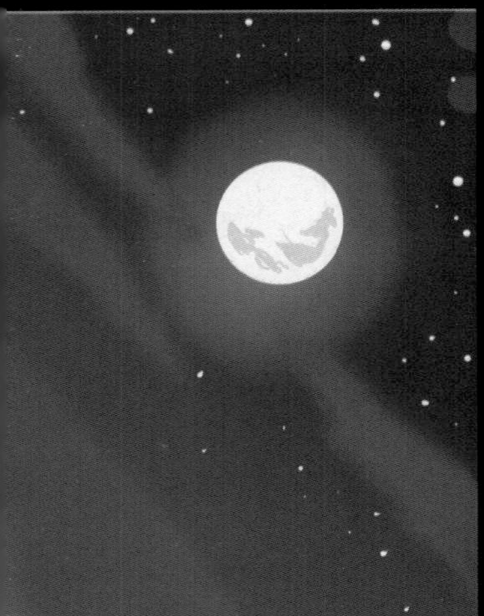

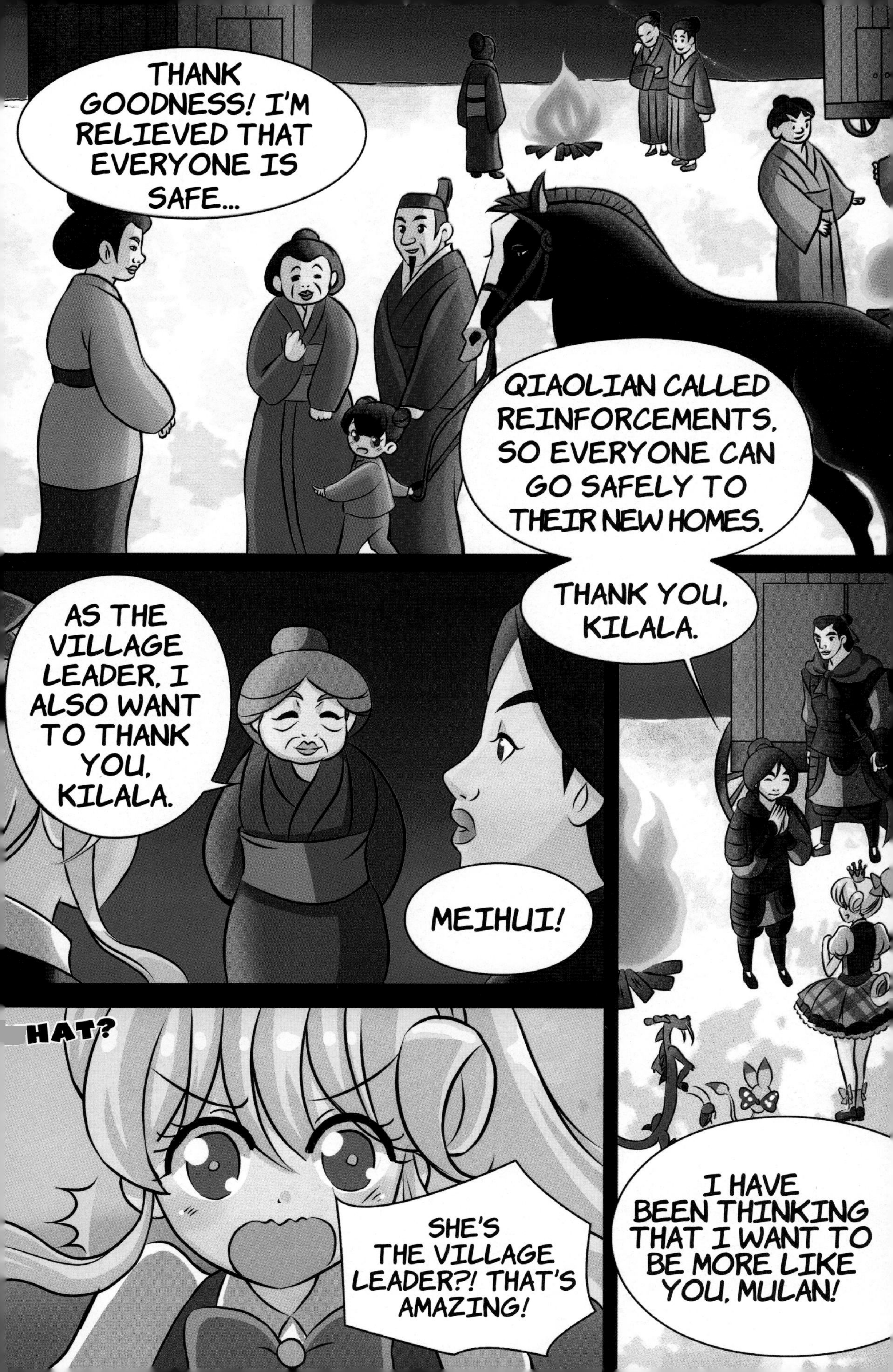
THANK GOODNESS! I'M RELIEVED THAT EVERYONE IS SAFE...
QIAOLIAN CALLED REINFORCEMENTS, SO EVERYONE CAN GO SAFELY TO THEIR NEW HOMES.
THANK YOU, KILALA.
AS THE VILLAGE LEADER, I ALSO WANT TO THANK YOU, KILALA.
MEIHUI!
HAT?
SHE'S THE VILLAGE LEADER?! THAT'S AMAZING!
I HAVE BEEN THINKING THAT I WANT TO BE MORE LIKE YOU, MULAN!

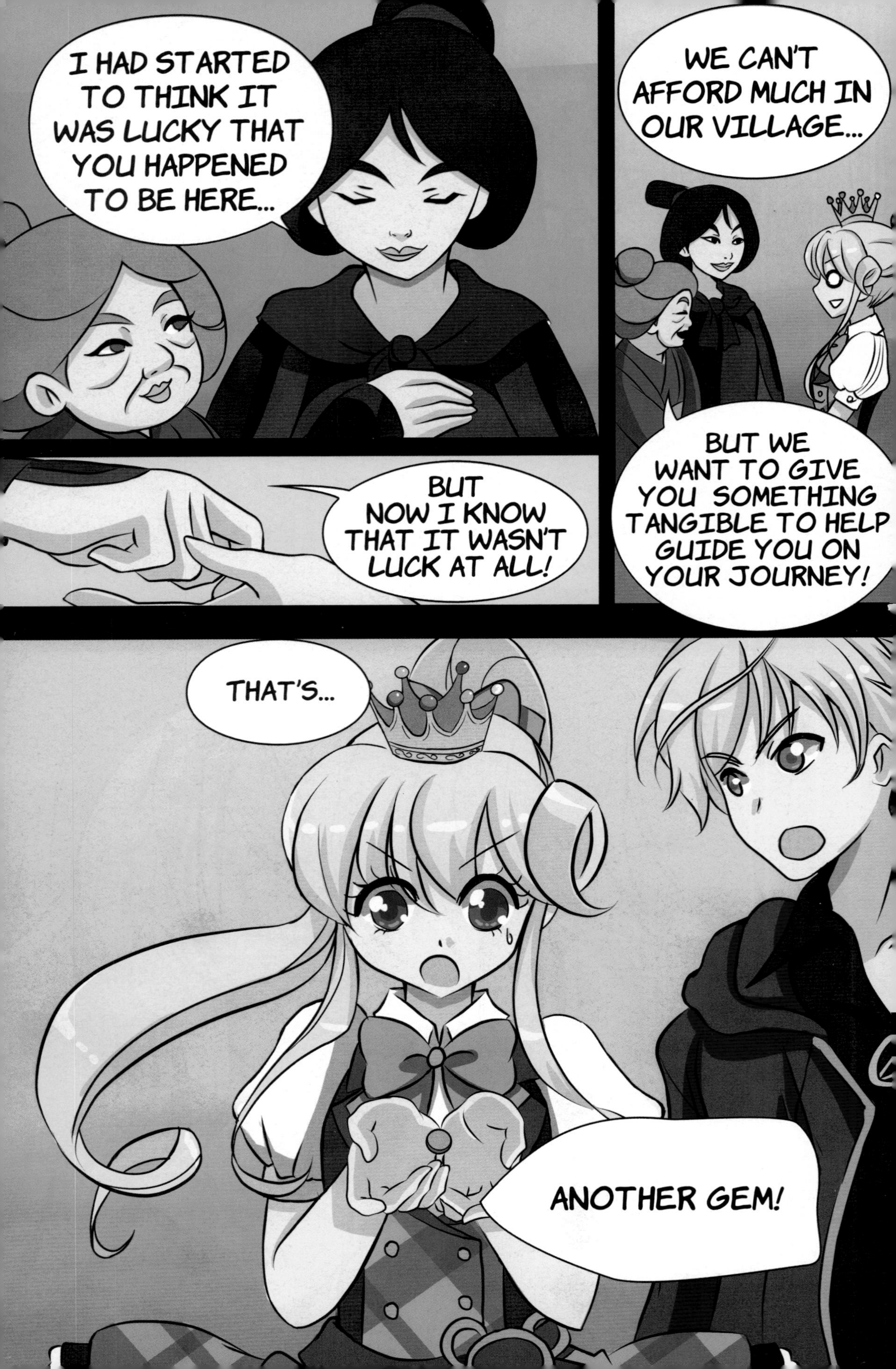
I HAD STARTED TO THINK IT WAS LUCKY THAT YOU HAPPENED TO BE HERE...
WE CAN'T AFFORD MUCH IN OUR VILLAGE...
BUT NOW I KNOW THAT IT WASN'T LUCK AT ALL!
BUT WE WANT TO GIVE YOU SOMETHING TANGIBLE TO HELP GUIDE YOU ON YOUR JOURNEY!
THAT'S...
ANOTHER GEM!

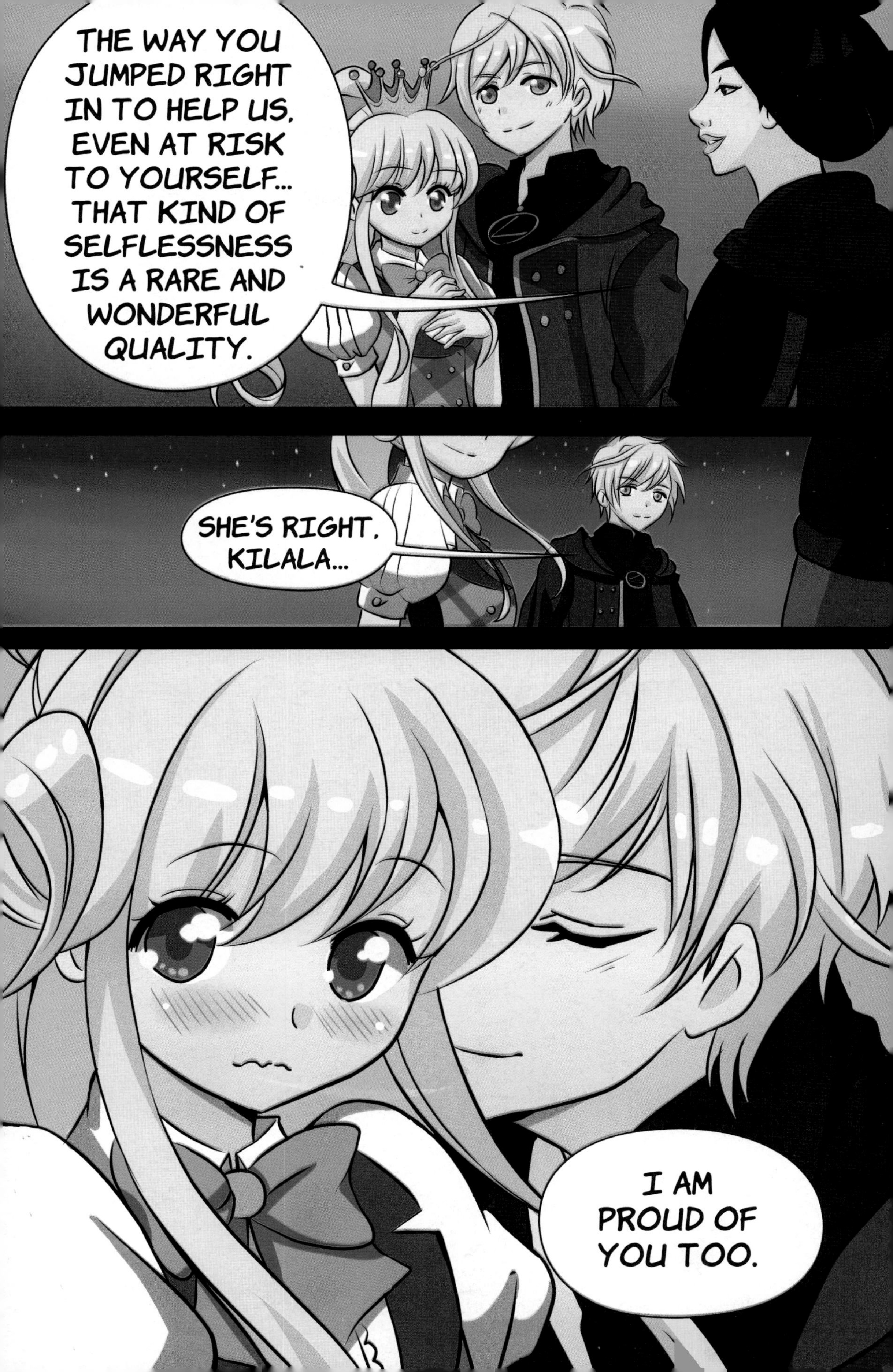
THE WAY YOU JUMPED RIGHT IN TO HELP US, EVEN AT RISK TO YOURSELF... THAT KIND OF SELFLESSNESS IS A RARE AND WONDERFUL QUALITY.
SHE'S RIGHT, KILALA...
I AM PROUD OF YOU TOO.

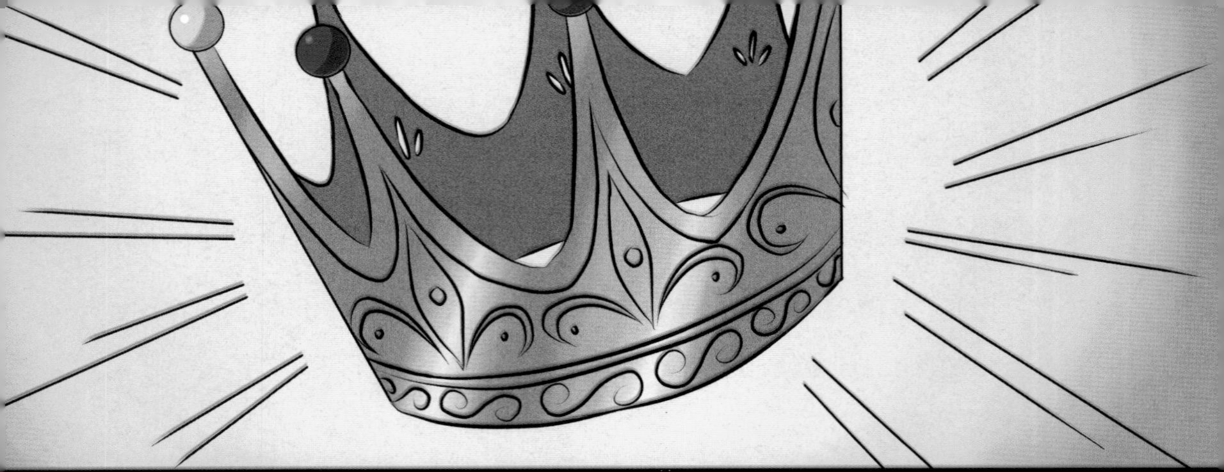

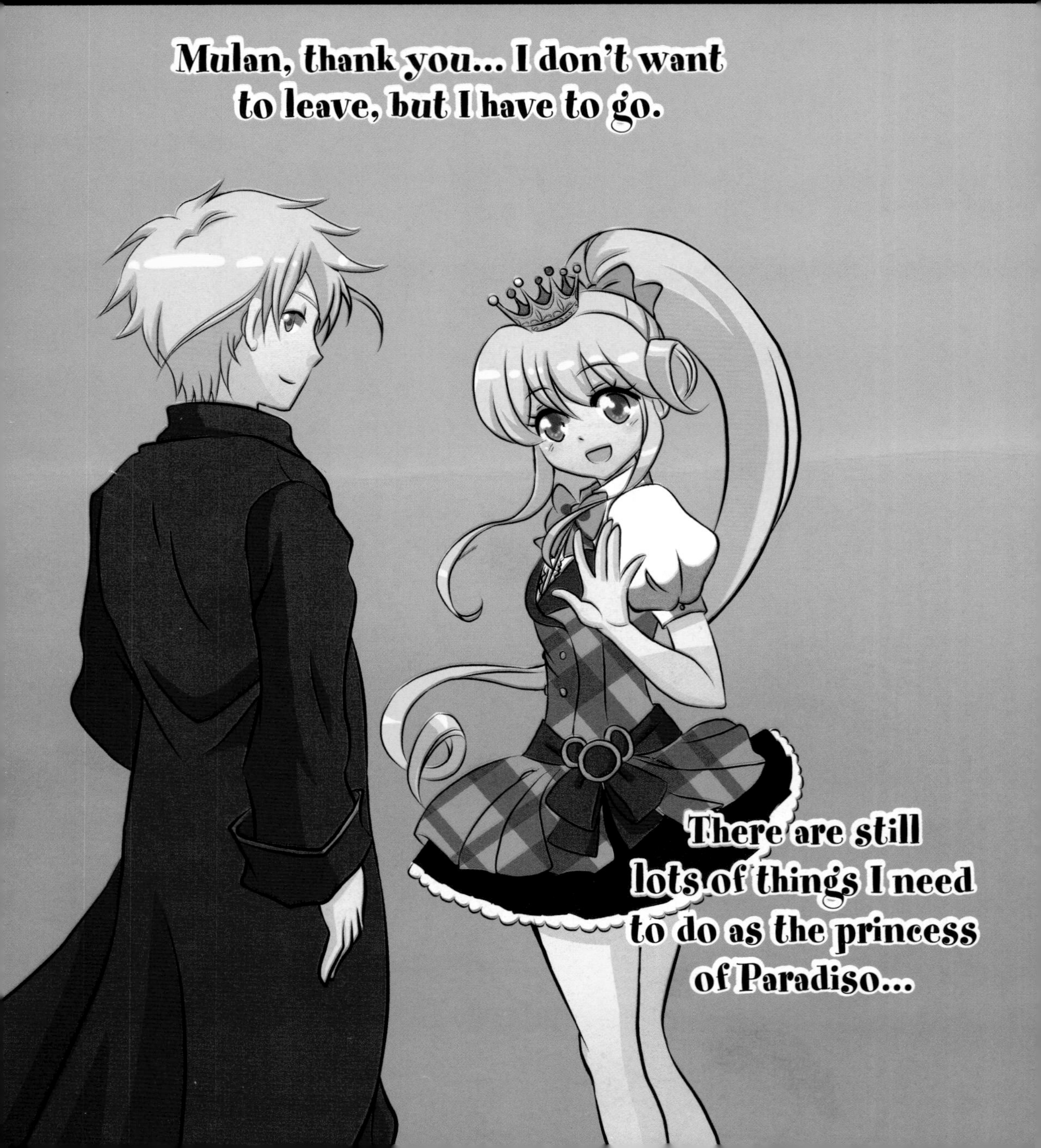
Mulan, thank you... I don't want to leave, but I have to go.
There are still lots of things I need to do as the princess of Paradiso...

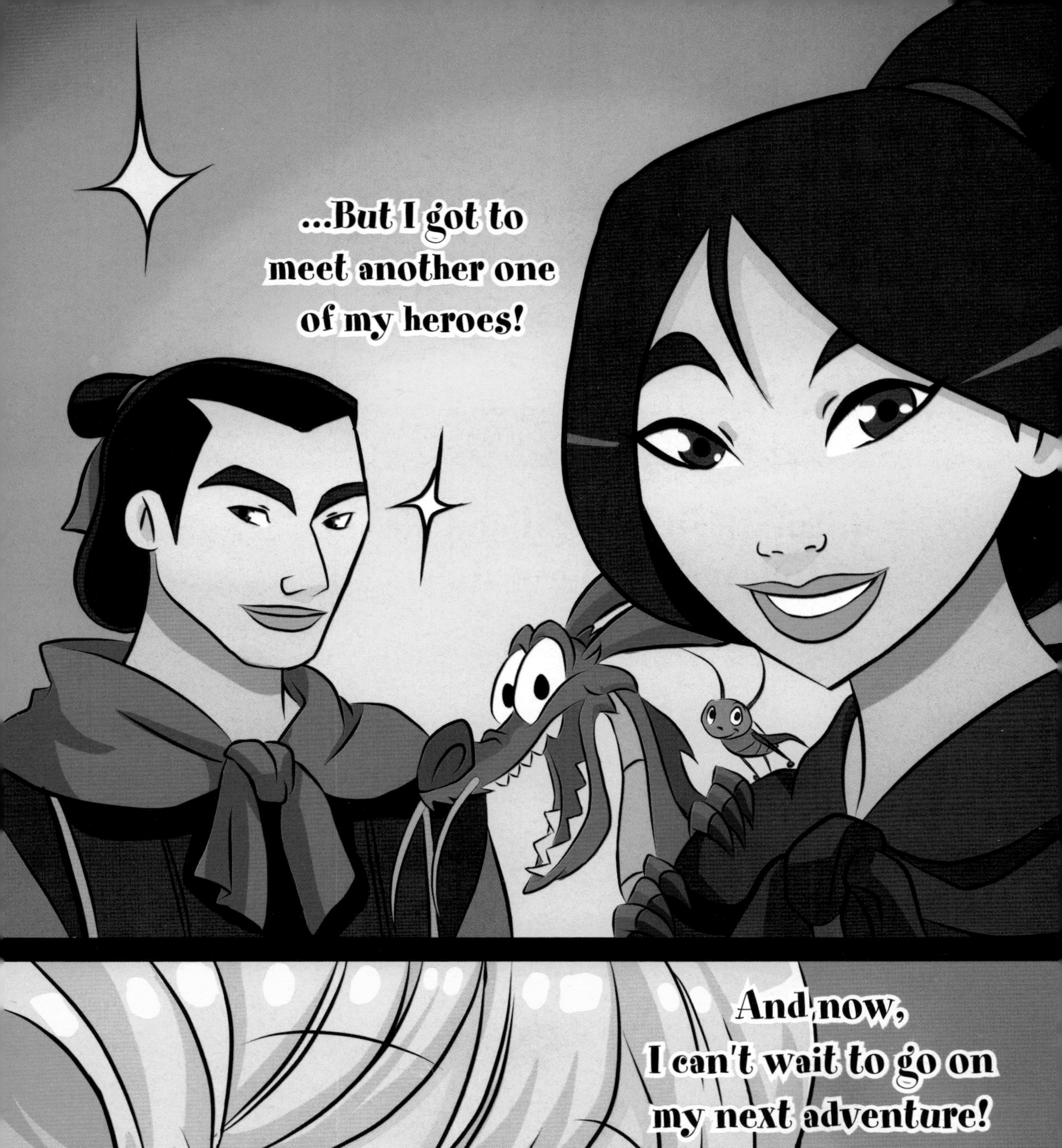
...But I got to meet another one of my heroes!
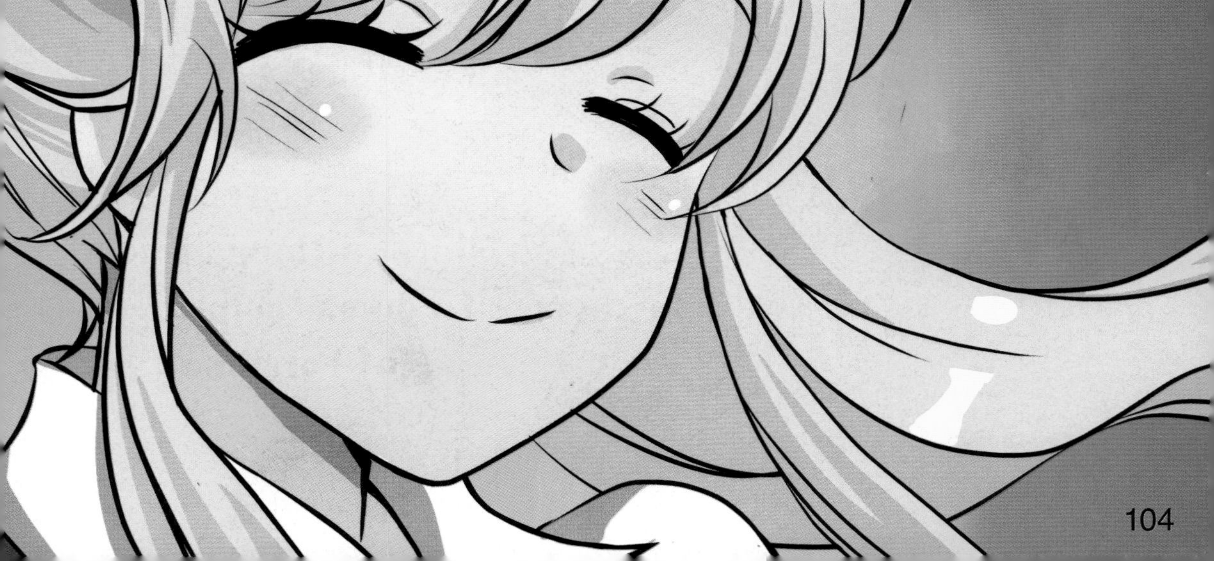
And now, I can't wait to go on my next adventure!

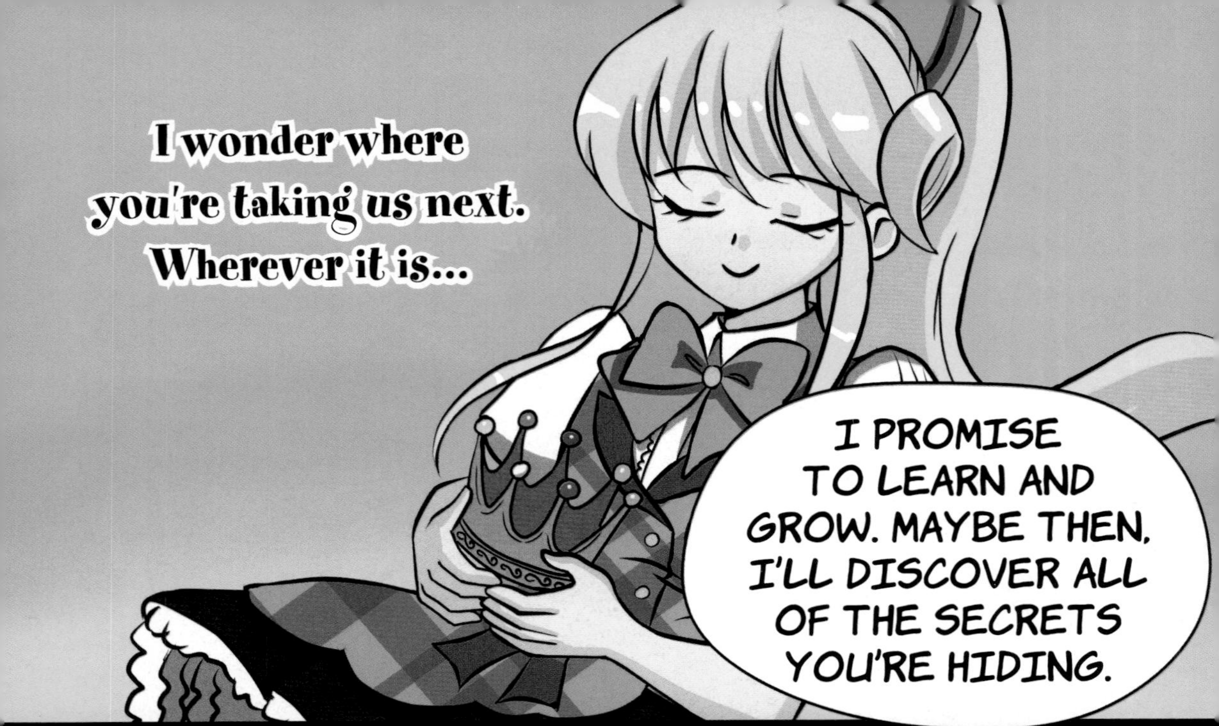
I wonder where you're taking us next. Wherever it is...
I PROMISE TO LEARN AND GROW. MAYBE THEN, I'LL DISCOVER ALL OF THE SECRETS YOU'RE HIDING.

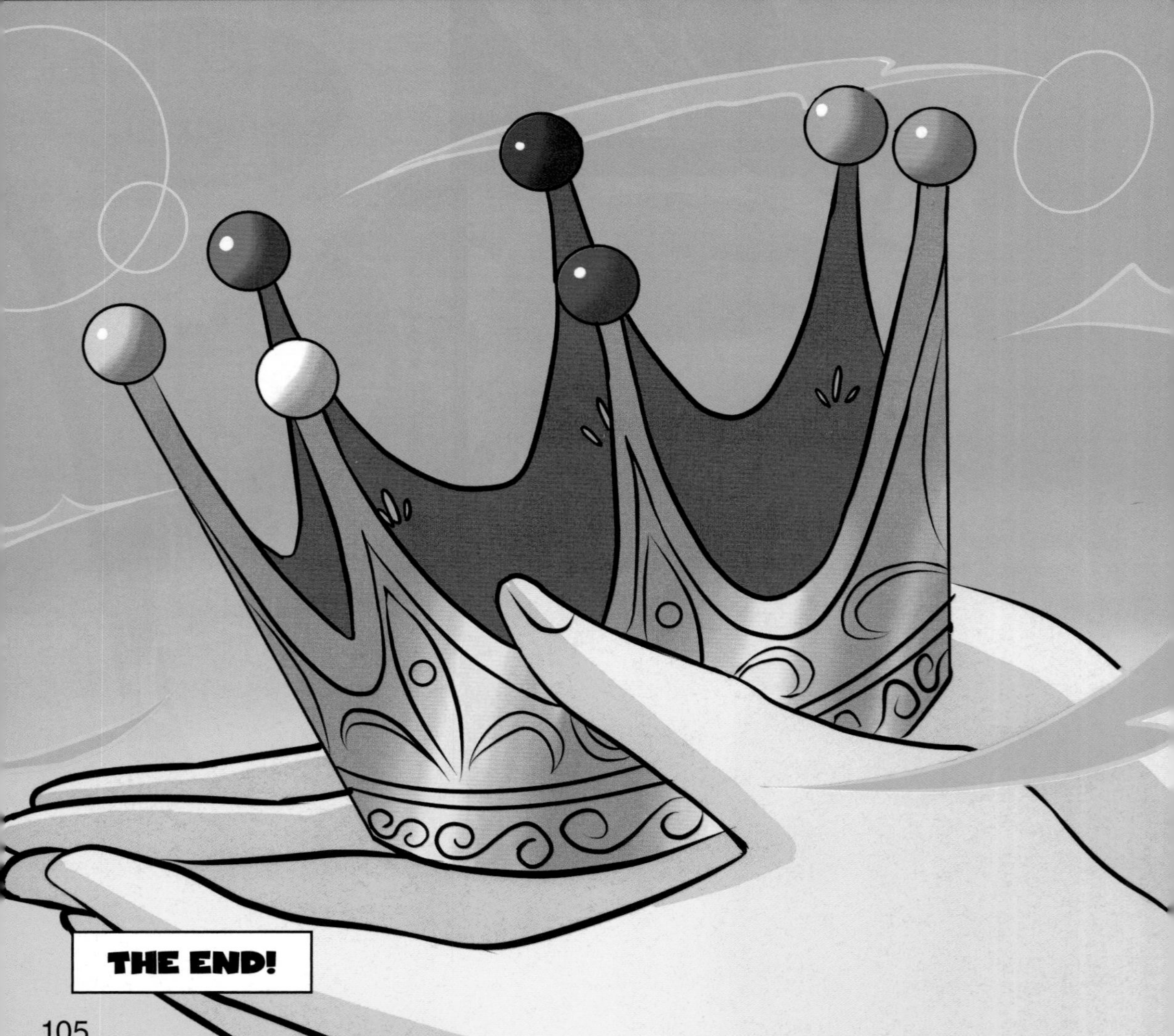
THE END!

GRAPHIC NOVEL: COVER ART

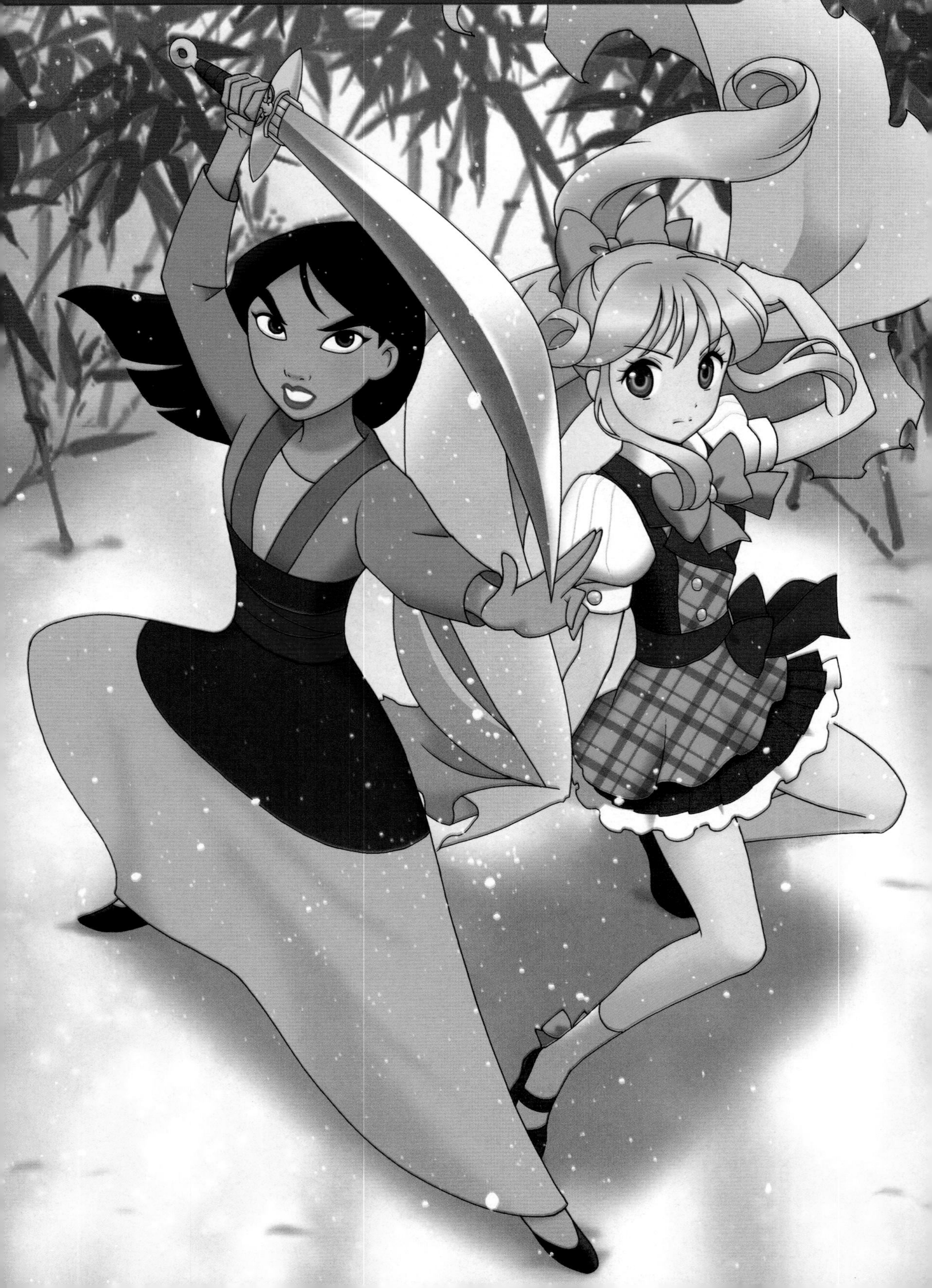

CHAPTER 1: DIGITAL EXCLUSIVE COVER

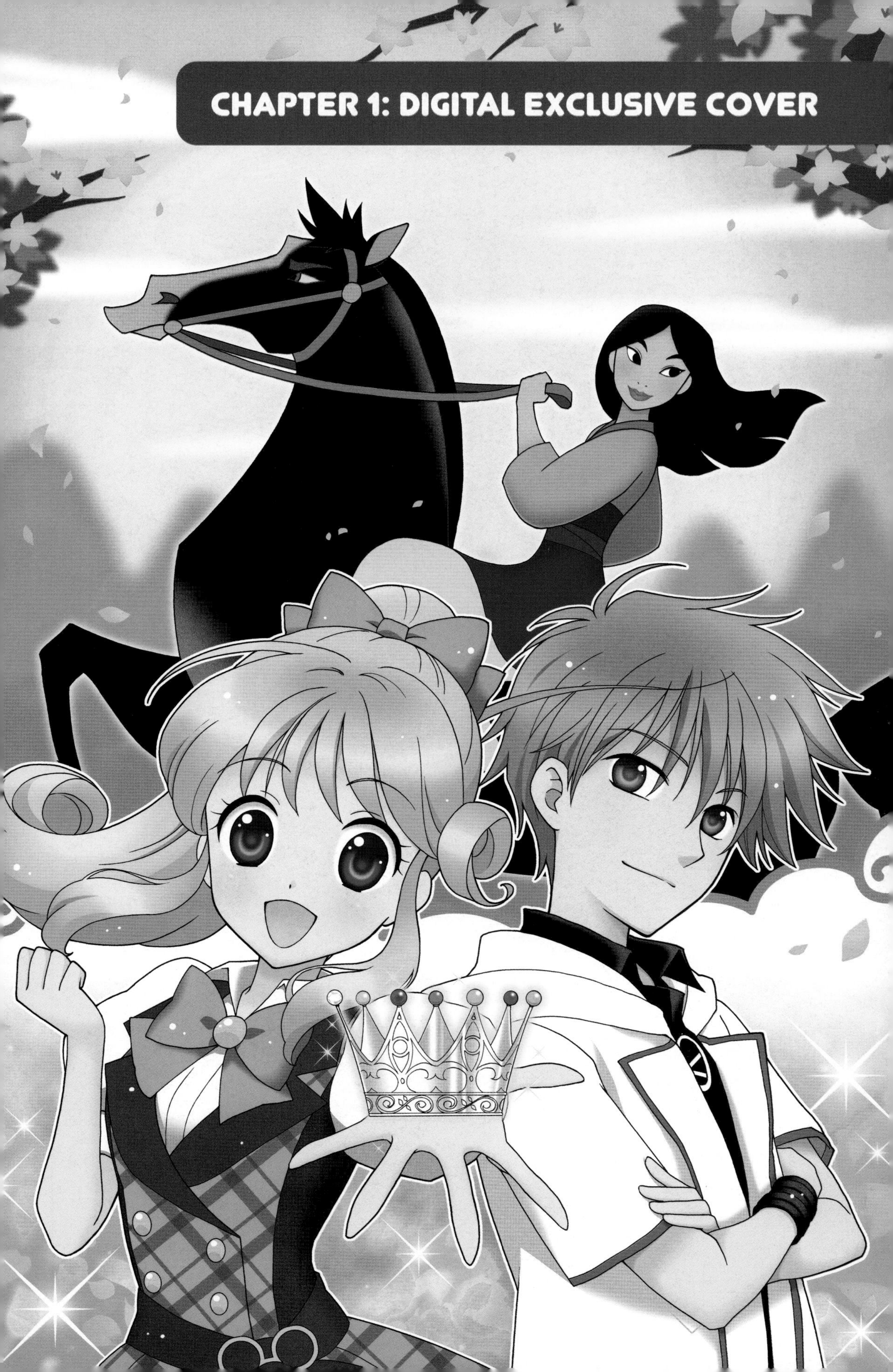

CHAPTER 2: DIGITAL EXCLUSIVE COVER

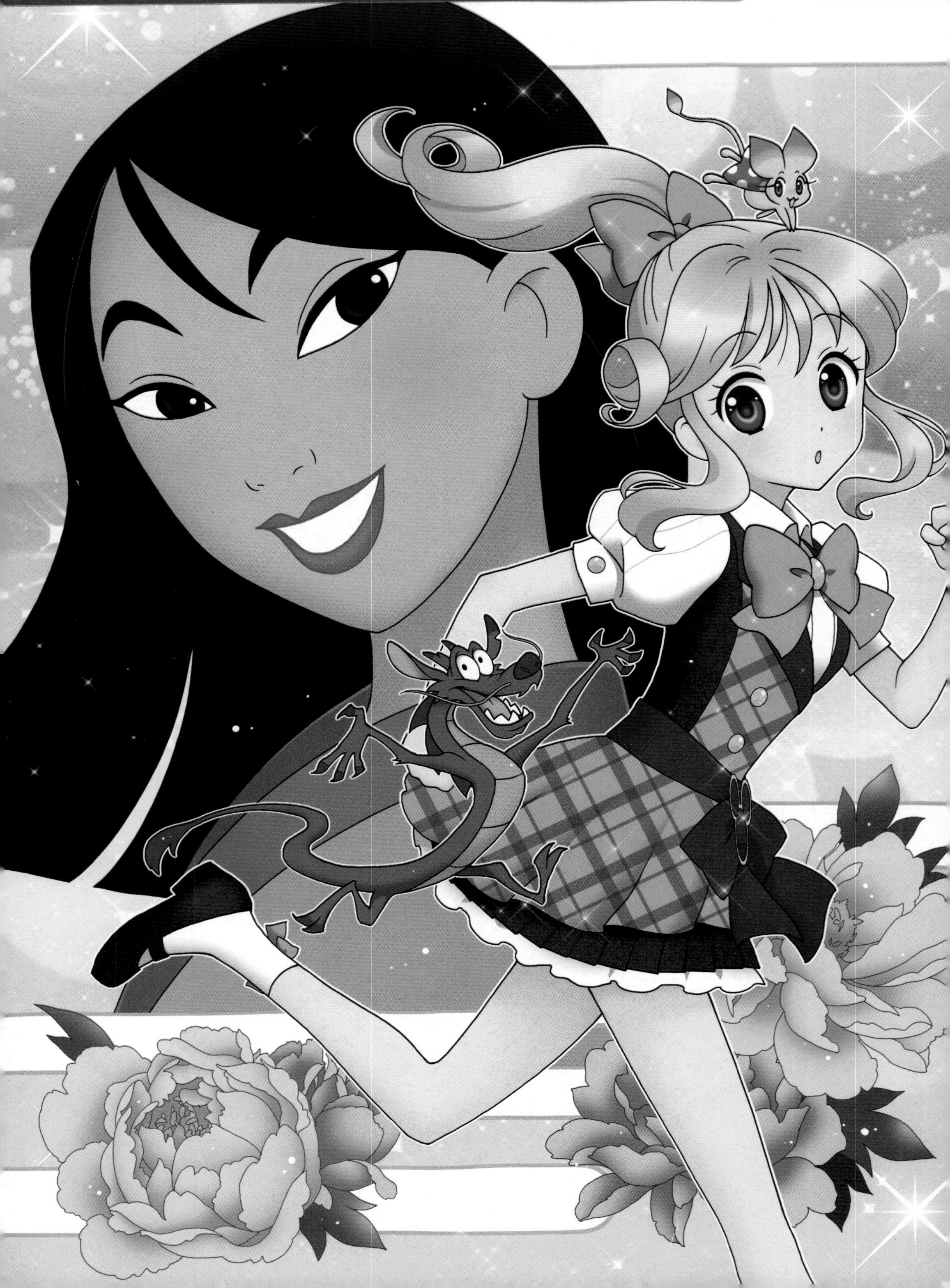

CHAPTER 3: DIGITAL EXCLUSIVE COVER

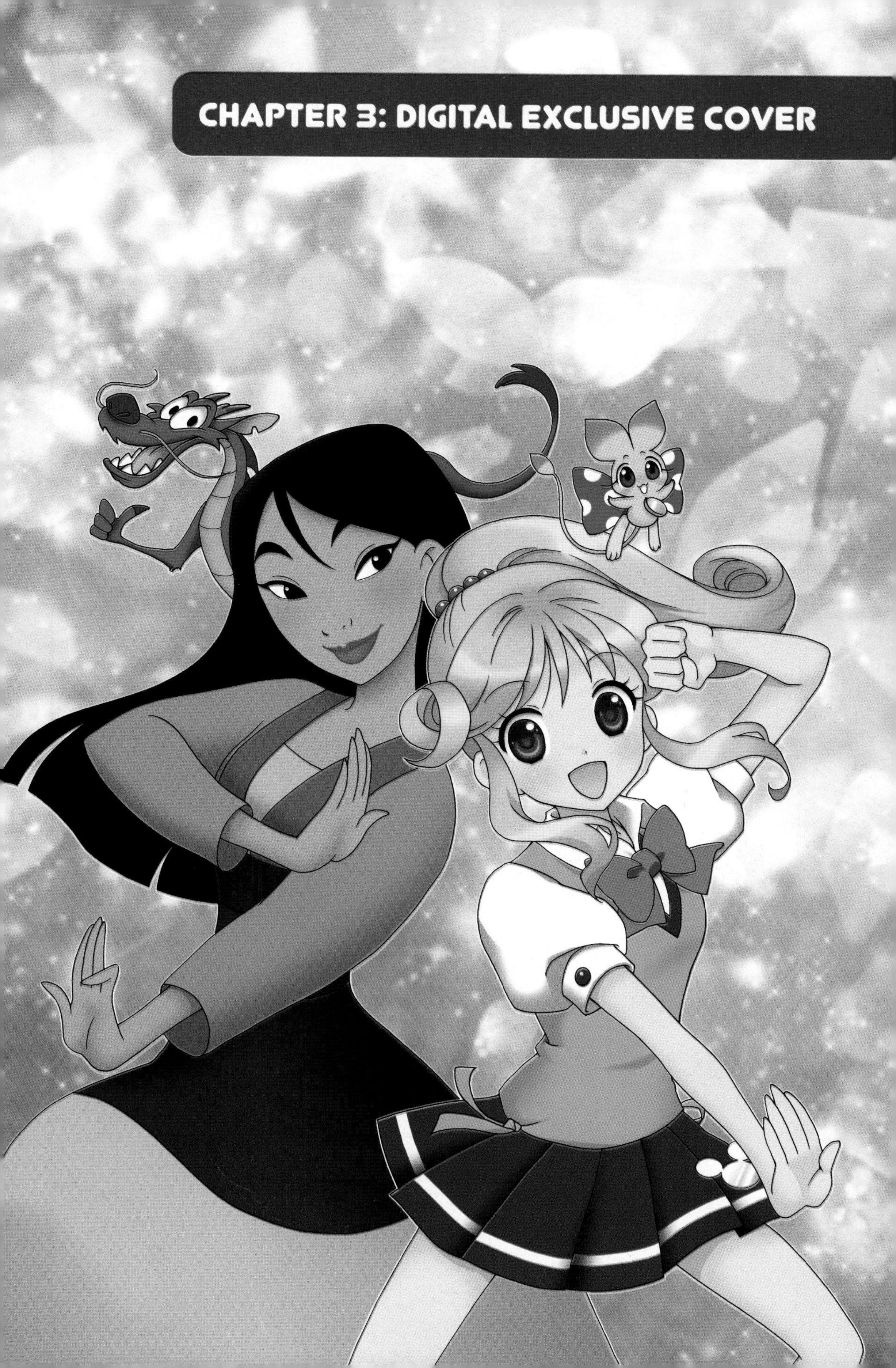

CHAPTER 4: DIGITAL EXCLUSIVE COVER

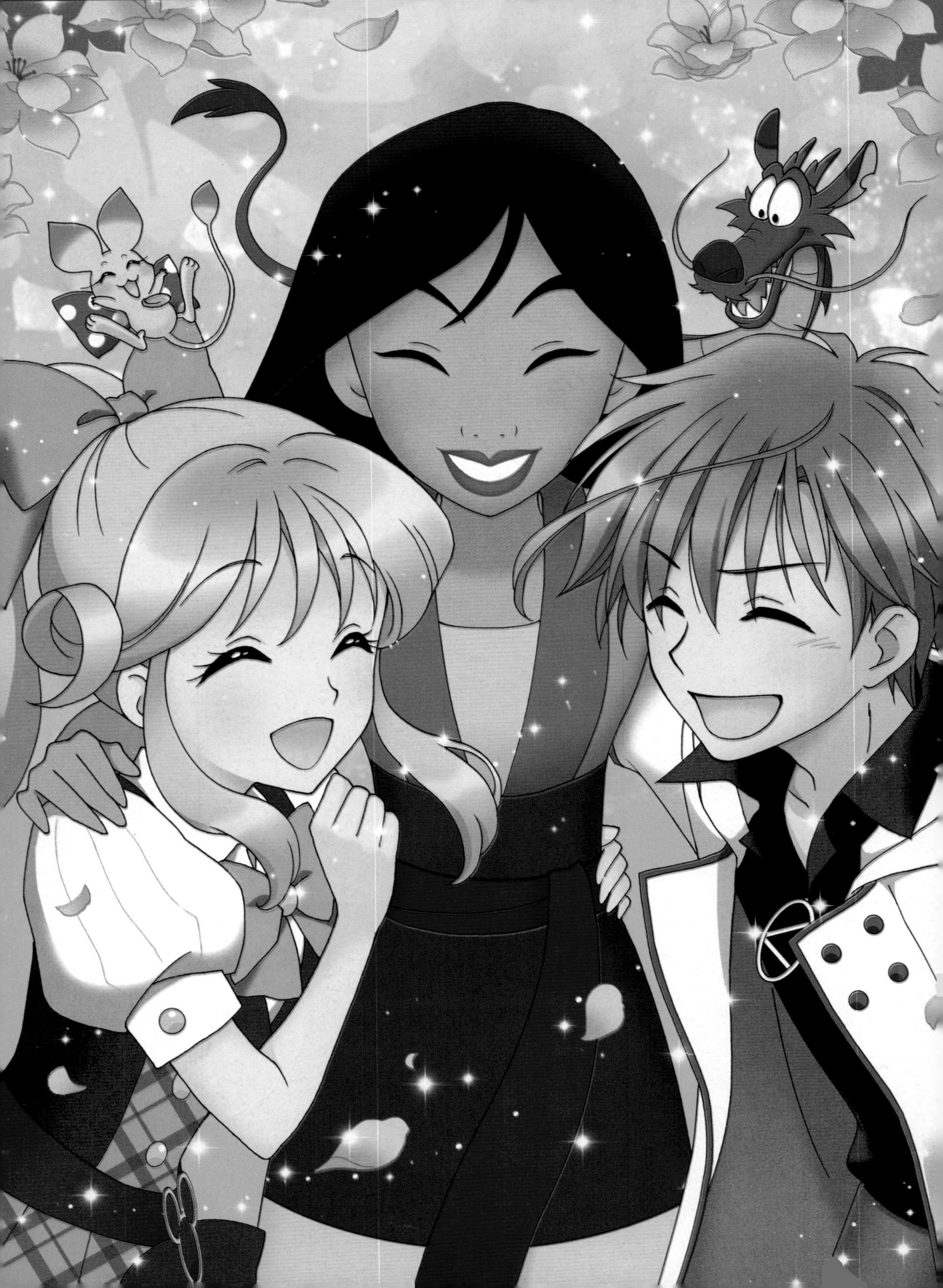

Add These Disney Manga to Your Collection Today!

SHOJO

- ☐ DISNEY BEAUTY AND THE BEAST
- ☐ DISNEY KILALA PRINCESS SERIES

KAWAII

- ☐ DISNEY MAGICAL DANCE
- ☐ DISNEY STITCH! SERIES

FANTASY

- ☐ DISNEY DESCENDANTS SERIES
- ☐ DISNEY TANGLED
- ☐ DISNEY PRINCESS AND THE FROG
- ☐ DISNEY FAIRIES SERIES
- ☐ DISNEY MARIE: MIRIYA AND MARIE

PIXAR

- ☐ DISNEY•PIXAR TOY STORY
- ☐ DISNEY•PIXAR MONSTERS, INC.
- ☐ DISNEY•PIXAR WALL•E
- ☐ DISNEY•PIXAR FINDING NEMO

ADVENTURE

- ☐ DISNEY TIM BURTON'S THE NIGHTMARE BEFORE CHRISTMAS
- ☐ DISNEY ALICE IN WONDERLAND
- ☐ DISNEY PIRATES OF THE CARIBBEAN SERIES

TOKYO POP

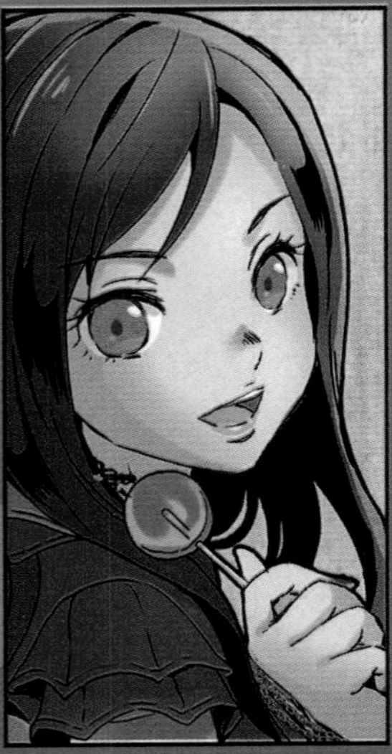
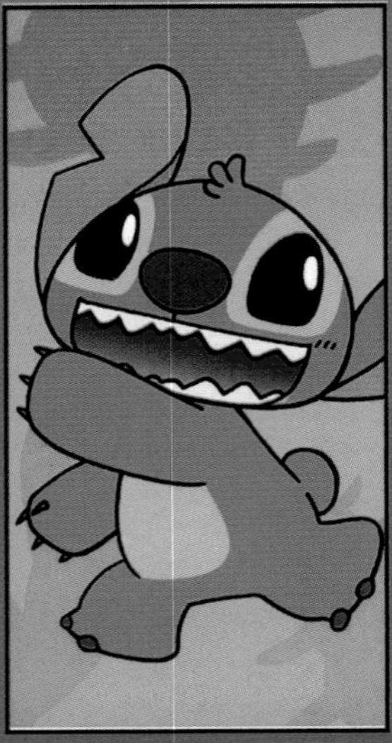
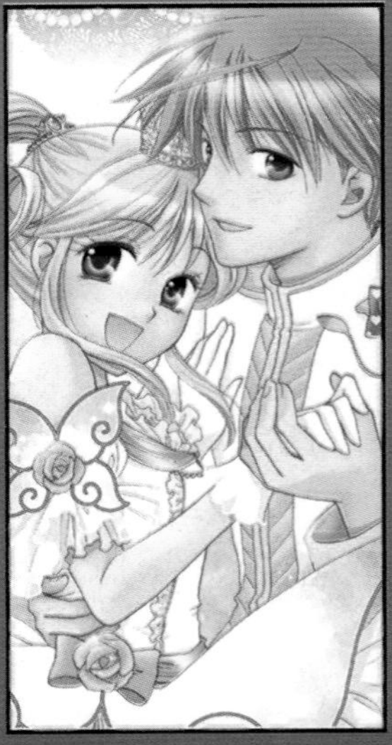
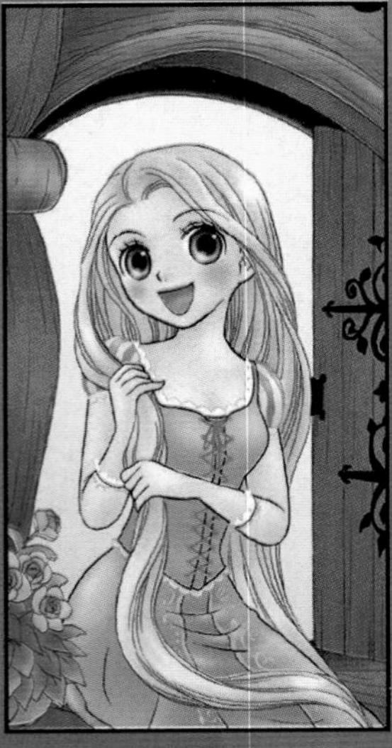
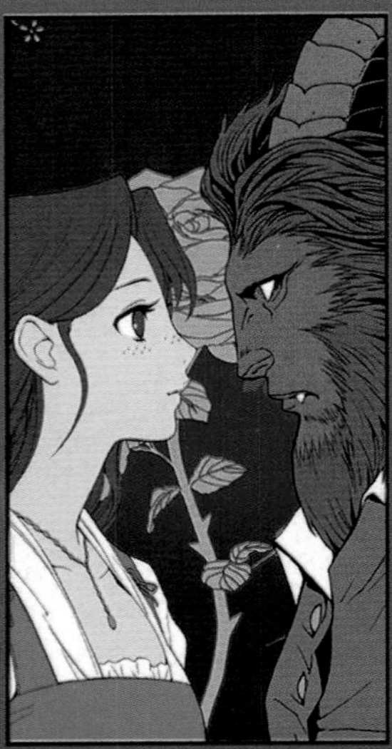
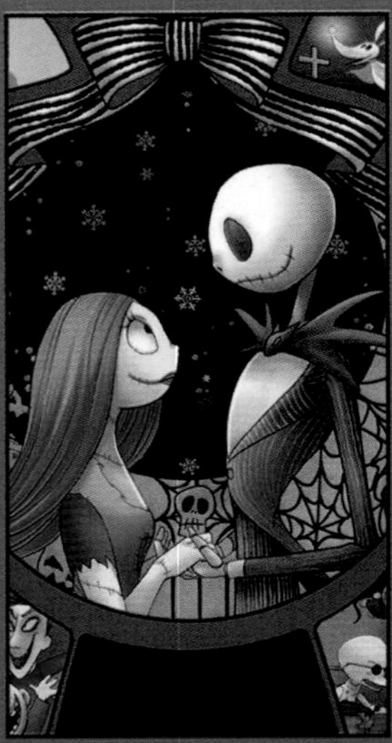
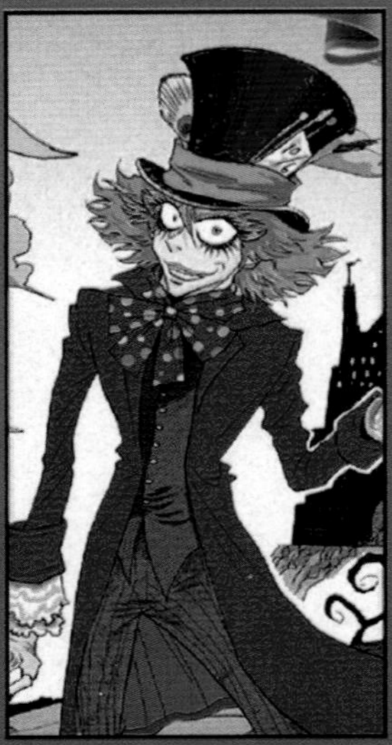
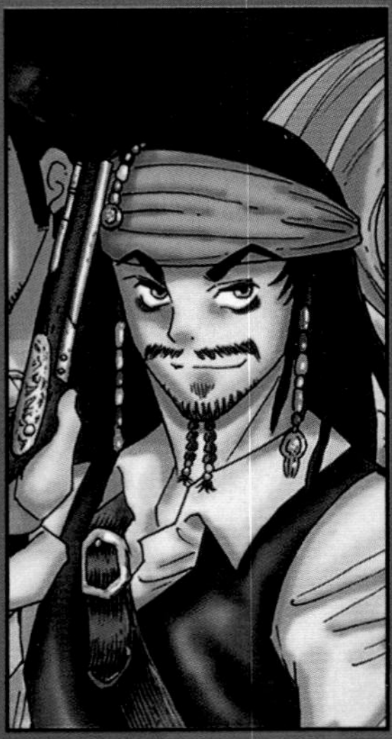
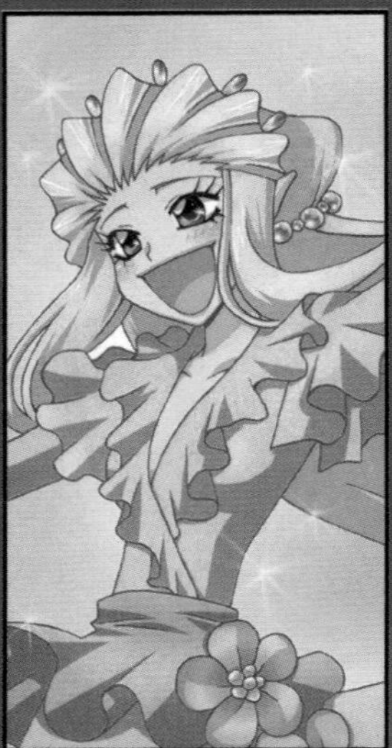
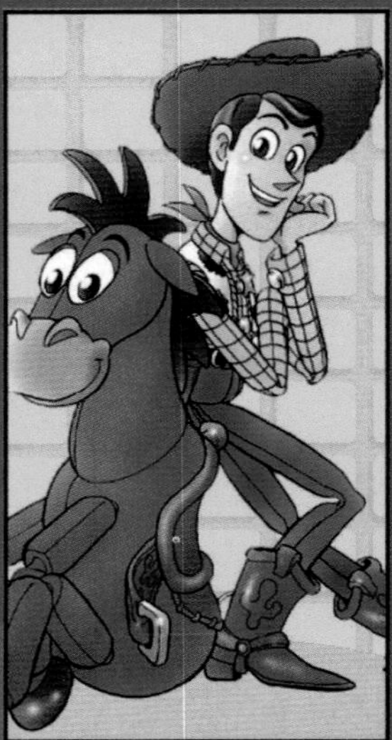
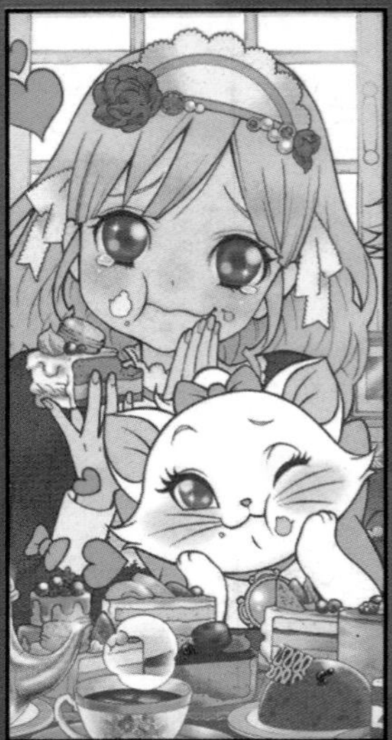
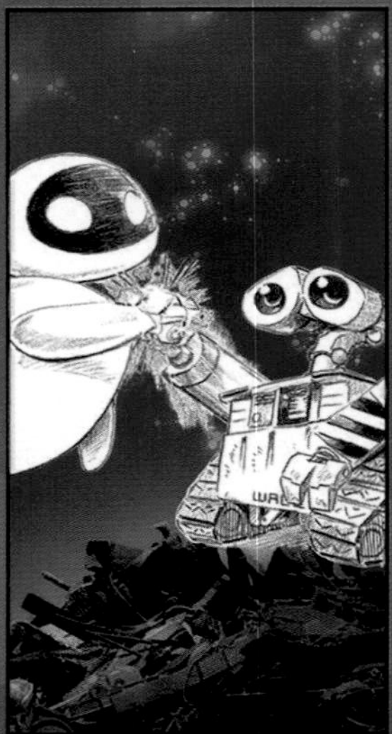

Disney Marie

MIRIYA & MARIE

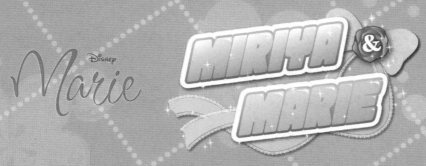

☆ Inspired by the characters from Disney's The Aristocats

☆ Learn facts about Paris and Japan!

☆ Adorable original shojo story

☆ Full color manga

Even though the wealthy young girl Miriya has almost everything she could ever need, what she really wants is the one thing money can't buy: her missing parents. But this year, she gets an extra special birthday gift when Marie, a magical white kitten, appears and whisks her away to Paris! Learning the art of magic is one thing, but getting to eat the tastiest French pastries and wear the most beautiful fashion takes Miriya and Marie's journey to a whole new level!

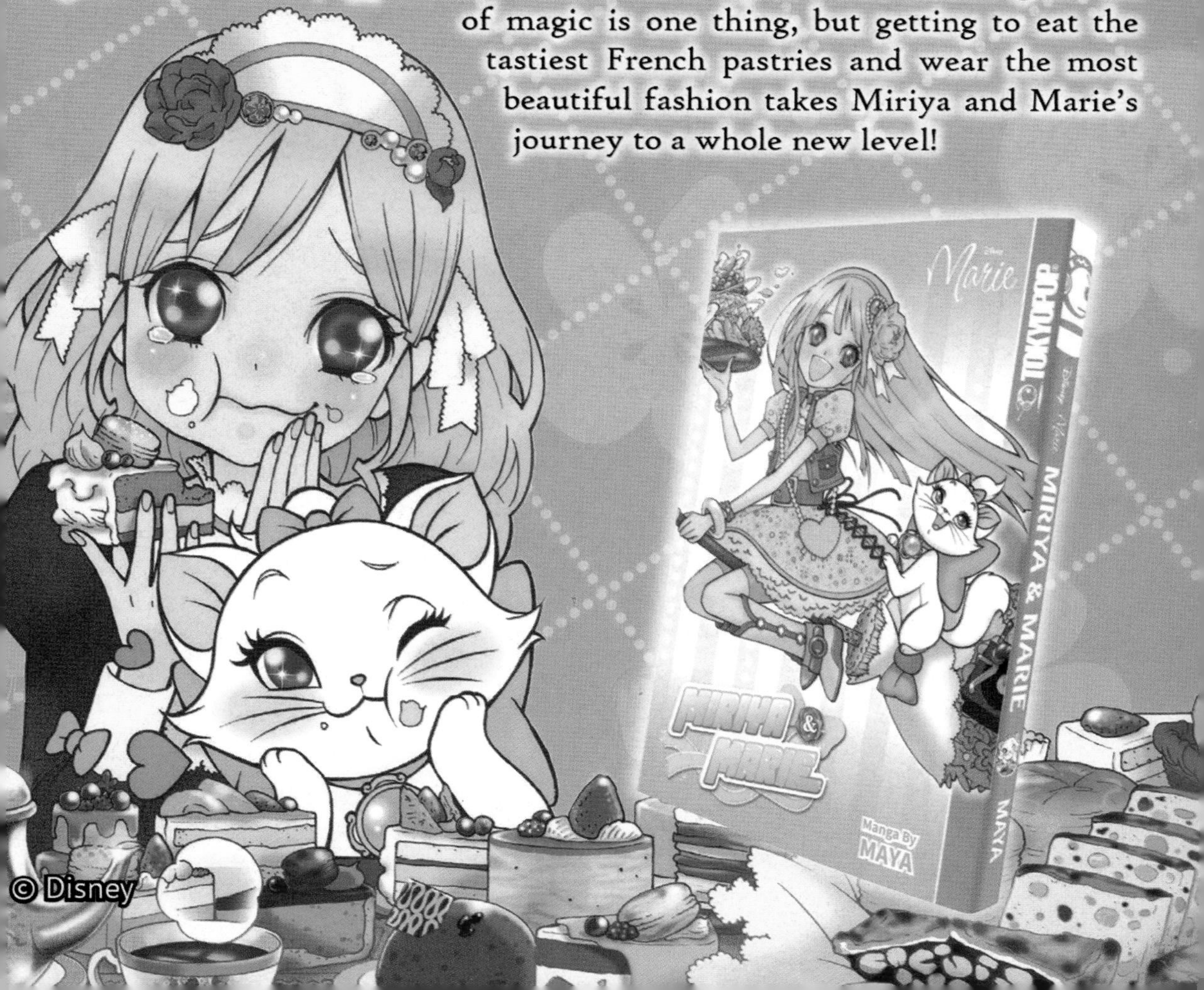
Disney Marie
TOKYOPOP
MIRIYA & MARIE
Miriya & Marie
Manga By MAYA
MAYA

DISNEY DESCENDANTS

Full color manga trilogy based on the hit Disney Channel original movie

Experience this spectacular movie in manga form!

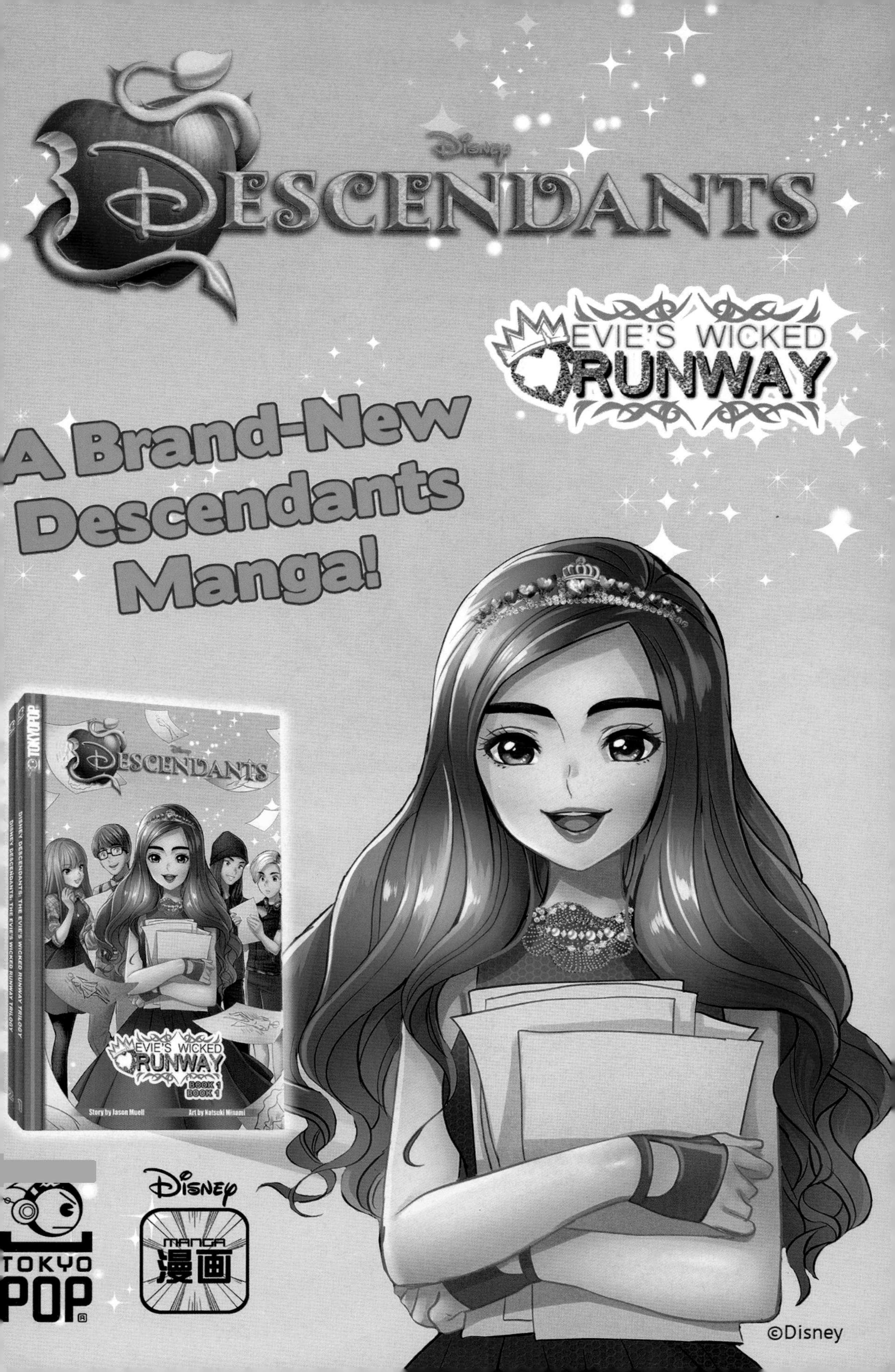
Disney
DESCENDANTS
EVIE'S WICKED RUNWAY
A Brand-New Descendants Manga!
Disney DESCENDANTS
EVIE'S WICKED RUNWAY
BOOK 1
Story by Jason Muell
Art by Natsuki Minami
TOKYOPOP
DISNEY DESCENDANTS: THE EVIE'S WICKED RUNWAY TRILOGY
TOKYO POP
Disney
MANGA
漫画
©Disney

Disney DESCENDANTS

DIZZY'S NEW FORTUNE

THE NEWEST DESCENDANTS MANGA WITH BRAND-NEW VILLAIN KIDS!

The original Villain Kids have worked hard to prove they deserve to stay in Auradon, and now it's time some of their friends from the Isle of the Lost get that chance too! When Dizzy receives a special invitation from King Ben to join the other VKs at Auradon Prep, at first she's thrilled! But doubt soon creeps in, and she begins to question whether she can truly fit in outside the scrappy world of the Isle.

TOKYO POP
© Disney

Disney MANGA 漫画

Disney CHANNEL

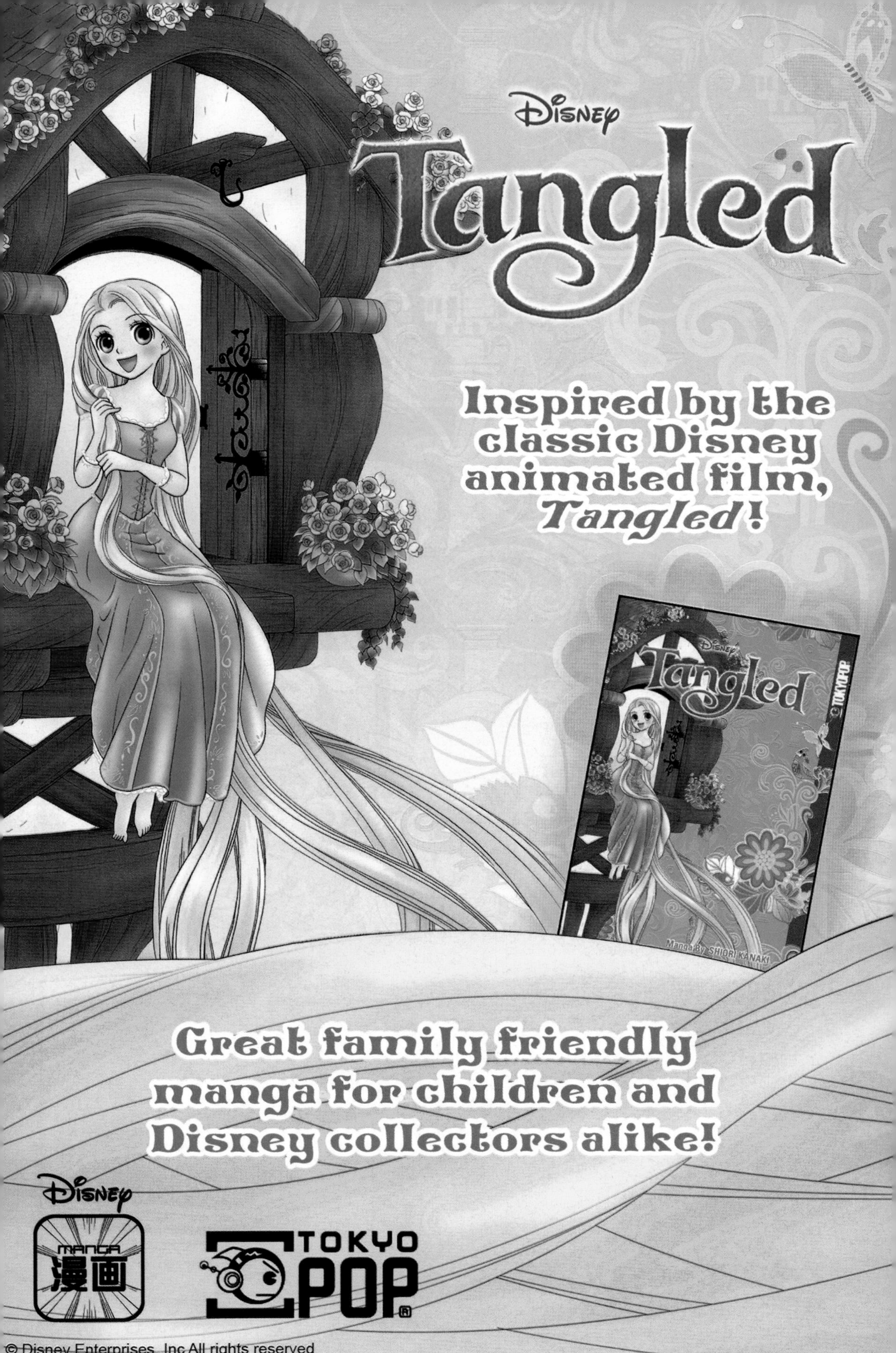
Disney
Tangled
Inspired by the classic Disney animated film, *Tangled*!
Disney
Tangled
TOKYOPOP
Manga By SHIORI KANAKI
Great family friendly manga for children and Disney collectors alike!
Disney
MANGA
漫画
TOKYO POP

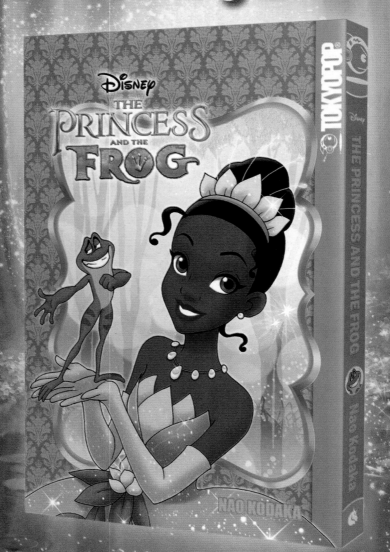

©Disney

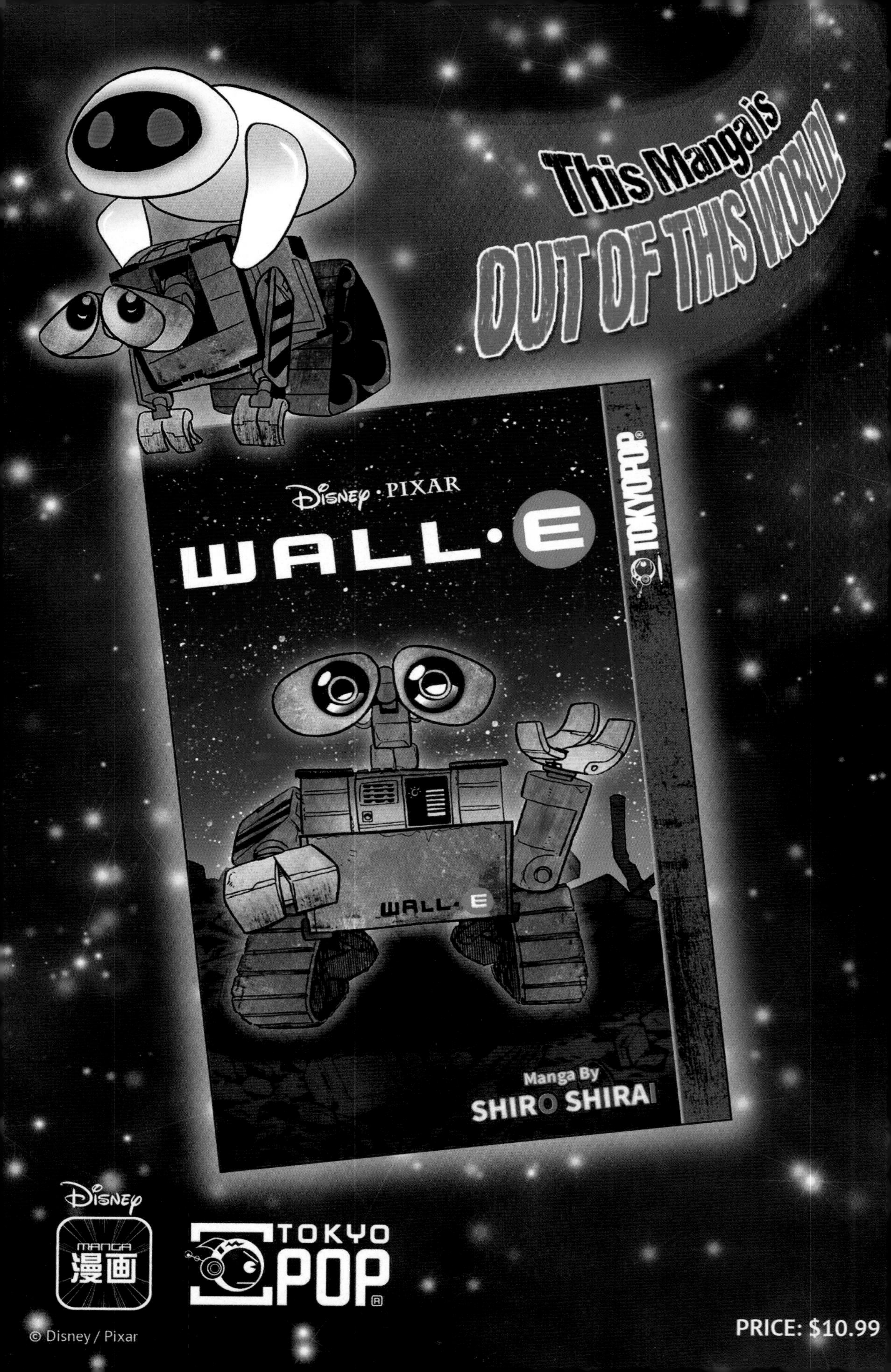
This Manga is
OUT OF THIS WORLD!
Disney · PIXAR
WALL·E
TOKYOPOP
WALL·E
Manga By
SHIRO SHIRAI
Disney
MANGA
漫画
TOKYO POP
© Disney / Pixar
PRICE: $10.99

DISNEY · PIXAR
TOY STORY

2-IN-1 SPECIAL
COLLECTOR'S MANGA

SPACE RANG • LIGHTYEAR

**TWO FAMILY-FAVORITE
DISNEY·PIXAR MOVIES
AS MANGA!**

TOKYO POP

Disney MANGA 漫画

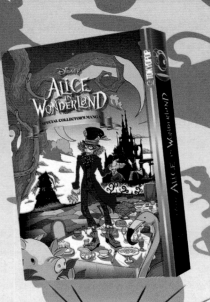

GRIMMS manga Tales

The Grimm's Tales reimagined in manga!

Beautiful art by the talented Kei Ishiyama!

Stories from Little Red Riding Hood to Hansel and Gretel!

The Fox & Little Tanuki

KORISENMAN

A modern-day fable for all ages inspired by Japanese folklore!

Senzou the black fox was punished by having his powers taken away. Now to get them back, he must play babysitter to an adorable baby tanuki!

Disney Kilala Princess
Rescue the Village with Mulan!

Written by: Mallory Reaves
Storyboards by: SAA
Cover Art by: Nao Kodaka
Pencils by: SAA, Angela Tan (Collateral Damage Studios)
Inks by: SAA, Michelle Tan Thing Siu (Collateral Damage Studios), Low Zi Rong (Collateral Damage Studios)
Colors by: James Perry II
Additional Colors by: Asuka Tun

Editorial Associate - Janae Young
Marketing Associate - Kae Winters
Digital Marketing and Content Associate - Shraboni Dutta
Technology and Digital Media Assistant - Phillip Hong
Translator - Mayu Arimoto
Editorial Coordinator - Daisuke Fukada
Artist Coordinator (Collateral Damage Studios) - KC Ng
Editor - Janae Young
Copy Editor - Lena Atanassova
Graphic Designer - Phillip Hong
Additional Design Work - Sol DeLeo
Retouching and Lettering - Vibrraant Publishing Studio
Domenico Guastafierro (Arancia Studio)
Editor-in-Chief & Publisher - Stu Levy

A TOKYOPOP® Manga

TOKYOPOP and are trademarks or registered trademarks of TOKYOPOP Inc.

TOKYOPOP inc.
5200 W Century Blvd
Suite 705
Los Angeles, CA 90045 USA

E-mail: info@TOKYOPOP.com
Come visit us online at www.TOKYOPOP.com

www.facebook.com/TOKYOPOP
www.twitter.com/TOKYOPOP
www.pinterest.com/TOKYOPOP
www.instagram.com/TOKYOPOP

ISBN: 978-1-4278-5844-3

First TOKYOPOP Printing: September 2020

10 9 8 7 6 5 4 3 2 1

Printed in CANADA

STOP

THIS IS THE BACK OF THE BOOK!

How do you read manga-style? It's simple! To learn, just start in the top right panel and follow the numbers:

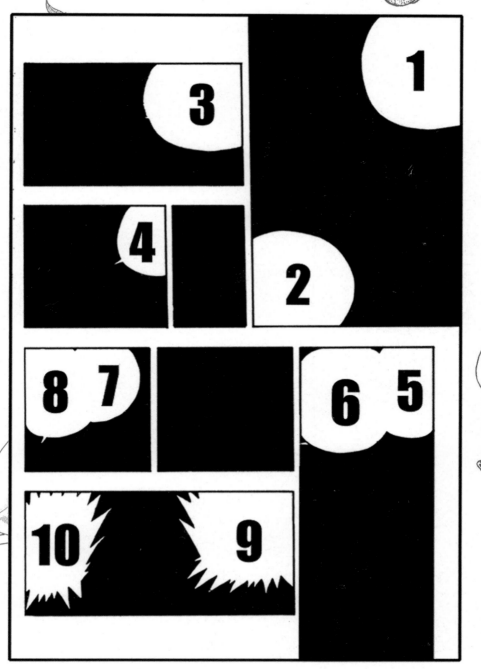